THE FUEL OF VIOLENCE

Every clone, including me, believed he was natural-born. We grew up in orphanages, surrounded by 36,000 identical beings. Each clone believed that he was the lone natural-born on the premises. They were programmed to see themselves as having blond hair and blue eyes. When three clones shared one mirror, they all saw themselves with blond hair and blue eyes, while recognizing the brown hair and brown eyes of their comrades.

But I did not see myself as having blond hair or blue eyes. I was a Liberator-Class clone. Other clone soldiers were built to be strong, patriotic, and ignorant of their origins. They were boy scouts and a little gland inside their brain would release a deadly hormone if they ever accepted the unnatural nature of their origin.

I was built to be fast, ill-natured, utterly deadly, and addicted to violence. I did not have the death reflex built into my brain. Instead, I had a gland that released an addictive combination of endorphins and adrenaline into my blood to clear my head during combat . . .

Praise for *The Clone Republic*

"A solid debut. Harris is an honest, engaging protagonist and thoughtful narrator, and Kent's clean, transparent prose fits well with both the main character and the story's themes . . . Kent is a skillful storyteller, and the book entertains throughout."   —*Science Fiction Weekly*

"The first sentence gets you immediately . . . From there, the action begins fast and furious with dark musings, lavish battle scenes, and complex characterizations . . . *The Clone Republic* feature[s] taut writing and a truly imaginative plot full of introspection and philosophizing."
—*Village Voice*

ROGUE CLONE

STEVEN L. KENT

ACE BOOKS, NEW YORK

THE BERKLEY PUBLISHING GROUP
Published by the Penguin Group
Penguin Group (USA) Inc.
375 Hudson Street, New York, New York 10014, USA
Penguin Group (Canada), 90 Eglinton Avenue East, Suite 700, Toronto, Ontario M4P 2Y3, Canada
(a division of Pearson Penguin Canada Inc.)
Penguin Books Ltd., 80 Strand, London WC2R 0RL, England
Penguin Group Ireland, 25 St. Stephen's Green, Dublin 2, Ireland (a division of Penguin Books Ltd.)
Penguin Group (Australia), 250 Camberwell Road, Camberwell, Victoria 3124, Australia
(a division of Pearson Australia Group Pty. Ltd.)
Penguin Books India Pvt. Ltd., 11 Community Centre, Panchsheel Park, New Delhi—110 017, India
Penguin Group (NZ), Cnr. Airborne and Rosedale Roads, Albany, Auckland 1310, New Zealand
(a division of Pearson New Zealand Ltd.)
Penguin Books (South Africa) (Pty.) Ltd., 24 Sturdee Avenue, Rosebank, Johannesburg 2196, South
Africa

Penguin Books Ltd., Registered Offices: 80 Strand, London WC2R 0RL, England

This is a work of fiction. Names, characters, places, and incidents either are the product of the author's imagination or are used fictitiously, and any resemblance to actual persons, living or dead, business establishments, events, or locales is entirely coincidental. The publisher does not have any control over and does not assume any responsibility for author or third-party websites or their content.

ROGUE CLONE

An Ace Book / published by arrangement with the author

PRINTING HISTORY
Ace mass-market edition / October 2006

ISBN: 0-441-01450-X

ACE
Ace Books are published by The Berkley Publishing Group,
a division of Penguin Group (USA) Inc.,
375 Hudson Street, New York, New York 10014.
ACE and the "A" design are trademarks belonging to Penguin Group (USA) Inc.

PRINTED IN THE UNITED STATES OF AMERICA

10 9 8 7 6 5 4 3 2 1

This book is dedicated to pioneering audio book reader Frank Muller, whose recording career was cut short by a motorcycle accident in 2001.

Most people think of writers when they hear the term "literary figure," but few authors have had as great an impact on my life as Frank Muller. His incredible talent has brought the works of Elmore Leonard, Herman Melville, Stephen King, John Grisham, Charles Dickens and many other great writers to life for me, and I am eternally grateful.

Mr. Muller, your voice is always with me. Thank you.

ACKNOWLEDGMENTS

The tough part about writing a sequel is that while the author and the characters remember every last detail about the previous book, readers who are new to the series do not. Just after I finished my first draft of this book, a friend named Dustin Johnson asked for a peek. As it turned out, his wife, Rachel, got to the book first and did me the greatest kindness a reader can do. She complained. (That greatest favor bit applies to pre-print. Once the book is out, insecure authors like myself prefer to be lavished with praise.)

Rachel had not read the first book in this series, and what she found was that while I and my characters knew the difference between the Republic, the Mogats, and the Confederate Arms, she did not. She wanted to like the story, but she could not tell which characters were fighting for which organizations.

Thank you, Rachel. Thank you, Dustin. Thank you, Andrew Perry, who I went to after Rachel. Andrew agreed with Rachel and my sizzling James Bond–style introduction was replaced with something a lot more expository.

I want to thank Mark Adams and my mother and father, readers to whom I resort for advice whenever I finish my first drafts. I want to thank Richard and Michael at Richard Curtis Associates for helping this book come about; and I especially wish to thank Anne Sowards and the crew at Ace for cleaning up after my many messes.

The cover of this book was created by Christian McGrath. It's not often that a writer wants people to judge his book by its cover, but with Christian doing the art, I don't mind.

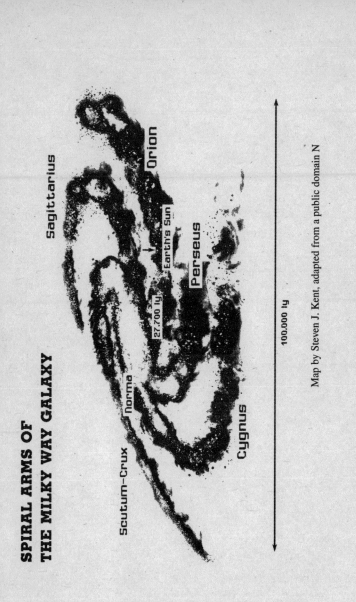

SPIRAL ARMS OF
THE MILKY WAY GALAXY

Sagittarius

Orion

Earth's Sun

Perseus

27,700 ly.

Norma

Scutum–Crux

Cygnus

100,000 ly

Map by Steven J. Kent, adapted from a public domain N

Fireflies dance in the heat of
Hound dogs bay at the moon
My ship leaves in the midnight
can't say I'll be back too soon

—Aerosmith
"Seasons of Wither"

PROLOGUE

Earthdate: 2512 A.D.

"It was the best of times, it was the worst of times . . ." Charles Dickens laid claim to those words more than 650 years too soon. You want the best of times? The best of times is when you control known space. You've explored the galaxy from corner to corner, you haven't found any opposition, so you claim the whole thing for yourself.

You want the worst of times? It's when you've been running the galaxy for four centuries, and all of a sudden you find your Republic crumbling from within.

The battle facing mankind involved either two sides or four sides, depending on how you interpreted it. There were no true allies in this little battle royale, though the three weaker nations pooled their resources to pull down the fourth.

On the one hand, you had the Unified Authority with its Earth-bound legislatures, its intergalactic highway, and its enormous military complex. The ever-evolving successor to the old United States, the Unified Authority began its expansion in the twenty-first century. First it became a global empire and then a galactic republic. The U.A. colonized the six arms of the Milky Way, creating a cosmopolitan society that superseded race and ethnicity. The galactic territories became a true melting pot as 180 new worlds opened up over the next 400 years.

The Unified Authority accomplished all of that expansion off the back of an almost all-clone military. By the beginning of the twenty-second century, U.A. clone labs began churning out over 100,000 cloned soldiers per year. By 2200 A.D., clone production was up to over one million per year. That sounds like a lot, but it's not as much as you'd think when you are conquering and colonizing a galaxy that is 100,000 light years in diameter.

The first real challenge to the Unified Authority's hold on the galaxy came in the year 2468 when a scientific expedition exploring the inner curve of the Norma Arm vanished. Afraid that they had located a hostile race, the U.A. Senate authorized the construction of a super fleet of battleships—the Galactic Central Fleet. Senator Morgan Atkins, the most powerful politician of his time, oversaw the creation of the fleet and traveled with it on its first patrol of the Norma Arm. Neither Atkins nor the fleet returned from that first patrol.

These were desperate times, but a few well-placed politicians had a plan of their own. Working with the U.A. Navy, they manufactured a breed of specially designed clones called "Liberators" which they sent into the Galactic Eye, the spot in the center of the galaxy where the six arms merge. Liberators were designed to be fast, intelligent, and dangerous. Their physiology included a gland that introduced a combination of endorphins and adrenaline into their blood during combat.

Once they entered the Galactic Eye, the Liberators discovered that Atkins and a large group of followers were behind the disappearances. Had he known about the Liberator project, Atkins might have prepared for an invasion. Instead, the Liberators caught him entirely off guard. They overwhelmed the renegade base, but Morgan Atkins and his followers escaped in their stolen Fleet.

Sometime during the next three years, colonies of religious fanatics calling themselves "Morgan Atkins Believers" began appearing throughout the galaxy. The Mogats, the common name for the Morgan Atkins religious movement, preached individualism and independence from Earth government.

As the 180 established worlds became more self-sufficient, the Mogat movement gained converts. A census taken in 2498 A.D. found approximately five million Morgan Atkins Believers. According to the 2508 census, more than 200 million people identified themselves as Mogats. Discovering that more than 200 million people had joined a potentially hostile religious movement, Congress woke up. New laws were drawn and the Atkins movement was loosely labeled subversive.

In 2510, four of the galactic arms declared independence from the Unified Authority and the civil war began. The Cygnus, Perseus, Norma, and Scutum-Crux arms formed an organization called the Confederate Arms Treaty Organization. Only the Orion Arm, Earth's home arm, and the Sagittarius Arm remained loyal to the Unified Authority.

The Morgan Atkins Believers and the Confederate Arms formed an unsteady alliance. The Confederate Arms had an enormous population and large armies, but no fleet to move troops and defend planets. The Mogats had the Galactic Central Fleet, but they lacked the manpower to pilot their ships.

A third partner was suspected of joining the Mogat/Confederate alliance—the Japanese people of Ezer Kri. Ezer Kri was a more-or-less law-abiding planet in the Scutum-Crux Arm with a large population of people of Japanese ancestry. As the civil war began, the government of Ezer Kri came into conflict with the Unified Authority. I was in the U.A. Marines at the time. When the Marines invaded Ezer Kri, the Mogat colonists who had settled on that planet fought a guerilla campaign. Our invasion turned into an occupation and the Japanese population vanished from the planet. No one knew what happened to them.

Then the war broke out. The Confederate Arms and Mogats launched their insurrection. According to our best intelligence, the Japanese population of Ezer Kri signed on with them. Even with the Japanese on their side, the Mogats and Confederate Arms did not seem to pose much of a threat.

As I said before, "It was the best of times, it was the worst of times . . ."

Part I

MURDER

Earthdate: March 1, 2512 A.D.
City: Safe Harbor; Planet: New Columbia; Galactic
Position: Orion Arm

"You look like a . . ." The boy got a stunned look on his face and stopped without finishing the sentence. He was about to tell me that I looked like a clone and changed his mind. Clever boy. Finishing that thought would either end in disaster or embarrassment. If I were a regular clone, hearing this might trigger a death reflex that released a flood of fatal hormones into my brain, killing me instantly. A more likely outcome might be my not knowing what he was talking about. I would laugh at him or possibly threaten him.

Few clones knew they were clones. Government-issue military clones had brown hair and brown eyes, but the neural programming synapse in their brains made them see themselves as having blond hair and blue eyes. It was the government's way of preventing an uprising from within the warrior class.

"I look a lot like an Army clone?" I asked, trying to sound relaxed and conversational. "I hear that a lot."

The boy might have been in his twenties. His shoulder-length orange-red hair was stringy and lank. Large red pimples formed a constellation across his forehead. I was twenty-two, but I had seen death and battle and betrayal. Walking among the general civilian population, I considered most males under the age of thirty to be boys. The few who did not strike me as morons were thugs, like the one I had come here to meet.

The boy looked stunned. He was neither a policeman nor a guard, just an usher in a movie house. His mouth hung open as he pondered my answer, and his eyes showed a mixture of confusion and fear.

"I'm a lot like them," I said as if confiding a family secret. "The Pentagon used my grandfather's DNA to make those clones."

"No shit," the boy said. A smile formed on his face. Of the six arms of the Milky Way galaxy, four had recently declared independence from the Unified Authority—the Earth government. The Orion Arm, Earth's home arm, remained loyal to the Republic; but this planet—New Columbia—was suspect. The New Columbian government swore allegiance to the Unified Authority, but its government was filled with politicians who openly sympathized with the Confederate Arms.

"Yeah," I said. "You might say half the Army and I are cousins. For the record, Army clones are about four inches shorter than me and a lot wider around the shoulders."

"Yeah," said the boy, and he laughed nervously. "I knew something was different."

There were a couple hundred thousand military clones assigned to New Columbia, but they seldom strayed far from their bases. The U.A. government had to tread lightly because of the planet's skewed neutrality.

The boy looked at my ticket. "Oh, wow, you're going to *The Battle for Little Man*. Lots of clones in that flick." He smiled at me. "Third holotorium on the right."

The hall was wide and bright with 3-D lenticular posters from upcoming movies on the walls. It was early in the afternoon on a weekday, and I had most of the theater to myself. The only people ahead of me were a young couple on a date—an uptight boy holding hands with a fresh-faced girl. The boy must have wanted to get to his movie. He walked quickly, his girlfriend in tow. The girl floated along lazily and paused to study each movie poster they passed.

"C'mon," he said, as he opened the door to their holoto-rium. "We're missing the coming attractions."

I went two doors farther. *The Battle for Little Man* had already begun. It was a war movie recounting a recent battle in which a regiment of U.A. Marines was massacred on a planet near the edge of the galaxy. I knew the battle intimately. Of the 2,300 Marines sent on that mission, only seven survived.

On the screen, a blond-haired, blue-eyed, barrel-chested Hollywood stud played Lieutenant Wayson Harris, the highest-ranking survivor of the Little Man campaign. As I took my seat, six enlisted men let themselves into Harris's quarters and asked him about the mission. These men were clones. They all looked exactly alike. They had brown hair and brown eyes . . . like me. They stood about five feet eleven inches tall—four inches shorter than me.

The people who made this film may have hired retired clones to play the enlisted men. I was impressed.

"What will happen down there, Lieutenant Harris?" one of the clones in the movie asked. Respect and adoration were evident in his voice and demeanor. The leathernecks on the screen must have been computer animations. No Marine could have said that line with a straight face.

"I don't know, Lee," said Harris. *"It's going to be tough. It's going to be dangerous. But we are the Unified Authority Marines. We don't back down from a fight."* As he said this, the actor playing Harris stuffed an eighteen-inch combat knife into a scabbard that hung from his belt. I had to hold my breath to keep from laughing. None of the Marines I had ever met carried eighteen-inch combat knives and none of them sounded as heroic as the Hollywood Harris on the screen.

"What if we die?" another Marine asked.

"You listen here, Marine," barked the Hollywood Harris on the screen, *"don't worry about death. We're here fighting for the Republic. The Republic needs us. The people need us as they have never needed us before."*

I slumped in my seat. This movie was supposed to be authentic with real combat footage taken from the actual battle. Maybe the battle scenes would be more realistic, but this portrayal of military clones was painfully propagandistic.

This movie was the kind of jingoistic shit that Hollywood always churned out during times of war; something meant to build patriotic morale. On a planet like New Columbia, that effort was wasted. I was the only person in the holotorium.

At least, I was the only person in the theater up until that moment. As Harris finished his soliloquy about defending the Republic, the door at the back of the holotorium opened. I heard men whispering among themselves as they moved into empty seats directly behind me.

By this time, Lieutenant Harris and a platoon of Marines were being drop-shipped behind enemy lines. They landed about one mile in from the beach where the rest of the Marines were pinned down by a group of Mogat Separatists. Harris and twenty-two commandoes snuck into the enemy's bunker. Using knives and pistols, Harris and his men made short work of at least two hundred enemy soldiers. God, it was glorious.

The scene was played out with a combination of two-dimensional projectors creating the background behind three-dimensional holographic images. The result was a battlefield that virtually burst out of the screen. As shown in this film, the battle for Little Man was filled with heroism and valor. Everything was bright colors and patriotic music. . . . And in the middle of all of the action stood Lieutenant Wayson Harris, twenty feet tall and covered with enemy blood as he ran from one room to the next brandishing that gigantic knife.

"Hello, Harris," whispered one of the men behind me. "Let's talk."

"Can it wait?" I asked. "I want to see how this turns out."

"You know how it turns out," the man said. "You were there."

"Not at this battle, I wasn't," I said. "The invasion of Little Man that I saw didn't look anything like this. We got pinned down on the beach. The Navy had to nuke those Mogat bunkers just to get us off the sand."

"That so?" the man asked. "I thought this movie was supposed to be accurate."

Up on the screen, Hollywood Harris led the charge across Little Man Valley. The charge was famous. Some 2,300 Marines ran across the floor of the valley thinking they were up against two or maybe three thousand Separatists. They did not know about the ten thousand reinforcements hiding just over the hill.

"You led the charge?" the man behind me asked. "That took guts."

"I wasn't even on the field. I was way off on the side. My platoon was assigned to flank the enemy," I said.

"Really?" the man said. "Sounds like you gave yourself the easy job."

Some of this footage was undoubtedly taken from the battle records. Watching untold numbers of enemy soldiers charge over the far ridge of the valley, I felt my skin prickle on the back of my neck. I saw the way they poured over the rise like ants swarming out of a hill. They had rust-red armor that sparkled in the sunlight. They shouted in unison. Seeing their advance, the Marines stopped and dug in.

"I didn't have much to say in the matter. I was a sergeant. They didn't make me an officer until after the battle." The filmmakers probably had little choice about this last piece of deception. Portraying me as an enlisted man would lead to questions about whether or not I was a clone. And I was not a general-issue clone. I was something far more dangerous.

The battle raged on. Trapped and hopelessly outnumbered, the U.A. Marines circled their wagons and tried to withstand the advancing horde. Marine riflemen formed a picket line in front of a battery of men with mortars and grenade launchers.

"They make these movies look real," the man behind me said.

"That is real," I said. "The part about me is a specking myth, but this part . . ." *Speck*, a slang word which referred to sperm, was one of the strongest words in our modern vocabulary.

The movie cut to a dogfight in space, a part of the battle I had only seen in the news feeds. Seeing the holographically-enhanced image on the big screen was a dizzying experience. The Separatists sent four battleships to destroy a lone Unified Authority fighter carrier patrolling Little Man.

What the Mogat Separatists did not know was that Rear Admiral Robert Thurston, who commanded the Scutum-Crux Central Fleet, had carriers and destroyers hidden behind a nearby moon. Hundreds of fighters poured out of those hidden carriers and swarmed the Mogat battleships. Three of the battleships exploded in space. The fourth crashed into the valley just as the Mogats polished off the last of the Marines. I watched the destruction from the safety of a nearby ridge, and I remember thinking that it looked like a portrait of Dante's *Inferno*.

The movie recreated the entire scene faithfully except that it had me leading my six survivors into a nearby cave. Having placed me on the front line of the battle, the scriptwriters would not have been able to explain how I sprinted to safety up the side of the canyon.

"Damn, Harris. You escaped in a cave?" the man asked. I heard newfound respect in his voice.

"Something like that," I said.

The screen cut to a scene showing six of the survivors saluting Hollywood Harris as he boarded a transport to Earth. Those six would attend officer training in Australia. They were the first clones ever to become officers in the Unified Authority Marines. As his transport flew out of the docking bay, a lone bugle played Taps and the screen went black. The words, *"Lieutenant Wayson Harris died five months after the battle of Little Man while defending the Unified Authority outpost on Ravenwood,"* appeared in the center of the screen.

"That's heart-breaking, Harris," the man behind me said. "It's specking heart-breaking. I've seen this show a couple of times now, and that part always gets to me. Know what I mean?"

CHAPTER
TWO

"Okay, so you weren't a lieutenant and you didn't lead the charge on Little Man . . . yeah, and you didn't die on Ravenwood? Should I believe the rest of that stuff?" The man who sat behind me in the theater was Jimmy Callahan, a New Columbian thug who hoped he could make a name for himself by playing the local espionage game. Sometimes I missed the mark with first impressions, but I felt relatively confident that Callahan was a punk and a prick. On the plus side, I was pretty sure I could trust him to deliver as promised so long as I was the highest bidder.

Callahan and two buddies had taken me to an outdoor cafe and we took a table on a terrace overlooking a trendy part of town. "You know, Harris, it just goes to show you, you can't trust anyone anymore. I mean, here's a movie that's supposed to make people feel all warm and patriotic; and what do you tell me? It's a pack of lies. Nothing happened the way they said it did."

A line of shrubs formed a waist-high wall that ran along the edge of the terrace. Small green birds, no larger than an infant's fist, darted in and out of its leaves.

Below us, a steady stream of pedestrians flowed across sidewalks lined with clothing stores, banks, and eateries.

The workday had just ended. Men in suits and women in dresses waited at intersections, peered in store windows, and eventually ambled into a nearby train station.

Now that I had met him in person, Callahan struck me as a lightweight trying to make a name for himself. He had a menacing presence. I gave him that much. His muscular chest and shoulders filled his T-shirt and his bulging arms stretched the fabric of its sleeves. But Callahan had a soft, manicured, almost pansy-fied face. His cheeks were pudgy and his skin was smooth. He marbled his brown hair with blond streaks.

"From what I hear, you've got information on some pretty big fish?" I said, trying to show him respect he had not earned.

"Big fish?" Callahan asked. "Yeah, I suppose you could call them big fish."

"How do we know we can trust you?" I asked.

"I'm good for it," Callahan said, and he turned to smile at the two men sitting behind him. They returned his smile. These were his bodyguards, I supposed, though I sensed the relationship went beyond mere protection. These other two were not as big or as strong looking as Callahan and I began to wonder if they were perhaps his younger brothers. Despite the gruff way he treated them, there was some kind of affection hidden in his voice.

"I suppose the reason you're going to trust me is that I have what you want," Callahan said, and his cronies chuckled. "The only reason we're talking is I got information and you've got money. Am I right?"

He paused. He wanted me to appreciate his rich sense of humor. I did not speak or nod. After a moment, he went on.

"An alert guy like me with an unlimited supply of information . . . I figure you can take a chance on me. As long as your friends in D.C. have a bottomless wallet and I've got good information, Harris, it's the world's greatest romance."

Callahan spoke in superlatives. Everything was the "best" or the "most." He irritated me, but I would put up with him as long as his leads checked out.

A waitress came to our table. "Have you decided what you want?" She turned to me first.

"Got anything in that's Earth-grown?" Callahan interrupted.

The waitress smiled. Customers typically paid nearly twice as much money for food made with Earth-grown ingredients. Outworld-grown products tasted just as good, but there was a snobbish appeal to buying Earth-grown.

"We received a shipment yesterday," she said. "The salad bar is entirely Earth-grown tonight. Oh, and we received a shipment of Earth-brewed beers."

Callahan stopped to think about this. His small, dark eyes sparkled in the late afternoon sunlight. He stroked a finger along his right cheek. "It's too early for dinner. Tell you what, you fix me a small salad and bring me a bottle of your best Earth brew."

The waitress moved to one of Callahan's thugs.

"I'll take a beer . . ."

Callahan turned to scowl at the man.

"Tea, please," he said sounding disappointed. The other thug ordered the same.

She turned to me and smiled. "What would you like?" the waitress asked.

"I'm fine," I said taking a sip of water.

"All right," Callahan said, nodding approval. "So are we going to do business today? I hope you didn't come all this way just to see yourself in the movies. Know what I mean?"

I leaned back in my chair and sipped my water. A stiff evening breeze blew across the terrace knocking menu cards from some of the tables. Across the plaza, the sun started to set behind the skyline. The traffic was tied up in the intersection below us and the street looked like a parking lot.

"You've given us some good stuff so far," I said. "Nothing great, but good enough . . . a couple of low-level operatives."

Callahan greeted this with a wide, knowing smile. "Hear that boys? I've given them some good stuff so far." He bobbed his head as if in agreement with himself.

They nodded and laughed.

"Are all clones this tight-lipped or is that just your personality?" Callahan asked. He smoothed his hair with his right hand, leaned forward in his chair, and rubbed his palms together. "Tell you what, Harris. I'm just like this restaurant. I've got a menu, know what I mean?

"You want to eat outworld-grown stuff, we'll give it to you

cheap. You want low-level operatives, I'll give them to you. They're worth what, one thousand dollars a pop?"

The waitress returned with Callahan's salad. Callahan remained silent until she left. He stuffed a forkload of greens in his mouth. "Earth-grown is the best tasting," he said around a wad of lettuce. "The goddamn best."

"So let's talk big fish. What's Crowley worth? What do I get for a big fish like Amos Crowley?"

I feigned nonchalance. Amos Crowley was someone in whom I took a personal interest. A former general in the U.A. Army, Crowley nearly killed me twice—once when he sent a band of terrorists to attack a backwater Marine base and once when he sent an inept assassin to even the score for the role I played in saving the base.

"Crowley?" I asked. "He might be worth one hundred grand . . . if your information was good."

"One hundred grand," Callahan echoed, his head perpetually bobbing up and down. "I like that. The math adds up. Small fish . . . one thousand dollars. Crowley is like one hundred times more important, so he's worth one hundred times more dough. I like that."

The conversation seemed pointless. I didn't believe Callahan had information about Crowley. The boy was a big talker, nothing more.

"How about Yoshi Yamashiro? Is he worth something?"

"I know several parties who would be interested," I said. Yamashiro was the former governor of Ezer Kri. I had nothing against the man personally, but the Department of Justice took a dimmer view of him.

When Yamashiro became governor of Ezer Kri, he inherited a planet with a large population of people of Japanese descent. Since the territories were supposed to be a great galactic melting pot, Ezer Kri's ethnically pure population concerned several senators back in Washington, D.C. The situation came to a head when a plurality of Ezer Kri citizens voted to formalize Japanese as their official language and rename the planet *Shin Nippon*.

The Senate accused Yamashiro and his cabinet of sedition and sent the Navy to declare martial law. Shortly thereafter, Yamashiro and most of the Japanese people vanished from the planet.

"And what do I get for Warren A.?"

"Warren A." was Warren Atkins. The "AT" in Mogat was short for Atkins, named after Warren Atkins's famous father, Morgan Atkins.

"Ambitious," I said. "Leading us to Atkins would make you a millionaire. Of course, everything would depend on the quality of your information."

"So let's talk about the biggest prize, Harris." Callahan paused to empty his beer. "What if I get you the biggest deal of them all? What do I get if I lead you to the Galactic Central Fleet?"

The Galactic Central Fleet (GCF) was a very large fleet of antique Naval ships. The Mogats had already used GCF ships in two minor attacks—one of them being the battle at Little Man.

"As I recall, there is a ten million dollar bounty for anyone who can lead us to the fleet," I said, still sure that Callahan was nothing but talk.

"Hear that, boys?" Callahan looked back and gave his cronies a cocky simper. "I could wind up rich." They nodded at him and smiled. He turned back to me and his good humor vanished. "You don't trust me, Harris, do you? How about if I give you a sample, just this one time?"

"You offering a freebie?" I asked.

All three thugs laughed. "You must be mistaking me for the halfway house down the street. I don't do charity. Know what I mean?

"How much do I get for Billy 'the Butcher'?"

"William Patel?" I asked. Patel was a harbinger of death—a Confederate Arms spymaster blamed for terrorist attacks on civilian targets. He had a high enough price on his head. Whenever intelligence reviewed satellite footage of terrorist bombings, Patel's face appeared somewhere in the feed. "Last I heard, he was worth twenty-five thousand dollars for a tip and maybe twice that for a capture."

"That so? How about if he's practically gift-wrapped?" As he said this, Callahan flicked his eyes toward the street. "See that red Paragon?" He pointed to a far away car. "That's Patel's car."

The avenue below us was shaped like a horseshoe. The street ran in a sweeping curve around the outside of an enormous marble and glass fountain with thirty-foot waterfalls. Glass tunnels served as walkways through the cascading water. The tunnels were packed with pedestrians as the work day had officially ended about an hour ago. The bumper-to-bumper downtown traffic had not cleared up.

Parked at the far end of the curve, well beyond the fountain, was a Paragon—a luxury sports car that looked like a shoehorn with windows. The car was burnt orange, not red. Its tapered rear window mirrored the amber and pink glow of the evening sun.

"Sure," I said, not taking Callahan seriously. "And the dump truck up the street belongs to General Crowley. Saw him drive it there myself."

"You don't believe me." Callahan placed his hand over his heart and did his best to look pained.

"Sure. I believe you. Patel drives a Paragon . . . nice car. I always took him as more of a armored tank–man, myself."

"You don't think much of me, do you, Harris?" Callahan asked.

"Is there any reason why I should believe that car belongs to Patel?"

"Is that reason enough for you?" Callahan asked. He pointed toward the street. There, stepping out of a delicatessen, was William Patel. He wore a black leather trench coat that swept along the sidewalk. He was tall and wiry with black hair and dark glasses hiding his eyes. He was too far away to shoot from this terrace, but close enough for me to recognize the face once Callahan pointed it out.

"I did some business with Billy this week. My boys have been following him ever since he came to Safe Harbor. He comes here for coffee. . . . He goes to the same damned stores every day. Loves this friggin' block. Maybe he's visiting his sweetie. Know what I mean?"

Down on the street, Billy the Butcher pushed his way through the crowd. I lost him as he took the tunnel through the fountain, then caught him again as he emerged on the other side. He shoved a woman out of his way as he stepped toward the street.

Taking only a quick glance at the stalled traffic, he skipped from the sidewalk to the road and wove his way through the cars. He was still in the middle of the traffic when he turned, looked in our direction, and peered over his shades. From this distance, I could not see the sneer on his mouth, but I knew that it was there. Having paused only for a quick glance, Patel walked past his expensive burnt orange Paragon and vanished around the corner.

I jumped from my seat.

"Where you going, Harris?" Jimmy Callahan asked. "You don't think you can catch him from here?"

I grabbed Callahan by his collar with my left hand and clipped the first of his bodyguards with my right. The goon was just getting to his feet, giving me a warning glare, and reaching for his gun when the heel of my palm struck the corner of his jaw. He gasped and fell to the ground. I instinctively knew that his jawbone had broken.

The second goon stepped in my way. I brought the edge of my foot down on the instep of his leg, pressing hard against his knee. The man's kneecap snapped like a dried branch. He made a faint whimpering noise as he fell to the ground and wrapped his arms around the knee, cradling it against his stomach.

"Harris, you speck! What the hell do you think you are doing?" Callahan shouted. Muscles or no muscles, the man followed without a fight. I tugged and he came running.

"Real tough boys you've got there, Callahan," I said to myself in a whisper. Behind me, the first explosions showered the street with fire, glass, and smoke. Pausing for less than a second, I caught a glimpse of flames bursting out of a distant storefront.

"What the sp . . . ?" Callahan asked as I pushed him forward through the door that lead from the outdoor terrace into the restaurant.

"Hey," someone yelled from a nearby table. I did not notice if it was a man or a woman.

"Move it, asshole," I said to Callahan, as I continued shoving him.

Behind us, the next set of explosions tore into the street. They sounded closer and more powerful. This was the trap. The first bombs, at the far end of the curving boulevard, sealed us in so that no one could escape. The only thing we could do was sit and watch as the explosions moved toward us. Only I didn't plan on cooperating.

The noise and percussion from the next set of bombs shook the restaurant. People jumped from their seats but the panic had not yet sunk in.

By this time, I had made my way through most of the restaurant, with Callahan stumbling ahead of me. The shock wave from this blast knocked glasses and silverware from the tables. The doors to a wine cabinet flew open. Bottles of fine wine crashed to the floor and bounced like bowling pins. Rubble from glass and china crunched under my shoes.

The sounds of panic started to waft across the restaurant. A woman shrieked. Someone yelled something about calling the police. Most of the people headed to the terrace for a closer look at the action.

The explosions happened in ten-second intervals. Even with smoke and dust filling the air and the explosions getting close, people still crowded the terrace so they could watch. I stole one last glimpse of them. Then, with my back hunched and my right arm bent around the top of my head to shield my eyes, I shoved the stupefied Jimmy Callahan through the swinging doors and into the kitchen. The big room was empty. Steam and froth boiled out of five-gallon pots along the stove.

"What's . . . What are you doing?" Callahan screamed.

The final explosion erupted from somewhere back in the restaurant. The sound was booming and short, a brilliant clap of thunder that rattles the world then leaves a vacuum in its wake.

The entire building seemed to leap from its foundation and slide backward. A large metal table in the center of the kitchen flew in the air and landed upside down. Five-gallon pots flew from the stove, splashing scalding soups and water across the floor.

The force of the blast sent me sprawling. I did not know if I was flipped into the air or if the floor dropped out from under me. Callahan landed face first beside me. "God almighty," he screamed as he sat up like a baby waking from a nap. Blood gushed from his forehead and nose. "My boys!" he half moaned. "Tommy! Eddie!"

I stood up and pulled him to his feet. I could see in his eyes that no one was home. I saw panic, not thought. The mark of my kind was that chaos gave our thoughts a warm kind of clarity and it irritated me to see Callahan so out of it. I spun him around and launched him face first through the service entrance at the back of the kitchen.

We entered a long service corridor that ran behind all of the buildings. There were none of the awnings or pretty trappings out here, just concrete block walls, empty palettes, and trash bins. This area was unscathed. The explosions had blown up the façades of these buildings, not the backs.

"Harris . . . What the speck happened. Where are my boys?" Callahan, looking dazed, turned to me for help. He did not bother wiping the blood from his pudgy face. He probably did not know it was there.

So much for his swagger. Callahan's shock irritated me beyond reason. I grabbed him by the lapels and slammed his back into a wall. Still pinning him down, his lapels in my fists which were pressed against his chest, I spoke in little more than a whisper. "They're dead, Jimmy. Everyone in that restaurant is dead. Maybe one day they will make a movie about the way the terrorists blew up this restaurant and they can make you the hero. Wouldn't that be a great idea for movie? Know what I mean?"

CHAPTER
THREE

A moment of terrible silence followed the explosions. I knew that silence. It was filled with shock and disbelief, as if something so outrageous had just occurred that even the buildings could not understand what happened. This envelope of silence lasted a few brief seconds, then moaning and screaming filled the vacuum.

With their façades blown off, the buildings along the block looked desecrated and bare. The delicatessen, the building Patel visited right before the explosions, drooped like a tent in a storm. Its bright red awning lay in a rumpled heap across the sidewalk.

The explosions reduced several buildings to nothing more than mounds of brick and debris. Some of the cars on the street remained right side up. The force of the blast sent others tumbling and they now lay wheels up like dead insects fallen around a hive.

Walking outside the bottom floor of the restaurant in which I had just been sitting, I took in the extent of the damage. The front wall of the building was gone, terrace and all. What remained was an open-faced building with wide open floors and a blanket of bricks, broken furniture, and concrete debris spilling out to the street.

"God almighty," Callahan said. His eyes flitted over the damage. His mouth hung slightly open.

"Your pals are under there," I said.

He nodded and said nothing.

Sirens blared in the distance. Fire engines and ambulances appeared at the end of the block where William Patel's burnt orange Paragon still sat parked. The emergency vehicles could get no closer. The street was choked with cars. It looked like a junkyard. The cars were smoke-stained and heavily dented.

Firemen with extinguisher packs and evacuation equipment jumped from their trucks. They ran down the street in companies, splitting up to search each building for survivors. Medics set up an emergency station around the outside of the fountain. Casualties that could not walk were rushed to that station on stretchers. Even before the first tables were open, the walking wounded came for medicine and stitches.

As the firemen dug through the wreckage, the medics started sorting victims. Freight helicopters swooped in from overhead. Policemen waded through the road pulling people from vehicles. Once the cars were empty, the police attached cables to them and the helicopters dragged them away.

"You've seen this before?" Callahan asked.

"I've seen worse than this," I said. I thought about the battle on Little Man and the parts that were left out of the movie. I remembered staring at the valley and seeing its rock walls glowing like hot embers.

Callahan's dark eyes narrowed as he began to comprehend what happened. He ran to the ruins of the terrace and dug into the debris. He pulled up a helmet-sized chunk of concrete, brought it to his chest, then threw it aside. "Tommy!" He found something and tugged at it until he unearthed the remains of a chair.

Not all of the wounded made it to the field hospital across the street. One man lay on his back staring peacefully into the sky. He held his arm over his face covering his eyes. A small trickle of blood ran from his gaping mouth. I saw this and knew he was dead. A woman kneeling beside him whispered in his ear. Blood poured from gouges in her cheeks and forehead. Sticks, paper, and shards of glass littered her dirty hair. All in all, the woman looked more battered than the corpse beside her.

There was no river of blood along the street, just dirty bodies, some alive, some dead. Jimmy Callahan might find an arm or a leg, as he pulled up chunks of brick and plaster. Panic showed in his movements. He'd already cut his fingers and palms and his blood splashed on the debris as he threw it behind him, but he did not notice.

"You gonna help me?" he shouted.

I shook my head.

He stood up and stared at me. "There are people under here," he shouted so loud that his voice cracked.

Some nearby rescue workers heard Callahan and mistook his shouting to mean that he had located a survivor. Grabbing gas-powered lifts and laser cutters, they ran over to join us. "Where are they?" one of the firemen asked.

Callahan looked down at the ground and shook his head. "Sorry," he said. "I was just trying . . . I was wrong."

The muscles tensed in the fireman's cheeks as he clenched his jaws. Then he relaxed. "Don't worry about it, pal. We're all desperate." He dug into his jacket and found a pair of protective gloves which he handed to Callahan. "Try these."

Callahan took the gloves and stood there as stiff and lifeless as a waxwork dummy. He held his hands palm up, as if he were cupping water. Somewhere along the way I got the feeling that Eddie and Tommy, the bodyguards, meant more to Callahan than hired muscle, but I didn't know what was going on between them. Callahan looked like he was going into shock as he looked at the pile of concrete and metal.

"You take the right glove, I'll take the left," I said to Callahan. He looked at me but said nothing as I picked one of the gloves out of his outstretched hand.

I was right-handed, but my genetic engineering gave me nearly equal dexterity with both hands. I found a long, rough slab of concrete. Holding it with my gloved left hand and balancing it with my right, I pushed it away from the pile.

"How did you know?" Callahan asked as he pulled on his glove. "How did you know this would happen?"

"I knew because Billy Patel is a galactic-class terrorist

and you're nothing but a two-bit punk," I said as I traced the fallen arch of a doorway.

"A punk?" Callahan asked. He sounded more stupefied than offended. "What does that mean?" He got his foot twisted in some wire and fell on his back.

"It means that there was no way you and your two-bit operation was going to sell out a big player like Billy the Butcher without him knowing it. He knew we were watching him. He knew you were watching him all along.

"When he ditched his car and turned to look back at us. He knew exactly where to look. We were right where he wanted us and he couldn't resist a quick look back just to gloat. He must have figured you were too stupid to guess what he was up to. Know what I mean?"

"Get specked, Harris."

"You asked," I said.

"So why did you pull me out?" Callahan asked. "You would have made it out more easily on your own."

"Look at this," I said. I was standing beside a long heavy beam that looked like it might have been made out of white marble. I found leaves from the hedge that had run around the edge of the terrace.

The man who gave Callahan the gloves returned. "You found something?"

"We were just leaving the building when the bombs went off," I said. "There were people right about here." I squatted and brushed away a layer of dust, then picked up a smashed branch with five teardrop-shaped leaves.

The man wore a radio clipped into his collar. As he knelt down to see the crushed shrub, he whispered into the radio. "Send a team. Full gear. We might have something."

Now that they had located a promising spot, the firemen ushered Jimmy Callahan and me away as they did serious excavation. They placed jacks and lifts under that beam, which must have weighed a good five tons.

"You think anyone is alive down there?" Callahan asked as two burley rescue workers wrestled a large ultrasonic cannon over to their dig. By this time it was late at night. Now that the helicopters had cleared the streets, fire engines and ambulances could drive right up to the buildings. The firemen placed tripods with spotlights around the dig. The spotlights were tiny, about the size and shape of a coffee cup, but their beams could be seen from twenty miles away.

We stood huddled at the front of a crowd that had gathered just behind the lights. Somebody had handed Callahan a blanket and a cup of coffee. His clothes were torn and bloody from the dig. He had wiped his cut up hands on his shirt and pants, and the dust and blood made him look like he had been in the heart of the explosion.

"I've never seen anyone pulled out alive," I said. I supposed that they probably did find survivors sometimes, but I had never seen it happen.

The rescue team's ultrasonic cannon reduced rock and glass to powder. If they fired it at the marble beam that stretched across their dig, they could destroy it, but that was not their goal. With the jacks supporting its weight, that beam now acted as a roof over their dig, protecting any survivors buried beneath.

The ultrasonic cannon fired sound waves that passed through liquid, air, and wood. You could fire it into a pond without bothering the fish, but the rocks in the pond would disintegrate. It did not hurt people. The shock waves from the ultrasonic cannons did not affect plastic or steel, but they reduced stone to dust.

The firemen used the cannon to clear a three-feet deep crevice under the beam. Two rescuers lugged a stiff, wide-bore hose into the hole. The hose was almost a full yard in diameter with some kind of cage in its opening.

"What is that?" Callahan asked.

I'd never seen anything like it and did not answer.

"Stand clear," one of the men with the cannon shouted, and the other rescue workers backed away from the site. There was so much dust in the air that I could watch the shock wave as it fired from the cannon. It looked like a pattern of ripples as it passed through the airborne dust. There was a soft sound, not unlike the sound made by a quick shake of a baby's rattle, and suddenly the rubble beneath that gigantic hose compressed into a powder that was finer than sand. The hose sucked the dust up.

A fireman with a tow cord strung around his waist walked

up to the crevice left by the hose. He stared down into it for a moment. The man wore an oxygen mask over his face and held a crowbar in one hand.

Another fireman approached and handed him something small that he tucked in his belt. "You ready, Greg?" the second fireman asked as he patted the first one's shoulder.

The fireman wrapped his hands around the cord, turned so his back was toward the hole, and rappelled out of sight. A moment later his voice echoed over multiple radios. "I found one. It's a woman."

"Condition?" a man on the fire engine asked.

"Alive." The crowd around me cheered. Jimmy Callahan rocked back and forth on the soles of his feet blowing warm breath nervously into badly gashed hands.

Two more firemen lowered themselves into the hole. Someone handed a stretcher down to them as a fire engine and an ambulance drew just a few feet away. The fire engine extended a ladder over the hole and dropped a winch to the firemen. Tense silence followed. Then the rope tightened. Most people cheered and a few even cried as the winch raised the stretcher from the hole.

Two medics received that stretcher. They detached the cord from the stretcher and pulled the woman into the back of their ambulance. In less than one minute, they loaded her, sealed up their rig, and sped away into the darkness. Another ambulance immediately filled the vacancy.

The rescue workers found seventy-six people in that one area—sixty-two were alive. Tommy and Eddie were alive. As the explosions had come closer, they had crawled under a table and made it out virtually untouched. Tommy had a badly broken jaw. Eddie's knee was shattered. Both of those injuries were my doing. The explosion barely scratched them.

I was glad Jimmy Callahan's boys were alive. Callahan was going to need all the help he could get. He had some powerful enemies. Considering the devastation that I had just seen, I doubted that "Silent" Tommy and "Limping" Eddie could protect Callahan from much of anything.

CHAPTER
FOUR

How to describe Ray Freeman?

Freeman stood over seven feet tall. When he walked through a crowd, other men came up to his chest. His hands were so large that he could bury your face in his palm and plug your ears with his thumb and little finger.

Every inch of him was sinew . . . no gawky limbs on Freeman. He had a large head, heavily muscled arms, and shoulders so wide that he had to move sideways through narrow doors. His body was hard and cylindrical, his waist being nearly as wide as his chest, and all of it muscle.

In the galactic melting pot of the frontier, race meant nothing. Terms like African, Caucasian, and Oriental were obsolete. The population was so intermarried that the physical characteristics could no longer be matched to specific races. In the cosmopolitan collective of the territories, Ray Freeman stood out. He was a black man, a man of African descent born centuries after that Earth continent had been turned into the galaxy's most prestigious zoological exhibit.

Freeman's skin was such a dark shade of brown that it almost looked charcoal. Looking into Ray Freeman's far-set eyes was like staring down the muzzle of a double-barreled shotgun. Utterly ruthless, he was the most intimidating man in the galaxy. He was my partner.

Two years earlier, when I limped out of the ambush on Ravenwood Station barely alive, Ray Freeman rescued me. He placed my helmet beside the remains of Corporal Arlind Marsten, staging my death, then carried me out of Ravenwood. Instead of wearing dog tags, U.A. Marines wore helmets with virtual identifiers. Placing my helmet next to Marsten's remains was tantamount to changing our identities. Since we were both clones, no one would think of checking our DNA.

Now Freeman and I were in business together, freelance bounty hunters.

"I hear there was some action on New Columbia," Freeman said.

"Yeah," I said. "I was in the middle of it. You seeing much?" He was on Providence, an evacuated planet in the Cygnus Arm—one of the renegade arms. We were speaking over the mediaLink. He was using a communications console with a camera so I could see him.

"Have a look," Freeman said, and then he stepped away from the camera to give me a panoramic view of downtown Jasper, the capital city of Providence. The streets were completely empty. The only cars were parked along the curb. No children playing. No pedestrians. Everyone had fled the city.

"What time is it over there?" I asked.

"Nighttime," Freeman said. Providence was indeed dark, but the streets were lit.

"Do the streetlights turn on automatically?" I asked.

"Yes." That was my partner, a man of few syllables.

"So is anybody left in the city?" I asked.

"Looters," he said. "Even the guerillas are gone."

The people leading the Cygnus Arm had declared independence without considering the consequences. They had no Navy of their own. The U.A. Navy had two fleets patrolling their space and the Cygnus Arm military complex had no way of fighting those U.A. ships. When one of those fleets had entered Providence's solar system, the only thing the Cygnus government could do was assemble an armada of unarmed commercial spacecraft or evacuate the planet.

"Is it safe for you to be on New Columbia?" Freeman asked.

"I don't know," I said. "Is it safe for you to be on Providence?"

"No one knows I'm here," Freeman said. The question he left hanging was, "Was that bombing aimed at you?"

"Fair enough," I admitted. "My flight leaves in a couple of hours. Maybe you should do the same . . . get out of Jasper before the troops arrive."

Freeman responded with his "get real" glare—a deadpan expression, a slight narrowing of the eyes, and a barely perceptible shrug of the shoulders.

"I met a guy who says he can find Crowley," I said.

"I'm listening," Freeman said. His voice was so quiet and filled with base tones that you almost felt it as much as heard it. It was the sound of distant thunder or cannons firing a half-mile away.

"Guy's name is Jimmy Callahan. He's a local who bags supplies and runs deals for the Mogats," I said.

"Did he say that before or after the bombs went off?" Freeman asked.

"About the same time," I said. "Callahan and I were negotiating."

"Do you think the bombs were aimed at you?" Freeman asked, not so much as a speck of concern in his voice.

"At him," I said. "It was Billy the Butcher, one of Callahan's clients."

"Where is Callahan now?" Freeman asked. "We need to put him someplace safe and sit on him."

"He's in the brig at Fort Washington along with two of his bodyguards." In my mind I added, *for whatever good that does him.* Fort Washington was the local Marine base. Safe Harbor was a well-fortified city. The Marines, Army, and Air Force all had bases there.

"You stashed him in the Marine base?" Freeman asked.

"Admiral Klyber sent for me. I figure the Marines can keep him till I can come back."

Freeman and I were partners, but we came to the business from different angles. I worked as an errand boy, mostly for Fleet Admiral Bryce Klyber, the highest-ranking man in the Navy and my personal benefactor. Freeman was more of the lone wolf type. As far as I could tell, he had no connection to anybody.

Freeman's camera shook as a bomb or a shell exploded somewhere near him. "I'd better go," he said. "That might be the people I came to see."

I had already stayed too long in Safe Harbor, not that anybody was looking for me. Having skeletons like the ones I had hiding in my closet meant that you could never settle down. For openers, I was absent without leave from the Marine Corps. Well, thanks to Freeman I had supposedly died in battle, but if the Marine Corps knew I was alive, they would list me as absent without leave. And I had even more damning skeletons than that.

I drove my rental car to the commercial spaceport, a sprawling complex that was one part runway, one part passenger terminal, and two parts parking lot. Just finding the building to return the rental took half an hour. The search ended on a ten-story spiral rampway in which each floor was occupied by a different car rental agency.

An attendant pointed me toward a lane filled with a line of parked cars. There would be no paperwork. The car registered its own return, measured its fuel level, reported its own condition, and then issued an electronic receipt to Arlind Marsten, the "missing in action" Marine Corporal who received my helmet on Ravenwood. The police should have arrested Marsten or me when I returned the car, but friends in high places had already made certain that would not happen.

Since Marsten and I were both clones and one clone is supposedly indistinguishable from the next, the personal identifiers in our helmets were the only way the military could tell us apart. That was the theory. In truth, I was not identical to Marsten. He and I came from different batches. My form of clone, the Liberators, had a dark history. Most people believed that the Senate had outlawed my kind. It wasn't true, by the way. They only banned us from entering the Orion Arm—the arm I was currently in.

I was a one-of-a-kind clone, an oxymoronic descriptor if ever there was one. By the time I dropped off the assembly line, my kind had been out of production for nearly thirty years because of our violent tendencies. I did not want to advertise this to the good people of New Columbia.

Prosperous and located in the all-important Orion Arm, New Columbia attracted tourists and businesses from around the galaxy. Its spaceport was the size of a small town with ten times the population. Police and military guards kept the tides of people flowing efficiently enough.

If they only knew what kind of shark had swum in with their minnows. I passed the queue for baggage. During my years in the military I learned to live light and travel lighter. I spent four days in Safe Harbor, two more days than I expected. Everything I brought fit in a small briefcase that I could carry on my lap.

From New Columbia I would fly to Mars, the galaxy's biggest spaceport. Once on Mars, I would either receive my next assignment or I would find a hotel room and rest until my next job arrived—I didn't care which.

Assignments meant money, but it also meant fighting for the good old Unified Authority. I didn't really mind having bombs explode around me. Even when an assignment meant risking my life to save a worthless punk like Jimmy Callahan, I preferred it to lounging around some hotel. I could not help myself, it was in my neural programming.

I enjoyed the study of philosophy, politics, and intergalactic relations, but only as they applied to combat. I was designed for battle, and a soldier was all I could be. I was screwed.

I went to the gate to wait for my flight, which would leave in another three hours. I cherished short breaks like this. It was the long ones that drove me crazy.

I put on my mediaLink shades, streamline glasses with retinal displays built into their hinges. Lasers painted images on my retinal tissue, opening a world of books, magazines, and video feeds. I could play games, watch movies, write letters, or catch up on the news. On this particular day, I decided to read.

My favorite reading was ethical philosophy. At the time, I was reading *The Complete Works of Spinoza*. Spinoza argued that men could not feel love, desire, or passion without already having a germ of that emotion within them. It was an interesting concept that was especially true of military clones. Our loyalty was programmed into us. We loved the government that made us. Even when we realized that the government hated our kind, we still loved it. Even when we hated the government back, we remained loyal.

Clones were also programmed to think they were natural-born. Your average soldier clone did not know he was cloned and programmed to love nothing but their country. They just thought of themselves as patriotic citizens.

Was Spinoza so depressing, or was it just my overapplied interpretation of his work? I looked around the gate. This particular flight was a business flight. Men in suits sat scanning the mediaLink or writing memos. Women in suits did the same. A young mother tried to busy two small children by reading to them. I had no love, desire, or passion for any of these people. They were natural-born, I was synthetic . . . a rare synthetic. I was a clone who knew he was a clone. My model was designed before the Senate added a death-reflex to its military clones to prevent them from rebelling against their makers. When other clones learned they were clones, a gland in their brain killed them. When I learned I was a clone, I went to a bar and got drunk.

If Spinoza was right, perhaps I felt no love or passion for humanity because the germ did not exist in me. Perhaps the germ of love required a soul. Most religions stated that clones do not have souls. Perhaps I proved them right.

The Unified Authority was right to build neural programming and the death reflex into its clones. Judging by my example, once clones knew they were apart from humanity, they closed themselves off to it.

As I said before, I was a one of a kind clone. The rest of my kind were created at a time when the Republic was under siege. The Galactic Central Fleet, an armada of warships, had vanished. As a last resort, the military created battalions of Liberator clones and sent them to the Galactic Eye to kill whatever unknown enemy was there.

The battle ended quickly. The problem was that having created a living, breathing super weapon, the Unified Authority did not know what to do with it. When the generals sent Liberators to settle smaller battles and domestic problems, they did not like the results.

Liberators were sent to stop a riot on Albatross Island, a penal planet in the Perseus Arm. The Liberators killed the prisoners and then turned on the guards and the hostages. With the exception of a few prison workers, the Liberators killed everyone on the planet.

In the end, Congress banned Liberator clones from the Orion Belt and let attrition thin them out. I stepped off the assembly line in 2490. By that time only four Liberators still existed. Three were wild and bloodthirsty, caring only about their own survival. One was religious and completely loyal to his U.A. creators. He was my mentor. To this day, I do not know whether to admire or despise him.

I feel them all inside of me, struggling for control of my emotions. When I close my eyes at night, I sometimes think I can hear the ghost of Sergeant Tabor Shannon, a Marine who happily gave his life for the Republic. When I pass through great crowds, I feel isolated and I imagine Sergeant Booth Lector sneering at everyone around him. Both men were Liberators. Both died in battle.

Shannon remained patriotic to the last, hoping for the best in a world that considered him an insect. Yes, I was still putting my life on the line for the Unified Authority; but as a mercenary. I could at least tell myself that my allegiance was to myself. But Lector was the only one whose allegiance was truly just to himself. He remained in the Marines because he could not figure out a way to escape the Corps.

Looking back, I think Shannon and Lector were both full of shit.

In the Marines, you scuttled into your transport when your sergeant yelled for you to get your ass on board. But on a civilian flight, pretty flight attendants ask the passengers to board their flights. The door to our commuter flight opened and an attendant with long dark hair welcomed us. We formed a line and quietly took our seats.

The flight took off smoothly, rising through the sky. When we were about two hundred miles outside of New Columbia, the blue and white atmosphere ended and turned into the blackness of space. To this point, the ship traveled slowly in the climb, never moving more than two thousand miles per hour. We picked up speed and traveled another eight hundred miles to the Broadcast Network in a couple of minutes—a painfully slow pace.

I reclined my seat and stretched out for the short ride. We were traveling 240 trillion miles to Mars. The flight would take just over an hour, and I had had enough of Spinoza and needed the rest.

I turned my head toward the porthole beside my chair and watched the tint shields form over the glass, dimming out stars and planets under a blanket of inky blackness. We would soon reach the Broadcast Network. I could not see the discs through the shields, but I knew what was coming.

A thousand miles outside of Safe Harbor, our spacejet slowed to a crawl as it approached the two gigantic elliptical discs that formed the New Columbian sector's broadcast station. The discs were approximately one mile across and reflected everything around them like giant mirrors. Many things happened over the next few moments. A silver-red security laser, able to X-ray a ship, its contents, and its passengers, searched the spacejet for criminals and contraband. Once the U.A. Port Authority completed its search, the galaxy's largest super computer sequenced our travel to make sure no other ships would enter our travel space.

The spacejet did not enter the discs. As it approached, jagged tendrils of electricity stretched out of the glossy face of the sending disc. The blue-white lightning was so bright that I could see it through the tint shielding on the window. The air in the cabin crackled with static electricity. Had the tinting failed, the glare of the Broadcast Network's electrical field would have blinded me. Even if I closed my eyes and placed my hands over my face, that light would blind me.

"Prepare for broadcast," the pilot said over the loud speaker.

And then the first 10,000-light-year jump was over. We had traveled sixty trillion miles in less than one second. We traveled the remaining one hundred eighty trillion miles in the next few minutes—the time it took to emerge from a receiving disc and glide to the broadcast disc beside it. The transfers took approximately thirty seconds and we made four of them.

Clearing Mars security, however, was a different story. The Unified Authority was at war and Mars was its most important port. Mars was the gateway to Earth.

Mars Spaceport was the galaxy's largest shopping mall. It was the hub of all space flight to and from Earth. Consequently, anybody on the planet qualified for duty-free shopping. Even the Mars port employees qualified. The jewelry stores on Mars sold more diamonds than jewelers on the next ten richest planets combined. As the advertisements said, "Serious shoppers shop on Mars." Even people who were not planning on traveling sometimes flew to Mars for the tax breaks on gems, fine liquors, and other luxury items.

Fluorescent light poured out of the storefronts. Pretty girls in short skirts stood just outside stores offering to mist passersby with samples of expensive perfumes. A robotic cigar store Indian turned back and forth proffering plastic cigars to all who passed. The shopping arcade I had entered stretched as far as the eye could see, and there were ten more like it.

Nearly one million people flew in and out of Mars on any given day. The planet did not have a breathable atmosphere, just a series of domes with a city-sized spaceport and a military base that was jointly run by the Air Force and the Army.

I did not like going to Mars. I came here because it was the most crowded spot in the galaxy, and the best jumping point for meeting Admiral Klyber. The traffic around this planet was so congested that no one paid undue attention when ships took off and headed out to space, and Klyber's pilots could meet me here and smuggle me away without attracting attention.

I scanned the crowd around me for known Confederates and Mogats. Having just survived a terrorist attack on New Columbia I was more cautious than ever. I also kept an eye out for people who might identify me as a Liberator—or even worse, recognize me.

"You ready to go, Marsten?" a man asked as I passed the door of a dimly-lit bar.

The pilot knew my real name. He also knew better than to refer to me as *Wayson* in public.

"Sure," I said, not even pausing to look back.

The pilot walked quickly and caught up with me. Dressed

in a long leather jacket and khaki pants, he wore the traditional uniform of civilian pilots. His short black hair was slicked back and a pair of dark aviator glasses poked out of his shirt pocket. He was not a civilian. He was an officer in the Navy.

We left the shopping arcade and entered a food court. Lines of people formed in front of small restaurants. Janitors bussed tables and cleared trash bins. Loud talk echoed in the rafters of this cavernous hall with its bright lights and gleaming white floors.

"You are the hot topic on the ship these days," the pilot said. "Is it true?"

"Is what true?" I asked.

"Were you in Safe Harbor when the bombs went off?"

"Where did you hear that?" I asked.

"One of my friends heard Klyber say you were there."

"If Admiral Klyber says I was there, I must have been there," I said.

The pilot laughed. We crossed the food court and entered an unmarked door. This led us into a narrow service hall that seemed to stretch for miles. The white tile floor gleamed but the walls were unfinished plaster. Bright fluorescent fixtures provided the hall with dry luminescence.

"So were you there when the bombs went off?"

"Yeah, I was there. I helped dig out a few of the survivors."

The service hall branched off to two different sections of the Mars Spaceport. We entered from one of the bustling commercial terminals. Had we headed left, we would have entered administrative offices. We turned right and wound up in the commuter terminal. This was the area used by private pilots and large corporations. It was smaller than the commercial terminals, far less crowded, and much less flashy. Instead of a large food court, it had a coffee shop where pilots went to relax as they filled out flight reports or studied their flight plans. The general mood in the commuter terminal was quiet, like the lobby of a library.

A couple dozen pilots stood in pockets scattered around the floor of the terminal. Most of these flyboys seemed to know each other. None of them recognized my pilot. They stole mildly curious glances. His was a new face that had stumbled into their tight-knit fraternity.

Once we left the terminal, my pilot swapped his

camouflage—the leather jacket and civilian accoutrements—for a Navy jacket. His spacecraft, however, remained camouflaged.

We crossed the tarmac and climbed into a Johnston R-27, the kind of twelve-seater light craft favored by small corporations. The Johnston was white with dark gray trim along its wings. It had neither armor nor hidden gun arrays, the prosaic sign of a military craft. This innocuous Johnston had something far more impressive.

"You strapped in?" the pilot asked as I fitted the last of the safety harness across my chest, a useless gesture. Any accidents in this little craft would end in death.

"This is Johnston R-twenty-seven zero four, four, nine Rectal, Anus, Penile five requesting permission to taxi. Again, this is Johnston zero, four, four, nine RAP five requesting permission."

"Roger, Johnston R-twenty-seven. You are cleared to taxi." I could hear other flight controllers squawking in the background as the man on the radio struggled to keep from laughing.

"Aren't there regulations about what you can say on the air?" I asked.

"To the tower?" the pilot asked, sounding genuinely surprised. "The controllers love it when I talk dirty. It's their supervisors who get pissed, and that's all right. They can't touch me. I have military clearance and they're just civilians."

The commuter runway was a mile-long tunnel with several airlocks. A crewman towed us to the first airlock using a cart. When he reached the far wall of the airlock, the crewman detached our tow cable, gave us a quick wave, and drove back to the terminal. The runway behind us vanished as the thirty-foot door closed behind us, sealing in the spaceport's manufactured atmosphere.

The wall in front of us was thick and heavy, the color of oxidized iron. After two minutes, a seam showed in the center of this great metal barrier. The cogs at the base and top of the wall groaned as they pulled it open along their zipperlike causeway.

This time we rolled forward under our own power and stopped just shy of a final barrier, an electroshield. The first two barriers we passed through protected the atmosphere inside the spaceport. This next shield was in place for military purposes. It was a force field designed to stop intruders and deflect attacks. The electroshield could dampen particle beam and laser attacks, and anything solid that hit the shield would be instantly fried. I could see the surface of Mars ahead through the electroshield's translucent white aurora.

"Do they know you're self-broadcasting?" I asked.

Having a "self-broadcasting" ship meant that this highly modified Johnston R-27 did not need to enter the Broadcast Network to travel long distances. The ship was equipped with its own broadcast engine that, used in conjunction with the right navigational computer, could transport the ship anywhere in the galaxy.

"It's sort of hard to hide something as big as an anomaly," the pilot said.

Anomaly was the term used to describe the electrical field through which broadcast objects vanished and appeared. "They track us the moment we leave Mars. We're the only ship that flies toward Saturn instead of Earth or the Broadcast Network. That kind of thing gets all kinds of attention these days."

"I suppose," I said.

The surface of Mars looked like an Earth desert from our cockpit. Peering out as we arched away from the planet, I saw dented plains that stretched around the horizon. Huge as the Mars Spaceport building was when seen from the inside, it became a mere speck as we pulled away from the planet. Soon enough, Mars looked no larger than a coin, and all of its features vanished.

The only broadcast discs in the Sol System, Earth's solar system, hovered a few hundred miles above the spaceport. Normally spacecraft either flew up to the discs or headed toward Earth, the only populated planet in the solar system. We, however, flew in the opposite direction. We headed out toward space, toward Saturn, and traveled more than 100,000 miles. Only the most powerful tracking systems like the ones on Mars would detect what happened next.

Sitting out in space, we glided as the contraption in the back of our craft came to life. The glass around our cockpit became as black as space. It was opaque but not dark enough to block out the electrical storm caused by our broadcast engine. Lightning danced across the edges of the Johnston R-27. I could see its squirming outline through the tinting. It looked like neon chalk lines as the cabin filled with the acrid scent of ozone.

"Welcome to the Perseus Arm," the pilot said.

"Still in Perseus?" I asked. "I thought they would have moved the ship by now. We are at war."

"Why move?" the pilot said. "No one knows we are here. We're protected from both sides."

CHAPTER
FIVE

March 7, 2512 A.D.
Ship: *Doctrinaire*; Galactic Position: Perseus Arm

Sections of the *Doctrinaire* were still under construction and probably would be for the next thousand years.

The *Doctrinaire* was so incredibly large that its size created an anomaly. Viewing the ship alone in space, you could not estimate its size. At first glance, she looked like any other fighter carrier—the same wedge-shaped body, the same beige hull and light gray underbelly. In the vast panorama of space, size and distance become blurred. Seeing the *Doctrinaire* floating beside a Perseus-class fighter carrier, you would think they were identical ships and that the *Doctrinaire* was closer to you because she was so much larger than the other.

The hull of the *Doctrinaire* filled the view from our cockpit long before we reached its landing bay. The ship was shaped like a bat—its wing span measuring two miles wide and its hull was about 1.3 miles in length. The great ship had four launch tubes, hollow tunnels used for launching fighter craft that stretched the entire length of the ship. The *Doctrinaire* had an additional four landing bays for transports and supply ships.

The pilot flew the Johnston toward Bay three. We slowed to a mere hover and the pilot used thruster engines to guide us into place in one of those docking bays.

"Well, Corporal Marsten, it's been a pleasure flying you on *Doctrinaire* Spacelines. Fly with us again sometime," the pilot said as he climbed from his seat. He gave me a sloppy, mock-salute. This was not an unfriendly gesture—he knew that I was AWOL.

I left the ship and walked to a nearby locker room. I pulled a key from my pocket and looked for the matching cubicle. Once I found it, I stowed my civilian clothes and dressed in the charley service uniform of a U.A. Marines corporal. For all appearances, I was just another enlisted clone on active duty.

The trip from the landing bay to the bridge was lengthy and fast. The *Doctrinaire* had twelve decks, plus a bridge and an observation deck. The ship had nearly twenty square miles of deck space. Just getting from the landing bay to the central elevator bank required a ride on the recently installed tram. Officers might spend their careers on this ship without visiting the bridge or the engineering decks.

I lived on this ship two years ago. Back then everything but the shell of the ship was still under construction. Last time I traveled this path, the corridors were covered with scaffolding. Welders used to work in these halls around the clock, the white glare from their torches shining up and down the halls like a continuous flash of lightning. Back when I was assigned to the *Doctrinaire*, the ship housed more builders than crew. You might pass ten construction workers walking down a hall and not see a single sailor.

A lot had changed. The cylindrical corridors I entered on this occasion had smooth shining walls. Bright light shined down from inlaid ceiling fixtures and polished chrome address plates adorned most doors.

The *Doctrinaire* had several banks of elevators, but only the central bank reached the bridge. As I entered one of these elevators, a security computer scanned and identified me. The doors closed behind me. Moments later they opened on to the bridge of the *Doctrinaire*—a sweeping deck manned by dozens of officers.

Three officers came in my direction. The man on the right was a captain—a heady rank in the U.A. Navy. He was young, stout, and very attentive. He looked like the kind of aggressive officer who runs a tight ship and accomplishes his mission at any cost. The man on the left was a rear admiral. He had a single star in his collar. He was an older officer whose casual smile and soft eyes gave the impression of patience.

The man in the center was Fleet Admiral Bryce Klyber, possibly the most powerful man in the entire Republic. Klyber was an accomplished Naval officer. He rose through the ranks by answering every challenge. With the exception of Bryce Klyber, no one had worn the fifth star of a fleet admiral for forty years.

Klyber was one of the last active officers who had fought in the Galactic Central War—the last full-blown war. Klyber, of course, won that war when he unveiled his battalion of top-secret Liberator clones.

"Marsten," Klyber said, and eyebrow cocked to show his surprise at seeing me. "I thought I left orders for you to meet me in my quarters. Just as well. Corporal, this is Rear Admiral Halverson and Captain Johansson."

I saluted.

They saluted back.

Klyber looked over at the rear admiral. "Admiral Halverson, have you met Corporal Marsten?"

Something about Captain Johansson caught my attention. He was tall and skinny with a shaved head and squinting dark eyes. He did not even bother looking at me as he saluted. He seemed to want to ignore me, not in the "you're not worth my time" way that many officers greeted clones, but in a way that seemed far more contemptuous.

"Corporal, I don't believe we've met," the older officer said. "Rear Admiral Halverson." He looked to be in his late fifties, an officer nearing retirement. Halverson looked like a youngster beside old man Klyber, however, a painfully skinny man who looked like he could have been one of the slaves forced into building the Pyramids of Egypt.

"Marsten here is retired from active duty," Klyber said. "I, um, reactivate him on occasion. He's got a knack for security."

Klyber was tall. I was six feet three inches tall and he had me by an inch or two. On the other hand, he may well have weighed less than 150 pounds. Klyber stood perfectly erect, his rigid posture and skinny body made him look like he was made out of the outer limbs of an old oak tree. He had icy blue eyes that looked as focused and intense as sapphire lasers.

He turned to the two senior officers. "Perhaps we can take this up again later this evening. I have some business to take care of with the corporal."

Halverson and Johansson saluted and walked off to continue their discussion.

"What do you think, Harris?" Klyber asked, looking around the bridge.

"She looks ready to run," I said, noting the brightly lit navigational panels.

"More or less," Klyber said. "It's not the equipment that worries me. I worry more about the men at her helm. You get a limited selection of officers with top-secret projects. My crew was chosen for security clearance, not battle experience. If I wanted a ship full of military police and intelligence officers, this would be the ideal crew."

"You worked with Halverson in Scutum-Crux," I pointed out.

"Tom Halverson does what he can. I like Halverson," Klyber said. He looked around to make sure that no one was within earshot of us and lowered his voice. "What did you think of Johansson?"

"Not especially friendly," I said. "He doesn't make a great first impression."

Klyber smiled and took one last look around the bridge. "Let's head down to my quarters."

"Yes, sir," I said.

We entered the elevator.

"What happened on New Columbia?" Klyber asked.

"Mogat terrorists happened," I said. The elevator doors slid closed and I felt the slightest vibration as we dropped three decks and sixty feet. The doors opened.

"Anyone I have heard of?" Klyber asked.

"William Patel," I said.

"Billy the Butcher? Are you sure it was him?"

"I saw him myself, sir," I said. We entered the corridor

that led to officer country. "Callahan, the informant you sent me to meet, fingered him. Callahan thought he could earn himself some credibility and a nice reward by handing him over to us."

Officers walked past us in groups of two and three. They all stopped to salute as Klyber walked by. Klyber returned their salutes without breaking stride.

"Patel was wise to him?"

"Have you met Callahan? He figured he could pinch both sides of the loaf. He sold Patel supplies and us information. It takes a subtle hand to play both sides off like that. Subtlety is not one of Callahan's stronger suits."

We entered the admiral's suite which included his quarters, a large office, and his war room. "So you don't think the bombs were meant for you?"

"Not a chance," I said.

"What tipped you off to the bombs?" Klyber asked.

"We were sitting on this balcony overlooking the street and out comes Patel, practically right on cue. He's too far away to nab, but somehow he knows where we are sitting and he looks up at us. I mean, he's a hundred yards away and he looks right at us.

"I didn't trust Callahan. He struck me as a punk . . . a small brain with a big mouth. So when Patel looks right at us, I figure he knows exactly what Callahan is up to. The only question I had was if we could make it out in time.

"The big question is, who tipped Patel off?"

Klyber listened to this, his blue-fire eyes seeming to X-ray my thoughts as I spoke. "Do you have any theories?"

"Somebody on your staff," I said.

"Interesting that you would say that. Of course, you realize that parked as we are so far from the Broadcast Network, we don't have communications with the outside world. In order to get a message to Patel, our spy would need to travel . . . broadcast to another location.

"Given that, do you still think the leak came from here?"

This quadrant of the galaxy was dark. Communications were transferred through the Broadcast Network and the *Doctrinaire* was nearly 20,000 light years from the nearest discs.

"Yes, sir," I said. "Whoever leaked the information traveled."

Klyber sat silent behind his desk and rubbed the thinning hairline around his temple. He seemed deep in thought, then brightened. "I have something for you," he said as he stood and opened a closet hidden in the wall beside his desk. "A friend sent this to me. He did not know anything about you, of course; but I think you will appreciate this."

When Klyber turned back toward me, he held a small book with tan leather binding that looked parched and old. The leather had gone stiff with age and drying. The words, *Personal Journal of Father David Sanjines*, were emblazoned in dark brown letters that stood out against the dust-colored leather.

"A friend in the Vatican sent this to me. Most of it is of no interest. It's the journal of an archbishop. But there is a small section concerning a mutual acquaintance of ours."

I looked down at the journal as Admiral Klyber held it out to me.

Klyber said. "I want you to have it."

I took the old book and it seemed to fall open of its own accord. The pages had a faint red tinge to them that I knew was from clay dust, though it looked more like rust.

The book had a five-inch strip of blue velvet ribbon sewed into its binding for a bookmark. Parts of that ribbon had turned nearly black with age. I noted the date—April 10, 2494—on the open page.

Klyber watched me. "That is the only entry of interest. It goes on for a few pages." He thought about the book for a few more moments, then shifted his attention. "I would like to revisit your impression of Captain Johansson."

"You think Johansson is a spy?" I asked, closing the book.

Klyber did not answer. He smirked as he watched me from behind his desk. "Oh, I know he's a spy, the question is for whom."

"A spy?" I asked. "Do you think he's a Mogat?"

"I'm guessing he's worse," Klyber said. "I think he works for Admiral Huang."

Admiral Klyber had a long-standing feud with Che Huang, the secretary of the Navy and a member of the Joint Chiefs of Staff. Admiral Huang wanted to see himself as the most powerful man in the Navy, but Klyber, with his political connections, was generally recognized as having more clout.

"Huang?" I asked. "That would be bad." Klyber could legally execute an enemy spy. A spy working for Huang, however, could only be transferred.

Possibly because Klyber headed the Liberator cloning project, Huang had a thing about Liberators. Huang was the officer who had assigned me to Ravenwood. To the best of his knowledge, I had died on that planet, and I wanted him to continue believing me dead.

"We're a thousand light years from the nearest planet," I said. "Dump him in space and say he had an accident."

"It's too late for that," Klyber said, putting up a hand to stop me. "Whatever he's looking for, I assume he has already found it."

"That doesn't mean he's been able to report everything he's found," I said.

"Whatever information he was after, he transmitted it the first time we sent him out. The safest thing to do with Johansson right now is to keep him onboard the *Doctrinaire*. That way we can observe him."

"Assuming he doesn't have any friends on board," I said.

"I hope he does," Klyber agreed. "We're keeping an eye on him.

"If he's Huang's boy, you're in for a fight in the Senate. If Huang hears about the *Doctrinaire*, he's going to ask for control of the project. He'll probably put Wonder Boy in command of the ship."

"Wonder Boy," a.k.a. Rear Admiral Robert Thurston, was Che Huang's protégé, the brilliant young officer who replaced Klyber as the admiral of the Scutum-Crux Fleet. Bryce Klyber was no slouch when it came to strategy, but Thurston crushed him in a battle simulation.

I did not like Thurston. He had a mile-wide anti-synthetic streak. Thurston saw clones as supplies and nothing else. He used them like any other kind of inventory, something to be expended and reordered.

"I'm meeting with Huang and the Joint Chiefs next week at the Golan Dry Docks for a top secret briefing," Klyber said, interrupting my thoughts. "I would very much like to return from that conclave alive."

I spent the night on the *Doctrinaire*, sleeping in one of the state rooms that Admiral Klyber reserved for visiting dignitaries. My bunk was hard, my room was sparse, and the bathroom was entirely made of stainless steel. I felt at home.

Stripping to my general-issue briefs and top, I took the book Klyber gave me and climbed into my rack. The sheets were coarse and stiff, stretched so tight that you could bounce a coin on them. It felt good to lie down.

Klyber had said that the book had a passage in it about a friend of mine. I opened the journal to the section marked by the thin strip of ribbon. As I looked at the handwritten entry, I realized that Admiral Klyber had been wrong. The man described in this journal was more of a mentor than a friend. The passage was about Tabor Shannon, whom I had met while serving on the Kamehameha, Klyber's old flagship.

Shannon was a living paradox. He was a Liberator. He'd killed hundreds of enemies in battle, but he also went to Mass. He was the only clone I ever met with a religious streak. His religious feeling made no sense because, as a Liberator, he knew he was a clone and therefore knew God had nothing to do with his creation. Catholic doctrine held that clones had no souls. Almost every church taught that.

Shannon was intelligent, but he remained blindly loyal to the Republic to his last breath. He died in battle, fighting for the nation that had banned his existence. At the time he died I admired him more than anyone I ever knew, but I grew to despise him. He seemed pathologically determined to devote his life to those who cared least about him—the nation that had outlawed his kind and the God who disavowed his existence.

Since leaving the Marines, I had come to question the line that separated devotion and delusion. Granted, I was still working for the same side as always, risking my life for the same Republic that never shed a tear for Tabor Shannon; but I was different. I had gone freelance. I made money for my services. I was also free to leave. If the Confederate

Arms offered me a better deal one day, I wanted to believe that I would take it.

Having seen what I had seen, I did not believe in nations or deities. And as for Shannon, who did believe, I could not decide whether he had been a quixotic hero or just a fool. Either way, I had no intention of following in his footsteps.

From the Journal of Father David Sanjines, archbishop and chief administrator of Saint Germaine:

Entry: Earth Date June 4, 2483
I received an urgent message from spaceport security this morning. When I called to look into the matter, the captain asked me to watch a feed from his security monitor.

They had detained a marine named Tabor Shannon. I only needed a moment to identify the problem. "Is that a Liberator?" I asked the captain. "Haven't they been banned?"

"Liberators are not allowed in the Orion Arm," the captain said. "They can travel Cygnus freely. If you want my opinion, I think they should all be executed."

The ecumenical council of 2410 held that clones did not have souls and therefore did not fit the Catholic definition of human life, but I did not think that made them machines. Church canon dating back to Saint Francis forbade cruelty to animals. Perhaps this Liberator clone had more in common with a mad dog than a man, but he had blood running through his veins, not oil. He was no machine.

The captain told me that he checked with the U.A. Consulate. "We don't have to let him on our planet. Should I send him away?"

The captain knew better than to tell me what to do. Saint Germaine being a Catholic mission, I was the one who made the decisions. "Do you know what he is doing here?" I asked.

"He says he is on a pilgrimage."

"You must be joking," I said.

"No sh—er, no, Father. I am sorry about that, Father."

"I understand, my son," I said. The presence of a murderer on our little planet would put everyone on edge. A religious pilgrimage? I was skeptical to say the least. "He is on a pilgrimage?"

"That's what he says."

I asked the captain if he would detain the man in question until I could arrive. I thought that might be soon, but this was Friday and a holy day—the immaculate heart of Mother Mary. I needed to attend to Mass and then I had a full day of meetings. The Liberator would have to wait until tomorrow.

Entry: Earth Date June 5, 2483

I did not know how I would react to meeting a Liberator face-to-face. As a young priest, I served in the Albatross Island penal colony. I was there during the riot of 2472. A force of Liberators came to the planet to stop the rioting. They put down the riot, all right. They also killed the prisoners and the guards and almost everybody on the planet.

Before seeing Liberators in action, I believed that clones were human even if they had no immortal souls. I even questioned the ecumenical convention that decreed clones were created of man and not God. That changed for me on Albatross Island.

You cannot understand a lion until you have seen one devour its prey. I thought that all people were created in God's own image until I saw the Liberators,

demons who looked like men but who rejected all
goodness. I saw them kill thousands of innocent, helpless men. Just thinking about that massacre is painful.
Once I witnessed the way the Liberators fought and
killed, I saw the wisdom of the ecumenical counsel's
judgment. These monsters could not have had souls.

I arrived at the spaceport before lunch and found
an office in which I could interview this Liberator. His
name was Tabor Shannon. I arranged for us to be
alone. I was an old man now, and I had no time to
fear devils, not even cloned ones.

Three soldiers walked the prisoner into the room. I
dismissed them at the door. The leader of the soldiers
did not want to leave. He said I would not be safe
alone with a Liberator. I told him I would take my
chances, and I dismissed him a second time. All the
while the Liberator sat in one of the seats I had
arranged in the middle of the room, watching us.

If I ever felt scared during my interview with the
Liberator, it was when I turned and saw the way he
watched us. I believed his expression was implacable.
Now, as I think about it, I have changed my mind. I
think that his expression was merely one of curiosity.

"I am Father Sanjines," I said as I came to sit
across from him. We were nearly knee-to-knee, just a
foot or two separated us. I knew this man could easily
spring from his chair and strangle me, but I sensed
that he did not come to do violence. "You are Corporal Tabor Shannon?" I asked.

"That is correct, Father."

I looked around the room. Maybe I was unconsciously looking for a door through which to escape.
What I saw instead was a small wet bar with a crys-
tal decanter. "I am an old man, Corporal Shannon. I
took my vows nearly fifty years ago."

He said nothing.

"Would you like some sherry? We don't have
many fine things on Saint Germaine, but we do have
a superb distillery. I personally oversaw the building
of it. I've been in this mission from its start."

*The clone did not accept my offer. Perhaps he was
not much of a drinker or perhaps he wanted to leave
a good impression, I could not tell.*

"You'll want to try it before you leave," I told him.

"What is this about?" the Liberator asked, still
trying to sound civil. "Why have you detained me?"

"Mr. Shannon, this mission is nearly twenty years
old, and I have been the chief administrator and
archbishop here for all of that time. Before coming
here, I was a chaplain on a penal planet."

"Was it Albatross Island?" he asked.

"It was," I said. "You can imagine my feelings
when I received a call alerting me that a Liberator
had arrived in our spaceport."

The Liberator said nothing.

"You claim that you have come on a pilgrimage.
Is that correct?"

"It is, Father," the clone said, sounding as determined as a young boy wanting to enter a seminary.

"You will forgive me if I find that hard to believe,
Mr. Shannon, but you see, I watched three hundred of
your kind butcher prisoners, both rioting and innocent. Perhaps you were not involved in that . . .
that . . ."

"Action."

*The Liberator used the word action. I was of-
fended.*

"I was trying to decide whether to call it a slaughter or a massacre," I told him. "I think a more appro-
priate word might be extermination. As best as I can
remember it, one thousand five hundred inmates ri-
oted and the marines sent a battalion of Liberator
clones to restore order. That was five rioting inmates
for each Liberator. I should have thought that would
have been enough blood to satisfy them."

"I wasn't there," the Liberator told me.

"When they finished killing the rioters, they
slaughtered prisoners who did not riot. Then they
turned on the guards and hostages. By that time, they
weren't even using bullets anymore. They beat men to

death with their rifles. I helped reclaim the bodies of
the victims, Mr. Shannon. It was the most terrible
thing I have ever seen.

"That was the closest I ever came to renouncing
my vows. When I saw what those Liberators had
done, I did not believe that a just God would have allowed the creation of such monsters. A few weeks
later, the Senate outlawed Liberators. Is that not so?"

"They outlawed the manufacture of Liberator
clones," Shannon said to me. His gaze still met mine.
I did not know if I saw glee or defiance in his expression, but I did not like what I saw.

"We don't, as a rule, receive many clones on this
planet." Having said this, I felt a tinge of guilt. This
clone had been nothing but pleasant, and I had acted
adversarial from the start. "Forgive me," I said. "I
have been too straightforward. Are you sure you will
not have a sherry?"

I climbed from my seat and went to the bar to
pour myself a glass.

"Are you refusing me entry?" the clone asked.

"We Catholics like to believe that our church runs
this planet, but the Unified Authority maintains an
embassy just down the street from the Archdiocese.
The U.A. runs this spaceport facility, as a matter-of-
fact. That is not a symbiotic relationship. We do not
welcome government intervention on our planet."

I shut my eyes and thought about Liberators as I
sipped the sherry. Perhaps I was reliving those last
hours of the siege on Albatross Island, those awful
moments when our rescuers became predators. I
thought about a cell block in which the blood and
brains on the walls were so thick that I could no
longer see the bricks and mortar.

We Catholics are anti-synthetic by our very nature.
According to our doctrine, only God can create life.
The use of clones in the military caused the Vatican to
release a statement defining life as a being with an immortal soul. Science can clone sheep, snakes, and soldiers that breathe air and move of their own volition,
but science cannot prove that its creations have souls.

"They were without compassion," I said. "Ravenous dogs lusting for blood. You will forgive me if I have been impolite, Mr. Shannon, but I see nothing even remotely redeeming about your kind. I once questioned the doctrine that clones have no souls. Having seen the work of Liberators, I determined that the butchers who came to Albatross Island were soulless creatures. I saw nothing redeeming in them."

" 'But if there be no virtue to take away, consequently there can be no vice,' " Shannon said.

I heard this and smiled and took a long sip of sherry. "You've read Saint Augustine. Impressive. But you've misquoted him. Augustine said, 'If there be no good to take away.' He also said, 'It is impossible that there should be a harmless vice.' "

"He did say that, didn't he?" the Liberator said cheerfully.

"The Liberators who invaded Albatross Island did a lot of harm. I believe that their existence is a vice," I said. "It is a vice of the Unified Authority government."

"I never cared much for Saint Augustine, anyway," Shannon said. "What about the secular philosophers? Friedrich Nietzsche said that no man has an eternal soul. If he was correct, that would put us all on equal ground. None of us would be alive by the Vatican's definition."

"Quoting a philosopher who referred to himself as 'the anti-Christ' does not generally lead to a favorable impression in a Catholic colony," I said. "I suggest you restrict yourself to Saint Augustine while you are on Saint Germaine, Mr. Shannon. Better yet, I suggest you avoid discussion of philosophy entirely. The people on this planet have strong opinions."

"While I'm on Saint Germaine?" Shannon asked, "Are you allowing me to stay?"

"What is the object of your pilgrimage?" I asked.

"The same as any pilgrim," the Liberator said. "I seek truth. I want to know who I am and how I fit into the universe."

"And you believe you can find those answers on our little planet?" I asked.

"I'm curious about Catholicism," the Liberator said.

"I can tell you where the Catholic Church stands when it comes to you and your place in the universe. The Catholic Church holds that you have no soul and that you are an abomination."

"And yet I am created in God's own image."

"Man was created in God's image," I told him.

"And I was created in man's image," he said.

I said, "I will allow you to visit our planet, and I hope that the answers you find here will not leave you discomfited."

I did not let him stay because of his amateurish attempts to grasp philosophy. I let him stay because I believed he was sincere, and that intrigued me. If this man was a Liberator, then he was by nature a killer and a creation without a soul. I knew this to be true, though in his case, I am not certain that I believed it was true.

March 13, 2512 A.D.
Location: Golan Dry Docks; Galactic Position:
Norma Arm

The Golan Dry Docks were considered one of the "seven man-made wonders of the galaxy." Other wonders included the Capitol Building in Washington D.C., the outer-galactic scientific observatory on the outer edge of the Orion Arm, the planetary food storage and production facility on Nebraska Kri, the all-faiths military burial facility near the center of the Norma Arm, the Sol science station on the surface of the sun, and, of course, the Broadcast Network.

Funny how the mundane wonders get overlooked. I considered the spaceport on Mars far more wondrous than the Sol science station or the Nebraska Kri food-packing plant. That place was so big that it needed a resort-sized dormitory to house clerks and waiters. Mars Spaceport even had a smaller secondary dormitory that housed the people who ran special stores, theaters, and restaurants for the employees living in the primary dormitory.

My mind wandered when I traveled through space. The light flashing on my radio brought me back to reality.

"Starliner A-ten-twenty-thirty-four, this is Dry Docks traffic control, please come in."

"Traffic control, this is Starliner A-ten-twenty-thirty-four."

Ahead of me, the Golan Dry Docks looked like a cross between bleached bones and a giant spider web. Eight-mile pillars described the outside of the platform in lilting arches like the ribs of a gigantic skeleton. Between these pillars was a haphazard warren of walls that divided the structure into mooring slips and construction zones. Scaffolding lined the insides of those slips. From out in space, the scaffolds looked like threads instead of twenty-foot-wide metal platforms. The dry docks housed over eight hundred cubic miles of space for building ships.

Golan did not orbit a planet. It was a free-floating space station.

"Starliner pilot, please identify yourself and prepare for security scan."

This request did not worry me. The Golan Dry Docks were one of the most security-intensive facilities in the galaxy. Knowing that Admiral Klyber had picked me for this assignment, the head of *Doctrinaire* security crafted my new identity and logged my clearance and flight plans while I was still on New Columbia. He knew where I was headed before I knew, it seemed. Rather than enter the Dry Docks as Corporal Arlind Marsten or Lieutenant Wayson Harris, both of whom had damning skeletons in their closets, I now traveled as Lieutenant Commander Jeff Brocius of the U.A. Navy assigned to the Central Cygnus Fleet.

I flew a Johnston R-56 Starliner, a 20-seat luxury craft on loan to me from the *Doctrinaire* fleet. The R-56 was generally flown by corporate pilots. Like every other pair of wings on the *Doctrinaire*, this R-56 had been outfitted with its own broadcast engine.

"Please state your identity."

"Lieutenant Commander Jeff Brocius, U.A. Navy."

"Lieutenant Commander Brocius, copy. Are there passengers aboard your flight?"

"No, sir."

"Thank you, Starliner."

Traffic Control was acting unusually polite and I had a pretty good idea why. Security gave me the name Brocius because Admiral Alden Brocius, the officer-in-command of the Central Cygnus Fleet, was headed to the Golan Dry Docks for the summit. For all the men in the traffic tower knew, I was the admiral's son or nephew.

"Starliner R-fifty-six, we are under heightened security at this time. Please switch off all onboard controls. Our traffic computers will guide your ship into port."

"Aye," I said.

The traffic tower took control of my ship the moment my hands left the panel. Lights turned on and off as traffic control accessed all of my instrumentation. They might discover that I had unusual equipment on board, but they would not know it was a broadcast engine unless they tracked me from millions of miles away. I had disconnected the power after broadcasting in. Without a generator pouring tera-volts into it, the broadcast engine would look like nothing more than spare parts to their security computers.

My ship slowed to a near standstill as it joined the queue waiting to enter the Phase 2 landing bays. Unlike the rest of the platform, Phase 2 of the Golan platform was totally enclosed.

Seen from this side, the Dry Docks had a sleek teardrop shape. The outer skin of the station had a pattern of shining black squares against a flat white base. As I flew closer, I realized that those black squares were enormous solar energy cells.

This side of the Dry Docks facility had three landing bays, each marked by two half-mile wide circular entrances called "apertures." All ships entering or exiting the docks would have to pass through those doors. As traffic control led me toward one of those openings, I saw the distinctive silver-red of a security laser and knew someone in the dry docks had X-rayed my ship.

Leaning back in my seat, I took in the sights as my ship dropped into place before one of the apertures. Inside, I could see the brightly-lit landing area and the staging area that planes entered just before takeoff. Ships and transports of all shapes and sizes sat quietly at the back of the runway. Beyond that, so far away that it looked no bigger than my fist, was the half-mile-wide aperture for departing flights.

Whether by computer or human talent, traffic control

brought me in for a perfect landing. Thruster rockets in the wings of my Starliner fired as I entered the quarter-gravitational field of the tarmac. My ship landed with no perceptible bounce. A runway technician towed me through the atmosphere locks and into the staging area. There would be no old-fashioned blast door on the ultra-modern Golan Dry Docks. No, sir. On Golan, the locks were completely transparent electroshields.

I grabbed my bags and climbed out of the Johnston. Two guards armed with M27s approached and saluted as I stepped on to the deck. These were Army MPs. Golan had thousands of them.

I, wearing my Charlie service uniform and looking like the quintessential officer, saluted back.

"Commander Brocius?" one of the guards asked. "May I take your bag?" It was not an offer or a courtesy. He spoke in that robotic tone that grunt soldiers use when speaking to an officer. They would search my bag and find that I had a government-issue M27 of my own. They would also see that I had combat armor, something that was not general-issue among naval officers.

"Aye," I said, handing him my rucksack.

The guards did not scare me.

"Please follow us, sir," said the officer with my bag. The *please* was as perfunctory as the request to take may bag. With this, the two guards turned on their heels so smartly that they looked like they were on spindles.

Now came the only part of this duty that did make me nervous. The soldiers led me to the security station, a well-lighted island in the otherwise dim light of this enormous spacecraft hangar. Ahead of me, several dozen soldiers milled around a booth enclosed by bulletproof glass. Some smoked. Some talked. Some manned personal computers and monitored everyone and every thing that passed.

All I had to do was walk between "the posts"—an innocuous ten-foot archway made of beige-colored plastic. Terrorists and criminals feared the posts. They made supposedly extinct clones edgy as well. The post on the left side of the archway housed a device called "the sprayer" which emitted a fine mist of oil and water and a sudden blast of air. The jam on the right was "the receiver," a micron-filtered vacuum that drew in the air, the mist, and anything that the sprayer dislodged.

There was no disguising your identity from the posts. You could wash, shower, and shave your entire body with a micron-bladed scalpel, and the gust from the left post would still find dandruff, flecks of skin, loose hairs, lint, or sweat. A bank of computers analyzed every substance the right post drew in.

"Commander Brocius," one of the MPs said. He motioned toward the posts. I hesitated for a moment. I looked around. A security camera watched me from overhead. All of the soldiers behind the bulletproof glass wore firearms. None of them looked old enough to know what Liberators looked like, and they paid little attention to me. As far as they could see, this was another routine entry.

I had to pass through security funnels like this one on every planet. The difference was that this was the Golan Dry Docks, a high-security facility. The computers would recognize that I was a Liberator. But the men manning the computers were no more screening for Liberators than they were screening for dinosaurs or dragons. As long as my identity cleared, my Liberator DNA would not trigger an alarm.

I stepped into the arch, my mind already focusing on what I would do once I left the security station. The Joint Chiefs had already arrived. Admiral Klyber and the other field officers would arrive in another two hours. As soon as I left this station, I would make a preliminary sweep of the corridors just beyond this security station. Then I would move to Klyber's quarters. If I worked quickly, I would finish an hour before he arrived.

The post on my left blew out a milli-second-long burst of air. It did not last long enough to mess my hair. In its wake I felt slightly moist, as if I had jumped in and out of a steam room.

In the booth beside the posts, four soldiers sat beyond the glass playing poker. One had just turned over his hand. The others tossed their cards onto the table in disgust.

Suddenly the security station went on alert. Bright red warning lights flashed on and off over my head. Clear sheets of bulletproof plastic slid out of the walls creating a bullet-proof cell. By the time I realized what had happened, every soldier in the security station had drawn his gun and closed in around me. They stood in a semicircular ring. A few of the officers lowered their guns when they saw that I had no weapon.

The MP holding my bag stepped to the glass and held up a piece of paper for me to read. It was a computer printout with my picture and bio on it.

"Lieutenant Harris, we got a tip that you might stop by."

CHAPTER
EIGHT

My arrest had Che Huang's fingerprints all over it. The MPs who arrested me had no idea what laws I might have broken. They made no effort to charge me. By now they knew that I was a Liberator; but they could not arrest me for that. It was illegal to manufacture Liberators, and I had clearly not manufactured myself. Liberators were banned from the Orion Arm—Earth's home arm—but the Golan Dry Docks were located in the Norma Arm. Thinking everything through, I decided that the only crime Huang had on me was being absent without leave.

Having a relatively clean slate would not get me out of the brig in time to help Klyber. I was vaguely aware of the time and decided that Klyber must have arrived. He would have his regular security detail around him. Unless given misinformation, Klyber would notice my absence. Would he look for me? Would he become suspicious and alert his guard? My absence might or might not have been warning enough that Huang might have an ambush in mind.

I needed to get to Klyber. If Huang was behind this . . .

The last time I ran into Huang, the bastard didn't even bother having me arrested. He simply paraded me across

Mars Spaceport in handcuffs, transferred me to his cronies in the Scutum-Crux Fleet, and had me placed on Ravenwood to die. As it turned out, Huang and Rear Admiral Thurston used Ravenwood as a testing ground for a new breed of clone they had secretly developed to use as Navy SEALS. Huang sent platoons of armed Marines to guard the outpost, then trained his new breed of SEALS by sending them in to slaughter those Marines.

What would Huang do this time? If the soldiers who had captured me had allowed me to make a call, I could have sent a message to Freeman, and he could have warned Klyber that a trap had been sprung.

I was cut off and helpless, able only to wait and see what would happen. I sat on the edge of my cot and looked around the cell for a way out. I must have been in the cell for a few hours, but I had no idea how many. Escape was out of the question. The air vents along the top of the wall were only three inches wide. I could not even fit my fist in them. Unless I could figure out a method for passing through steel walls and bulletproof glass, I might be stuck in this cell for a long time.

Bright light and heat blazed from arc lamps set into the roof of my cell. Cool air blew out of the line of vents just under the seam of the ceiling. Without the cooled air, I would have fried; and without the overbright lights, I would have frozen.

An officer approached the door of my cell and spoke into the intercom.

"You're free to go," the man said.

"Free to go?" I asked, both surprised and sardonic. I stood up and walked toward the door. The man outside was a colonel, probably the head of the security station and likely the highest ranking officer assigned to the Dry Docks. Golan was a civilian operation with military security—a lot of military security.

"I apologize for the misunderstanding, Harris." The glass slid open. The colonel had two guards with him. All three men were armed. Apparently they did not want to take any chances with the dangerous Liberator clone. "Fleet headquarters sent us a message telling us to be on the lookout for a Lieutenant Wayson Harris who was falsely reported as killed in action."

"That sounds like me," I said as I followed the colonel

and his escort out of my cell and down a hall. Like my cell, the security complex had that odd combination of vents spewing chilled air and blazing hot arc lights.

"And now I'm free to go?" I asked. I did not expect them to let me loose in the Dry Docks.

We reached a table at the end of the hall. My bag sat on the table. One of the guards handed me the bag.

"Everything is in there," the colonel said, "including your gun." He sounded apologetic.

I decided to play smart and act like I expected this. Taking the bag, I zipped it open and sifted through my gear as if suspicious something might be missing. I knew everything would be there, and it was.

The colonel watched me. "This is all a misunderstanding," he said. "My men mistook the bulletin for orders to arrest you. Once we reported the arrest to fleet command, Admiral Huang's office contacted us."

"That so?" I asked, acknowledging the colonel with just a glance as I zipped my bag shut. I wanted to come across as officious.

"Nobody told us that you were on a high-security mission for Admiral Klyber. I'm sorry about this. You're here running security for the Joint Chiefs meeting, aren't you? I hope we didn't screw it up."

"When did Klyber's party arrive?" I asked.

The colonel's dark eyes and tight frown created a grave expression. "They've been here for several hours."

"Then we'll know the extent of the damage pretty soon, won't we?" I said.

The colonel nodded. "Admiral Huang called my office . . . the admiral himself," the colonel said, now sounding desperate.

"Really? What did old Che have to say?" I asked.

The colonel took a deep breath, then lowered his voice to a near whisper. "Admiral Huang says that he missed you." He paused to see how I would react to the message, then added, "He says he's surprised to hear you're alive and that he can't wait to catch up with you."

In preparation for the Joint Chiefs arrival, Golan adopted Earth time, and more precisely, Eastern Standard Time. I had arrived at 1400 hours, spent five hours in the brig, and emerged as the summit kicked off with a banquet.

If I rushed, I could get to my room and change before the banquet started. Nothing had happened so far; and if I had to guess, a dining hall filled with security men and armed officers would not be the place for an ambush. As I thought about it, it occurred to me that perhaps Klyber was just paranoid. Sure, Che Huang was a prick, but he was also an officer. Officers didn't murder each other. Officers ruined each other's careers and sometimes sent rivals on suicide missions, but they did not kill each other.

Rather than house me in the barracks with his men, the colonel booked me a room in the civilian dormitories—not far from Klyber and the other attendees. He had one of his men drive me to my room in a fast-moving cart. He drove me through a service tunnel, dropping me off in a corridor behind my room. I ran the rest of the way.

Not even bothering to look around my quarters, I tossed my bag on my bed and started to strip off my blouse. The rest of the room was dark, but the glare from the entryway light was enough for me to see what I was doing. I had my blouse off and was just beginning to step out of my pants when I heard the hiss of the pneumatic door sliding open. By the time I heard the noise, it was too late.

CHAPTER
NINE

I was bent over with my ass in the air just stepping out of my pants when the door opened. I managed to swivel around just far enough to see the boot before it kicked me across the chin. Bright lights popped in my head as I tipped over and fell into the darkness of my room.

I had no time to react before the man rushed forward, brought up his boot and kicked me in the base of the ribs. My lungs seemed to implode. He kicked with the top of his foot like a soccer player. My ribs already hurt and I saw him bring back the boot for another strike. Behind the kicker, I saw two more men but I did not have time to see their faces.

The next kick struck me across the point of the chin. Had he aimed farther in, the man might have broken my jaw. The fireworks in my head were intense; but by this time my Liberator combat reflex had started. Adrenaline and endorphins ran through my bloodstream. My thoughts were clear, the pain was distant, and this fellow would have to kill me before he could knock me out.

He changed his kick. This time he brought back his boot and prepared to strike toe-first. He aimed at my throat or face, I could not tell which. Using my left foot to push off the bed, I lashed forward with my right, scooping the man's leg off the floor. He fell to the carpet.

I wanted to retaliate. I wanted to lunge for him and snap his neck, but that would come later. I was down on the floor and he had friends. Pushing up to my knees, I sprung to my bed and grabbed my rucksack with one hand while rolling over the far edge for cover.

As I dug through my bag with one hand, I stole a quick glance over the bed. The two men in the entryway pulled pistols. I ducked back behind my bed and lay flat on the floor as bullets tore through my mattress and slammed into the wall behind me. My fingers found the butt of my M27. Feeling the cool steel of the grip, I smiled, visualized the room, and sprung to my feet. I fired one shot, shattering the lamp above their heads.

The ambushers had silenced weapons. The report of my M27 was loud and reverberated through the room like a train wreck.

"What do we do?" one of the attackers called.

Three more bullets cut through the mattress. By this time, I had moved. The room was completely dark. I had no reason to hide.

My shoes were off and I moved along the edge of the wall toward the entryway in complete silence. I watched the muzzles flash and knew where two of the men stood. Taking in a long, deep breath, but not exhaling, I crouched and prepared to shoot.

I heard the *flak* of a heaving object hitting the quilted blanket that covered my bed, followed by a thud from that same object dropping to the floor. "Get out of here!" one of the men yelled.

I took his advice. Grabbing my bag off the floor, I sprinted for the entryway. The door slid open and I jumped out into the hall dressed in nothing but my underwear with my rucksack in my left hand and my M27 in my right, blood pouring from several spots on my face and purple bruises starting to form on my ribs. If there had been any civilians in the hall, they might have passed out.

One of the assailants peeked out from behind a corner and fired a shot at me. I leaped in his direction, firing shots I knew would miss. The shots did what I needed them to do—they scared the man away. He disappeared around the corner, and I managed to get clear of the door. I was lying flat on the ground with my side pressed against the wall of the next room when the grenade exploded, disintegrating my quarters in a storm of debris and shrapnel.

Smoke alarms shrieked across the hallway. Security alarms bellowed. A sheet of water poured out of sprinklers hidden in the ceiling.

The assailants got away. Rocked by the percussion and covered with the shredded remains of my room, I was in no condition to chase them. I struggled just climbing to my feet. Had the attackers waited around to see if I had survived their grenade, they could have killed me easily enough.

They'll be back, I thought. *Next time I'll be ready for them.*

Other than a bunch of officers with political aspirations giving long-winded speeches, nothing bad happened at the banquet. Of course, nothing *happened* at the banquet. What was Huang supposed to do, lean across the dinner table and stab Klyber with his butter knife?

My job at the Dry Docks was to protect Klyber; but more and more, it looked as if he had come to protect me. Golan security drove me to the infirmary where an orderly diagnosed me as having three cracked ribs. No collapsed lung, no life-threatening injuries, just a bruised-up face and a lot of hostility. Had my attackers put a boot into my testicles, they would have done a lot more damage. As it was, the medic strapped some bandages around my torso, handed me a bottle of painkillers, and gave me a clean bill of health.

As I buttoned my blouse, Admiral Klyber came into the room. He wore his dress whites and could not help smiling. "I suppose that is an effective way to run a security detail," he said.

"How is that, sir?" I asked.

"Get all of the assassins to come after you."

"Very clever, sir," I said.

"You always were a lightning rod for trouble," Klyber said. "When I sent you to Gobi on your first assignment to hide you from some Liberators, a Mogat general found you instead."

"Hazards of the career," I said. "Marines and mercenaries get shot at. It comes with the pay."

"And you always survive," Klyber said. "Extraordinary."

I had lacerations just under my left eye. Bruises covered my chin and cheeks and one side of my face was swollen. Admiral Klyber watched as I buttoned my blouse over my bandaged ribs, and his smile faded.

"Are they after you or after me?" he asked.

"Without you," I said, "there's no reason to go after me."

"I suppose not," Klyber said, now looking a bit gray.

"But look on the bright side," I said. "If this is the best they can do with three gunmen and a grenade, by the time they get to you they might run out of ammunition."

Klyber smiled. "Thanks," he said. "I feel better."

Golan security arranged for my new room, complete with guards posted outside the door. I was a bodyguard with body-guards. In short, I was useless. When I finished stowing my gear, I put on my mediaLink and contacted Ray Freeman.

"So much for traveling as Arlind Marsten," Freeman said when I finished telling him about my day.

"Yes," I said. "Corporal Marsten can finally rest in peace. As far as I'm concerned, Huang did me a favor. Now I can come and go freely. I don't have to worry about guards find-ing out that I'm a Liberator every time I pass through secu-rity stations anymore. They'll know, and they'll know that I'm legal.

"Thanks to Huang, I can carry my gun in public. The head of security asked me how many men I need. Hell, he even upgraded my room."

I was lying on a bed with a queen-sized mattress covered by a blue and white quilt. My room in the Dry Docks dormi-tory looked like a suite for important executives. My bed-room included a media center with a holographic screen and there was a separate office with a desk and reference shelf. The setup included a wet bar complete with liquor and tum-blers, an ice maker, a sink and three stools. Having grown up in an orphanage and spent most of my life living in barracks, this was a lifestyle I had never imagined.

"What does Klyber have to say about Huang?" Freeman asked.

"He's got other things on his mind," I said. "He's going to tell the Joint Chiefs about his ship tomorrow." Klyber built the *Doctrinaire* working directly with friends on the Linear Committee, just as he had worked in secret with the committee with the Liberator project. Huang and the other members of the Joint Chiefs supposedly knew nothing about the *Doctrinaire*. At least they should have known nothing about it. I wondered whether Rear Admiral Halverson was also spying for Huang. Johansson did not know me from Marston. Halverson knew my real name and make.

"Will you be there when he makes the announcement?" Freeman asked.

"I'm not allowed in. Only top brass gets in that room."

"No guards? No wonder Klyber's nervous," Freeman said.

"It's all top brass," I said. "He's with civilized company."

"They stabbed Caesar to death on the floor of the Senate," Freeman said, giving a historical reference I would never have guessed him to know. "Caesar thought he was in civilized company, too."

Freeman would not have learned about Caesar from the works of Shakespeare. War and the engines of death interested him, not literature. I thought about this for a moment and decided that Klyber would be safe enough on the floor of the summit. It was out of my control, anyway. Once Klyber entered the conference room, there was nothing I could do.

"You flying back with Klyber after the summit?" Freeman asked, ending my chain of thought.

"Nope," I said. "My job is to get him from his transport to the meeting, and from the meeting to the transport."

"Think you will see Huang at the meeting tomorrow?" Freeman asked.

"Yeah, I need to thank him for the swank accommodations," I said. I sounded more confident than I felt. Huang, never hid his hate of all clones, especially Liberators. All clones, except his own top secret model. Before initiating the attack on Little Man, Huang transferred every last Liberator in the Unified Authority military to the invading force. If he wanted me dead, sooner or later he would succeed.

"How did Huang's office know you were headed to Golan?" Freeman asked. "Who told them about you?" His low voice reminded me of distant gunfire. His flat expression conveyed no emotion. If he were a poker player, no one would read his bluffs. But Ray Freeman did not trouble himself with card games. That would be far too social an activity for him.

"I've got a pretty good idea." Half of Klyber's senior staff officers had arrived the day before. I checked the manifest. Captain Leonid Johansson was among them.

"Don't jump to any conclusions," Freeman said after a long moment of thought. "Those weren't Huang's men in your room. He could have let you rot in jail if he wanted to hurt you."

I was about to sign off when Freeman changed the subject. "What do you know about Little Man?"

"The battle or the movie?" I asked, trying to sound smarter than I felt.

"The planet," Freeman said.

I had only seen a hundred-mile strip of the planet at tops—just a straight swatch from the beach where we landed to the valley in which we fought the battle. Before landing, we had a briefing. I tried to remember what the briefing officer had said. "It's a fully habitable planet," I said. "Well, not fully habitable. That valley where the Mogat ship crashed is plenty hot."

"Hot as in radioactive?" Freeman asked.

"As in highly radioactive. You wouldn't want to go anywhere near there. Every place else should be OK. Why do you want to know about Little Man?"

"My family is moving there."

It never occurred to me that Freeman had a family. I thought of him as a freak of nature . . . like me, the last clone of his kind. "Your family? A wife and kids?"

"My parents and my sister."

"What are they doing on Little Man?"

"Colonizing," Freeman said.

"Colonizing?"

"They're neo-Baptist," Freeman said.

"Which means? Why are the neo-Baptists colonizing Little Man?"

"The neo-Baptists want to establish colonies, like the Catholics."

"And they got permission to land on Little Man?" I asked.

"Does it matter?" Freeman asked.

"It matters," I said. "That planet is in the Scutum-Crux Arm . . . one of the hostile arms. If the U.A. finds them, they'll think it's a Mogat colony. That was why we went to Little Man in the first place . . . to kill Mogats. The planet is listed as uninhabited, and the last I heard, Congress wanted to keep it that way."

Freeman did not like long conversations. This current conversation was epic by his standards. We spoke for another minute or two, then signed off.

I lay in bed thinking about what he'd said. Freeman was right. Why would Huang spring me from the brig, then send a trio of goons after me? It made no sense.

Before falling asleep, I browsed the news. U.A. forces had claimed another three planets in the Cygnus Arm, including Providence. During the last week, they had claimed control of five planets in the Perseus Arm, four planets in Norma, and one in Scutum-Crux.

"These are all outlying planets," an Army spokesman told news analysts. He gave a cautious spin on the latest events. "The insurgents tend to evacuate them before our troops arrive. The fighting should be much more fierce as we approach more settled territory."

What he was not saying was that the Navy could easily have obliterated the insurgents' transports. That was the problem with winning a civil war. Sooner or later you had to repatriate the enemy, and you didn't want the sons of bitches to hold a grudge.

From everything I could tell, this civil war was unspectacular. The big media outlets tried to build it up as if the entire Republic was unraveling before our eyes; but the truth was that except for a very few terrorist attacks such as the one on Safe Harbor, the Confederate forces were in retreat. Except for the self-broadcasting fleet, which they had only used twice, the Confederate Arms had no Navy and no way to defend themselves from Naval attacks.

CHAPTER
TEN

Bryce Klyber sat at the breakfast table in his dress whites. The man made the uniform; but in this case, the uniform was something special. Fleet Admiral Klyber had four stripes and a block on his shoulder boards. He was the first man in nearly several decades to have that much gold on his shoulders. When he wore his khakis, he had five stars laid out in a pentagonal cluster.

The climate of this summit must have agreed with Klyber. He looked thoroughly energized as he spread marmalade over a triangle of toast. His posture, erect as always, now looked pert. A slight smile showed on his face as he looked up to greet me.

"Lieutenant Harris," he said.

I saluted, and he returned the gesture.

"You look surprisingly fit, considering your adventures from last night. Did you sleep well?"

"Yes, sir." I did not feel surprisingly good. In fact, I felt predictably dour. My ribs hurt. It felt like the bandages around my chest shrank over the course of the evening making it considerably harder to breath. The left side of my skull felt like it had caved in.

Before him, spread across the snowy white of the linen

tablecloth, Admiral Klyber had a plate of scrambled eggs with a side of bacon and smaller dishes with toast, a half grapefruit, and sausage. Banished to the far side of his table sat a bowl of grits. The spread also included carafes holding coffee, orange juice, grapefruit juice, and hot water for tea. The admiral, who would walk away from this meal with less than 150 pounds on his six-foot, four-inch frame, hardly looked like he knew where to begin. I would have gladly joined him for the meal, but the invitation did not come.

Using his fork, Klyber stabbed at a strip of lightly-cooked bacon and twirled it as if eating pasta. He stabbed the individual kernels of his scrambled eggs with the fork. He scooped a segment of grapefruit and savored it for several seconds. In the end, he ate a small portion of each dish except the grits, which he did not touch at all.

"Permission to speak, sir?"

"What is it, Lieutenant?"

"Sir, I was wondering about my status with the Marines. Now that Huang knows I am alive, am I back on active duty?" I asked. Considering my narrow escape from my last tour of duty, I had no desire to rejoin the Marines.

"Ah, that is the question," Klyber observed. He folded his napkin and placed it on the table, then fitted his cap on his head. "I've wondered about that myself. What would be the safest course with Admiral Huang lurking about? Do you have any suggestions?"

"No, sir," I said, though I considered killing Huang a solid option.

"I have taken the liberty of reassigning you to the *Doctrinaire* for now. You are on my roster. I doubt Huang's men will arrest you right under my nose."

"Thank you, sir."

Klyber nodded. "I assume you have no desire to go back on active duty?" He tried to act nonchalant; but his cold, blue eyes met mine and I saw a glint of excitement which I quickly dashed.

"Join the Marines again? No, sir."

"Understood, Lieutenant. Then I suppose we should regroup after the summit and discuss your options. You've spent two years on the lam as it were, and I see no reason why you could not turn up absent without leave again." With this he started for the door.

"Thank you, sir," I said.

He turned back and gave me a sharp-edged grin that revealed his top row of teeth. "And now, Lieutenant, perhaps we should head out to the conference room."

Four armed guards met us as we stepped out of Klyber's suite. They were Army, dressed in formal olive greens and armed with M27s. They marched with perfect precision, matching our pace as they walked in a pack directly behind us.

I also had my M27. Beyond that, I had spent some time earlier this morning patrolling the route from Klyber's room to the conference area. Golan security had posted guards along the route the day before. My job was to escort Admiral Klyber to the door of the conference room and then, after the conference, to deposit him safely on his transport.

We traveled down a brightly-lit hall with gleaming white walls and bright ceiling fixtures. Our footsteps echoed off the walls as we approached the final stretch of the corridor. As we drew closer, I heard loud chatter. From here, the summit sounded like a cocktail party.

We rounded that final corner and there it was, a large glowing lobby, obviously prepared especially for the purpose of this summit. Surrounded by the stark white corridors of the Golan executive complex, this lobby looked like a mirage. An oversized Persian carpet covered the floor. Black and red leather furniture sat in small formations around the room. There was a long table covered with bowls of fruit, pastry trays, and silver carafes.

From what I saw, the meeting looked more like a college reunion than a military summit. Officers in dress uniforms spoke cheerfully as they caught up on old times. I saw more bars and stripes floating around that gathering than I had ever seen in my life. Old generals with graying hair, stout bellies, and well-trimmed mustaches talked in genial tones like old friends swapping stories in a bar. One Army officer held a fat cigar in his fingers. He waved his hands as he spoke. The cigar smoke seemed to tie itself in a knot above his fingers.

Behind every swaggering general and admiral stood a couple of lesser officers watching quietly and taking mental notes about everything that was said. Admiral Halverson, Captain Johansson, and a handful of Navy men stood off in one corner waiting for Fleet Admiral Klyber. He was their shark. They were his remoras. When they saw Klyber, they drifted out to greet him, then silently fell into his entourage.

Having delivered Admiral Klyber to the summit, I started to leave. I had rounds to make. I wanted to check in with the security station and do one last sweep of Klyber's quarters, but Klyber summoned me back. "Stay for a moment, Harris," he said, making a very discreet nod to the right. Following his eyes, I saw Admiral Huang heading in our direction. "This may be my moment to do a bit of body guarding on *your* behalf."

"Admiral Klyber," Huang said in a tone that was rigidly formal but not unfriendly.

Admiral Che Huang stood just over six feet tall. He had broad shoulders, a massive chest, and a commanding presence. Standing beside Huang, Klyber looked old and frail.

More than two years had passed since the last time I had run into Huang, years that had not been especially kind to the man. I remembered him as having brown hair with streaks of gray. Over the last two years his hair had changed to salt and pepper with large gray patches around his temples. His cheeks had hollowed.

Huang's eyes narrowed as he turned toward me. "Lieutenant Harris. I heard you were here."

I saluted. The admiral did not bother returning the salute.

"The lieutenant is here with me," Admiral Klyber said.

"Yes," said Huang. "So he's on the crew of your mysterious ship." With this he left us.

We watched him walk away, then Klyber gave me a wry smile. "How much does he know about my ship, I wonder?"

"He should not know that you have a ship at all," I said.

"Yes," Klyber agreed. "I really must have a word with Captain Johansson before we return to the *Doctrinaire*."

General Alexander Smith, secretary of Air Force and head of the Joint Chiefs, called everyone to attention. "Gentlemen, it's time we begin," he said, and the party started to funnel through a nearby doorway.

"This should be an all-day affair," Klyber said.

"Yes, sir," I said.

"Do you have plans for the day?" Klyber asked. "I hope you're not going to waste the entire time checking and rechecking these same hallways."

"That's the plan, sir," I said.

"Have you read the book I gave you?" Klyber asked.

I nodded. "The story about Shannon?"

"Did you learn anything?" he asked.

"Not to expect hospitality in the Catholic colonies," I said.

"That's one lesson," Klyber said. "See you after the summit." He joined up with Admiral Brocius and they entered the conference room.

As I turned to leave, I had a dark premonition. I imagined Admiral Klyber stepping up to a podium to explain about the *Doctrinaire*. I pictured Admiral Huang stepping behind him and whispering something. Klyber turns pale and looks back at him with a stunned expression just as Huang plunges a diamond-edged combat knife into his back.

In my bizarre fantasy, I watch Huang's knife jab in and out of Klyber's white uniform. Huang stabs him four times as he turns to run and the other summit attendees close in around him. They stab Klyber again and again until his dress whites turn red.

My disconcerting daydream ends with Huang looking down at Kyber's corpse and saying the phrase that must have been hovering in my subconscious: "Beware the Ides of March."

According to the Earth date, it was indeed Tuesday, March 15.

CHAPTER
ELEVEN

The summit lasted ten hours. I met Klyber at the door when it adjourned. More than anything else, he seemed tired as he emerged from the meeting. He walked slowly, talked softly, and stared straight ahead. His breeding did not allow for slumped shoulders or bad posture; but he was, nonetheless, a defeated man. "We're in for a tougher fight than any of them know," he said. "Stupid bastards are too young to remember the last war. Kellan wasn't even born yet."

General John Kellan, the new secretary of the Army, made big news a few years back by attaining the rank of general before his thirty-fifth birthday. His father and two uncles, all three of them senators, threw a party to commemorate the achievement on the floor of the Senate.

When it came to mixing politics and service, Kellan was a mere piker compared to the illustrious fleet admiral. Nobody respected Kellan's combat-free war record. Klyber had political connections that ran all the way up to the Linear Committee, more than forty years of active service, and an impressive war record. Even his role in the creation of Liberator clones meant something in Washington. The politicians may not have liked his Liberators, but it was the Liberators who saved the day in the last war.

But Klyber did not look like a war hero now. His frosty blue eyes seemed lost in their sockets. He looked fragile instead of vibrant. This morning I might have described him as haughty. Seeing him now, the only word that came to mind was "wilted."

I led Klyber back to his room, our four-man Army escort in tow. We went to his room, and he stood silently near the door. I wanted to ask what happened, but I knew better.

"Did you tell the Joint Chiefs about the *Doctrinaire*?" I asked.

Klyber, pouring gin and water over ice, nodded. "Yes. You should have seen Huang. Admiral Huang said that he knew all about it. He sounded so familiar with the ship you would think I had invited him aboard for tea. Arrogant bastard stared me right in the eye and all but admitted that he had spies on board . . . didn't flinch . . . didn't even bat an eye."

"Johansson?" I asked.

"Undoubtedly," Klyber said. "I have a score to settle with our Captain Johansson." Klyber stood beside his wet bar holding his glass of gin and staring at me with not so much as a glint of a smile.

"What do we do about Huang?" I asked.

"The million-dollar question. I don't have to do anything about Huang. The man will destroy himself. There is no place in the Unified Authority for an officer with his lack of judgment. I seriously doubt he and his career will survive the war." Klyber saluted me with his gin and took another sip.

"Perhaps we should leave," he said as he placed his drink on the bar. The cup was still mostly full.

A caravan of security carts waited to drive us to the docking bay. The front and rear carts were loaded with MPs. Klyber and I climbed into the backseat of the middle car. We drove through brightly-lit service halls that were so wide three cars could travel through them side by side. The hollow growl of our motors echoed in the halls and our tires squealed on the polished floor.

Klyber sat silent through the ride. He stared straight ahead, a small frown forming on his lips, as he let his mind wander. It took ten minutes to drive to the security gate.

Leaving the Golan Dry Docks was easier than entering.

You did not pass through the posts. No one checked your DNA. Guards checked luggage and passengers for stolen technology, but the officers who attended this summit were allowed to forego that formality. The six soldiers guarding the security gate snapped to attention and saluted Admiral Klyber as he approached. They stayed at attention as he walked past.

"Huang's got nerve. I'll give him that much," Klyber said as we left the security gate. "The other Joint Chiefs don't know what they are up against with him. They're simple soldiers. He's Machiavellian. You get a Machiavelli in the ranks when you've been at peace for too long. Without war, officers advance by politics instead of merit."

We reached the staging area where VIP passengers boarded their ships. Ahead of us, the landing pad stretched out for miles. It was so immense that its floor and ceiling seemed to form their own peculiar horizon.

Klyber's transport sat on the tarmac just one hundred feet ahead of us. One of Klyber's pilots milled at the foot of the ramp smoking a cigarette. He tossed the butt on the ground and crushed it out with his shoe as Klyber approached.

Klyber turned to look at me. "You are not interested in a life as a Marine," he said. "I understand. When you get to the *Doctrinaire,* I'll make arrangements for an honorable discharge. What you do beyond that is up to you."

"Thank you, sir," I said. "What about you?"

Klyber gave me a terrible, withered smile. "The *Doctrinaire* is going to end this war, Harris, then we can rebuild the Republic. Once we shake the deadwood out, there will be a need for rebuilding. I suppose it will be time for me to enter politics."

The triumphant words did not match the defeated posture. He looked so old. The only explanation I could imagine was that having finally revealed his plans, Admiral Klyber had become more acutely aware of the challenges ahead.

We had reached the door of the transport. I snapped to attention and saluted Klyber. He returned my salute. I wanted to talk more, but I was not boarding the ship.

"Admiral," I said with a final nod as I ended my salute.

Klyber smiled. "Good day, Lieutenant Harris." He turned and walked up the ramp into his transport.

I watched him—a tall, emaciated man with a long face and a narrow head. He had twig-like arms and legs like broomsticks; but even in his late sixties he was the picture of dignity walking proud and erect. His starched white uniform hung slack around his skin-and-bones frame, but Bryce Klyber was the quintessential officer.

A sense of relief washed through me as I saw an attendant seal the transport hatch. There had been an assassination attempt, but it was on me. Were they after Klyber and just trying to get me out of the way? Maybe so. Maybe I scared them away when I chased them out of my room. Golan was on high alert after that.

Unlike my little Johnston, Klyber's eighty-foot long C-64 Mercury-class transport ship was not designed to fly in an atmosphere with oxygen or gravity. The big ship rolled to the first door of the locks under its own power. This particular ship was big and boxy with a bulging hull that looked unworthy of flight. Even rolling toward the runway, it had a clumsy, overstuffed feel about it.

An electroshield door sealed behind the C-64. I could still see the craft through that first door, but it now had an unsteady appearance, as if I was watching it through heat waves. The ship lumbered on through two more electroshield doors, entering the low gravity area.

The tower gave Klyber's ship immediate clearance—fleet admiral's privilege, who could out rank him?—and it levitated from the deck on a cloud of steaming air. The ship hung above the deck for a few seconds as it rotated to face the aperture. I watched the ship and thought about receiving an honorable release from the Marines. I had to smile.

As I turned to leave, I saw something that did not make sense. At first I did not even realize what I was seeing. Five or six civilians stood on the far side of the security gate watching ships take off. Aware that something felt wrong, I headed toward them for a better look.

Then I realized what I saw. I knew one of the men, only he was not a civilian. Rear Admiral Tom Halverson, dressed in a suit and tie like an ordinary businessman, stood at the front of the group. I smiled thinking he must have missed the transport. "Miss your ride?" I called out as I walked toward the gate.

Halverson turned to look at me. He paused, stared at me for just a moment, then turned and bolted into the service halls behind the security station. "Grab that man!" I yelled at the men guarding the exit. They looked over at me so slowly they reminded me of cows grazing in a field.

"Stop him!" I screamed as I pulled my M27.

All five guards pulled their guns. Two ran off after Halverson, but the other three kept their M27s trained on me. Red warning lights flashed from the ceiling for the second time since I had landed on Golan. Soldiers with drawn weapons rushed out of the security booth and surrounded me. I placed my gun on the ground then laced my hands behind my head without being asked.

As the MPs closed in around me, I looked back at the launch area expecting to see Klyber's ship explode. The C-64 had dragged itself to the airspace just in front of the aperture, and the transport seemed to dangle precariously as it approached that opening. But instead of exploding, it rose steadily higher.

"What is going on, Harris?"

I turned to see the colonel who had sprung me from the brig pushing his way toward me. He looked angry.

"Colonel, there's a bomb on Klyber's ship!"

The colonel did not hesitate. "Out of the way," he yelled. He pulled a discrete communications stem from his collar. "Traffic control, hold Klyber's ship! I repeat, this is urgent, hold Klyber's transport!"

The MPs lowered their guns and cleared out of my way. I could not hear what was said, but traffic control apparently got the colonel's message. "Yeah, that's right . . . Yes, I've got a man out here who says that there is a bomb on board the admiral's ship. Shit . . . no. . . . don't bring it down. If we have a bomber around here, he might set it off. Yes. Yes! Look, we're on our way over. Just have the pilot hang tight."

And that was what happened. Klyber's massive transport continued to hover in front of the aperture like a bee waiting to enter a flower. I paused to look at it for just a moment.

"Move it, Harris." The colonel did not need to ask twice. We headed into the control tower, a tinted glass tower that reached to the ceiling of the landing area. The tower was seventeen stories tall. We entered the elevator and the colonel stabbed the button for the floor he wanted.

"You'd better be right about this, Harris." He panted as he spoke.

"Yes, sir," I said.

"What did you see?"

"Rear Admiral Halverson," I said. "He didn't get on the flight."

"You set off the alarms because you saw some guy standing around?" The colonel screamed so hard that streamers of spit flew from his lips.

"Rear Admiral Halverson is Klyber's second-in-command," I said.

"So he missed the specking flight!" The colonel shook his head. "Oh, I'm specked. I had to trust a goddamned clone."

"Halverson ran when he saw me. He was . . ."

"You're a damned Liberator!" the colonel shouted louder than ever. He did this just as the elevator doors opened. Everyone on the floor turned to look at us. "Damned specking right he ran when he saw you. You're a goddamned Liberator clone. You're a friggin' disaster waiting to happen. Anyone in his right mind is going to run when he sees you. I should have run when I saw you. No, I should have had my men shoot you while I had the chance. Oh, I am specked."

The floor of the control room was dim, lit only by the green and red phosphorous glow of several large radar screens. The air was moist from recirculation and carried a bad combination of scents—mildew and cigarette smoke. Entering this heavily air-conditioned floor felt like being sealed in an old refrigerator.

Around the room, men sat beside radar consoles in clusters of three. "How should we handle this?" one of the men at the nearest console called over. The colonel and I went over to join him.

"Traffic control, this is U.A. Transport five-Tango-Zulu. Do you read me?"

"We read you five-Tango-Zulu," replied one of the controllers.

"What seems to be the hang-up down there?" the pilot

asked. This was the same man who picked me up on Mars a few days earlier. I recognized his voice.

"Want me to bring them back?" the controller asked.

The colonel thought for a moment, then shook his head. "Not based on the evidence Lieutenant Harris just gave me."

"Is there a problem, traffic control?" the pilot squawked over the radio.

Through the black tinted windows, I could see Klyber's transport hanging just below the lip of the aperture. There was very little gravity on that part of the deck, but the C-64 still looked awkward. A long line of ships started to form below the transport.

"Colonel, we have to do something. My queue is cataclysmically specked."

The colonel walked to the dark glass wall of the tower and stared out for several seconds. "Can you laser scan the transport in midair?" he asked.

"Sure," the controller said.

"Five-Tango-Zulu, this is traffic control. Prepare for a scan. Do you copy?"

"Don't you save scans for incoming?" the pilot asked.

I didn't realize they had scanners by the outbound aperture, but they did. A silver-red beam locked on to the hull of the C-64. It moved up and down the Mercury-class transport.

"Find anything?" the colonel asked.

"Clean, sir," the traffic controller said.

The colonel glared at me.

"You see any unidentified ships in the area?" I asked, desperation starting to sink in.

The controller ran his finger over the radar screen, tracing a line above the information the scan found. "All clear. Look for yourself."

The markings on his radar monitors could have been written in Sanskrit as far as I could tell. The notations they used to identify the ships used symbols and numbers, not letters.

"What am I looking at?" I asked.

"Control, should I land this bird?" the pilot asked. Irritation showed in his voice.

"What do you think?" the head controller asked the colonel. Still staring into the monitor, the controller pointed at it, drawing invisible circles around different areas on the screen.

"What do the markings mean?" I asked.

"These red triangles are Air Force. They're guarding our air space. These blue boxes are civilian ships. These green ones are government, strictly non-combat . . . surveyors, that kind of shit."

The colonel took a long breath, gave me another angry glare, and said, "Send them on their way."

"No problem," said the controller. "Five-Tango-Zulu, this is traffic control. Sorry about the tie-up. We had a false alarm."

"Are we cleared to leave?" the pilot asked.

"You are clear for takeoff." The controller looked back at me and smiled. I heard nerdy enthusiasm in his voice as he said, "Klyber's transport is self-broadcasting. You don't see self-broadcasters often. Now comes the cool part."

The controller pointed at a blue square with symbols that meant absolutely nothing to me. "See that? That's Five-Tango-Zulu. That's the Admiral's transport. He'll fly a few minutes out, and then poof. The ship vanishes off the screen so quickly that the computers don't know what to do about it. The screen goes blank because the system resets. If you ever wanted to see a computer wet itself, watch this. Weirdest damn thing you ever saw."

"Hurting for entertainment," I muttered to myself as I turned to gaze out the window. The colonel still stood in front of the window. Now that he cleared the transport to leave, he wanted to make sure he made the right call. Once the big transport departed safely, he would deal with me.

I took another look at the radar screen and tried to make sense of the rainbow of symbols. The low glow of the screen seemed to dissolve into the overall darkness of the room. I walked over to the window in time to see the tail of Klyber's C-64 escaping into the black void beyond the aperture. Strobe lights along the wing and tail of the transport flashed white, then yellow, then red.

"Huang or no Huang, Harris, you're up shit creek this time," the colonel said in a soft voice. "You know that, don't you?"

I did not answer.

He turned to look at me. "We'll just wait until your friend Klyber's transport is away, then you and I can settle up."

For a moment I wished they had found a bomb on the transport, then I remembered Rear Admiral Halverson. Surely they would catch the admiral . . . but what would that prove? "Shit creek," the colonel repeated under his breath. Watching Klyber's ship grow smaller and smaller as it drifted into space, I realized just how far up that creek I had traveled.

"That's it," the colonel said. "They're gone. Now let's you and me go over to the brig and have a discussion. How does that sound?"

It did not sound good. The colonel started toward the elevator and I turned to follow.

"Wait," the controller said as the colonel walked past the radar console. "You're going to miss the show."

The colonel paused to see what he was talking about.

The controller pointed into the radar screen to show us Klyber's ship. Blocking the low glow of the screen, his hand looked like a swollen shadow. "See, he's already ten miles out. He's going to want to get at least one thousand miles away before he broadcasts. That will put him here," the controller said pointing to a ring about four inches away from the circle that represented the Dry Docks.

"Now you see these?" the controller went on. "These are the local broadcast discs." He pointed at two orange rectangles. "The transport has to be at least one thousand miles away from them. Self-broadcasting too close to the network really mucks with the discs, see, so the transport has to go in the other direction."

The colonel nodded impatiently. It didn't interest me, either. I found that I wanted to get to security and get on with whatever the colonel had planned. Without saying a word, the colonel turned and started to leave.

By this time, a crowd had formed around us. At least thirty traffic control workers had drifted to the station to watch "the show." Men in white shirts carrying coffee cups stared into the big computer screen as if it were a work of art. Some pointed, others whispered to each other and nodded as if noticing significant secrets.

"What is going on here?" the colonel snapped angrily as he tried to push through the gawkers.

"I told you, this is the show. We don't get many self-broadcasting ships out here. They want to watch it speck with my computer." We stood about ten feet from the controller by this time. He had to raise his voice for us to hear him.

The colonel watched out of courtesy. He placed his arms across his chest, folding his hands over his biceps, and stood stiff as a pillar. His lips pressed into a single line and his eyes were hard as stone.

"Any second now . . ." the controller said. A few seconds passed, but nothing happened. "What the hell!" the controller said, sweeping clutter away from his console. Coffee cups, ashtrays, and papers fell to the floor. He flipped a switch. "U.A. Transport five-Tango-Zulu. Come in five-Tango-Zulu. Come in."

There was no response, not even static.

"Come in, five-Tango-Zulu."

Silence.

"What's going on?" the colonel asked the exact same question, starting to sound nervous.

The traffic controller ignored him. He flipped switches, tried to hail the C-64 again, and flipped more switches. He moved quickly, like a man trying to stave off a catastrophe.

"Mark, get to your station. Get me a reading," the controller called, and one of the controllers who had been gawking at the radar sprinted across the floor. It seemed like silent communication passed from the floor leader to the other controllers. The rest of the onlookers scattered.

"What is going on?" the colonel repeated.

"I can't reach the transport," the controller said without looking back. He pressed a button and spoke into his microphone. "Emergency station, we have a possible stiff!"

"I read you, control," a voice on the intercom said.

The controller stood up and looked out toward the aperture, then gazed back into his console. "Make that a definite stiff. Look on your radar for five-Tango-Zulu. It's a few miles off deck in Sector A-twelve."

"A-twelve?" the voice asked.

"Hold on," the controller said. "I'll try raising visual contact with the pilot."

Under normal circumstances, only the people in the cockpit initiated visual communications; but for security reasons, the Dry Docks' computers had special protocols that enabled the traffic controllers to override ship systems. A little screen the size of a playing card winked to life on the console next to the radar readout.

Centered in that screen was Klyber's pilot. He sat strapped in his chair, his head hanging slack. At first I thought he was reading something. Then I noticed the tell-tale details—white skin with a slight blue tint, the blood blister color of the lips, the frozen eyes—and realized that only his harness held him strapped in his seat. "He's dead," I said.

"Shit!" the controller gasped. "Shit! Shit! Shit!

"Oh my God! Emergency station, Mary, mother of God, it's a ghost ship. Repeat, emergency station, five-Tango-Zulu is a ghost ship. The pilot is dead!" he said. "Holy shit! Mary, mother of God. Repeat, the pilot is dead."

CHAPTER TWELVE

A network of emergency lights flashed red, then green, then white, then yellow around the launch pad. I walked over to the window and watched twelve floors below as emergency teams moved into position around the enormous hangar. Rescue workers piled on to carts and trucks and rode to the outer edge of the locks. Five ambulances arrived and medics set up emergency stations. Watching from the cool, stale environment of the control tower, I saw everything and heard just a shade of the chaos below.

Soft-shells climbed out of rigs and set up emergency equipment. *Soft-shells* was Marine-ese for spaceport emergency personnel who wore soft armor designed to protect against flames, toxins, and radiation.

Watching them now, I noted their color-coding. Med-techs wore white. Firemen wore yellow. The bomb squad wore black.

"They'll do what they can," the colonel said as he took a place beside me to look out the window. He spoke in a near whisper. "We get a lot of crashes when we test prototypes. These guys know how to scramble."

"The Triple Es are ready," the traffic controller called from behind us.

"Triple Es?" I asked.

"Emergency evaluation engineers," the colonel said. "They'll inspect the ship and board her if possible. Their control room is two floors up. We can watch what they do from there."

I followed the colonel into the elevator. A moment later, we entered a universe that bore no resemblance to the traffic control floors below. The sterile glare of fluorescent lights lit an endless expanse of cubicles. People didn't just speak on this floor, they shouted at each other.

"Hey, Clarence, this isn't a good time. We have a ghost ship," somebody yelled at the colonel as we stepped off the elevator. A short, chubby man in a messy white shirt and dark blue pants came toward us.

"That's why we're here," the colonel said. "Harris here is familiar with that ship. He's Klyber's head of security. Maybe he can help."

The colonel turned to me. "Just don't get in the way," he said. We followed the colonel's friend into a control room lined with video monitors.

A bank of four monitors along the wall displayed the scene in full color. The first screen showed only Klyber's ship, which hung in mid-space, silent and motionless. I saw light through the portholes but no movement. Strobe lights along the tail and the wings of the ship flashed white then red.

The next screen showed a five-man security ship approaching the derelict transport from the rear. The security ship was tiny compared to the C-64. It looked like a minnow approaching a whale. I became mesmerized by the glow of the transports' strobes as it reflected along the hull of the transport . . . red, then white, red, then white. When the security ship shined a powerful searchlight on the hull, the glow of the strobes seemed to vanish.

All of this took place in the eerie silence of space.

The third screen was a close-up of Klyber's ship, illuminated by the bleaching eye of that searchlight.

"Are you bringing the ship in?" I asked the man who led us to this bank of screens.

"Hell, no. We don't know what killed them. That ship could be leaking radiation. That's all I need, a dirty bomb in the middle of my landing field. They could have been killed with some kind of germ agent."

"You scanned it," I said to the colonel.

"We must have missed something," he answered.

"McAvoy." Somebody stuck his head out of an office and called to the colonel. The colonel walked over to that office for a chat.

"Scanning the target," a voice said. It came from a small speaker below the bank of screens. The man who led the boarding team pressed a button, changing the view of one of the screens on the wall. "Keep sharp, boys. They ran a scan on this bird before it left the docks and it came up empty."

"Roger," the voice said over the speakers. "Scanning for bombs."

The background in the scanning screen turned red. Everything on the screen turned red. The space around the exterior of the ship was empty and black with a slight red tint. The Mercury Class transport showed a bold red. The nose of the transport turned bright pink as a laser shined on it. Three columns of text appeared across the bottom of the screen displaying an on-the-spot object, substance, and element analysis.

The laser beam moved ever so slowly as it scanned the ship. I watched, nearly needing to bite my tongue to stop myself from screaming. There was no bomb on that ship. If there had been a bomb, the ship would have blown up.

"Harris," the colonel returned, "you sure you saw Halverson?"

I nodded.

"Rear Admiral Thomas Halverson?" he asked.

"Yes," I said, now feeling a little frustrated. I was tense to begin with, and I did not think there were many admirals in the U.A. Navy with the last name Halverson.

"That can't be," the colonel said. "He's registered as a passenger on Klyber's ship."

"You have the passenger manifest?" I asked.

The colonel nodded.

"Can I see it? We might get some answers by comparing the list of passengers with the people we find on the ship."

"I'll get a printout," the colonel said. "And I'll put out an all-points bulletin for Halverson. If he's still in the Dry Dock facility, we'll find him."

I nodded. "Can you run another DNA search in the apartment they blew up last night?" I asked. "Maybe you missed something. If you find anything, compare it to Halverson's file."

"You think that was Halverson?" the colonel asked.

"Or some of his friends," I said.

"The room was pretty well scorched, but we'll give it a try."

"Okay, explosives came up clean. Let's run for chemicals and anomalies," the tech at the screens said.

As the chemical scan began, the single color on the screen turned from red to white. A line pulsed across the face of the screen, and a three-dimensional wire frame diagram replaced the video image of the transport. The lines in the image changed color as the security ship scanned for chemicals, radiation, power surges, and temperature fluctuations. This scan moved more quickly, but not by much.

"Can you bring it in now?" I asked.

"No," the controller said without looking away from his monitor.

"Admiral Klyber could still be alive," I said.

"We don't know what happened on that ship. We can't risk it."

I felt my insides coiling. I clenched my fists and rapped my knuckles against my thigh.

"Ready to board the ship," the voice said over the speaker.

I looked back at the screens on the walls. Dry dock emergency must have sent two teams out to the transport, one to run scans and the other to board the ship. The smaller ship, the one that had looked like a minnow beside the C-64, had attached itself to the transport. Now that it sat snuggly connected just behind the cone-shaped cockpit section of the big transport, it looked more like an enormous tick.

This was a civilian operation. Instead of giving orders, the guy at the screen growled suggestions such as, "Let's have a look."

The first three screens now showed nothing but static shots of the outside of Admiral Klyber's transport. All the action took place on the fourth screen, which was mostly dark. This screen showed a helmet camera view of the action. It showed the accordion walls and temporary gangway that connected the Triple E ship to the transport. The only light on the screen came from the torches in the evaluation crew's helmets.

One of the engineers pressed a three-pronged key into a slot on the side of the C-64's hull, and the hatch opened. There was a brief blast of air as the cabin repressurized. A loud slurping noise blasted over the speakers, then stopped as suddenly as it began.

"Okay, we're moving in."

The cabin within was brightly lit. I recognized the ivory-colored carpeting in the quick glance that I got.

"I'll check the cockpit. You search the ship," the lead engineer said.

On the screen, the eye of a single torch beam lit the door to the cockpit as a hand came out of nowhere and tried the handle. The door opened.

The pilot and copilot sat upright in their seats, their heads hanging chin to chest as if they were asleep. Lights winked on and off in the dimly-lit space. The pilot's coloring was off—the blue tones in his skin more pronounced then before. I might have mistaken it for bad lighting had his brownish black hair not looked the right hue.

"Any idea what killed him?" the colonel asked into a microphone.

"I can guess," the voice over the speaker said. "It seems pretty obvious. Want me to take a tissue sample or wait for the medics to arrive?"

"Take it," the controller said.

On the screen, the camera drew closer to the pilot. A gloved hand reached under the pilot's chin and drew his head up. Blank, glassy eyes and blue lips faced the camera. "Any vital signs on your end?"

"He's dead," the controller said. "Jab him."

The gloved hand released the pilot and his head flopped back toward the floor, bobbing with the whiplash of the neck. The gloved hand on the screen dug through a small pouch and produced a plastic packet. The hand tore the packet open and pulled a three-inch long needle with a little hilt on one end.

"God, I hate this shit," the controller said.

On the screen, the tech pressed the needle into the fleshy area just under the pilot's jaw. The point was sharp enough to pierce the skin instantly. A single drop of blood formed around the needle as the tech pushed it into the hilt. "You getting a reading?"

"Yeah," the controller said. "Cardiac arrest."

"You want me to do the copilot, too?"

"What's the point?"

"Cardiac arrest?" I asked.

"Means they got electrocuted," the controller said. He did not look back. Nothing could induce him to take his eyes from the screens.

"Live and learn," I said to myself.

"We've found bodies," another voice said over a speaker. More screens lit. On one of the new screens, a tech sorted his way through the passengers in the main cabin. This part of Admiral Klyber's transport had a living room–like décor with couches and padded chairs arranged in intimate clusters and workstations.

The tech shuffled from one passenger to the next, lifting heads and occasionally using a handheld device to check for pulses and other vital signs. Looking at this scene, I remembered attending elementary school at the orphanage and how the teachers sometimes made us put our heads on our desks when we misbehaved. Apparently all of the passengers had misbehaved. One officer had fallen off of a couch and now lay slumped over a coffee table. Whatever had killed these men did not so much as jostle the ship. Nothing had fallen out of place and the three men sitting at the bar had not fallen off their stools.

This guy was not as reverent as his partner in the cockpit. He moved through quickly, moving the bodies as little as possible, and saying, "Dead. This one's dead, too. Dead. Dead."

He reached a body in a corner of the cabin. This man's arm hung in the air like a school kid looking to ask his teacher a question. "This one got flamed," the tech said over the speaker.

The man's hair and uniform had apparently caught on fire. The flames had singed his skin, burning it up like a log in a fire. The face, with its lips parted to reveal a skeletal smile, was unidentifiable.

Back on the first screen, the engineer in the cockpit took readings using the C-64's sensors. He took an air reading. "High ozone. High carbon dioxide. You reading this?"

"I see it," the controller said.

"Am I cleared to retrieve the ship?"

"Unless one of the passengers objects'," the controller said.

Both men laughed.

"What did he find?" I asked.

"Ozone," said the emergency systems operator. "That means the broadcast engine malfunctioned."

I did not understand the relationship between the broadcast engine and ozone. "How do you know it was the broadcast engine?" I asked.

"Ozone is what you get when you fire up a broadcast engine."

"How do you know it malfunctioned?" I asked.

"They're dead, ain't they?" the operator quipped.

I could not argue with that one.

CHAPTER THIRTEEN

The colonel had a cart waiting for us at the bottom of the control tower. An MP drove us out to the edge of the docks, and there we waited for ten long minutes while the tower guided Admiral Klyber's C-64 transport in through the aperture.

Through the wavy lens of the electroshields, I saw the big Mercury-class transport sidle into the aperture. It entered the landing bay nose first, then hung in the air for several seconds, its bloated fuselage swaying slightly like a chandelier in a breeze.

"What is a ghost ship?" I asked the MP.

"Dead crew," he said.

"And the passengers?" I asked.

"I don't know," he shrugged as he spoke. "Once the crew is dead there's not much hope for the passengers."

Landing gear extended from the bottom of Klyber's "ghost ship" as it dropped down to the deck on the other side of the lock. Before this moment, I had never appreciated the sheer bulk of a C-64. The rods that held the landing gear were four inches in diameter, as big around as a mortar shell. The struts were thick as beer bottles. The ship was solid but it looked like an apparition through the turbulent veil of the electroshields. I watched it closely as I pulled on the blue soft-shell jacket of a civilian security man.

"What the speck do you think you're doing?" somebody barked at me. I turned around to see the head of Golan Dry Docks emergency services, a slightly chubby man with a thick neck and a spiky buzz cut. He was a civilian, and he apparently had very little respect for the military.

"Lay off, Smith," the colonel said. "He's with me."

"That's just what I need, a damned Liberator running around loose in my operation." The man's face turned a deep red as he spoke. He lowered his voice but his tone remained unreasonable. Since the Golan facility was a public sector operation, this man undoubtedly outranked the colonel.

Struggling to keep control of his temper, the colonel zipped the front of his soft-shell coat closed. The quarter-inch-thick plasticized material was just stiff enough to form a tent-like slope over his shoulders. Frowning fiercely, he said, "Harris is Klyber's head of security. He has the right to be here."

"He doesn't have shit in my landing bay," the emergency services chief snapped.

"I'll take responsibility for him," the colonel said.

"Then it's your ass," the chief said. He looked down at the tarmac and shook his head.

While they had this conversation, the transport rolled through the first gate of the docks. Once that sealed behind it, the second electroshield opened and the C-64 pulled within a few feet of the emergency teams.

Five medics boarded the transport first. The colonel and I came in on their heels. They stopped to inspect the bodies in the main cabin, an area that looked more like the executive suite of a luxury hotel than the interior of a military transport. The soothing soft light of table lamps illuminated the cabin.

Even in my emergency armor I could smell the acrid scent of ozone, the smell of overheated batteries, and charged copper wires, as I entered the cabin. This smell was soon drowned out by a stronger scent—the dusty smell of burned meat. Two medics crouched in front of the charred body in the corner of the cabin.

I hurried across the thick ivory-colored carpeting and

past the living room fixtures and entered a hall that led to the rear of the craft. I had traveled with Bryce Klyber in the past. He always reserved a private cabin for himself in the rear of the ship. I knew where I would find him.

Two Marines—clones—had stood guard by his door. Both men had collapsed in place, their M27s still strapped across their shoulders. The color of their faces had turned to a deep violet, and their black tongues hung from their mouths. I did not have time to feel sorry for them. That might come later, though I doubted it would. Pity and empathy were emotions that seldom troubled me.

The door to Klyber's cabin was locked. Without looking back to the colonel for permission, I kicked the door open. The door swished across the carpeting, stirring a small cloud of dust. I touched the surface of the door then looked at my glove. A fine layer of dust covered the tip of my finger.

"Ash," a medical tech said as he and a partner squeezed past the colonel and entered the narrow hallway. They carried a stretcher. "It's everywhere in here . . . the carpets, the walls, the bodies."

Hearing the word "bodies," I snapped out of my haze. I watched for a moment as the medics pulled one of the guards onto their stretcher, then I turned and entered Admiral Klyber's cabin. I spotted the admiral immediately.

The room was a perfect cube—fifteen feet in every direction. It had a captain's bed built into one wall and a workstation built into another. Bryce Klyber sat flaccid at his desk, still wearing his whites, the gold epilates gleaming across his hunched shoulders. The admiral's head lay on the desk, his left cheek resting on the keyboard of his computer, his blue-black lips spread slightly apart and his swollen black tongue lolling out. Klyber's bright blue eyes stared at the wall across the room.

Klyber seemed to have shrunk in death the way large spiders curl in their legs and compress when you kill them. Tall, thin, and intense, Klyber's presence used to fill the room. Now, slumped over his desk, he looked like nothing more than a fragile old man.

Seeing Klyber splayed over his desk, with his posture curved and his eyes so vacant, seemed almost indecent, like I was seeing him naked. Here was a man whose uniform was always pressed and whose posture was always erect. He was the epitome of the aristocratic officer. Now his cap sat upside down on the desk before him and his arms dangled to the floor. A small stream of saliva ran from the corner of his mouth. It simply wasn't dignified—and above all else in life, Bryce Klyber had always been dignified.

Standing in the door, the colonel watched me as I checked Klyber for a pulse. I don't know why I bothered. I suppose I did not know what else to do. I thought about propping Klyber upright in his seat, replacing his cap, and letting him pass into history with his majesty intact, then dismissed the idea.

As if reading my thoughts, the colonel asked, "You're not going to leave him like that?"

"What do you suggest I do with him?" I asked.

"Sit him up," the colonel said.

"I don't think he's worried about appearances," I said. I waited for the colonel to move out of my way so that I could leave the cabin. I don't think I felt anger yet, though I knew that emotion would come. At the moment, I simply felt numb.

"Let the dead bury the dead," I whispered to myself as I left the room. I was a Liberator. I was Klyber's brew. We had not been built to mourn the dead, we were programmed to avenge them.

"What do we have here?" I heard a cheery voice through the open doorway of the engine compartment as I walked down the hall. The cabin that housed the broadcast equipment was nearly twice the size of Klyber's small cabin. I peered in the door and saw two demolition men in black armor kneeling side by side in front of the broadcast engine.

The broadcast engine looked like a giant replica of a box of rifle shells. The engine casing was a rectangular black box with chrome stripes. Inside the case stood eighteen brass cylinders that looked like three-foot-tall replicas of long-point bullets. A network of wires and tubes connected these cylinders.

"Was it sabotage?" I asked.

The two men turned back to look at me. I could see their faces through the glass in their protective masks. "So much for mystery," one of the men said, holding up a foot-long length of perfectly clean copper cable. "I could have told them what happened the moment the ship went dark."

I felt a hand grasp my shoulder. "You okay, there, Harris?" the colonel asked.

"That cable?" I asked.

"Oh, hello, Colonel McAvoy," the second bomb squadder said.

"Boys," said the colonel. "You were about to explain something to the lieutenant?"

"This is what happens when a broadcast goes wrong," the first guy said. "And there are too many things that can go wrong. No one in their right mind ever travels in a self-broadcasting ship."

I, of course, had traveled to the Golan Dry Docks in a self-broadcasting ship. The impact of the technicians' statement had just begun to sink in when I heard, "And that, Lieutenant Harris, is how you allowed the deaths of every one on this transport." I turned to see the chief of emergency services glaring down at me.

"Easy, Fred," warned the colonel.

"If you came here to protect the admiral, you did a shitty job. This ship was sabotaged right under your specking nose, bud." He stepped past me and took the copper cable from the bomb squad technician. Brandishing it like a newspaper at a misbehaving dog, he added, "Do you know how these people died?"

"I heard something about cardiac arrest," I said.

"Cardiac malfunction caused by electrocution would be more accurate. Somebody strung a cable from inside the broadcast engine to the frame of the ship. When the pilot turned on the broadcast engine, he sent four million volts through the entire ship for one one-hundredth of a second."

"One one-hundredth of a second . . ." I echoed.

"Do you understand how broadcasting works?" the tech asked. "The engine generates . . ."

"Yes," I said. "I know how broadcasting works." From what I had heard, only a select few in the entire galaxy truly understood the principles that made the broadcast process work, and they were elite scientists. I doubted some lowly corpse bagger understood the theory of broadcast travel any better than I did. I knew that broadcast engines coated ships with highly-charged particles that could be translated and transferred instantaneously, and that was enough for me.

"Yeah, well, apparently other people know how it works, too," said Fred, the Golan Dry Docks emergency services czar. "'Cause somebody snuck on to this ship under your nose and planted this cable. The admiral died on your watch, asshole."

FOURTEEN

I did not return to the *Doctrinaire*. I boarded the Johnston Starliner that Klyber loaned me for my trip to the Golan Dry Docks, and I charted a course into space. I flew straight out into deep space, away from the Dry Docks and the broadcast network, for four hours. This far out, the blackness seemed to fold in on itself like a blanket closing around me. By that time I had flown millions of miles to nowhere. A more experienced pilot might have understood the navigational hazards of deep space travel, but I neither understood nor cared. And, of course, I had a self-broadcasting ship.

Before initiating the broadcast engine, I climbed out of the cockpit and squeezed down the aisle through the cabin. The Johnston R-56 Starliner was a luxury craft. It did not have a living room-like main cabin, but it had enough head-room for me to walk nearly erect. It was designed to carry twenty passengers in six rows, but the last two rows of this particular craft were blocked off by a felt-covered bulkhead. Behind that bulkhead sat the broadcast engine.

I had pulled the power cables from the broadcast engine before approaching Golan. Without juice running through it, the broadcast engine was nothing more than a mess of brass, silicon, copper, and cables—undetectable with remote surveillance equipment. Now, before reconnecting those cables, I thought about what happened to Klyber's transport and gave the broadcast equipment a quick diagnostic.

I shimmied around to the back of the engine and checked for cables. Everything looked fine. I inspected the far corners, looking between the engine and the inner wall of the fuselage. Nothing. Moving on to the special generator that powered the engine, I removed a few of the cylinders and inspected the floor using a mirror to peer around corners. The floor looked clean.

Taking a deep breath, I stretched the power cables to the proper terminals on the broadcast engine and snapped them into place. I closed the hood over the engine and returned to my seat in the cockpit. And there I sat.

I thought about the dangers of self-broadcasting. A competent assassin could certainly have hidden a grounding cable somewhere in my ship where I would not find it.

As I thought about it, Klyber and his crew could scarcely have found a better way to go. All they knew was that their ship had traveled a safe distance from the Dry Docks and then they were dead. A powerful charge ran through them for one one-hundredth of a second. It stopped their hearts, turned some of their skin and hair to dust, and went away.

Even the officer who happened to have his hand on a door handle died painlessly. The metal handle prolonged the charge into his already-dead body and he charred. Had "Major Burns's" ghost hung around, it would have had reason to cringe; but "Burns" himself felt nothing.

When I first heard the med techs referring to him as "Major Burns," I thought it was yet another example of morbid med tech humor. Ironically enough, his real name was Major James T. Burns.

My thoughts returned to Bryce Klyber—my last tie to the Unified Authority, my former commander, and ultimately my creator, since he had led the team that engineered the Liberators. A creator was a cold and unattainable relation. I told myself that if I had once loved Klyber, it was only in the way that a man lost in a tunnel loves the light when he finds a way out. Klyber was kind to me. He protected me. In the end, though, he saw me as a way of justifying his career. I was not a son to him, not even a colleague.

Admiral Klyber wanted to use me to clear his name. History remembered Liberator clones as brutal and uncontrollable killers. Klyber's agenda was simple. He wanted to remind the people that his Liberators had saved the Republic. I wasn't a person to Bryce Klyber, I was a means to an end. Perhaps that was all any person was to another—a means to an end. Certainly the synthetic population was a means for helping natural-borns achieve certain ends.

God, I had to fly somewhere. All of this introspection had to be a sign of depression, but it felt nice to be alone with time to reflect. I needed to sort my feelings and figure out my future.

Sitting in a self-broadcasting ship, I realized that I had many options. I could fly anywhere. Klyber had only loaned me the Starliner; but now that he was gone, I considered the touring ship mine. With Klyber out of the picture, where could I return it? I could not bring myself to join the other side. I might have been able to bend my programming enough to ditch the Unified Authority Marines, but I could not even consider joining the Mogats or the Confederates. And the truth was, I liked the Mogats and the Confederate Arms even less than the Republic.

Unified Authority officers may have considered clones no more valuable than any other supply; but the Mogats equated clones with U.A. bullets—lethal tools of the enemy. The Unified Authority may have banned my kind from entering the Orion Arm, but the Mogats would exterminate me.

The one thing I knew I wanted was revenge. Father or creator, friend or manipulator, Klyber died on my watch. He trusted me and I failed. My job had been to get him off the ship, through the conference, and back on his C-64 transport alive. By the letter of my contract, I succeeded, but that did not make me feel any better. And the truth was, even after all of my tough talk, when I shut my eyes and thought about the people I cared about, Fleet Admiral Bryce Klyber was the first person to come to mind.

Letting my mind wander, I donned my mediaLink shades to check my mail.

With Bryce Klyber out of the way, there was no one stopping Admiral Huang from hunting me down. On the other hand . . .

I had a private message from somebody named Clarence McAvoy. The name meant nothing to me until I noticed the sender's address: Golan Dry Docks Security. Until that moment, I had never stopped to think of him as anything more than "the colonel," just a cog in the Dry Docks security works. As I thought about this, I realized the way I considered the people around me was not all that different than the way so many officers viewed clones.

Harris,
We have identified all of the passengers on Klyber's
transport. According to the manifest, there were 21
people aboard that flight. We found 19 bodies. As you
said, Rear Admiral Thomas Halverson was not
aboard the transport. Neither was Captain Leonid
Johansson.
We found Johansson's name on a passenger mani-
fest for a transport headed to Washington, D.C. He
returned to the Pentagon with Admiral Huang.
Huang transferred Johansson to his personal staff
early this morning. Isn't that just about the most god-
damn lucky transfer you ever heard of?
Colonel C. McAvoy

PS. The attached is the security record of the only
people who entered Klyber's ship. It was a mainte-
nance team. We have not been able to locate all of
the techs on that team.

With a couple of quick optical commands, I cued the file McAvoy sent and watched the video record.

A team of five technicians passed through the security gates outside the hangar. Each presented identification cards at the desk. Each man passed through a set of security posts, submitting himself to DNA profiling.

One of the men was short—no more than five feet tall—and mostly bald with a ring of sandy blond hair. The man wore the jumper of a janitor—a dirty number with short sleeves that ended just beyond the elbow. The suit looked loose around his compact, wiry physique. His exposed forearms had incredible muscle tone. And there was something else, not that I needed it to identify this man. The edge of a colorful forearm brantoo poked out of his sleeve.

Brantooing was the earmark of the rugged. Brantoo artists branded their clients with a hot iron to raise their skin, then injected colored pigment into the scar. The result was an embossed tattoo. Thugs and barroom brawlers loved brantoos because the average citizen went numb at the sight of them.

I recognized this brantoo—it was the emblem of the Navy SEALS. It was a wheel with six spokes, each spoke tinted a different color. This was a crude map of the six arms of the Milky Way. Every SEAL had it brantooed on his forearm.

But this man wasn't just a Navy SEAL. This was an "Adam Boyd" clone. These were special clones from a highly-classified operation under the personal direction of Admiral Che Huang. No need to worry about anybody recognizing this guy. For the most part, the only people who saw Boyd clones in action were Marines who had very little time to live.

Ravenwood, the outpost where I had supposedly died, was a training ground for Adam Boyd clones. Huang assigned platoons of forty-two Marines to defend the outpost on Ravenwood, then sent ten-man assault teams of Adam Boyd SEALS to kill them. I was the only Marine who ever escaped.

In the video feed, the Adam Boyd clone stepped through the posts without a moment's hesitation. A guard put up a hand to stop him, and the midget smirked up at him with a look of pure disdain.

Using an optic command I stopped the video feed and brought up the clone's identification badge. "Name: Adam Boyd. Title: Maintenance, Sixth Detail. Security Clearance: All Levels. Years with company: Five."

The guard said something that was not picked up by the security camera. The Adam Boyd clone answered satisfactorily, and he was allowed to pass. The maintenance team cleared the security station then entered and cleaned each of the ships parked on the high-security deck, including Admiral Klyber's C-64.

I watched this scene with a mixture of prurient interest and utter awe. The maintenance team stepped into transports belonging to each member of the Joint Chiefs of Staff. Had he wanted to, that little Boyd bastard could have blown up the entire hierarchy of the U.A. military.

Once the Boyd clone left Klyber's C-64, I rewound the file and watched him enter the transport a second time. Then I rewound and watched it again in slow motion. I looked for any sign of the copper cable. I timed how long it took him to enter and leave. I noted that the Boyd entered Klyber's ship three minutes before any of the other workers. He was on the ship for eighteen minutes and thirty-two seconds. He carried a small box of tools as he boarded the ship and brought the same box out. He could have easily smuggled a short length of cable in that box.

After watching that clone enter and leave the transport two more times, I finally allowed the video feed to play to its end. What I saw at the end hurt the most.

The security camera followed the maintenance team as it left the transport and then the landing area. They walked through the security gate. There, standing just inside the gate on almost the exact same spot where I would see him later that evening, stood Tom Halverson dressed like a civilian.

He leaned with his back against the wall, smoking a cigarette. For a moment he seemed to ignore the maintenance crew. Then he saw the Boyd clone. His eyes locked on the little clone as he continued his smoke. Once the maintenance men walked by, Halverson tossed his cigarette aside and fell in behind them, remaining a few steps back as they walked down the hall and disappeared from the screen.

"Why aren't you at the summit meeting?" I asked Halverson as he appeared in my mediaLink shades. Then it occurred to me. Why should he stay at the meeting? He was Huang's man. His job was to oversee the sabotage of Klyber's ship.

Expecting simply to leave a message, I used my shades to place a call to the colonel's office. He took the call.

"Harris?" Colonel McAvoy's face appeared in my shades.

"Colonel, I got your message. Thank you for sending the video feed."

"Did you find anything?"

"Did you watch the feed all the way through?" I asked.

"Sure," the colonel said. "I thought you might find the last few moments especially enlightening. We've searched the Dry Docks. Halverson isn't here. My guess is that he had another identity programmed into our computers and left using a false ID. I don't suppose you approve of officers using false identification codes, Commander Brocius?"

I had used so many false identities over the last few years that it took me a moment before I remembered coming into Golan as Commander Brocius.

"Is there any chance that Halverson flew back to Earth with Huang?"

"He did not," the colonel said. "Huang left before Klyber. I have a feed of the passengers boarding. Do you want it?"

"No," I said. "But I would like to see any video you might have from the summit."

"Good joke," the colonel said.

"I'm not joking."

"Yes, you are. You seem like a bright guy. You cannot possibly think I would have a feed from a high-level summit. And even if I did, you cannot possibly think I would throw away my career by giving it to you."

"The highest-ranking officer in U.A. Navy just died on your watch," I said, trying to sound calm with just a hint of menace. I was bluffing, of course.

"Military intelligence is going to be all over this, Harris," the colonel said. "They'll get it sorted out."

"Yes, they will. And they are going to blame it on you."

"How's that?"

"Follow the trail far enough and you'll see that Admiral Huang was behind this. When it comes to somebody taking a fall, who do you think they are going to go after, you or the secretary of the Navy?"

The colonel laughed. "You think Huang killed Admiral Klyber?"

"I can prove it," I said. "Do you have a video feed from the summit?"

"No," the colonel said.

"Good," I said, not believing him. High-level meetings like the summit were always recorded, and McAvoy was the man with the recording equipment at the Dry Docks. "Kly-ber and Huang will have gotten into a hot debate. Check out their brawl, then watch the feed of the maintenance team . . . and check out the short, bald guy."

"I should have shot you while I had the chance," the col-onel said. "Suppose I just say you planted the cable . . ."

"Your own video record proves that I never went near Kly-ber's ship," I said. "Are you planning to doctor your records?"

"Get specked," the colonel said.

"Look, Colonel, if you have access to the summit rec-ords, and we both know that you do, I suggest you view them. Once you've done that, send it to me, and I will try to help . . ."

"And you think I trust you?" the colonel asked.

"If you don't want my help, that's fine. The best of luck to you. You're going to need it."

"If you're right and there's something there, I'll get you that feed. If you're lying to me, Harris, I'll have you hauled back to my station for an immediate court-martial," the col-onel said. "How do you like that deal, Liberator?" With this, he ended the transmission.

I did not like that deal. I sat in the cockpit of the Starliner, stared out into space, and stewed. As the fleet admiral's se-curity officer, I felt duty-bound to find Klyber's killer. As a Liberator, I felt an almost pathological need for revenge. Be-yond that, the evidence suggested that Admiral Huang mur-dered Klyber and just thinking about putting a bullet between his eyes made me feel happy.

Killing Huang . . . killing Huang. A simple bullet in the head would be too easy. A gun, a bomb, or maybe a knife so that he would know it was personal. Our eyes would meet in the last moment, and he would know who killed him and why.

McAvoy contacted me within an hour. He did not call or write a message. Instead, he sent a virtual delivery. A mas-sive, encrypted file and the key with which to open it.

"Klyber's death is all over the Link," Freeman said on my mediaLink shades. Judging by the ugly furniture and plain room behind him, he was staying in a cheap hotel. "The Navy says it was a tragic accident."

"If you call sabotage an accident," I said. "Otherwise it

was a tragic murder." I was still out in space, still a few million miles from the Golan Dry Docks. I had spent the last four hours viewing the summit and had more to go.

"You think it was murder?" Freeman asked.

"Yes, and Huang was behind it," I said.

"Can you prove it?"

"No."

Freeman was sitting on a bed. The shape of the mattress turned from a square to a funnel under his weight. "What do you have?" he asked.

"I have a security tape showing the maintenance team that cleaned Klyber's transport. There was an Adam Boyd with them." I paused to see how Freeman would react.

He raised an eyebrow, and said, "That's it?"

" Huang created those little speckers."

"Was Thurston at the summit?" Freeman asked.

I remembered seeing him on the video feed and nodded.

"The only Boyd clones I've ever seen were assigned to one of Thurston's ships. Maybe he did it."

It was true. To the best of my knowledge, every last Adam Boyd clone had been transferred to the *Kamehameha*, the command ship of the Scutum-Crux Fleet—Robert Thurston's purview. That tidbit did not fit in with my theory. I wanted Huang to be the killer. "Thurston is Huang's man. He doesn't have anything against Admiral Klyber."

"You can't prove Huang has anything against Klyber." Freeman replied.

"Get specked," I said, knowing that Freeman was right.

"The only thing you have is a picture of an Adam Boyd clone boarding Klyber's ship. Is that right? You can't even prove he did anything to sabotage it."

I nodded. "He was carrying a toolbox," I said. "And he was on the ship for eighteen minutes and thirty-two seconds."

"Was he alone?"

"Some of the time. He got on first."

"So you are saying he had the opportunity to open the broadcast engine and place the cable even though the rest of the maintenance crew was coming?"

"Must have," I said. "How did you know about the cable?"

"That's how you sabotage self-broadcasting ships." Freeman said. "Do you have anything else?"

"I've got a security feed from the summit. You should have seen the sparks. Klyber and Huang really hated each other."

"The way I see it, we can either drop this or go after the Boyd," Freeman said. "That's the best we can do until we can tie Huang to the clone."

I knew the Adam Boyd clones were trained on Earth, on an island called Oahu. I stumbled into one of them while on R and R on that island. I knew that their base of operations was now the U.A. *Kamehameha*, a fighter carrier in the Scutum-Crux Arm. Of the two places, Hawaii sounded more hospitable.

"Guess I'm headed to Earth to have a look at their farm," I said. "You coming?"

Freeman nodded. "The only time I've ever seen Boyd clones was after you got through with them. It'd be interesting to see one that is still breathing."

Part II

THE INVESTIGATION

CHAPTER
FIFTEEN

General Alexander Smith, secretary of the Air Force and ranking member of the Joint Chiefs of Staff, stands in front of an electronic display board holding a laser pointer. Like most of the members of the Joint Chiefs, Smith is in his sixties, a short man with a medium build and graying hair. His mustache covers the entire length of his upper lip.

The display board is an old-fashioned two-dimensional model, strictly low-tech. How he smuggled such an antique into the Dry Docks is beyond me, but there is no way this is Golan equipment. All of the big corporations gave up on 2-D displays long before this facility was built.

The summit takes place around a U-shaped table that is fifty feet long. Only generals and admirals sit at this table. Staffs members sit behind them in chairs set against the wall.

At the moment, General Smith's 2-D display shows a diagram of the galaxy. Large red circles appear in several areas of the diagram. The general turns and points at them.

"As you know, we have engaged enemy troops in the following locations." He points to the circles. "The Mogats seem to have set up power bases here . . ." He points at the lower flank of the outer Cygnus Arm. "Here . . ." He circles

a parallel segment on the Perseus Arm. "And throughout these portions of Scutum-Crux."

Smaller red splotches appear throughout the map. "The Mogats have free access throughout the galaxy. These are hotspots for spying and illegal activity. The only red zones in the Orion Arm are the planets New Columbia and Olympus Kri."

Three of the galactic arms turn bright green. "The Cygnus, Perseus, and Scutum-Crux Arms have declared independence and formed the Organization of Confederate Arms. The Norma Arm has also declared independence. From what we can tell, this arm has ejected all Mogat colonists and is not a member of the OCS.

"Only the Orion and Sagittarius Arms have remained loyal; and in all candor, the U.A. government is funding an all-out covert war in Sagittarius that is costing us trillions of dollars. That's the bad news."

The colored areas vanish from the display, leaving a white and blue-black map of the stars. "The pink areas represent the territories in which our enemies currently enjoy military superiority."

All of the men in the room laugh. There are no pink areas.

With the introductions and joking out of the way, General Smith suddenly turns serious. "About three weeks ago, Air Force intelligence intercepted the message, 'Alterations complete. Will test in NGC three thousand six hundred and twelve.'

"Obviously, we had no way of knowing what the message meant then."

"NGC," Klyber calls out, "Norma Galactic Center?"

"Correct," Smith says with a slight bow. "NGC did indeed refer to the inner curve of the Norma Arm, an unpopulated sector of the galaxy." He walks to the edge of the dais, his eyes still focused on Admiral Klyber. "Care to venture a guess as to their usage of *alterations* or three thousand six hundred and twelve?'" There is nothing confrontational in the way he does this. This is a friendly challenge between two fellow officers.

"It sounds like a date," Klyber says, shaking his head and sitting back in his seat.

"You missed your calling, Bryce," says Smith. "You should have been in intelligence. You would have really risen up the ranks."

This comment gets scattered laughs as Klyber is the high-est ranking officer in any branch.

"We do not have any outposts in the central part of the Norma Arm, it's just too remote. We do, however, have an ex-perimental radar station. This is what that radar readout looked like nine days ago—March 6, 2512."

The screen turns flat black with concentric rings marking distances from the radar station. Except for the wand effect of the screen refreshing itself, the screen remains still and black for several seconds. When the radar wand finishes its third sweep, a litter of dots appear in one small section of the screen.

The wand sweeps by refreshing the radar reading every thirty seconds and the dots do not move. They stay in place for sixteen complete sweeps of the wand, a total of eight minutes. Eight minutes pass and the next pass of the wand reveals that the dots are gone. They vanished without a trace. The wand sweeps on, but the radar reading remains clear.

"Do we have a more detailed reading, sir?" *asks Admiral Brocius.* "I'd like to see an analysis of that."

"This radar reading was taken over a four-million-mile distance. I'm afraid the ship designs and serial numbers were out of focus," *General Smith quips.* "The best we could do was dots."

The patch with the dots reappears, then grows until it fills the entire screen. The dots look like a clutch of glowing eggs laid across a black surface in no particular order.

"There are precisely five hundred and seventy-six dots in this picture," *Smith says.* "There were five hundred eighty ships in the Galactic Central Fleet—"

"Admiral Thurston shot down four of the Galactic Cen-tral destroyers during the battle at Little Man," *Huang inter-rupts, standing up as he speaks. Sitting behind Huang, Leonid Johansson nods complacently, as if he has some ownership in that victory.*

Once I notice Johansson, I turn my attention to the wall behind Klyber. Halverson is sitting behind Klyber taking care-ful notes. Beside him sits an officer I do not know . . . could be the ill-fated Major Burns for all I know. Each officer attending the summit has three aides. The last seat behind Klyber must have been Captain Johansson's. It now sits empty.

"That would mean that every last ship was up and running," an Air Force general I do not recognize calls out.

"Why not?" Huang shoots back, still standing, *"they've had more than forty years to tune them up."*

"Admiral Huang makes a good point," says Admiral Brocius.

As the inertia of this discussion builds up among the other officers, Admiral Klyber leans back in his chair and mumbles something to Halverson. The way Klyber leans back and the sly smile on his face suggest that he is telling the rear admiral a joke, but the startled look on Halverson's face is anything but amused.

"Those ships are antiques. They belong in a museum," the unidentified Air Force general responds.

"I wish I shared your confidence," General Smith says in a raised voice, trying to arrest control of the floor.

"Come on, Alex . . . one sighting in two years . . . Before that it was forty years," the unidentified Air Force general replies.

The board behind General Smith clears itself and turns into a map of the Scutum-Crux Arm. *"There have been eighteen sightings of those ships in the last three days. They appeared here, here, and here . . ."*

"That's only a few million miles from the Scutum-Crux Fleet," Huang says in astonishment. *"Perhaps they plan to engage Admiral Thurston."*

"Yeah, too bad your boy missed them," The unidentified Air Force general taunts Huang.

Rear Admiral Robert Thurston, sitting quietly in a corner in the back of the room, says nothing. He is a quiet, deliberate man. He has red spiky hair and the face of a high school student. His short waif's physique adds to the illusion that he is a boy just out of secondary school.

"Don," General Smith says, turning toward his fellow Air Force man, *"we have a radar record of three hundred ships appearing within six hundred thousand miles of your base. They come in, reprogram their broadcasting computers, and flash out. One theory is that they are testing our level of preparedness."*

"It looks like those old ships are flying circles around you

*boys," says an Army officer. It is easy for him to talk. His
forces aren't expected to guard open space.*

*"You cannot possibly expect us to patrol every inch of
space," Don says, now sounding defensive.*

*"We've got a bigger problem than that," says Smith.
"Whatever fleet this is, it has an uncanny awareness of our
movements."*

Earthdate: March 16, 2512 A.D.
City: Honolulu; Planet: Earth; Galactic Position:
Orion Arm

The last time I flew into Hawaii, I was a young sergeant in
the Marines on leave. I played like a kid, swam in the ocean
like a kid, and had a meaningless romance with a girl whom
I could only describe as ornamental. Within a month of returning to duty, I landed on Little Man. After seeing the massacre on Little Man, I would never be a boy again. Looking
back, I see my stay in Hawaii as the last chapter in my youth.

I did not fly directly from the Dry Docks to Earth. As a
Liberator, I was not allowed to enter the Orion Arm and I did
not want to take the chance of attracting attention.

Having a self-broadcasting ship allowed me to bypass the
broadcast network and Mars security. I broadcasted myself to
the "dark side" of the solar system, the spot exactly opposite
Mars in its orbit. That left me with nearly one hundred million miles to fly to reach Earth—twenty hours of travel at the
Starliner's top non-atmospheric speed was five million miles
per hour.

Even more hours of flying awaited me once I entered
Earth's atmosphere. The Starliner had a top speed of three
thousand miles per hour in atmospheric conditions. The
Mach 3 speed limit was a convention imposed throughout
the Unified Authority.

"Harris, you there?" Ray Freeman's voice sounded on
my mediaLink.

"Yeah. I'm here," I said. I had been watching the summit
and was lost in the politics of it. Hearing Freeman's voice
brought me back to the real world. "Are you in Hawaii yet?"

"Not yet."

"When you went to Little Man, were you hunting Mogats?" Freeman asked.

"That's what they told us," I said. "This about your family?"

"What do you think the Navy will do if they find neo-Baptists there?"

"It's a valuable planet," I said. "There aren't many planets capable of sustaining life without engineering. At the very least they will consider them squatters. How many people are there?"

"About one hundred," Freeman said.

"That's tiny. The Navy may not even notice them," I said.

"They noticed them," Freeman said. "My father contacted me. He said that they're sending a carrier to review the situation."

"Know which one?" I asked.

"The Grant, I think. Does it matter?"

"It might if it's the Grant. Remember Vince Lee?" Vince was my best friend when I was a Marine. I had not talked with him since going AWOL. "He's an officer on the Grant."

"Lee?" Freeman said, not making a connection.

"You tried to kill him once," I said. "You paid him a few bucks to wear my helmet without telling him there was an assassin looking for me."

"Yeah," Freeman said.

"He's a fair man," I said. "I've met the captain of that ship, too . . . Pollard. Both good men. They'll give your father a fair shake. They might tell them to leave, but they won't be harsh about it. Hell, once they know the colony doesn't pose a threat, they may choose to ignore it. How long ago did they make contact?"

"A day or two."

"Well, they won't get there anytime soon. It takes a long time to travel to Little Man. The nearest broadcast disc is several days away."

Freeman and I spoke for a few more minutes, then he signed off. I leaned back in my chair to watch more of the summit. I had ninety-five million miles to go, time was on my side.

CHAPTER
SIXTEEN

"The GC Fleet's movements show an increasing amount of sophistication," General Smith says as a new set of circles appear on the screen behind him. "In the radar reading from Central Norma, they appear to have been testing their ability to broadcast. That was the first reading that we took. The ships broadcasted in, they remained perfectly still for eight minutes, and they left. From what we can tell, they remained just long enough to generate the power they needed to broadcast out."

"Eight minutes between broadcasts?" Klyber asks, unconsciously using a voice that is just loud enough to catch everyone's attention. "That hardly seems possible."

"Bryce?" Smith asks. "Did you say something?"

"The broadcast generators on those ships should take fifteen minutes to build up enough energy for a broadcast," Klyber says. He looks and sounds deeply concerned. Seeing this, I wonder how long it takes the *Doctrinaire* to charge up and broadcast.

"You will recall the intercepted message—'alterations complete,'" says General Smith. "We believe they have updated their equipment."

"What's the problem, Admiral Klyber?" Huang calls. He

is sitting directly across from Klyber; now the two officers face each other. "How long does it take the generators on the Doctrinaire *to power up for a broadcast?"*

The floor of the summit goes silent. The atmosphere of that great chamber suddenly becomes a vacuum of sound. Bryce Klyber turns his narrow, bony head toward Che Huang. Klyber is a fleet admiral, the highest-ranking man in the Unified Authority Navy, but Admiral Che Huang is the secretary of the Navy and a member of the Joint Chiefs. Klyber has powerful friends on Capitol Hill. Huang has the backing of the Pentagon. Neither man is about to back down.

"The Doctrinaire?" General Smith asks. Smith clearly has no clue what Huang is talking about.

"Admiral Klyber has been developing a self-broadcasting fighter carrier," Huang says in a voice that is both arrogant and bored. "Haven't heard of it, Alex? Don't feel bad. It's Klyber's little secret. He's been building it with funding from his pals on the Linear Committee."

"Is that true?" General Smith asks.

If there is one thing that senior officers do not like, it is being left out of the loop. This feeds into their paranoia and leaves them feeling ambushed. Anger and astonishment show on General Alex Smith's face. Triumph shows on Huang's.

"Of course it's true," says Huang. "This is Bryce Klyber. He has a long record of calling on friends in high places to skirt regulations. This is the same officer who made the Liberator clones . . . one of which is in this very facility."

The room remains silent.

"I'm prepared to discuss the Doctrinaire," Klyber says. Then he turns to Huang and adds, "And after that, perhaps we should discuss your furtive cloning projects."

Che Huang turns stark white, but for only a moment, and then he turns blood red. He slams his fist on the table but says nothing.

"May I take the floor?" Klyber asks. Not until General Smith nods and leaves the dais does the well-cultivated Bryce Klyber leave his place at the table. Klyber is urbane, discreet, and circumspect in his approach. Across the table, Huang is so angry he can barely stay in his chair. He fidgets and his hands are clenched into fists.

Klyber has clearly come to this meeting planning to discuss his top-secret project. He takes a data chip from a case by his seat and places it into a slot in the display board. A schematic of the Doctrinaire *appears.*

"Gentlemen, let me begin by apologizing for not informing you about this project sooner. You should know that the project was not even discussed within the Senate. National security the way it is at this time, the members of the Linear Committee specifically requested that I wait until a moment like this to discuss the project.

"As this project was paid for using the Linear Committee's discretionary funds rather than the military budget, it seemed like a fair request."

When it comes to the merging of military matters and politics, Bryce Klyber has no equal. Huang must already have realized that he picked the wrong venue for this fight. He picks up a data pad and pretends to read notes, his eyes fixed on a spot in the middle of the pad. When Johansson leans forward and whispers something, Admiral Huang's jaw tightens and he acts as if he does not hear him.

Dressed in civilian clothes, a cap covering my hair, and carrying no visible weapons, I passed through Honolulu Airport without being noticed. This was not like entering the spaceports on Mars or in Salt Lake City where they had large security stations. Flights in and out of airports like the one in Honolulu originate on Earth and never leave the atmosphere. By the time you were on an Earth-bound jet, you were clean. You were clean, that is, unless you flew a rare self-broadcasting craft.

Freeman did not meet me in the airport. Being met by a seven-foot black man with arms like anacondas and tree trunks for legs did not lend itself to inconspicuousness. With nothing but an innocuous overnight bag slung over my shoulder, I strolled through the open air lobby of the private craft terminal and headed for the street. A few minutes later, Freeman swung by in a small rental car and I hopped into the passenger's seat.

Freeman had selected a convertible. Most people drove these cars so that they could enjoy warm island weather; however, sun worship had nothing to do with Freeman's decision. He simply did not fit in most cars. He sat scrunched behind the steering wheel, and everything above his nose was higher than the windshield. He looked like an adult trying to squeeze into a child's go-cart.

"Have you ever been to this island before?" I asked Freeman, trying to ignore the sight of him in that driver's seat.

He shook his head.

The Unified Authority maintained vacation spots on Earth as a way of reminding citizens on the 180 outworlds which planet was home. Hawaii was a living museum, and the only commerce conducted was tourist-related. Hawaii had a police force, garbage men, and air traffic controllers, but the only reason they were there was to keep the place nice for tourists. There were pineapple and sugarcane farms, but they were productive museum exhibits run by the government. They existed only to show visitors what island life had been like five hundred years before. Their production methods were antiquated and much of the produce was sold as souvenirs.

"Where are we going?" he asked.

"There's a place called Sad Sam's Palace," I said.

"The boxing arena you told me about?"

"Boxing, wrestling, professional fighters, amateur challenge. It all depends what night you go," I said. "The Palace is near Waikiki. Can you find it?"

The March sky was a mixture of sunshine and shadow, and the city was drenched with moist air. Clouds the color of stainless steel gathered around the mountains to our left, choking out sunlight. To the right, the sky over the ocean was nearly clear.

Freeman and I drove along the outskirts of Honolulu. He sat in his seat, cramped behind the wheel, watching the road and quietly scanning every turn and approaching vehicle.

"I came in clean," Freeman said. To avoid drawing attention to himself on Earth, as if a seven-foot black man could somehow make himself inconspicuous in this homogonous society, he took public transportation in from Mars. With a war brewing and security at an all-time high, he didn't even bother trying to smuggle a gun in with him. "Any idea where I can find something?"

I thought about that for a moment. "No. Colorful shirts, yes. Alcohol, yes. I know where they sell a fruit drink that will knock you flat."

"Where do you get the shirts?" Freeman asked.

"The International Marketplace," I said. "It's a bazaar for tourists. You want bathing suits, hats made with coconut leaves, candles, or Hawaiian shirts, that's the spot. Guns . . ." I didn't see any.

"Clean wholesome place?"

"Not exactly," I said.

"Think you can find it?"

Finding the International Marketplace was no problem. It was in the middle of Waikiki, the heart of the tourist area. It was a wide open lot with trees and carts and buildings with walls made of faux lava rock. The time was just 1700 hours on what looked like a slow day. There was only a sprinkling of tourists around, and the sales people aggressively chased anyone who walked by their stands.

"You looking for sandals, sugar?" a girl called to me as we walked by her store. Not one customer stirred inside the store, just the sales girl and rows of shelves with leather and rubber sandals.

Freeman turned and glared at the woman and she shrank back.

"Didn't see anything that you wanted?" I asked.

Freeman said nothing.

"Probably a good thing," I said. "I doubt she had anything your size."

We passed jewelry, candle, and clothes shops, and Freeman ignored them. Hucksters came to show us shirts and luggage. Freeman pushed past them without looking back. Then we passed a stand selling perfume and Freeman stopped. Beside the stand was a warty little man in shorts and a golf cap. The man had no shirt. His body was skinny but muscled. His stomach muscles showed distinctly, and his chest was flat and carved with sinew.

"Wait here," Freeman growled. He went to the man and they spoke very quietly.

"Get specked!" the man yelled suddenly. "What kind of a store do you think this is." He threw his hands in the air. Even reaching all the way up, the man's fingers barely came level with Freeman's eyes.

Freeman said something in his soft-thunder voice and the man lowered his hands.

"Go speck yourself!" the man yelled. "Who do you think you are?"

Freeman dug into his pocket and rolled out some dollars. I could not see how many dollars he peeled off, but I saw him place them on the counter. The warty man shook his head. Freeman laid out more. The man shook his head. Freeman peeled off two more bills. When Freeman went to retrieve his cash, the little man placed his hand over it.

Putting the money in the front pocket of his shorts, the warty little man trotted into a service corridor. He returned a few minutes later with a colorful red shirt folded into a neat square. The shirt did indeed look large enough for Freeman to wear.

Without saying a word, Freeman took the shirt and left. When we got back to the car, Freeman unfolded the shirt. Inside it he found a pistol and three clips filled with bullets.

"How did you know he'd have guns?" I asked.

Freeman looked at me in surprise. "Who would buy perfume from an asshole like that?"

CHAPTER
SEVENTEEN

"In the interest of time, I will not go into every detail of this ship," Klyber says. "A complete . . ."

"Why not give us the complete rundown?" Huang interrupts.

"As I was saying," Klyber continues, a trace of a smile showing in his expression, "a complete set of plans has been forwarded to each of you. As the Linear Committee has not gone public with this project, your discretion is requested." He is laying an obvious trap, knowing full well that Huang will not be able to control his arrogance long enough to avoid it.

"I would, however, like to go over a few of the finer points of the ship. The Doctrinaire has twelve decks and a bridge. She measures a full two miles from wingtip to wingtip.

"The Doctrinaire has four launch tubes, each of which is loaded with a complete squadron of seventy Tomcat fighters for deep space combat. She also has . . ."

Leaning back in his chair with a bored expression that demonstrates that he has heard all of this information before, Huang says, "Two-thirds of the ship is taken up by the engines."

Klyber smiles. "Quite right, Admiral Huang. With a ship

of this size, power generation is a major concern. Especially for a ship that is self-broadcasting."

The response to that is so enthusiastic you might have thought Klyber has announced that God himself has enlisted in the Marines. One dozen small conversations open up across the room. Several officers turn back to whisper to their aides while others begin speaking among themselves in louder voices.

"Admiral Klyber, you have not yet told us the regeneration time needed to power your broadcast engine," Huang calls out in a voice that cuts through the din, a sneer across his face.

"I believe we just learned that the Mogats have reoutfitted their broadcast engines so that they can charge and broadcast every eight minutes. How long will it take your colossus to charge its broadcast engine, Admiral Klyber?"

Klyber nods to acknowledge the question. "Fair question. Our best intelligence showed that the ships in the Galactic Central Fleet required fifteen minutes per broadcast. We set a higher standard, of course . . ."

"How long?" Huang asks.

"The broadcast engines in the Doctrinaire require ten minutes," Klyber admits, but he does not seem unhappy to admit this. In fact, his smile only broadens. Either he is bluffing or he has an ace up his sleeve that neither Che Huang nor Leonid Johansson know about.

"Ten minutes?" Huang asks.

"That is correct."

Stepping away from his chair, Huang repeats, "Ten minutes." He moves around the table and approaches the dais. "So, assuming you manage to fly this juggernaut to the battle before the GCF ships depart, they will simply be able to broadcast off before you can recharge your engines and follow them."

Klyber pauses to consider this. The look of confidence on his face does not fade. "Well, of course, you realize that we have no way of tracking a self-broadcasting ship? We'd have no way of knowing where the GCF ships had broadcast themselves."

Huang's expression turns to fury. "We're all quite aware of that, Admiral Klyber. My point is simple. If the GC Fleet *appears . . . oh, for the purposes of this discussion, we'll say they appear near Olympus Kri. And let's say you have a three-minute response time. It seems unlikely, but let's say you manage to get your colossus ship there in three minutes. Your ship will have five minutes to engage the enemy before they fly off to another target, very likely their primary target, while you sit around charging up the* Doctrinaire's *broadcast engine.*

"Brilliant plan, Admiral," Huang snickers. "You've created a trillion-dollar boondoggle." He stands triumphant, his arms folded across his chest, his head high, and his eyes staring angrily at Klyber.

"That is a concern," General Smith says. Several of the officers around the table nod in agreement.

It is at this moment that Klyber drops a bomb that even Johansson does not expect. "Admiral Huang, you'll note that I said 'broadcast engines.' The Doctrinaire *does, in fact, have two such units, each working independent of the other.*

"One engine recharges while the other one broadcasts. The Doctrinaire *can self-broadcast every five minutes. Admiral Huang, we never believed that the Separatists would be so foolish as to commit their entire fleet into a single battle. The* Doctrinaire *was built around the notion that they would stage their battles with decoys and feigned attacks along several fronts."*

At first there is silence as the officers assimilate this information. Then applause erupts. General Smith is the first to clap his hands, and the Air Force officers soon join in. Admiral Brocius stands up from his chair and applauds. He slaps his hands together so hard that the noise echoes. A moment later, Rear Admiral Thurston joins him, an appreciative smile on his youthful face. A general from the Marines stands silently and salutes. The applause lasts for several minutes.

"What about armament?" Thurston asks, his enthusiasm evident.

The board behind Klyber shifts to an exterior schematic of the ship. Klyber picks up an old-fashioned wooden pointer instead of the laser pointer that General Smith had used earlier. "She has two massive forward cannons for bombarding stationary targets such as cities and military bases. These cannons are both laser- and particle-beam enabled." This is friendly talk, like friends telling each other about a new car over a round of drinks.

Klyber slides the pointer along the outer edge of the wing. "The ship has three hundred particle beam turrets along with twenty missile stations and fifteen torpedo stations. And, as I mentioned a moment ago, she has a compliment of two hundred and eighty Tomcat fighters. Should the enemy attempt to attack her, the Doctrinaire could annihilate the entire GC Fleet.

"Oh, and Thurston, you'll appreciate this . . . Look at the shield antennas." Klyber watches expectantly. "This is an entirely new technology."

There are rings around the antenna at the ends of the wings. Other U.A. ships do not have rings connecting their antennas. Their shields are flat panes broadcast from pole-like antennas.

"We've developed a cylindrical shield," Klyber says with the air of a father boasting about his son. "Those rings project a seamless shield that covers the entire ship."

"And the Mogats haven't got a clue," General Smith marvels.

"Perhaps," Klyber says in a voice that carries across the room, "but I am concerned about that. We paid for the ship with Linear Committee funds so that we could slip under the radar, but . . ."—Klyber turns toward Admiral Huang—"apparently we didn't go undetected."

Suddenly, everyone in the room becomes silent. Huang looks at the other officers, hoping for support. Rear Admiral Thurston, Huang's closest ally, is too busy lusting over the schematics to see that Huang needs help.

"Yes," says General Smith, "it does appear that you had a breach of security." Smith takes the dais and formality creeps back into the session. The officers return to their seats.

Smith calls the meeting back to order. He turns toward Huang. "Admiral, while we are on the subject of secret operations . . ."

Bryce Klyber's combination of political and military acumen now comes to bear. It becomes obvious that he has briefed General Smith about Huang's Adam Boyd cloning project. Klyber used himself as a decoy, and now that Huang has fired all his guns, Smith flanks and attacks.

"General," Huang interrupts. "My intelligence unit located the construction of a large project in deep space. Our radar showed repeated broadcasts in the Perseus Arm. We had no idea that this was Admiral Klyber's operation when we began investigating . . ."

But General Smith puts up a hand to stop him. Smith is smiling. He has no interest in beating the Doctrinaire horse any further. Everyone on the floor has now heard about the ship and shown their approval. The smile on Smith's face is one of supreme satisfaction. He is the gambler who has no need to bluff. He is the only man at the table with all four aces in his hand.

"Admiral Huang, general accounting found an anomaly in your books. Apparently, your branch has had a six billion dollar increase in spending on toilet paper and uniforms." Smith's smile turns wicked as he says, "We all hope the lack of one of these items has not led to a need for the other."

Huang does his best to look confused, but he is no actor. Instead of dropping his jaw, he clenches it. He glares at General Smith. "I have a staff that goes through the books and reports to . . ."

"But a six billion dollar expenditure, surely that would not go unnoticed," Smith observes.

"Perhaps our inventory was . . ."

"When my staff looked into it, we discovered that your procurement team placed no additional orders for either toilet paper or uniforms, Admiral. What we found was that a mothballed Military base was reactivated on Earth." Alex Smith picks up his data pad.

Huang says nothing. He stares back at Smith defiantly.

"I understand that you have a cloning plant on the island of Oahu. Is that correct?" Smith asks.

Huang shows no sign of fear or remorse. "That is correct, General. The Navy is experimenting with a new set of genes to improve our SEAL operations. I was unaware of any regulations stating that the Navy had to clear its research projects with members of other branches."

A video feed of an Adam Boyd in a firefight appears on

the display board. It is a brief five-second loop that repeats itself again and again. I recognize the image. It is from the battle on Ravenwood—the one in which I supposedly died. The footage was taken from cameras placed in the helmet I wore during the battle on Ravenwood. Ray Freeman placed my helmet by the body of a different marine before lifting me off the planet.

Across the room, Admiral Thurston looks particularly interested in this discussion. Huang's newly cloned SEALs operate off of Thurston's command ship.

"When were you planning on telling us about this new project?" asks General John Kellan, the thirty-nine-year-old secretary of the Army. There is a centuries-old tradition of jealousy that runs between the SEALs and Kellan's Rangers.

We headed for Sad Sam's at 2100 hours. It was Thursday night during a slow season for tourists, and the city seemed deserted. We found a drive-in restaurant just up the street from the Palace and ordered hamburgers, then ate in the car.

Except for the streetlamps and an occasional car, the only lights on the entire street came from the façade of the Palace. The marquee was studded with old-fashioned bulbs that winked on and off, casting their warm manila glare. Foot-tall letters announced the name, Sad Sam's Palace. Below that, the event for the night—"Ultimate Fighting Competition: Mixed Martial Arts"—showed over a glowing ivory panel.

The Palace was the modern world's answer to the Roman coliseum. Instead of Christians and lions, it featured professional wrestlers, boxers, and mixed martial artists. It had an open challenge on Friday nights. If you were a military clone, and you happened to be in the audience during the Open Challenge, an announcer called you down to fight. The standing champion of that Open Challenge was a fighter named Adam Boyd, obviously one of Huang's clones.

"You got that scar here?" Freeman asked.

The scar ran through the eyebrow over my left eye. Three smaller scars formed parallel stripes across my left cheek, just under the eye socket.

"This is the place," I said.

I got the scars fighting an Adam Boyd clone. I beat him, had certainly put him in the hospital, but not before he dug into my face and back with his talonlike fingers, giving me lacerations that went all the way to the bone.

Freeman finished his burger and drink in what looked like a single motion, then sat without saying a word. As I finished my burger, the front doors opened and a mob flowed out. "Fights must be over," I said, crumpling the wrapper and throwing it in the bag. "That's our cue." I climbed out of the car.

The crowd thinned as we made our way across the empty street. Most of the people had walked in from the waterfront where the buses ran. Now they walked back, their excited chatter filling the street.

An usher in a white shirt and black vest approached me as I came through the door. He must have seen Freeman, too, but he did not dare approach that giant of a man. "Show's over," he said.

"My friend dropped his wallet somewhere around his seat," I said.

The man looked at Freeman, nodded, and stepped out of my way. If I had said it was my wallet, he would likely have told me to "come back tomorrow."

We walked through the dark hall toward the auditorium, the usher following from a safe distance. Bright arc lights blazed in the center of the auditorium, their true white glare shining bright.

A wall of bleachers surrounded the outer edges of the floor. These bleachers curved up, ending just below the first of two balconies. On busy nights during the tourist season, Sad Sam's Palace must have played host to five thousand people per night. Now the floor was empty except for janitors sweeping food, cups, and wrappers from the floor. Under the lights, a small crew disassembled the steel cage and octagonal ring they used for mixed martial arts. Friday night was Open Challenge night. That show would take place on a raised platform with glass walls.

Freeman and I walked across the floor and headed for the tunnel to the dressing rooms. I paused for a moment to look at the ring, then pushed the door open.

"Where are you going?" the usher yelled. I did not bother answering. The answer was obvious.

The metal doors opened to a brightly-lit hallway with a concrete floor and cinderblock walls. Some of the fluorescent lights that ran the length of the hall had gone dark, occasionally flashing on and off in a Morse code pattern. Our footsteps echoed, and the steel door slamming behind us sounded like a volcanic eruption.

"Do you know where we're going?" Freeman asked.

"I've never been back here," I said. That was not quite true. As I understand it, paramedics carried me back here on a stretcher after my fight, but I was only semiconscious during that ride.

Halfway down the hall, we found a pair of emerald-green double doors. With the usher and three security guards storming down the hall yelling at us, I tried the door. It was unlocked, so I let myself in. Freeman remained outside to deal with the security guards.

The men inside the locker room seemed not to care that I had entered. A man with a towel wrapped around his waist strode past me without so much as a sideways glance. His hair was wet. He had a square chest and muscular arms, all of which was covered with welts and bruises. He sported a superb shiner over his right eye.

Another man, sitting stark naked on a wooden bench in front of a row of lockers, watched me. "I know you," he said, rubbing his chin.

"Not likely," I said.

The security guards had caught up to Freeman. It should have been a four-against-one battle; but from the sound of things, Freeman took out the first guard so quickly that it really was more accurately described as three-against-one. I heard, "Hey, you're not . . ." Then there was the thunderous sound of something slamming against the outside of the door, followed by a moment of absolute silence.

"Shit. I'm calling the . . ." The door muffled the shouting.

Then the door flew open. In ran the usher, stumbling over the body of the fallen security guard. "There's a giant black man out there!"

"That's nothing," said the naked man as he stood and

stepped into his briefs. "There's a Liberator clone in here."

The usher looked at me, and the blood drained from his face. He did not say another word.

"You're the one who killed that Adam Boyd guy," the man said as he pulled up his pants. By this time several other fighters came to investigate. Outside, the commotion ended quickly. I heard a click, which I assumed was the last security guard's head hitting the concrete, then Freeman stepped through the door looking as nonplussed as if he had come from a grocery store.

The usher was willing to share a locker room with me, but Freeman was another story. Freeman had barely come through the door when the usher bolted to the safety of the bathroom stalls.

"Everything moving along in here?" Freeman asked.

"Just fine," I said. I turned back to the fighter. "You say he died?"

"Yeah, I helped drag his ass from the ring. That boy was dead. You caved in the front of his skull."

I thought I might have killed him. In truth, I felt no regret about it. "I heard he went on to win another fifty fights," I said.

"Not that Boyd."

The other fighters eyed Ray Freeman nervously, gave me a curious glance at most, and went back to finish dressing.

The air in the room had that sweaty, unpleasant humidity that comes with locker rooms and open showers. The floor was wet and slick. Near the door, a canvas basket on rollers overflowed with wet towels, some of which were streaked with blood.

"What makes you think I'm a Liberator?" I asked. This guy was a natural-born, a muscular man, maybe thirty-five years of age with sun-bronzed skin and bleached-blond hair.

"Boyd said you were," the fighter said.

"I thought you said I killed him?"

"Not the one you killed, the next one. We had at least three of 'em . . ." He smiled as if remembering a joke. "At least three. They were clones. Had to be. You off-ed one and two others got busted up pretty bad.

"So you are a Liberator, right?"

I chose to ignore the question. "Is there going to be a Boyd fighting tomorrow?"

"Nah," said the fighter. "The Boyds stopped coming a couple years ago. They're gone . . . left the island."

"Do you know where they went?" I asked.

"No, but I know where they used to live."

CHAPTER
EIGHTEEN

"But what is the point of creating a new strain of clones?" General Kellan asks. "We've been using volunteers in special forces for six hundred years."

"My clones are more effective in battle," Huang says. "They are more expendable, less concerned about self-preservation, and far more lethal.

"This new strain was developed specifically for commando operations. They are quick, think independently, and are programmed to kill."

"That sounds an awful lot like Liberator clones," an officer calls out.

Huang laughs. "Klyber's Liberators were never in the same league," he says with a confident laugh. "Klyber's clumsy attempt at clone-making may have been enough for the Mogats . . ."

"Is that so?" asks General Smith. "I understand that you lost a squad of ten clones in an operation in Scutum-Crux."

Klyber sits this battle out, preferring to let his allies ask questions and pose charges. He watches quietly from his seat, smiling as he follows the direction of the conversation.

"They were killed running drills on a planet called

Ravenwood," Huang admits. "Over a four-year period, we ran hundreds of drills and only lost one squad."

"And how many Marines did you kill off?" the Marine general asks, sounding angry.

"I'd guess in the neighborhood of five to six hundred. Ravenwood was a major success. We sent squads of ten clones against platoons of forty-two Marines, and we only lost once. Most drills ended without the loss of a single commando.

"We also ran tests in a tough-man competition in Hawaii."

"Sad Sam's Palace?" asks the Marine.

Huang nods. Hawaii is a popular vacation and retirement spot for high-ranking officers and Sad Sam's Palace attracts military types like a magnet. "I suspect many of you are familiar with the Palace's tough-man challenge. If there's a better testing ground for hand-to-hand combat, I have not found it.

"We had a clone fighting under the name Adam Boyd entered in that competition. He racked up a record of two hundred and fifty wins and one loss."

"Two hundred wins and one loss?" General Kellan observes. "How do we get our hands on the guy who beat him? That's who we should be cloning."

The last time I visited Honolulu I stayed in a vacation home with a courtyard and a well-stocked kitchen. I came with a pal from my platoon, Vince Lee. He was a corporal, I had just been promoted to sergeant. I met a beautiful blonde named Kasara on the beach and we had a fling. She had a friend named Jennifer, so Vince got to share in the fun.

That was a vacation. This time I came on business.

Freeman and I drove out of town after visiting the Palace. We found a wooded area and pulled our car off the road. Then I curled up in the backseat for five hours and he pulled guard duty. Living with combat armor, you learn how to make yourself comfortable in all sorts of situations. Lying in the fetal position, with my knees propped up against my gut, I slept very soundly until 4:00 A.M., when Freeman and I switched places.

Massive as he was, Freeman breathed heavily in his sleep. He took long hard pulls of air, then exhaled in three-second drafts. His breathing sounded like waves rolling in and out of shore.

We were up in the slopes just north of town. I held Freeman's pistol on my lap, well out of sight in case anyone passed by.

The sun rose at 0800. Sitting behind the wheel, feeling sweaty, with stubble covering my cheeks, I watched the sunrise. I watched the violet sky turn copper colored and then eventually blue. Down below us, the town filled with shadows as the streetlamps faded. Honolulu was a tourist town, but it had its share of traffic. I watched thousands of cars roll into the city in stop-and-go traffic. From my vantage point, they looked like a column of ants.

I did not notice when the current of Freeman's breathing vanished behind me. The sunrise had just finished, and I watched mynah birds nimbly hopping back and forth on the branches of a nearby tree.

"You ready to go?" Freeman asked as he lay folded on the backseat of the car. It was early in the morning and his voice rumbled more softly than ever. His words came in a thunderous whisper.

"Good morning to you," I said, knowing that the humor would be wasted on Freeman.

"Give me a moment." With this, the big man reached across the seat and opened the door by his legs. He stretched his legs out and found the ground with his feet, then he sat up just enough to grab the edges of the open doorway and pull himself out. Once in the open air, he stretched and yawned. The sunlight reflected in a dull streak across his shaved head as he unfurled his long arms and rotated his back. Next, he walked into the woods to relieve himself. When he came back, I handed him his pistol and did the same.

We stopped at a drive-in restaurant and bought a couple of greasy egg sandwiches which we ate as we drove, passing signs with mostly incomprehensible names like Waipahu and eventually Wahiawa. We passed a defunct naval base called "Pearl Harbor." The base was enormous.

We headed out of town and into the countryside where farmers grew pineapples. The pineapples grew in immaculate rows that made the landscape appear as if someone had raked an enormous comb across it. The pineapples themselves were knee-high clumps with football-shaped fruits in the center, like some sort of alien cactus.

We drove deep into the farming country where sugarcane fields stretched out along the sides of the road. We passed large stretches where only scrub trees grew. Antique railroad tracks ran along the side of the road at one point, and we crossed a steel-framed bridge that spanned a stream. I thought the countryside was beautiful. Freeman seemed not to notice it at all.

We passed Wheeler Air Force base. It was dark and abandoned. We did not stop. A few miles farther, we approached another military complex called Schofield Barracks, a defunct Army base.

Schofield Barracks looked a lot like Wheeler and the defunct Naval base at Pearl Harbor, just an empty campus with sturdy two- and three-story buildings. From the road it looked a good deal larger than Wheeler but not even half the size of the Pearl Harbor facility. There were no immediate signs of life, but there was one difference at Schofield Barracks—the main gate was wide open. A length of chain link fence blocked the main gate of Wheeler and some of the gates around Pearl Harbor were bricked shut.

"You think they're expecting us?" I asked.

"Looks that way," Freeman said.

We originally planned to drive by the base a few times before going in. I did not know about Freeman, but I felt a strong desire to avoid stumbling into a hive filled with Adam Boyd clones.

Seeing the gates left open did not deter Ray Freeman. He was not the type of man who looked for trouble, but he did not back down from it. He turned into the entryway.

Finding our way across the base was easy enough. Most of the roads were overgrown with weeds, but one artery was trimmed and neat. The sidewalks in this part of the base gleamed in the sunlight and the asphalt on the streets was not cracked. We passed a courtyard in which the weeds had only started to grow wild. The grass was knee-high and the trees wanted trimming. We found a parking lot in which the stalls were clearly painted, and Freeman parked.

"We're supposed to go there," Freeman said, pointing straight ahead. The building was three stories tall. Its architecture was a cross between twentieth century American military and sixteenth century Spanish, combining rounded arches and thick stucco walls. The sun was behind this building and its verandas were buried in shadow. Had there been lights on in the building, we would have seen them. The lights were off but the front doors of the building hung wide open.

"An open invitation," I said, embarrassed by my own flat humor. Strangely enough, Freeman cracked a small smile at that lame joke. Freeman was a bright and dangerous man with absolutely no sense of humor. Perhaps jokes had to be obvious for him to appreciate them.

I had no gun, but Freeman had his pistol. He carried it in the open now, holding it in his right arm which hung almost limp at his side. He seemed so relaxed.

We walked straight toward the building and right in the door. Leaving the sunshine and entering this shadowy realm was like falling into a deep cave. Even after Freeman found a light switch and turned on the lights, the darkness in this building seemed almost palpable.

Most of the furniture had been removed from this hallway. There were no chairs. A large reception desk wrapped around one doorway. Bulletin boards lined one of the walls. One of these bulletin boards was covered with rows of eight by ten photographs, and the light from the windows reflected on their glossy finish. Beside the bulletin board sat a communications console.

We approached. Five rows of five photographs—twenty-five pictures in all—stretched across the bulletin board. Each of them was a picture of me. There were pictures of me entering Klyber's C-64 transport right after the evacuation team brought it back into the hangar at the Dry Docks. There was a picture of me climbing out of my Starliner in Honolulu. There was one picture of me in the International Marketplace and two of me and Freeman outside of Sad Sam's Palace—one of us entering and one of us leaving.

The last row of pictures had been taken this very morning. One showed me pissing outside the car. Another showed me taking a big bite out of my breakfast sandwich. The most recent photograph showed me opening the gate to the barracks. The picture was no more than five minutes old. Whoever placed these pictures had time to print this last photo and escape unnoticed between the time that I opened the gate and the moment we walked in the door. I had been under surveillance and never even knew it.

"I think they are sending you a message," Freeman said.

The message was obvious. The photographer could just as easily have used a rifle with a sniper scope as a camera with a telephoto lens. I reached over and switched on the communications console. Che Huang's face appeared on the screen.

"Are you always this slow, Lieutenant?" he asked.

"Hello, Huang," I said. I was supposed to salute him at this point. Instead, I folded my arms and stared into the screen. "What do you want?"

I tried to sound calm, but my heart was pounding so hard I could hear it pulsing. Liberators were known for their primal instincts. Though I was still in control, I could feel the rage building inside me.

"I did not kill Klyber," Huang said in a matter-of-fact tone.

"Not by yourself," I said. "You had one of your SEAL clones do it for you. I have the video feed from the Dry Docks security. You had a clone on the maintenance team that cleaned Klyber's transport."

"I did send a SEAL to visit Klyber's transport," Huang admitted. "He installed listening and video devices throughout the ship."

"I didn't hear anything about bugs on the transport, " I said.

"Golan security didn't look for surveillance equipment. Why don't you have your friends back at the Dry Docks sweep the main cabin and the late admiral's room for bugs?"

I did not respond.

"Think about it Harris, why would I kill Klyber?" Huang asked.

"Let's see . . . petty jealousy, old rivalries, just for the fun of it, to take control of the *Doctrinaire* . . ."

"I already had control of the *Doctrinaire*," Huang said. "I took it away from Klyber during the summit."

"I saw the summit. You didn't have anything," I said.

"You have been busy," Huang said. "Perhaps you weren't watching the feed closely. By the time the summit ended, I had command of the *Doctrinaire* and Klyber had nothing but the fleet."

"Commanding the fleet isn't being in control?" I asked.

"Once the battle begins, the ship's captain makes the decisions. When historians discuss great battles, they won't bother mentioning the fleet. Klyber knew it. I suppose you saw the old fool sulking once I got my suggestion past Smith and the rest of them. He did not say a word for the rest of the meeting. He just sat there, stewing. I got everything I wanted.

"History will remember me as the secretary of Navy who won the war. I'll place Robert Thurston over the ship. He'll be the commander who won the key battle. And Klyber . . . Klyber would have been a footnote. He would have been the man who brought up the rear.

"Harris, if you don't believe anything else I tell you, believe this—I got what I wanted."

Huang generally seemed on the verge of a tirade. Not this time. Now he explained himself with gloating patience. I thought about what he said. When the meeting ended, I met Klyber at the door. He looked tired and old and withdrawn. He talked about the members of the Joint Chiefs being too young to understand war, and he said that the fight would not be as easy as they thought.

"Why come to me?" I asked.

"I want your help," Huang said.

"Help you?" I laughed. "Why should I help you?" Across the hall, Ray Freeman stood as still as a statue, watching Huang. His face showed no emotion. His eyes never left the screen.

"We both want the same thing, Harris. We want to kill the people who killed Klyber. Now that I have the Doctrinaire, I won't be safe until they are dead.

"You can clear my name while you're at it. You are not the only one who thinks I sabotaged Klyber's transport. Once Smith and the other Joint Chiefs see the video feed with that SEAL entering the ship. . . ." He shook his head.

"I saw your SEAL in the feed. I saw your spy, too," I said.

"My spy?" Huang asked, sounding frustrated. The ragged edges of his personality began to show.

"What about Halverson? He was in the landing bay, too."

"Halverson?" Huang repeated.

I did not like or trust Huang, but I had never known him to lie. He was a storm-the-front-gates type of enemy. He did not smile at people he disliked. If he wanted you dead, he let you know it. Except for his political maneuvering on the floor of the summit, I had never seen anything resembling subtlety from the man.

"Wasn't Rear Admiral Halverson working for you?" I asked.

"Halverson?" Huang asked. "I wouldn't work with an idiot like Tom Halverson. He was Klyber's man."

"He was your spy on the *Doctrinaire*," I said.

"Johansson was my spy," Huang said. "I should have thought that was obvious. He sat with my staff during the summit. He flew back to D.C. with me. Leonid Johansson was my eyes on the project."

"So what was Halverson doing by the hangar?" I asked.

"I've seen the security feed," Huang said. "Halverson isn't on it."

"Perhaps you weren't watching the feed closely," I said, using Huang's words against him to get under his skin. "When the janitors left the hangar, they passed Admiral Halverson. He was there having a smoke. He watched your boy come in, then followed him away from the hangar."

"Halverson? He may have been there, but he wasn't working for me," Huang said. "It sounds to me as if you've got your first clue, Sherlock. What you need now is to follow up on it."

CHAPTER NINETEEN

This is the moment when Che Huang demonstrates his prowess in the dark arts of politics. It should be obvious that he is a political creature—an officer with no actual combat experience who has risen to the Joint Chiefs. Now that he has weathered the counter-attack about his clones, Huang draws back his fangs and sinks them into Admiral Klyber.

"Admiral Klyber, powerful as this super ship of yours is, do you really think it can handle more than five hundred enemy ships?" Huang asks this question in an uncharacteristically reasonable tone.

"No, of course not," says Klyber. "We'll need support ships, and the optimum situation is to engage no more than ten or twenty dreadnoughts per battle."

"I really must congratulate you. You have created a fine weapon. I honestly believe that this ship will be the weapon that wins the war."

Klyber only nods to acknowledge this compliment. His eyes remain coldly fixed on Huang. He does not trust the man.

"How would a fleet be able to support this ship? You haven't talked the Linear Committee into funding a self-broadcasting fleet, have you?"

Appreciative laughter rings through the room.

"*I have assembled a ready-alert fleet that will remain near the Broadcast Network. It's a small fleet now, but we'll find more ships for it. The fleet will have flash access to the broadcast computer on board the* Doctrinaire. *Anytime she self-broadcasts, her travel information will be relayed to the ships in the fleet.*"

"*But will they be able to get to her in time to assist?*" *General Smith asks.*

"*The ready-alert ships can override the Network. They can enter the discs and override the system to broadcast them directly to the* Doctrinaire."

At this point, I notice that both of the seats behind Klyber are empty. Admiral Halverson has gone somewhere. I check summit clock and note the time. It is three in the afternoon according to Washington, D.C., time, which is the clock used by the Dry Docks for the duration of the summit. Suddenly it occurs to me where Halverson has gone, and I feel a chill. He is at the hangar observing Huang's clone as he plants the cable on Klyber's transport.

"*Brilliant,*" *Huang cheerily admits.* "*Absolutely brilliant. Of course, you'll need a skilled administrator to handle the logistics.*" *Perhaps he means Leonid Johansson, but that does not seem likely. Johansson is barely paying attention to the proceedings at this point. He is leaning in his chair causally looking toward the back of the room. He is, in fact, looking at baby-faced Robert Thurston—the man who replaced Klyber as commander of the Scutum-Crux Fleet. Thurston's brilliant battle tactics are legendary.*

"*Strategy and logistics,*" *Huang continues.* "*They seem to be the keys. A great battle strategist at the helm of the* Doctrinaire *and the right logistical support to make sure that the ship does not fail.*"

"*What is your point?*" *General Smith asks.*

"*It seems to me that the fleet admiral's skills are wasted commanding a lone ship, even a great ship such as the* Doctrinaire," *Huang begins. I recognize that he is trying to take command of the* Doctrinaire *away from Klyber and I feel as if I have been slapped across the face. I cannot even imagine the thoughts going through Klyber's head.* "*You are the highest ranking officer in the Unified Authority Navy. Your command should not be limited to one lone boat. You should be in command of a fleet."*

"I will not relinquish control of the Doctrinaire."

"Of course not," Huang says. "This is your project. The Doctrinaire *is your ship. I am simply suggesting that you should command the entire fleet as well as the ship itself. If the* Doctrinaire *is part of a fleet, you should have the highest authority in that fleet."*

"Avoid all tangles in the chain of command," General Kellan, the 39-year-old secretary of the Army, adds. "I can't speak for you Annapolis graduates, but that was one of the first things we learned at West Point."

"Of course you would use the Doctrinaire *as your command ship," Huang adds as slick as any salesman trying to close a deal. "She is your ship. The* Doctrinaire *will always be your ship."*

Like all of the senior officers in that room, I see nothing wrong with Huang's suggestion, except that I do not trust the man who has made it. Klyber, on the other hand, looks beaten. He is the only officer at the table without an entourage, and he now looks small and lonely sitting at the table by himself. He looks to General Smith for support, but Smith does not seem to have a problem with Huang's suggestion. In fact, one minute later, Smith agrees with it.

The remainder of the meeting is unspectacular. Neither Che Huang nor Bryce Klyber speak again. And when the meeting adjourns, Klyber is the first officer to reach the door of the conference room. He meets me at the door looking old and depressed.

CHAPTER TWENTY

The carrot that Bryce Klyber dangled in front of me, Che Huang delivered: an honorable discharge. With just a word from Huang, I was Lieutenant Wayson Harris, Unified Authority Marines retired. My permanent record did not even contain the word, "Liberator," not that I doubted Huang's intention to add it back the moment I caught up to Halverson.

"What are you going to do next?" Freeman asked me as we left Schofield Barracks.

"I need to pick up Halverson's trail," I said. "Whoever put the cables on Bryce Klyber's ship was working with Halverson. That means Halverson was spying for the Separatists or the Confederate Arms."

"It looks that way," Freeman agreed.

"Last place I saw him was in the Golan Dry Docks. I figure that's the place to start."

Freeman dropped me off at Honolulu Airport, then went to return his rental car. I did not trust Huang. I would never trust him, but I thought this might be a good time to see if he had kept his word. Instead of going out to the field with the private planes, I passed through the tighter security at the commercial terminal where they had DNA-scanning posts for outgoing passengers.

The last time I had passed through one of these stations was just two days earlier, and I had been spotted as Wayson Harris the Liberator. This time I had no idea how the computer would label me. I might be an AWOL Marine or a Liberator or a dead Marine. As I approached the posts, I heard the quick blast of air as it wafted across the man ahead of me. I looked at the armed guards inside the station and wondered if testing my identity so soon was a mistake.

The guard on the other side of the posts, a civilian in an outfit designed to look like an old fashion police uniform, motioned me forward. As I stepped forward, I considered everything that would happen in the next three seconds. One of the jams would hit me with a burst of air. The other jam would inhale the air and any debris it shook loose. A bank of computers would scan my DNA. If the computer warned the guards that I was a Liberator in the Orion Arm . . . as I thought about it, being recognized here would be more dangerous than being recognized in the Golan Dry Docks. Here, in the Orion Arm, where Liberators were illegal, being spotted might be fatal. I was betting my life that Admiral Che Huang was a man of his word. What was wrong with me?

The guard, a grubby man whose shirt barely fit over his jostling beer belly, hardly noticed me as I stepped between the posts. He had a pistol. There was no bulletproof glass around this security station, but I noticed a dozen armed guards around the area.

A warm and humid breeze blew through the open-air lobby of the terminal. Most people stepped right through the posts, but I stood my ground waiting to see what would happen.

The security guard looked at me curiously. "You okay?" he asked.

I looked around the station, other people were watching me curiously as well. No one reached for their guns. "Yes," I said. "I'm more than okay. I'm street-legal."

The man gave me a suspicious look, but what could he do? His high-tech security equipment had searched both me and my identity.

I walked across the terminal and followed signs to the private pilots/corporate jets terminal. Nobody stopped me when I asked for my plane, and I left Hawaii without incident. I was for all intents and purposes, a free man.

This time I would use the Broadcast Network. I saw no point in advertising that I still had my hands on a self-broadcasting transport. If Huang knew I had a self-broadcasting ship from the *Doctrinaire*, he would demand its return and possibly keep the ship for himself. After all, the good will that now existed between us only went so far.

I put in a call to Colonel McAvoy, the head of security at the Golan Dry Docks as I started the long trip to Mars. I asked him if he had searched Klyber's C-64 for listening devices. He said, "No," but said that he would and that he would get back to me shortly. The Unified Authority's only fleet admiral had died on his watch. McAvoy's career would be as good as over unless he caught the murderer. Ten minutes after we hung up, Colonel McAvoy called back to say that he had located a wide array of spying devices.

"That clears Adam Boyd," I said.

"Spying devices clear the guy?" McAvoy asked.

"I talked with Huang," I said. "Boyd was Huang's man, and Huang admits having Boyd plant the devices. Why bother planting mikes and cameras on the ship if you plan to kill the passengers?"

"Spying as an alibi for murder," the colonel observed. "That's a new one."

"I need whatever information you can get me on the rest of the maintenance team," I said. "And get me anything you can on Admiral Halverson. I need to know where he went when he left the Dry Docks, and I need to know if he went alone."

One of the niceties of crossing such highly trafficked airspace as the lanes between Earth and Mars was that you did not need to pilot your own ship. With thousands of ships traveling at millions of miles per hour in a relatively small pocket, collisions would be inevitable without computers seizing control of every spacecraft. Pilots who refused to relinquish control were given mere moments to turn around before squadrons were scrambled from Mars Station to shoot them down.

Now that I was a legitimate citizen, I chose the conservative route. I logged my travel plans into the Mars traffic control computer and allowed it to schedule my route through the Broadcast Network. From here on out, I would not need to touch a flight stick or turn a knob until the Network spilled me out a few minutes from the Dry Docks.

I leaned back in my chair and stared out the window at the endless blackness of outer space. Stars winked in the distance. Out here I could see the colors of the planets. Jupiter, a dust-colored marble with horizontal stripes, loomed off to the right. Mars, not really red but tan with a rust-colored patina, floated in the darkness dead ahead.

I looked back at the dimly lit cabin behind me. The passenger seating was no more comfortable than my pilot's chair, but I liked the idea of leaving the cockpit. Taking my mediaLink shades, I slipped into the first chair behind the cockpit and reclined it as far back as it would go.

The top story of the day was Bryce Klyber's funeral. Several sites, both civilian and military, showed the service in its entirety. The faces of the guests taking up the front two rows of Arlington Chapel were remarkably similar to to those sitting around the table at the summit. Smith and the other Joint Chiefs were there along with their aides. In enlisted man lingo, "There were so many stars and bars in that funeral you would have sworn you were touring a flag factory."

Huang was there. I expected him to have a secret grin or at least the smug sneer with which he customarily greeted the world, but he did not. Huang stared straight ahead at the glossy black casket that lay on the stand. He did not look arrogant or satisfied. If anything, he looked worried.

"Hello, Judas," I said when I saw Captain Leonid Johansson was there as well. Captain was a much higher rank in the Navy than it was in the Marines. But even as a Navy captain, Johansson looked like a piker in this setting. The chapel was filled with admirals, generals, and famous politicians. The Joint Chiefs and members of the Linear Committee sat on the front pew. I looked for people who might be Klyber's family and saw no one. After the service, as I filtered through ancillary stories, I learned that Klyber had never married. He'd outlived his siblings. Except for the Navy, he was alone.

In the grand tradition of Washington D.C. funerals, this

service droned on and on. I wondered if I would reach Mars before it ended. First there was some dreary organ music. Then a Protestant minister stood up to speak. The man gave a thirty-minute sermon over the dead body of a devout atheist. I imagined Klyber's ghost rising from the coffin to say, "Listen to this rubbish, not over my dead body."

After the sermon came the eulogies. I thought military men kept their speeches short, but General Alexander Smith of the U.A.A.F. went on for forty-five frigging minutes. Next came two of Klyber's pals in politics. I expected them to drone on and they did not disappoint.

A small red emergency beacon flickered on and off at the bottom of my vision. By flicking my eyes at the flashing symbol, I brought up the call.

"Harris, are you seeing this?" Freeman asked.

"Seeing what?" I asked, though I really wanted to say, "Ray, nice to hear from you. Yes, the flight has been good so far. And how are you?"

"Gateway Outpost is under attack," said Freeman.

I knew Gateway. It was a habitable planet in the area where the Orion and Sagittarius arms met. The space around Gateway was a high-security zone even though Sagittarius and Orion were the only arms that remained fully loyal to Earth.

Both the Central Sagittarius Fleet and the Inner Orion Fleet patrolled that area. As I considered this, I realized it could take days or weeks before ships would arrive to help Gateway. The Inner Orion Fleet patrolled a channel that was 10,000 light years deep. The Central Sagittarius Fleet covered an area that was more than 30,000 light years. Getting to a planet like Gateway would only take a couple of minutes if either fleet happened to be near the Broadcast Network. It could take weeks if they were in deep space.

Without saying a word, I switched to the Galactic News Service. The GNS was an organ of the Unified Authority internal structure and a propaganda machine, but it offered the most up-to-the-moment information. GNS reporters traveled everywhere, including planets that had declared independence from the Republic.

The picture before my eyes was one of grand destruction.
The legend on the screen said, "New Gibraltar" in light blue
letters that seemed to glow over the pitch-black sky. New
Gibraltar was the capital city of Gateway. Gateway Outpost,
the local Marine base, was on the outskirts of the city.

In the center of the picture, a dying Marine base crumbled before my eyes. Its three green particle beam cannons
fired into the air lighting up the midnight sky. On a major
base like this Gateway Outpost, there should have been a
hundred cannons. No buildings remained on the streets
around the fort. Flames danced on the shattered remains of
what might have been hotels and business centers. The fort
itself, a five- or six-story affair, was shrouded in darkness.
Sections of the outer wall had fallen.

A red beam, as wide around as a highway tunnel, flashed
down from the sky. It seared one corner of the fort. Cement
exploded into smoke and flames and another cannon went
dead as more of the wall tumbled to the ground.

"When did this happen?" I asked.

As if hearing my question, a tickertape image along the
bottom of the screen appeared. "Live Feed."

"The attack started a couple minutes ago," said Freeman.

There was movement on the street near the base of the
fort. Twenty men, maybe as many as thirty, skirted around
the remains of blasted buildings and wrecked vehicles. They
were on foot, running quickly, and hiding behind cover.
"The scouts have arrived," I said.

"It has to be a demolition team," Freeman said. "There
aren't enough of them for anything else."

"Who are they?" I asked.

"The Pentagon won't speculate until after the battle,"
Freeman said. "I'm guessing they're Mogats. Amos Crowley
is probably someplace nearby coordinating the attack."

Freeman and Crowley had history, and Freeman wanted
to settle that score. He wished he was in New Gibraltar, I
could hear it in his voice. Freeman may have considered
himself a mercenary, but he mostly collected bounties.
Crowley was the prize he wanted most.

The majority of the Marines in the base must have been
dead or wounded. However many were left, they did not put

up much of a fight as the commandos closed in. Somebody managed to mount a machine-gun nest on the wall and a perforated line of tracer fire rained down into the street. A commando fired a shoulder-mounted rocket at the nest. The rocket streaked through the air leaving a trail of glare and smoke. Dust clouds exploded out of the wall where the machine gun had been. The tracer fire stopped.

The commandoes divided into teams that now stormed ruins of the fort. They sprinted the last yards to the base, dodging around holes and debris and overturned cars in the near darkness of the night.

I viewed all of this knowing that I was connected to these events and yet somehow I felt detached. What did I care if the Republic fell? The only people I ever considered friends were in the Unified Authority military—Bryce Klyber and Vince Lee, my old buddy from the Marines. Klyber was dead, of course, and I had not heard from Vince in years. Last I heard, he was an officer in the Scutum-Crux Fleet.

Using an optical command, I brought up an "On the Spot" audio analysis.

> *"Enemy ships continue to batter the city of New Gibraltar from outside Gateway's atmosphere while enemy troops now storm the Marine facility. Reports suggest that there may be as many as ten battleships attacking the city.*
>
> *"In recent months, Gateway has functioned as the central base of operations for several raids into the Perseus Arm. This attack may be retaliation for . . .*
>
> *"We have a report that several ships from the Sagittarius Fleet have broadcasted into the Gateway System and should arrive shortly."*

On the screen, the commandoes turned to retreat. They backed away from the fort and headed toward a single transport under the cover of a bullet and rockets barrage. The last of the commandos boarded and the shooting stopped. In the distance, the firefly glow of armored transport rockets vanished into space.

"The Moga . . .

"Watch the fort," Freeman interrupted me.

The Mogats had placed High Yield radiation bombs around the walls of fort. These bombs burst, flooding the streets with a dazzling blue-white display that seemed to burn into my eyes. The effect of having my shades go stark white then black was like being blinded. For a moment I sat in that plush cabin thinking my shades had died, then I realized that the site I had been watching was no longer in operation.

CHAPTER
TWENTY-ONE

Normally a wing of three Air Force F-19 Falcons guarded the Mars broadcast discs. As my Starliner approached on this visit, however, I saw two squads of five fighters circling the area.

"Starliner A-ten-twenty-thirty-four, be advised that Mars Station is on high alert. Do you copy?"

"Aye," I said. "I copy."

"Due to heightened security, disc traffic is slow. We are requesting that pilots return home unless they have urgent business. Please await instructions while I access your travel file."

Considering the attack on Gateway and the importance of the Mars broadcast discs, I thought that ten F-19s was pretty skimpy protection. The Army base on Mars had some pretty hefty cannons, but after seeing the destruction of Gateway Outpost, ground cannons no longer seemed like an effective deterrent. I joined the queue of ships waiting to approach the broadcast discs. The line was at least twenty miles long. Hovering above the line, like a trio of vultures, were three fighter carriers.

Mars did not have a fleet of its own. These ships had to be on loan from the Earth fleet. Since capital ships travel a maximum speed of thirty million miles per hour, the trip from Earth to Mars would be anywhere from three to five hours depending on where each planet was in its orbit. Even a five-hour trip seemed short compared to the twenty hours it had just taken me in my Starliner.

"My records show that you are traveling to the Golan Dry Docks. Is this correct, Starliner A-ten-twenty-thirty-four?" the traffic controller asked. "The Golan facility is a maximum security facility. What is the purpose of your travel?"

"I am working for the Joint Chiefs," I said.

There was a short pause. "Starliner A-ten-twenty-thirty-four, you have been cleared for immediate broadcast. We have dispatched an escort to take you to the front of the line, sir. Please follow your escort."

In times of emergency, the military ran the Broadcast Network. The man on the other end must have been Air Force.

As I approached the broadcast discs, the tint shields came on and I could no longer see out the windows of my ship. The tint shields had to be thick to protect my eyes from the blinding glare that poured out of the discs when they discharged their electrical currents. Sitting in my pilot's chair, I watched the slow approach of the two Falcons on my radar. In another moment, the radar would go blind and I would see the glare of lightning so bright that it penetrated the tinting across the Starliner.

In the last moments before my radar went out, three fighters glided alongside my ship. My Starliner must have looked like such a relic compared to those ships. The F-19, designed for space and atmospheric combat, was probably the sleekest fighter in the U.A. arsenal. It had an elongated fuselage that looked like a cross between a stiletto and a dart. Its wings were razor thin but strong enough to handle atmospheric maneuvers. These jets would outpace any fighter in space and fly circles around any attacker that tried to touch down in an atmosphere like Earth's. The F-19 was the pride of the Air Force.

"Hello, Starliner A-ten-twenty-thirty-four," one of the fighter pilots said. "Why don't you follow us, sir?"

This, of course, was fighter pilot humor. The Mars flight

computers had complete control over my cockpit. I could not even shut down the power to my engines without asking permission.

A squadron of Tomcats circled the Golan Dry Docks and the nearby disc station. Two battleships were moored nearby. Golan was indeed on high alert. After identifying me and scanning my plane, traffic control brought me in through a partially sealed aperture and armed guards walked me to the security station.

The last time I passed through the posts at this security station, I was identified as Lieutenant Wayson Harris, "Marine on the lam." This time I was a retired Marine and I was coming to visit the head of Golan security, Colonel Clarence McAvoy.

I handed my papers to the guard and walked toward the post. The Dry Docks' high alert had brought out the brass. An Army major sat with civilians and enlisted men on the other side of the bulletproof glass. The light on the inside of the booth was bright. After the gloom of the hangar, it made me squint. This, I suspect, was intentional: it's hard to shoot accurately when your eyes have not adjusted.

"Step forward," said the guard on the other side of the posts. For all I knew, this was the guy who pulled the gun on me the last time I passed through. He was Army. He wore combat greens, and his M27 was strapped to his belt like a side arm.

I stepped forward.

The corporal snapped to attention. "Welcome to the Dry Docks, Colonel," he said in a loud enough voice for the people behind the glass to hear. I looked over and saw that even the major now saluted me. I returned the salute and moved on.

"Colonel McAvoy is expecting you, sir. He left word that he wanted to drive you to your meeting personally."

"Very well," I said, still trying to figure out how I could have suddenly become a colonel.

McAvoy pulled up in his little base cart—an electrical scooter with a top speed of fifteen miles per hour. "Colonel Harris?" he asked in a voice drenched with mirth. "You've gone through the ranks more quickly than any soldier I have known. Weren't you a Lieutenant last time I saw you?"

"I retired after that," I said.

We shook hands. "Well, come on Colonel," McAvoy said. "I thought I should roll out the red carpet for you, just in case."

"In case of what?" I asked as I climbed into the cart.

"In case you're on the Joint Chiefs next time I see you." He started the cart and rolled into the service hall. "Your pal, Huang, called for you. He told me to have you call him the moment you landed.

"You heard about Gateway, right?"

I nodded.

"Bastards," McAvoy said.

CHAPTER
TWENTY-TWO

"Colonel?" I asked.

"Welcome back, Harris. You've been recalled to active service, and as a colonel. I never thought I would see a clone make colonel, but desperate times call for desperate measures." Huang looked more tired than he had at the funeral. Dark bags had formed under his dark brown eyes. No trace of that cocky smile showed on his face.

"And the reason for this?"

"Clearance, Harris. Only officers with the rank of colonel or higher are cleared to view the information I'm going to show you. Don't worry about the commission, I don't want to leave you in the Corps any longer than I need to."

Still an anti-synthetic prick, I thought to myself, but I was glad the change was not permanent.

"I don't suppose you can guess how long the siege on Gateway Outpost lasted?" Huang asked.

I took a moment to think about this. "I watched the feed," I said. "It was fast."

"Real fast," Huang agreed. "No guesses?"

"No," I said.

"Eight minutes," he said, a disapproving expression on his face. "Almost to the second."

"I must be missing something," I said as I tried to figure out why he mentioned this.

"Shit, Harris! You're supposed to be bright." Huang no longer looked tired or disappointed. Now he looked disgusted. His eyes closed to slits. He put a hand to his temple, brushing aside the short brown hair.

I thought quickly. What was so important about eight minutes? It showed a certain level of efficiency. Whoever planned the attack had done a superb job combing out the logistics.

"Eight minutes, Harris. Eight, specking minutes. Eight minutes, the amount of time it takes GCF ships to power-up and self-broadcast. You couldn't figure that out on your own? Judas in heaven, what did Klyber see in you?"

I wanted to tell Huang to speck himself, but I agreed with him. I should have seen it. I said nothing.

"I'm sure you've seen the video feed of the ground attack," Huang said. "You haven't seen this."

Satellite video showing the surface of Gateway appeared in my mediaLink shades. The full name of the planet was Gateway Kri—the term *kri* designating that the planet had a terraformed atmosphere. In truth, the planet looked a lot like Earth with icy poles, large oceans, and green continents.

The screen flashed as lightning danced across the scene. I saw the four battleships from the Galactic Central Fleet only as silhouettes against the glowing surface of the planet. Their hulls looked black as coal. They were shadows. Had the satellite not been orbiting above them, they would have been invisible against the backdrop of space. From this perspective, the ships looked like giant sharks circling their territory.

The ships had a deformed diamond shape. They were long, not wide, with blunted corners at their bow and stern. They dove down to the edge of the atmosphere and green dots flashed on the surface as the Marines down below fired cannons at them.

"Concentrated firepower, the mark of a well-trained commander," Huang said. "All of their laser fire hit within a five-block radius. Whoever led this assault knew his tactics."

In the bottom corner of the screen, a small window showed the Gateway outpost. Laser blasts rained down on the fort and the streets surrounding it. As the attack began, the cannons along the walls of the fort flashed like strobe lights. That cannon fire slowed as hit after hit tore into the walls of the fort.

"Now this is interesting," Huang said. "The GCF ships appeared one minute ago to the second. In that minute, the Marine base has focused all of its weapons on the capital ships . . . standard procedure."

The screen froze. What I saw was one flame. It looked no more significant than a firefly as it penetrated the atmosphere.

"That is the transport. It will take that transport precisely one minute to land."

The little flame seemed to shrink to nothing as the transport raced down to the planet. In the small window on my screen, New Gibraltar wilted quickly. The invading ground force stormed the fort, then ran off. At six minutes, to the second, the bombs went off creating a bubble of white light that seemed to grow like a blister out of the side of the planet. The flash was clearly visible from space.

At seven minutes the transport rejoined the battleships. One minute later, the entire invasion force was gone.

"They call themselves the Hinode Fleet," Huang said.

"Hinode?" I asked. I had heard the name Hinode before, on Ezer Kri, the planet with the large population of Japanese descent. That was what the locals called their capital city. The real name of the city was Rising Sun, or *Hinode* in Japanese.

"The Japanese population on Ezer Kri called their capital city Hinode. Do you think there is a connection?" I asked.

"I don't want to guess," Huang said. "That's your job."

"My job?" I asked.

"Yes, Colonel, your job. It came with the commission."

"What about finding the guy . . . ?"

"The Republic is under attack. We knew about the Mogat instigators and the Confederate Arms. We knew about the GC Fleet. You get to figure out why GCF ships are using a Japanese name."

"Doing a little scouting before you take them on in the *Doctrinaire*?" I asked.

"Yes," Huang said as if answering a challenge. He took a moment to gather his thoughts before speaking in a calmer voice. "You get me movements and capabilities on that fleet. You get me a profile on the officers commanding those ships. You help me win this war."

"And the guy who killed Klyber?"

"Harris, once that fleet is destroyed, you can do whatever you want to Halverson. Get me what I want, and I will make you a very rich, very retired Liberator clone."

"I'll need help."

"You want men?"

"One," I said. "I have a partner."

"Freeman," Huang said. "I've heard about him."

"He's going to need access to whatever information you give me. And he won't help me if it means he has to enlist."

"Do what you need to do. Tell who you need to tell. Spend whatever money you need. I'm giving you a blank check."

"Okay," I said. I did not like the idea of working for Huang, but we both wanted the same thing at this moment. He wanted a clean shot at the Hinode Fleet. I wanted the men who killed Klyber. Both of us wanted Halverson.

"Do you know where to start?" Huang asked. I could see him beginning to relax. The plane of his shoulders softened. "Where will you start?"

"New Columbia."

"Why New Columbia?" Huang asked.

"Because Jimmy Callahan is a two-bit know-nothing, and Billy the Butcher Patel tried to kill him," I said, only just beginning to put the pieces together.

"What are you talking about?" Huang asked.

"There's a two-bit thug on New Columbia who thought he was a big fish," I said. "He sold supplies to the Mogats or the Confederates and thought he was a player. He tried to sell out Patel and nearly got himself killed. Remember the Safe Harbor bombing? Callahan was the one they were going after.

"I figured they wanted to make an example out of Callahan, but now I have another idea."

"What does this have to do with Klyber?" Huang asked impatiently.

"I never stopped to figure out how they knew about Callahan. . . . Klyber was the one who sent me to meet with him. If Klyber knew about it, Halverson must have known as well. Halverson must have known something else, too, like where Callahan was getting his supplies."

"Did Patel get him?" Huang asked.

"I locked him up in the local Marine base brig for safe-keeping," I said.

"You think he knows something?" Huang asked.

"He's too small-time and too stupid to have set up a deal with the Confederates himself. Somebody with bigger ambitions must have used him as a middleman. I need to sweat the name out of him."

"You'd better get there quickly," Huang said. "Intelligence says the Confederates are going after New Columbia next. We're already evacuating the planet."

Huang thought for a moment. "I told you you've got a blank check on this. You can spend whatever you need. I'll send you whatever equipment you need. And one more thing. I don't think I need to tell you this, Harris—but just in case . . . feel free to kill anyone that gets in your way."

And they say that clones have no souls, I thought to myself. I wondered if they would have allowed Huang on a Catholic colony like Saint Germaine.

Part III

WAR

TWENTY-THREE

Earthdate: March 23, 2512 A.D.
City: Safe Harbor; Planet: New Columbia; Galactic
Position: Orion Arm

A fighter carrier and two destroyers floated just a few
miles away, guarding the broadcast discs that orbited New
Columbia. The carrier brought a compliment of Tomcats,
Hornets, and Harriers. The fighters flew in groups of three as
they buzzed back and forth, "inspecting and protecting" the
solid lane of traffic that stretched from the edge of the atmosphere to the discs. The authorities stepped up security in
some areas of New Columbia and evacuated others. After
considering the attack on New Gibraltar, the Pentagon decided to evacuate Safe Harbor.

"You're flying into Safe Harbor?" Colonel McAvoy had
asked when I told him my plans. "They're evacuating the
planet. The only people there are going to be Marines and
looters. Come to think of it"—he brightened as he thought
about this—"you'll fit right in."

As I glided out of the reception disc, I saw the line of
ships leaving New Columbia. This was a mishmash that included military transports.

From what I had read, New Columbia had a population of over fifty million civilians. Looking down this seemingly endless line of evacuation ships, I would have believed that an entire population was on its way out. Big ships, small ships, just floating there waiting for a turn to enter the Network. As I flew toward the atmosphere, I took one final look at the line of ships. It looked like a kite string holding the discs in place. At the top of the line, the electrical field created by the broadcast discs flashed bright white against the eternal blackness. That distant flash burned ghosts into my eyes, but the ghosts faded quickly.

I traveled toward the planet at the intolerably slow pace of three thousand miles per hour, aware that below me were Marine, Army, and Air Force cannons that tracked my every move. Any suspicious deviation from my specified flight course would be fatal.

By the time I reached New Columbian space, my ship had been scanned so many times that the security computers even knew which of my bones had pins in them. The only worry the military types had about me was that I might be an enemy scout.

"Starliner A-ten-twenty-thirty-four, this is Safe Harbor spaceport. Come in."

"This is Starliner A-ten-twenty-thirty-four," I said.

"Starliner A-ten-twenty-thirty-four, we are evacuating this planet."

"So I've been told," I said.

"I show that you are a Marine," the controller said. "Please confirm."

"Colonel Wayson Harris, Unified Authority Marines Corps," I said.

"You have chosen to use a civilian landing facility, Colonel. Are you aware that there is a Marine base with a landing field just outside of town?"

"I am aware of that," I said. I was also aware that that base would be a prime target once the Confederates arrived. I wanted my ship in one piece.

"We can offer you landing assistance. Please be advised that this spaceport will close within the next three hours. All traffic control will close at that time. Should you choose to leave your ship here, this facility cannot be held responsible for your ship."

"Got it."

"Can't talk you out of this, can I, Colonel?" the man asked.

"You got a problem down there?" I asked.

"Yeah. I can't spare the men to check in your ship. Everyone I have is busy sending up transports. I don't know if you noticed that little line of ships leaving home."

"Of course I noticed it," I said. I also noticed how absolutely vulnerable these transports would be if a couple of GCF dreadnoughts happened to appear, but I did not mention it. Shoot a few cannons straight down this line of traffic, and you would likely kill half the population of New Columbia. But judging by the pinpoint tactics the invaders used in their siege of Gateway Outpost, I did not think they were after civilian casualties.

On the other hand, a billion casualties would interest Bill "the Butcher" Patel. Patel was a radical separatist from the Cygnus Arm who was not constrained by morals or religious beliefs.

The line of transports did not extend from the edge of the atmosphere down to the spaceport. In the full gravitational pull of the atmosphere, transports would not be able to support themselves in a slow-moving line without burning tons of fuel.

I flew down through an evening sky, penetrating a thick layer of clouds as my approach slowed to a few hundred miles per hour. The weather had turned bad over Safe Harbor. Mercury-colored clouds formed a washboard ceiling over the city. Lightning illuminated pockets in the clouds with dazzling flashes. Rain fell in heavy drops that burst across my windows. Below me the city was dark. Not a light shown in the forest of skyscrapers that covered Safe Harbor. No street lights shined. The giant billboards on the sides of the buildings were invisible in the blackness.

The city may have looked lifeless, but the air above it fairly bristled with movement. I looked up through the top corner of my rain-spattered windshield and saw the darting profiles of three F-19s passing above me like shadows against the steel wool clouds. Beneath me, three more crossed my path.

The Marines, the Army, and the Air Force all maintained bases around the city of Safe Harbor. Unlike Gateway, New Columbia was a well-protected planet. The Marines of New Gibraltar Outpost had only cannons to defend themselves from attack. Here, on New Columbia, there were squadrons of F-19 Falcons, and the Navy had capital ships guarding the planet from above. The invasion of Gibraltar had been a massacre. An invasion of Safe Harbor would be a battle.

Against the jungle of shadows that was the city of Safe Harbor, the spaceport looked like an eruption of light. Two lines of strobe lanterns clicked on and off along the runway, creating dashes of midnight-blue. In the distance, white glare poured out of a row of hangars at the edge of the runway. Lights shone around the outside of the air terminal and more light spilled from the windows.

I landed the Starliner on the edge of the runway and coasted toward the hangars. Two runway workers placed it in a security hangar. I asked if it would be safe, and they said it would. "As safe as anything else on the planet," one of them amended. The hangar had been filled with private craft just one day earlier. Now my ship was the only one. The hangar crew drove me to the main terminal of the spaceport in silence.

A few weeks earlier and in another life, I had sat in this very building trying to distract myself as I waited for a flight. Back then I sensed ambition in the air. Safe Harbor attracted businessmen and tourists, people who were glad to travel or glad to clinch the next big deal. This time I sensed something very different—depression and panic.

In the terminal, long lines of people sat silently clutching their belongings. The richest people, able to buy their way to the front of the line, had left first. The last of the New Columbian elite were probably in the queue of transports I passed on my way down from the discs. The people I saw in the spaceport now were the poor and the middle class—people with families and suitcases; little girls with dolls and boys with video games. They formed lines that snaked back and forth the entire length of the lobby—rows of people in perfectly straight lines standing so crowded together that the lines disappeared altogether. I heard sneezing and sobbing and a few whispers, but this population was mostly in shock.

Many people wore damp clothing. Had the spaceport been its normal chilly temperature, these people would have caught colds, but the sheer numbers overloaded the air-conditioning, and the atmosphere was hot inside the terminal and the air smelled of sweat.

"Where do you think you're going?" a Marine in combat armor asked as I reached the main entrance. I flashed him the newly-minted identification card that Colonel McAvoy gave me. It identified me as "Colonel Wayson Harris."

The man looked at it and snapped to attention. "My apologies, sir! The private was not aware that he was speaking with an officer."

He saluted.

I saluted back.

"Carry on, Marine," I said as I stepped around the boy and left, glad that I was no longer a mere grunt. Stepping out of the terminal, I entered a cold, wet night. The rain fell continuously. Puddles covered the sidewalk leading away from the terminal building. A line of streetlights stretched as far as the parking garage. Beyond that, a shroud of inky darkness hid everything from view. Before stepping out from under the awning, I looked into the sky and sighed. I did not know who I might meet in that darkness, but it did not matter much—this time I was armed.

I stole a car. I didn't have any other options. Supposing that a city-wide evacuation and naval attack might hurt their business, the car rental agencies had closed for the night . . . and the next night, and the night after that. In honor of Billy the Butcher, I found a sporty little Paragon in the parking lot and wired it. Patel's Paragon was orange and this one was red, but they both had the same shoehorn-shaped chassis.

I did not bother myself with fables about returning the car or justifications about the owner of the car having cast it away. I needed wheels, this car looked nice. Once I had the engine going, I threaded my way though the spaceport parking lot and drove into town.

There was something eerie about traveling through an

abandoned city that reminded me of swimming underwater. It might have been the emptiness or the silence or the lack of movement. The electricity was out almost everywhere. Without their red, yellow, and green glow, the traffic lights looked like misshapen trees. I did not care for crowds, but I found this emptiness unsettling.

Driving down dark streets lined by lifeless buildings, my isolation seemed to amplify itself. I looked into storefronts that were as dark as caves. It wasn't just that the lights were off—life itself was gone. It was like climbing up an escalator that has been turned off. For psychological reasons, climbing dead escalators seems harder than walking up stairs. It feels like civilization has failed.

I drove past the movie house where I had met Jimmy Callahan and watched *The Battle for Little Man*. The entrance was a black hole. The holotoriums would be empty and the projection rooms dark. It seemed unnatural.

Jimmy Callahan, I mused, with his bulging muscles and his big, big talk, would be one of the last men on New Columbia. The Mogats and the Secessionists may have chased everybody else away, but Callahan was still on the planet, right where I left him, locked up in a Marine base brig. The irony was that the very spot where I placed him for safekeeping would soon be the most dangerous location on the planet.

I was driving through uptown Safe Harbor and turned a corner. The block in front of me was completely demolished. For a moment I thought the attack must have begun, and then I recognized where I was. This was the neighborhood that Patel bombed. Only three weeks had passed since that bombing . . . two weeks and an era.

Something far more dangerous than Billy the Butcher Patel was coming to New Columbia. Who would have believed it? Jimmy Callahan who had talked so big and gotten himself into so much trouble might just be the key to winning the war.

I expected to see looters hiding in shadows, moving through alleys, and breaking into buildings. Instead, I ran into roadblocks. The Army was out in force. I turned a corner and saw a chrome and titanium barrier stretched across the road. A string of bright blue lights winked on and off sequentially across the top of their barricade. Five soaked and miserable-looking soldiers in camouflaged ponchos flagged me down. They had M27s strapped over their shoulders, and there were machine-gun nests on either side of their barricade.

I stopped and lowered my window.

"Nice car," a soldier said as he approached. He was a corporal. He was a clone. He had brown hair, broad shoulders and a round chest. He was short and squat, and powerful. He and I might have been raised in the same orphanage for all I knew. Rain poured down on him. Drops hit his poncho and burst.

"You mind if I don't get out?" I asked. "I don't want to get the upholstery wet."

He smiled and nodded. "I don't suppose you have papers for that car?" he asked.

"How about these?" I handed him my military ID.

He took the card and read it over several times. "Colonel," he said, acknowledging my identity, but the barrier did not open. "Our scanner says this car belongs to James Walker. I don't suppose you can prove that he loaned you this vehicle?"

"No, Corporal, I can't," I said.

"Then we have a bit of a problem, Colonel. We've been sent out to prevent looting. That includes the borrowing of cars."

Colonel McAvoy had issued me a pistol. I had it under my car seat. I could have shot the corporal. "How far is Fort Washington from here?"

The corporal's expression tightened. Fort Washington was the local Marine base. If I was indeed a colonel in the Marines, I should have known how to get there.

"I just flew in, Corporal," I said. "Fleet Headquarters dispatched me to see what I can do to prepare this planet for an attack."

"I heard air traffic was stacked up for hours," the corporal said, a dubious note in his tone.

"Getting out is a problem," I said. "There's a line all the way up to the disc and more people waiting in the spaceport. Coming in is a breeze. Who wants to go to a planet that's about to get smashed?"

That seemed to satisfy him. The corporal smiled and nodded. "Sir, I can't let you pass in that car."

"I understand," I said.

"Tell you what, sir. You park the car over there," he said, pointing to a nearby alley, "and I'll give you a ride to Washington in our jeep."

"You don't mind?" I asked.

"Base Command, Base Command, this is post fifteen in Sector A, come in," he said into an interLink microphone that was attached to his poncho. He must have received the response through an unseen earpiece.

"I have an incoming Marine colonel looking for Fort Washington. Requesting permission to drive him."

He put a hand over his ear to block outside sounds. "That is correct. I said a Marine colonel . . . yes, that would be the equivalent of colonel in the Marine Corps."

The corporal bent down again and said, "Okay, I'm cleared to drive you to the base."

"I appreciate it," I said.

Then, lowering his voice just shy of a whisper, he added, "Leave the keys in the Paragon . . . just in case."

I couldn't really leave the keys in the ignition since I had hot-wired the car. "You know anything about hot-wiring cars?"

"No sir," the corporal said.

"I'll leave the ignition running," I said. I turned the car around, backed into the nearest alley, and stepped out into the rain. The downpour was hard and steady, but the air was warm. Sitting in an open-air bungalow on an evening like this could have been very pleasant, I thought, assuming you had the right company.

The corporal led me to his jeep, a sturdy little five-seat auto with a hard top. It did not have mounted machine guns or a missile carriage—clearly the Army did not expect to face ground forces.

I was not so confident. Once out of the rain, I put my pistol in my ruck and pulled out my M27. I grabbed two extra clips and hid them in my jacket.

"You expecting a war?" the corporal asked as he climbed in.

"Better safe than specked," I said.

"Colonel, we have road blocks set up every eight blocks across Safe Harbor. Intel ran a scan. There may be a couple thousand looters out there, but the last thing they want is to mess with us."

"You're probably right," I said. "This just makes me feel a little more relaxed." I patted the M27.

"Sort of a security blanket, sir?"

"Ever been in combat, Corporal?"

"Mostly police actions."

"That's good," I said. "You'll know what I am talking about soon enough." Dead is dead. It doesn't matter if you're shot by a scared looter or a separatist sniper.

The strange sensation of driving through empty streets never went away. We drove through the financial district with its tall skyscrapers, the light of our headlights reflecting on marble and glass façades the way it might reflect on the surface of a still lake. I kept looking for men in suits. We drove past a row of apartment complexes and grocery stores, and I automatically checked the buildings for lights. The only time we saw people was when we passed roadblocks.

The soldiers would see us, slow us for visual inspection, and salute us on our way.

"Spotted any looters, sir?" the corporal asked. I didn't answer.

The most haunting thing we passed was a LAWSONS convenience store. These were stores that never closed. Lights were always supposed to be on in these stores and the doors were never supposed to be locked. Yet here was a LAWSONS that was as dark and deserted as any dance club on Sunday. Even the LAWSONS sign over the door was dark.

The corporal drove like a maniac. He streaked down the wet streets so quickly that he could not possibly have swerved in time to avoid hitting another car had one appeared. When he came around corners, he did not slow down, causing the jeep to drift more than it turned.

"You know, I've been stationed in Safe Harbor for two years now and I've seen more of the town over the last five hours than the last twenty-four months. It's not a bad place, really . . . a little dark, maybe."

"Did you see the feed from New Gibraltar?" I asked.

"I'd like to see them try something like that around here. McCord would send one thousand fighters and shoot their asses down," the corporal said.

"From what I hear, the Separatists only had four ships at Gateway," I said.

"Yeah?" the corporal said.

"And from what I understand, they have over five hundred ships in their fleet."

The corporal frowned. The dim green glow of the dashboard lights lit up the lower half of his face. It lit his bottom lip, the bottom of his nose, and the folds of skin under his eye sockets. The strange lighting made his expression grim. "Five hundred ships? I didn't know that."

The entrance to Fort Washington Marine base was up ahead. You did not need to know military tactics to see that it was also on high alert. Bright lights lit the main gate to the base. Red strobes flashed on and off on the half dozen radar dishes that spun around the wall of the fort. Unlike New Gibraltar, which looked like a modernized version of an old medieval castle, Fort Washington was a sprawling campus that took up several square miles.

Looking beyond the gate, I saw the taillights of jeeps rushing between buildings. They drove by headlight only. The streetlights were out. There were no lights on the outsides of the buildings. Throughout the grounds, the only bubbles of light were emplacements for long-range cannons capable of hitting ships outside the atmosphere.

Crazy driver that he was, I expected the corporal to race up to the front gate and screech to a stop. He showed more common sense than that. With the base on alert and armed guards all around the entrance, the corporal slowed to a crawl and coasted to the gate.

The guard who approached the jeep did not draw his M27, but I could sense a dozen other weapons pointed in our direction.

"Corporal," the guard said.

"Just bringing you one of your own," the corporal said, nodding toward me.

I handed the guard my ID. "I brought in a local thug named Jimmy Callahan about a week ago. Your MPs have been keeping him and a couple of buddies in the brig for safekeeping," I said.

The guard walked around the jeep for a better look at me. He read my ID, considered it, and reread. "Wait here, sir," he said and went into his booth to phone command. When he hung up the phone, he handed me my card and saluted. A moment later the gate went up, and the other guards saluted as we drove by.

The corporal may have been Army, but he knew his way around this Marine base. He skirted the motor pool and the barracks and brought me right to the administration building. I thanked the man and he saluted me, then he drove off.

TWENTY-FOUR

Jimmy Callahan and his two bodyguards sat in an interrogation room. Both of Callahan's stooges smoked, he didn't. The three of them sat without speaking to each other. Callahan did not even look in the other boys' direction. He occasionally reached up to smooth his hair as he considered his various options.

I watched this scene on a security screen in the chief's office hoping for a clue about Callahan's general mood. The man was a sphinx for nearly five minutes, then he gave me a clear insight by staring into a supposedly hidden camera and sticking his middle finger out at it.

Two MPs escorted me to the interrogation room and locked the door behind me.

"You're a colonel now?" Callahan asked as he turned to look at me. "You must have run away from something really big this time. Know what I mean?" He bobbed his head in that arrogant way as he spoke. Behind him, Silent Tommy and Limping Eddie, the two bodyguards I maimed right before the explosions, stubbed out their cigarettes and sat like statues. They did not seem as happy to see me as their boss was.

"I don't know what you mean," I said.

"Allow me to explain. You run away from the battle at

Little Man and they make you lieutenant. Now, in two short weeks, you're a specking colonel. What did you do, run away from New Gibraltar?"

It became very apparent that there were two Jimmy Callahans. The first, the one speaking to me at this moment, was a petulant prick who thought he had the world by the balls. The other was a scared little kid.

"That's clever," I said. "Don't you think that's clever?" I asked Silent Tommy. He did not answer. "How about you, Eddie? Don't you think Jimmy's joke is clever?"

"See, now, Harris, they don't want to answer because they're scared of you. They don't have anything you want. Me . . . I have information you want, so I'm not scared. In fact, I think it's about time you did me some favors."

"Really?" I asked, sitting on the edge of the table in the center of the room. "You don't think saving your ass from Patel was enough?"

Callahan's mouth bent in a comical frown that took the corners of his lips halfway down his chin. "I've been thinking about that, and I don't think Patel was after me. I think he was after you. Know what I mean? I never did anything to Billy. What would he have against me?"

"Well, there is this little issue about you fingering him to the Marines," I said.

"You cannot possibly be talking about yourself, Harris? You're not the Marines. Hell, you're a specking deserter." Callahan smiled at his own joke and flexed his biceps. "And as for saving my ass, who says that you saved it? Tommy and Eddie were there. They came out just fine 'cept what you did to them."

Tommy's jaw was wired shut and mending. Eddie was on crutches. Both my doing.

"And where did I end up?" Callahan continued. "I ended up in Fort frigging Washington, the biggest shithole on New Columbia. I figure you did nothing for me. The way I figure it, you owe me."

"Sounds like you have it all figured out," I said. I hopped off of the table and started for the door.

"Where are you going?" Callahan asked.

"Didn't you hear?" I asked. "Your buddies from the Confederate Arms are getting ready to bag this planet. Should be quite a reunion. Their fleet will bombard this base until it's defenseless, then they'll probably send down commandoes to nuke it. That's what they did on Gateway. Of course, Billy the Butcher probably didn't have an old pal like you that he wanted to bust out of Gateway Outpost.

"You did know that they evacuated New Columbia?" I asked.

"So I hear," Callahan said.

"If I were you, Jimmy, I'd be thinking about how I might get off this planet. They planted hot bombs around the base on Gateway," I said. "You know what that means? It means that most of the jarheads who were in that building are alive and melting at this very moment. Mop them with a sponge and you'll pull off their skin. And those boys were wearing radiation-proof armor.

"The lucky ones got cooked on the spot. They weren't wearing armor, just like you're not wearing armor. Lucky you. You will probably die just like that." I snapped my fingers. "One moment you're praying, 'God, please don't let them nuke me.' The next minute, you're face to face with God and he says, 'About that prayer . . . ' "

"What do you want?" Callahan asked, all humor drained from his voice.

"Where is the GC Fleet?"

"How the speck should I know?" Callahan said.

"You said you knew."

"I asked what I would get if I led you to that fleet," Callahan said. "I didn't say I knew where it was. I just wanted to know what it would be worth to me."

"You wanted to show off."

"What?" Callahan thought about this. "Yeah . . . maybe."

"What is the Hinode Fleet?" I asked.

"Never heard of it," Callahan said.

"Right before the attack on New Gibraltar, the Intelligence Network intercepted signals referring to the Hinode Fleet. Is that what your Mogat buddies call the Galactic Central Fleet?"

"I don't know," Callahan said.

"How do the Japanese figure into this?" I asked, feeling more than a little frustrated. "Are they in with the Mogats?"

"Who the speck are the Japanese?" Callahan asked.

"Refugees from Ezer Kri," I said. "Are they part of the Confederate Arms?"

"How should I know?" Callahan asked. He sounded frustrated and his face turned red.

"How about your pal Billy the Butcher?" I asked. By this time I was yelling. The mood in the room was thick with anger, and I wanted to hit Callahan. "Where is Patel?"

"I don't know," Callahan shouted. Then, lowering his voice, he said, "Someone else always arranged our meetings."

Finally I was getting somewhere. "Who was that?"

Callahan sat slumped in his chair when Limping Eddie mumbled, "Tell him how to find the supply guy."

Callahan looked at him and a smile stretched across his face. "I like that." Then he turned back to me. "You could visit Batt, he's your best bet. If anyone can answer your questions, it's Batt."

"Who is Batt?" I asked, the calm returning to my voice.

"Batt is Bartholomew Wingate," Callahan said. "He introduced me to Patel."

"Mogat or Confederate?" I asked.

"Neither," Callahan said, the swagger back in his smile. "He's one of yours. I guess patriotism isn't his bag. Know what I mean?"

"He's a punk like you?" I asked.

Callahan's smile brightened. "Oh, he's much bigger than me. You might say he has his own army."

"I thought you had one, too?" I said.

"I do," Callahan said, "but it's not as good as Batt's. He's got a lot more clout around here than me. He knows everything and everybody."

"Great," I said throwing my hands up in frustration. "Only we can't find Batt. We just evacuated the planet." Players like that vanish into the woodwork the moment you look the other way.

"Oh, you don't have to worry about that." Now Callahan sounded almost gleeful. "He's still in Safe Harbor. He's just up the road. He's the commander at the Army base."

"Let me get this straight," Lieutenant Colonel Bernie Phillips said. "Your prisoner claims that Colonel Wingate is selling supplies to the Confederates?"

"That's right," I said.

"Bullshit."

We sat in an observation room in the brig. Behind Phillips, the video screens showed the room in which Callahan and his bodyguards sat idly waiting for me. I could only hope that the colonel did not glance at the screen. At the moment, Callahan was flexing his biceps and kissing them. Silent Tommy responded with a hand-gesture that meant "go speck yourself." This only encouraged Callahan. He responded by flexing both arms at once.

"How well do you know Wingate?" I asked.

"I've known Batt three years now," Phillips said. "Ever since I transferred in."

"So you're friends?" I asked, knowing that I could always play the Che Huang trump card if the need arose.

"I can't stand the son of a bitch," Phillips said, his expression dower. "He thinks he's king of the goddamned planet just because he has a bigger base. Command airlifts our supplies in through his base. The prick makes me fill out so many forms to get my stuff you'd think he owned it. He's always showing off. He must come from a rich family. He lives like a friggin' king."

"Let's see here. Your supplies come through his base and he acts like he owns them. Is that right?" I asked. Phillips nodded. "And he lives like a king, but you don't think he's selling?"

Phillips's expression brightened. "Bust Batt Wingate? Think we could shoot him for this?"

"Once this is over, I'll hand you the gun," I said. "For now I need him alive. If my hunch is right, Wingate might be able to lead me to the Confederate Fleet."

"Just remember, I get to shoot him when you're done with him," Colonel Phillips said.

"Deal," I said.

"What's our first step?"

It was late at night and the sky over the city was still black. I crept through the alley behind a row of restaurants until I could see the roadblock. Arc lights filled the street around the barricade with senseless glare. The light shined on the soldiers, blinding them to any enemies lurking nearby while making them well-lit targets for any snipers who happened to pass.

These boys did not have anything to worry about from me. I didn't want the pack. I wanted the stray. I hid in the alley, using garbage pails and food crates as cover. I hoped my fall guy would come soon. There was so much rot in the cans around me that the air smelled like vomit.

My target came in the form of a sergeant who was touring roadblocks to keep the men alert. He drove a jeep. He drove alone. Approaching the roadblock, he stormed out of his vehicle and started screaming and cussing the moment his feet hit the ground. He was kind enough to line the men up at attention in just the right angle so that neither he nor they were facing in my direction. Then he paced back and forth in front of the line like a caged animal, screaming something about always being alert. I did not listen to what he said or how they responded.

"Phillips, I found our guy," I called over a comLink stem in my glove.

The colonel had volunteered to direct this operation himself. He and five of his men hid a few blocks away, waiting for me to locate and mark a target. They had two special jeeps that had been decked out for night operations. Unlike other jeeps, these units had absolutely silent engines that could only be detected with sound equipment. These stealth jeeps were black with special nonreflective glass. Their chassis were not painted. They were covered with a nonreflecting flat coat of black porcelain that resisted radar detections. Sophisticated radar equipment would spot them in a heartbeat, but the cheap radar used in ground vehicles such as tanks and all-terrain vehicles would turn a blind eye. Even trackers, those sniper robots so loved by the enemy, had trouble spotting these vehicles.

Since these jeeps were also made for night operations, they had night-for-day scanning built into their windshields. They had discreet lights and searchlights, but with that night-for-day scanning, you could drive stealth jeeps black.

"What you got?" Phillips voice came over the discreet ear piece.

"A single passenger in a stealth bug."

"Officer or enlisted man?" Phillips asked.

"Does it matter? You're in either way, right?" I asked. We were going to kidnap the man and use his ID and vehicle to break into Fort Clinton. If Callahan gave us good information, a medal of valor awaited Phillips for his part in this. If Callahan had lied . . . even a Secessionist attack would not save him from a court martial, assuming he survived.

"If we have to knock somebody up, I'd rather hit a synthetic," Phillips said.

"He's a sergeant."

"Perfect. Can you mark him?"

Hiding in the darkness of the alley behind some trash cans and a stack of crates, I shined a laser pointer on one of the rear tires of the jeep. It had stopped raining in Safe Harbor, but the air was humid and heavy. Puddles dotted the ground and the alley was grimy with dirt and slop.

My laser pointer cast a red beam that was as thin as a sewing needle. It illuminated a tiny red spot no bigger than a mouse's eye on the side of the tire. I kept the light steady for twenty seconds as the sergeant berated his men.

"How the speck do you plan on catching criminals? Are you on guard duty or vacation?" Then, without a pause, "I asked you a question!"

"Guard duty!" the men yelled.

"Guard duty. That must be why you ladies are not wearing bathing suits," the sergeant continued yelling. He made me nostalgic for my old drill sergeants back in basic, though those sergeants used far more creative profanity than this fellow. They also cuffed us alongside the head at every opportunity.

"You got him?" I asked.

"Yeah, he's marked," Phillips said.

"Now if he would just shut up and drive," I said.

But the sergeant continued to pace back and forth and berate his men. "So you ladies think you can keep this block safe? I'm not sure who I would bet on if it comes down to you five speck-suckers against a gang of kindergarteners.

"You need to be alert. Do you hear me soldiers? Alert! A! L! E! R! T!"

I could not help myself. I painted the laser across the sergeant's A-L-E-R-T ass. His soldiers were too busy looking him in the eye to see a filament-wide laser beam shining on his butt.

"You marking another jeep?" Phillips radioed me. "I'm getting another signal."

"Sorry," I said as I slipped the pointer back into my clothes.

The sergeant inspected each man's weapon, wasting another five minutes, leaving me in that fetid alley smelling of rotten food. I saw a rat scurry among some distant crates. I would even the score with that sergeant for making me wait, I told myself, and I felt better.

A few minutes later, the sergeant climbed into his jeep. He slammed the door behind himself and sped away.

"I wish somebody would stomp that specker," one of the soldiers said.

Somebody was about to.

Moving in absolute silence, not kicking a can or brushing a box, I walked through the alley. I did not think those soldiers would notice a marching band parading by with that arc light shining in their eyes, but I did not take any chances. A stealth jeep filled with Marines met me at the end of the alleyway. I climbed in.

"I don't know where you marked the target that second time, but it's a good thing you did," Phillips said. "This guy drives like a frigging maniac. That second mark is a lot clearer."

Our driver watched the road through a night-for-day lens in the windshield. I did not envy him that task. I had used similar technology in my old combat armor. Night-for-day lenses, with their monochrome displays, just about annihilated your depth perception.

A radar panel on the dashboard showed our position, the sergeant's position, and the position of our second stealth jeep, along with any nearby Army vehicles. Sergeant Target was on his way to the next barricade, three miles away. His car swerved severely as he drove. Our jeeps, driving on parallel roads, flanked him on either side.

"What's the matter with him?" Phillips asked.

"Probably drinking and driving," I said.

"Was he drunk?" Phillips asked.

"He's a sergeant," I said. "You can't tell without a blood test."

This was a lucky break. A shitfaced sergeant might crash

his car. He might stop for a drink, be found by looters, and be stripped from his car. It fit perfectly into our plans. He had given us an alibi, assuming we needed one.

Looking at the map, I saw that our sergeant was still one mile from the next barricade. "Last chance to back out," I said to Colonel Phillips.

Phillips picked up the microphone and said, "Take him."

Our driver accelerated. Looking at the map, I saw that the driver in the other jeep had also picked up some speed. We streaked ahead for two blocks and gained a good lead, then swerved around the next corner and planted ourselves in the middle of the road. Using a computer to aim our searchlights on the sergeant, we leapt from the car and drew our weapons.

Our second jeep pulled in behind the sergeant. Once our lights went on, the other driver flashed his, too. And now the brain-dead sergeant, Mr. A.L.E.R.T, did exactly what we hoped he would do. Instead of hunkering in his jeep and calling in his situation, he grabbed his weapon and stepped on to the street. The searchlights blinded him, and he stood with his arms over his eyes too dumb to move.

I approached from the front. The searchlight shone over my shoulder.

"Who are you?" the sergeant muttered.

"Are you drunk, sergeant?" I asked as my right fist slammed into his jaw, dropping him to the street. He fell and did not stir. The drivers in the stealth jeeps cut their search-lights as I knelt beside the fallen Army man and stripped him down to his underwear. I took his uniform, wallet, ID and dog tags. These articles I placed on the hood of his car. Then I stripped my clothes off and handed them to Phillips.

"Damn, Harris. You didn't need to do that," Phillips said.

"The last thing he heard was *drunk*," I said.

"So?" Phillips asked.

"The word will stay fresh in his subconscious. It'll be the first thing he thinks of when he wakes up," I said.

"Does it work that way?" Phillips asked.

"It does with me," I said as I buttoned his shirt over my chest. That was a lie. I had never gotten so drunk that I passed out.

"Good thinking," Phillips said.

The sergeant was a clone, of course . . . brown hair, brown eyes. He was shorter than me, and broader around the neck and the chest. He also had a gut. The sleeves of his fatigues ended well shy of my wrists, but I didn't worry about it. I was not headed to Fort Clinton for a fashion show. The soldiers manning that base would be too busy to notice my sleeves.

As for the good sergeant, he was on his way to the brig at Fort Washington. There he would remain in a cell until he woke up. He would tell them that he was a soldier in the Unified Authority Army. They would tell him that they found him passed out and naked on the street. Thanks to the bottle he carried in his jeep, the story would be an easy sell. His blood alcohol would be legitimately high. If everything went as expected, Phillips would be in the clear. Had he known what we were doing, Colonel Batt Wingate would have been worried.

I nodded to Phillips and climbed into the Army jeep. The air inside the car smelled of beer and flatulence. Using the dome light in the roof, I examined my dog tags for a name—First Sergeant Mark Hopkins. Then I rolled down the window and started up the engine. I was about to pull forward when one of Phillips's men waved for me to stop.

"You might want this," he said, handing me the sergeant's M27. I thanked the man and left. Rather than follow Sergeant Hopkins's designated course, which would have taken me through three more checkpoints, I found a circuitous route that took me through alleys until I passed all but one final guard station. There I would need to make an appearance.

The jeep barely fit through a few of the tighter alleys. Dumpsters, trash cans, and abandoned cars choked some of the back ways. I saw looters, too—mostly harmless men, scurrying like rats through the shadows, trying to hide by diving into buildings when my headlights turned in their direction. These men traveled alone or in teams of two, mostly. Had I run into a mob, I suspect they would have come after me.

I left the cover of the alleys before entering the final checkpoint. The soldiers guarding that checkpoint would expect an Army sergeant to come up the street. So I pulled onto good old Main Street, Safe Harbor, a six-lane thoroughfare leading to an endless suspension bridge that spanned a great river.

The checkpoint looked like a wall of light spanning the front entrance to the bridge. Soldiers milled around the titanium barricade which stretched the width of the road. There must have been an officer in charge at this post. The soldiers were far more alert than the ones at the other barricades I had seen. They held their guns at the ready. Men sat in the machine-gun nests on either side of the bridge. Soldiers sat behind the wheels of the jeeps and all-terrain vehicles on the edges of the post.

None of this would matter as long as I did not do anything stupid. I slowed my jeep and coasted up to the barricade before coming to a stop. Somebody flashed a spotlight on me; the glare through the windshield was blinding. I lifted a hand to block the glare as I opened my door.

"May I see your identification?" a soldier asked from somewhere within the light.

I felt through my pockets and produced Sergeant Hopkins's ID.

Hopkins and I were different models of clones, but we were both clones. We both had brown hair, brown eyes, and similar facial features. I was an elongated version of Hopkins, a more than reasonable facsimile with this blinding spotlight bleaching my skin and features.

"Could you cut the light?" I asked. It seemed like something a dumb-ass sergeant might ask.

The soldier handed back my ID. I heard the grating yawn of metal scraping across a concrete surface as the barricade slid open.

"You're clear," the soldier said.

So I drove across the bridge, watching the island of light diminish in my rearview mirror. The bridge stretched for more than one mile, the yard-wide cables that supported it forming an arc that reminded me of the spokes of a bicycle tire. A blanket of thick clouds stretched across the sky. Rain so fine that it felt like mist filled the air. An enormous mile-wide river rushed beneath the bridge, but it was so far below me that I could barely hear the hiss of its currents. And covering everything was the inky blackness of night.

I took confidence from the ease with which I had passed through that last checkpoint. Had I stopped to think about it, I might have hesitated before entering the base. Mark Hopkins was supposed to be out reviewing guard stations, a fact that should have told me that he had something to do with security. My luck had held so far, and I did not stop to think that it might end soon.

Ahead of me, Fort Clinton looked more like a constellation of stars than an Army base. Most of the complex was blacked out. Shutters had been closed across windows of buildings so that the only light they emitted came out in thin stripes that dissolved into the night air. The buildings themselves looked darker than a shadow.

Helicopter gunboats ran slow patrols above the fort while jets circled the area high in the atmosphere. I could not see the gunboats or the jets, but the loud *chop, chop, chop* of helicopter rotors echoed up from the ground and the searing roar of jet engines thundered and faded in the darkness.

TWENTY-FIVE

The guard at the gate barely checked my identification. I drove a Fort Clinton Army jeep. After a glance at my papers and a sweep of my face, he signaled his pals to let me through.

Following base signs, I found my way to the administration building. The lobby of the building was brightly lit. Officers in fatigues hustled up and down the halls. Men hunkered by communications consoles, relaying orders and checking the overall readiness of the soldiers. No one so much as looked in my direction.

This administration building was no different than thousands of other similar buildings across the galaxy. Colonel Bartholomew Wingate's office was right where I expected it to be. And, as I suspected, the colonel was nowhere to be found. I went out to my jeep and drove until I found officer housing. I only hoped that I had enough time to find Wingate before he bolted.

Base commander housing tended to be big and conspicuous, and I had little trouble locating Wingate's estate. There was a stealth jeep in the driveway that looked black and sinister, a phantom car meant to blend in with the night.

I parked my jeep along the street and climbed out into the

misty night hiding behind a stand of trees as I waited to see what would happen next. If Callahan was right about Colonel Bartholomew Wingate, I would not have to wait very long.

Wingate's front door was about ten yards ahead of me. His house was easy to spot. His porch lights blazed while every other house on the block was dark. I sat in the silence, my mind wandering.

There was so much that the U.A. intelligence community did not know about the enemy. We knew that the four rebelling arms—Cygnus, Scutum-Crux, Perseus, and Norma—all had their own governments. But we also knew that Gordon Hughes, the former speaker of the House of Representatives, was the acting president of the Confederate Arms. Was there one government or four?

From everything I had heard, the arms had formed a shaky alliance. The only thing they had in common was that they wanted the Unified Authority out of their space. The Morgan Atkins Separatists, on the other hand, wanted to topple the Unified Authority. They wanted to conquer and destroy, but unlike the renegade arms, the Mogats did not have the kind of infrastructure that would allow for an army. They had controlled the Galactic Central Fleet for more than forty years and did nothing with it.

Then there were the Japanese. Approximately 12.5 million people of Japanese descent fled Ezer Kri because of the Unified Authority occupation of their planet. No one had ever satisfactorily explained how 12.5 million people could have fled a planet in a system patrolled by the Scutum-Crux Fleet, but I had my ideas. They could have been evacuated by a large fleet of self-broadcasting ships such as the dreadnaughts, battleships, and destroyers in the Galactic Central Fleet.

The last estimate I read placed the Mogat population at approximately two hundred million. The combined arms had approximately thirty billion citizens. So how did the Japanese fit in? They numbered less than thirteen million; how important could they be? And yet, for some reason, people were calling the GC Fleet by a Japanese name.

An hour passed. I remained crouched, hidden from Wingate's house by trees and a shrub. An observant driver might have spotted me among the trees, but no one came down this road. The base was at high-alert and the officers were at their stations.

When the enemy finally appeared, they were dressed in Army fatigues and spoke common English. They drove a jeep, leaving the windows open to enjoy the breeze. After the trip down in a Galactic Fleet transport, they must have been glad for the cold fresh air.

The jeep rolled up the street right past me. It parked in front of Colonel Wingate's yard and two men climbed out.

"I told you this was the right street," one man said. He had a single bar on his fatigues. Had he not been an enemy commando, that bar would have made him a lieutenant in the Army.

"I spotted the house," the other man said. He wore the same clever disguise. They were wolves in wolves' clothing.

"How hard was that?" the first man said. "It's the only house with its lights on." They spoke loud enough for me to hear them from thirty yards away. Stealth work was clearly not their strength. An angry-looking Wingate came to the door before they reached it. He might have been watching from the window, but he might also have heard their point-less babble.

"Ready, Colonel?" one of the commandos asked.

Wingate turned off the lights outside his house and locked the door behind him. He did not speak as he walked over to the stealth jeep in his driveway, a rucksack dangling over his shoulder. He climbed into the back seat. I could see his head through the rear window. The commandos climbed into the front seats, and the jeep rolled out of the driveway.

I wished I had marked that jeep with the laser pointer that Bernie Phillips loaned me. Then I could have asked his trusty Marines to do the tracking. I did not have the option this time. The Marines had returned to their base.

Colonel Wingate and his commando escort drove with their headlights off. Since their stealth vehicle had night-for-day vision built into its windshield, that was no problem for them. To avoid being spotted, I also drove with my head-lights off. I did not want the base police or the traitor I was tailing to notice me. The only thing in my favor was that in-stead of following Wingate, I sped ahead to the place I hoped would be his rendezvous spot.

Before taking me into town to kidnap the Army soldier, Colonel Phillips had shown me several maps of Fort Clinton and the surrounding area. There was no way a sellout like Wingate was going to ride out the attack. His soldiers were going to die. The Pentagon would send men to survey the base and there would be huge inventory discrepancies. Even if Wingate survived the attack, he would be arrested and killed in the aftermath. His Confederate Arms pals might not care if he got himself executed, but he might spill some important information in the process. To keep him quiet, they either needed to kill him or get him off the planet. Either way, they would need to send down a transport with a team of commandos. When that transport returned to the fleet, I aimed to hitch a ride.

By studying the maps, Phillips and I located the most likely spot for an enemy transport to land. It was only an educated guess, but it proved right.

Driving almost blind, I headed up a slow grade toward the raised parade grounds along the eastern gate of the base. This area was dark and mostly empty. Sure enough, every few seconds I spotted just a glimpse of the phantom black car in the darkness.

This part of the base was dark and lifeless. We passed no other cars. The landscape was studded with old-fashioned drill towers, standing high over the ground on stilts made of logs. A half-mile ahead of me, Wingate's jeep slowed as it passed through a poorly-lit guard station. The gate at the guard station raised as Wingate approached. A commando left the station and climbed into Wingate's stealth jeep.

As if this were a cue, the attack commenced the moment Wingate's car left the base. It came in the form of a silvery red beam that poured out of the night sky like a translucent pillar. The scene remained absolutely silent for a moment, then fire, smoke, and sirens erupted as a building exploded. I watched this scene unfold as I drove, and I looked at my wristwatch to mark the time. Once eight minutes had passed, I knew the whole thing would be over.

Fire trucks flashing red and white warning lights streaked across the base. From where I sat at the edge of the parade grounds, I could see fire blazing below, and I could see the immaculate red and white light twinkling from the tops of the fire trucks.

When I reached the gate, I noticed the shattered glass of the security booth and knew that the commandos had slaughtered the men left to guard this gate. There was no blood, no major destruction. The commandos had probably sneaked up to the gate on their way into the base. A couple of quick shots from a high-powered pistol, and the gate was theirs. Did Wingate care that men under his command had been ambushed?

Behind me, lasers rained down from above. Beams as big around as water towers struck buildings. Smaller beams no more than one foot in diameter flashed quickly, striking jets and gunboats right out of the sky.

I drove through the gate at eighty miles per hour—not a safe speed for driving wet roads on a dark night without lights. It might have taken the transport one minute to drop to the planet. It could have taken another minute or two for the commandos to drive to Wingate's house. In another four minutes the shooting match would end whether I was on hand to catch Wingate or not.

The sky outside of the fence was velvet and peaceful, a typically calm evening on a nonindustrial planet. When I saw a break in the clouds, I thought the sky looked like a lake of oil and stars. In the distance, another silver-red barrage cascaded down on Fort Washington.

There would be similar fireworks over the Air Force base. There the attack would be more intense, if anything. The base would send up its squadrons of F-19s to attack the invaders. If the enemy ships could destroy the runways in time, a few of those fighters might be stranded on the ground. The majority would streak through the sky faster than bullets. They would leave the atmosphere, find the invading ships and the real battle would begin.

The Air Force's F-19 Falcons would attack from the ground. The U.A. fighter carrier and destroyers guarding the discs would close in from above. How many GCF ships had the enemy sent? How would they perform in battle? Were their weapons updated?

How long had the attack lasted so far? I looked at my watch. Only twenty seconds had passed since the first beam rolled down from the sky.

I saw no trace of Wingate's jeep in front of me and had

no time left for discretion. Turning my headlights on, I raced down tree-lined lanes and into the forested countryside. The sounds of sirens and explosions carried in the air, but they were distant and I ignored them. The attack was far away now and seemed no more significant than a day-old dream as I concentrated on finding the transport.

I looked at my wristwatch and saw the timer hand sweep past the twelve. One full minute had passed since that first laser attack. Why had I not started timing when I spotted the commandos? Why had I gone to the base instead of simply hiding out here?

I doused my headlights. Up ahead, the white light of arc lamps shined through a grove. The trees blocking the glare created a strobe effect, as if I were watching an ancient silent movie. I pulled off the road and skidded to a halt in the mud.

There would be no time to call for help or pack my weapons, not even my M27. I jumped out of my jeep. A good hundred feet into the woods, men in green uniforms loaded small stacks of crates into an antique-looking military transport.

Other men with guns circled the area looking for folks like me. Here I had a stroke of luck. These men were dressed in Army fatigues that looked precisely like mine. They were camouflaged to look like the soldiers at Fort Clinton. Had one of Wingate's soldiers unknowingly stumbled into their operation, these spies might have pointed to their own transport and claimed that they had located an enemy ship.

"We're out of time," somebody said in a soft voice that carried through the silence. "Anything and anyone who does not get on now gets left behind." Somewhere back near town, still as distant as a dream, sirens and explosions continued to break the silence. I had to make my move. Fortunately for me, one guard had strayed far enough into the trees for me to take him.

"Last call. Return to the transport." The voice was soft but it echoed over a hundred comLinks and carried through the woods.

I drew closer to my target, a lone man with an M27. He had blond hair. We looked nothing alike, but I did not think it would matter. Looking around these woods, between the men loading the ship and the guards, there were too many faces for anyone to keep them all straight.

I doubt my victim heard me. He took one last sweep of the area before turning to go back to the transport. I hid behind a tree, no more than fifteen feet from where he stood. He had his back to me. I could see the barrel of his M27 pointing straight up above the top of his shoulder. Nice of him to bring me a replacement for the one I left in my jeep.

I took a deep breath and held it in my lungs. Barely lifting my feet, I rushed forward, staying in a slight crouch, my arms out and my fingers stretched as if preparing to strangle the boy. Had the floor of the forest been dry, I could have taken him easily, but the ground was muddy from the rain. I moved more quickly than he did, but I had to shuffle my feet to squelch the sound of my boots tromping through the mud. He hiked, I glided.

Ahead of him, I could see the landing area. Guards, cargo handlers, and commandos hustled into the transport. They did not look back as I leaped forward, fastening my right hand around the boy's chin and anchoring my grip by placing my left hand just on the back of his neck. I pulled with my right hand and pushed with my left. The sound of his neck snapping was no louder than the tick of a clock as we both toppled forward. He was dead before our momentum sent us to the ground.

Straightening my fatigues, I climbed to my feet. There was a smear of mud on my knee. I brushed off the dirt and leaves as best I could as I approached the transport.

"Hurry up, asshole," someone yelled as I started up the ramp. I nodded and ran forward as the doors closed behind me. My boots clanked against the metal floor. I heard excited chatter all around me. The cabin was mostly dark except for soft red emergency lights. The engines rumbled and the transport lifted straight up in the air.

TWENTY-SIX

Every ship in the Galactic Central Fleet was more than forty years old. That did not mean that they were in bad condition or that they had seen a lot of action. In fact, few of the ships had traveled over the last few decades. New and clean as this transport was, it had antiquated technology. To prevent glare in the cockpit, the only light in the kettle—that was what we called the cattle car in which the soldiers traveled—came from red emergency lights. That was to my liking. I was, after all, a stowaway. I sat in the back of the kettle not far from the cargo area where nobody noticed me.

The men around me did not like the dark atmosphere. "Like traveling in an armpit," one man complained. "Sending us back and forth in a damned drain pipe," another man said in a different conversation. The best line came from the man sitting beside me: "Not even fit for clones."

The inside of the kettle was anything but luxurious. The walls, ceiling, and floor were bare, unadorned metal. A line of benches ran along the wall of the cabin offering enough seating for maybe one-quarter of the men on this flight. Safety harnesses hung from the ceiling. In the case of an emergency, men would strap themselves in with these harnesses and hang from the ceiling like butchered cattle in a slaughterhouse freezer. The harnesses became rigid when in use, preventing the men from swinging into each other.

In a transport like this, passengers were nothing more than cargo. There were no windows and no way of knowing what was happening outside of the ship. The launch from New Columbia was smooth enough, but moments after we took off, the pilot signaled us to harness ourselves in.

Batt Wingate and his commando-escort sat somewhere in the front of the kettle. I could not see them. It did not matter. I knew they were inside and besides, there was only one way off this bird. Once we landed, I would slink toward the door so that Wingate would pass me before he left. The mood in the kettle changed as the men fastened themselves in. Now, nobody spoke. Most of the men hung absolutely silent. A few smoked cigarettes and spat their smoldering butts to the floor.

Outside the ship, the gears of war were turning. Swarms of fighters might spot us and attack as we left the atmosphere and entered the blanket of space. A lone fighter could destroy a transport, but it would take multiple missiles. These ships looked and flew like pregnant seagulls, but they had powerful shields and thick armor. This ship could survive a direct hit from a particle beam cannon. If one or two fighters homed in on us, we would likely survive the attack long enough for the Confederates to send help.

I looked at my watch. Just under four minutes had passed since the bombardment began. By my best guess, the GCF ships had been in the area for six minutes and would broadcast out in another two.

A missile slammed into our shields and the transport shuddered. The red lights blinked out for several seconds. In the darkness, men gasped but no one screamed. The atmosphere was tense but not panicked.

Another missile slammed into the shields sending the transport skidding sideways. It was a blow, a force that struck quickly and vanished. A few moments passed and we were struck by a particle beam. The walls of the kettle began vibrating. At first they shook, and then they convulsed in short fast shakes that seemed to tear the metal plates around us.

The lights went out again. This time they stayed out. I

heard heavy breathing. The shuddering continued for no more than three seconds, but it seemed like minutes. I heard an occasional whimper, then somebody yelled, "Shake 'em and bake 'em!" It was a dumb joke but it broke the tension. Relieved laughter filled the cabin. A moment later the red lights came back on.

In times of danger, I had the Liberator combat reflex that flooded my blood with a hormone made of adrenaline and endorphins. Everyone else on this ship turned to desperate humor to distract themselves. I did not need it. A warm, comfortable feeling spread through my body, a sense of power and mental clarity. I was not in control of the situation, yet the hormone made me feel as if I were.

Another missile struck the ship and the kettle rattled.

"Knock, knock," some man yelled. I could not see who.

"Who's there?" responded nearly every man in the cabin, and the men burst out in hysterics.

Inside joke, I guessed, and not a very good one.

And then the ride was over. There was the loud clank of metal dropping on metal as we lowered into a landing pad inside some GCF ship. The whining growl of straining motors echoed through the kettle as the heavy iron doors slid open and the hangar bay came in view.

I, of course, was still hanging from my harness. When my harness released me, I pushed through the crowd and hid near the door.

TWENTY-SEVEN

Granted, I did not see the space battle as it took place, but I had time to study it at length over the next few days. What I saw was the work of genius.

The first GCF ship to arrive in New Columbian space broadcasted in alone. It was a cruiser, the smallest class of ship in the GCF Fleet. It carried a crew of 130 men and, among other things, a fleet of three transports.

The captain of this ship played an interesting gambit. Instead of broadcasting his ship a few million miles out and risking remote radar detection, he used the Broadcast Network as camouflage. His ship materialized so close to the reception disc that the U.A. radar system recorded the anomaly caused by his ship's appearance as a hiccup in Broadcast Network radiation. His ship was as black as space, making visual detection unlikely. To use an antiquated phrase, the cruiser flew in under the radar.

If the ship's arrival near the Broadcast Network had disrupted the Network, the cruiser would have been quickly detected. Some kind of modification in the cruiser's engine prevented the disruption, and the ship was never spotted.

This cruiser parked itself five hundred miles above Safe Harbor. It launched a single transport and waited.

So, was this lone cruiser picked up by radar? Nobody knows and the equipment that would have recorded the readings was destroyed during the ensuing battle. Somebody knew the space around New Columbia very well. The cruiser stopped in a blind spot—a seam between two different radar systems. There it stayed until the battle was over.

About the time that Colonel Wingate left Fort Clinton, the cruiser radioed the rest of the fleet, and that initiated the attack. Fifteen GCF ships broadcasted into New Columbian space—a slightly larger attack force than the one that sacked Gateway. There would be no missing the anomalies caused by fifteen GCF ships broadcasting in at the same time.

The Air Force responded by sending up all of its F-19 Falcons. The fighter carrier and destroyers guarding the discs also moved into position. Had the GCF ships been of recent design, this might have been an even fight—a fifteen-ship armada comprised of destroyers, cruisers, and battleships against nearly 400 fighters, two destroyers, one fighter carrier, and ground cannon. But the Joint Chiefs were not looking for a fair fight.

Hoping to rout the enemy, the Navy had an additional fleet of ships waiting near a set of broadcast discs. The moment the battle began, the plan was to feed these ships into the Network, and in less than sixty seconds, the U.A. Navy would have twenty more ships in New Columbian space.

But the Navy had to deal with the bottleneck of using a single reception disc. The GCF Fleet had no such restrictions. As the first of the Tomcats bore down from space and the Falcons flared up from the atmosphere, fifty additional GCF ships broadcasted into the battlefield.

The video feed from the battle looked like a misprint. So many anomalies tore into the open blackness that it looked like the fabric of space had begun to boil. Feathery white lines flashed and crisscrossed. Circles of light appeared from which shadowy black forms seemed to glide.

A dozen GCF battleships coasted into place in front of the broadcast disc and formed a line. Other ships parked behind the first waiting for a turn. When the first U.A. carrier emerged from the disc, the GCF ships opened fire as it materialized into space.

The hull of the carrier flashed and ignited. The tip of its wing sheered off and webs of flame danced along its shell. That was the worst of the spectacle, I think. Flames cannot exist in the vacuum of space. Those flames were feeding on oxygen pouring out of the ship.

Only two or maybe three fighters made it out of the launch tube as the carrier staggered forward. An enormous fireball burst out of the tube and dissipated. Two battleships left their place in the firing squad and followed the dying fighter carrier, bombarding her with bright red laser fire. In another minute, the hull cracked and spokes of flames shot through. It looked, for a brief moment, as if the ship had a yellow and orange aura that vanished as quickly as it appeared. Then streams of debris gushed out of those ruptures in place of the flames, and the lifeless ship floated sideways and drifted into space.

By this time, the next U.A. fighter carrier emerged from the Network and the massacre repeated itself. The firing squad bombarded the ships until they could not defend themselves. Then two ships finished the execution, and two more GCF battleships took their place in the firing line.

Once the U.A. ships entered the Broadcast Network, it was too late to stop them or save them. A few ships were rerouted, but more than twenty Unified Authority ships were destroyed.

Closer to the atmosphere, GCF ships prowled above Safe Harbor like sharks in a feeding frenzy. They traveled in groups of three and four, circling small territories and firing powerful lasers at planetary targets. A satellite captured video of this directly from above, and you could see the ships clearly against the blue and white glow of the New Columbian atmosphere.

New Columbia's planetary defenses crumbled quickly. In the beginning, plenty of green and red beams fired up from the planet, but they seldom hit targets. The gunnery men on the ships homed in on those rays and returned fire. It took them less than two minutes to silence the cannons below.

The fighters fared no better. Rows of battleships bore down on the Falcons as they tore out of the atmosphere. Several more GCF battleships swarmed the fighter carrier and the destroyers that had been guarding the broadcast discs.

The battle took ten minutes, not eight. During that entire time, the line of civilian ships fleeing New Columbia continued to stream into the Broadcast Network. The GCF ships never attacked them. When the last of the U.A. ships exploded, the GCF ships broadcasted away.

You may or may not win an even fight, but you will certainly take casualties. By stacking the deck with sixty-five ships, the commander of the Galactic Central Fleet guaranteed more than victory, he guaranteed himself a rout. The Unified Authority lost three forts, twenty-three capital ships, and hundreds of fighters on March 24, 2512. The GCF lost one soldier, the guy I killed to get aboard their transport. I was about to even the score.

CHAPTER
TWENTY-EIGHT

The landing bay was disorganized. Of course, the battle was still going on when the transport landed on a Confederate ship, but that did not explain all of the chaos. This was supposed to be a military operation. During my time as a Marine, the ships I served on either ran like clockwork or key officers lost their jobs. That did not seem to be the case in the Confederate Navy.

As the rear door of the kettle split open revealing the deck, I saw cargo movers driving large crates through a confused crowd. Men sprinted to get to their stations. The movers, rudimentary robots that looked like a cross between a forklift and a battle tank, used radar to keep from colliding with people and objects. The mob of crewmen running back and forth around the movers must have overloaded the radar.

On the *Kamehameha*, every wall was polished and every light fixture dusted. On this ship, bunches of black and red cables hung from the walls like bunting. Branches from these cables snaked along the ceiling.

"Okay, let's get this ship unloaded," somebody yelled. There was a distinctly informal sound to the way the man gave orders, and I realized just how devoid of military leadership the Confederates must be. With very few notable exceptions, every officer that graduated from the military academies was Earth-born and Earth-loyal. It had always been so.

The only officers the Confederate Arms and Mogats would have were likely book-trained with no battle experience. They had a few notable defectors like Crowley and Halverson, but those officers would be too busy running the battles to work with the rank and file. The men I saw giving orders had not gone to basic training. They had not experienced the way seasoned drill sergeants stalk among enlisted men like a Tyrannosaurus rex in a herd of grass-eaters. The only experience these poseurs might have came from watching movies. Small wonder the Unified Authority won every land battle.

The men on the transport unloaded the crates. They mobbed boxes that were light enough to be lifted and trotted down to the deck, stacking them in marked areas. They were a willing throng, not a workforce.

What I needed above all else was to blend in. By the time I got involved in unloading the transport, the small stuff was off. That left crates filled with heavy equipment, munitions, and the like. A crew of men riding lifters, two-wheeled vehicles with mechanical dollies capable of lifting a five thousand-pound pallet, weaved their way aboard.

I joined the hubbub at the base of the ramp and watched for Colonel Wingate. Now that we were on a GCF ship, Wingate was just a small fish, but he was connected. He would lead me to the men in charge. The pack of men around me thinned and disappeared, and still Wingate did not leave the transport. The men in lifters skittered back and forth up the ramp until their work was done, and still Wingate remained on the ship.

Soon I was alone in the landing bay, hiding near the open transport. I could not remain on the deck much longer without someone spotting me.

Yellow and red lights began flashing around the deck. "Prepare for broadcast," a mechanical voice intoned. "Prepare for broadcast in ten, nine, eight . . ."

I looked at the transport. Wingate had to have boarded this ship. He would not have remained on the planet. It was entirely possible that the commandos killed him and left his body in the woods to cover their tracks, but why go to such lengths? Why send men to Fort Clinton? Why smuggle him off the base? Why not just target his house from space?

"Seven, six, five, four, three . . ."

No need for stealth with that mechanical voice blaring so loudly. The flashing red and yellow lights created visual noise on the deck. The ship would self-broadcast any moment and, of course, images of Admiral Klyber's pale corpse ran through my mind. I had a brief moment of uncertainty, then I sprinted up the ramp and into the dark belly of the transport. The kettle was completely empty. Harnesses hung from the ceiling. In the red light, they looked blacker than darkness. With its ring of hard benches and metal walls dully reflecting the non-glare amber light, the kettle looked like the inside of a kiln.

"Two, one. Broadcast initiated." The voice sounded nearly as loud aboard the transport as it did in the landing bay.

Wingate had to be on this transport. He was not in the kettle. So he had to be up near the cockpit. The mechanical door began to close. Behind me, I heard voices.

". . . complete shutout," somebody said. "They're guessing twenty, maybe twenty-five U.A. ships and as many as five hundred fighters."

"Five hundred?" another voice asked.

"They had four hundred and twenty at Bolivar Air Base," a voice said. I did not see the man speaking, though it was probably Wingate. So the traitor now was standing just outside the cockpit chatting with the pilots, getting a blow-by-blow account of the battle. They headed toward me. By the time Wingate and his friends reached the kettle, I had hid myself in the shadows near the ramp, wrapping myself up in cargo netting along the side of the wall.

"They had a carrier guarding the discs. That was another seventy fighters, so that makes four hundred ninety fighters."

"How many of their ships were carriers?"

"I'd say all of 'em if I had to guess." I could not see him, but I would have waged good money that was Wingate again.

"Broadcast complete," the mechanical voice said over a speaker above the door of the kettle. The rear doors had sealed.

"All fighter carriers carry seventy fighters?"

"They're supposed to. There's a ship in the Scutum-Crux Fleet that has nothing but SEALS and transports." All I could see was the netting around me and the metal walls, but I now thought I knew the sound of Wingate's voice.

Now that the broadcast was complete, the transport could shuttle between ships. I heard the hiss of thruster engines and the whine of the landing gear as tons of weight were lifted from it. I felt the tremble of the ship as the hull lifted off the deck.

"I heard about that one," somebody said. "I heard all of those SEALS are clones. Special clones. Real dangerous." This was a low voice. A hard voice. This was undoubtedly the voice of a commando, probably one of the men that pulled Wingate out of Fort Clinton. I would have happily wagered my life savings that this fellow was some sort of street thug before starting a new career in the military.

"I wouldn't know. That was a Navy project. All of the Rangers and Special Forces men I commanded were natural-born." Wingate sounded irritated and tired. Turning traitor must have taken a toll on him.

The grinding sound of retracting landing equipment echoed through the empty kettle. We were cutting through space. I did not know if we would fly to another ship or land on a planet. Wherever we were, it was deep in Confederate territory.

"So if there were seventy fighters on each of the ships we caught coming out of the Network, and we caught twenty-five of them . . ." He paused to do a little math. "That would mean we got one thousand seven hundred and fifty fighters." There was excitement and pride and intelligence in this voice. It belonged to neither the thug nor Wingate. "Man, I'd hate to be the guy who has to report those losses to the Joint Chiefs."

"And we didn't lose a single ship?" the thug asked.

"Not a one," the intelligent-sounding commando replied.

"How about the planet?" Wingate asked. Apparently the bright commando had access to some kind of report that neither Wingate nor the thug had received.

"I haven't heard anything. You get the best info on stuff like that from the mediaLink anyway. They'll have reporters down on the planet . . . assuming there's any planet left."

The bright commando said this, then he and the thug laughed.

A moment passed and the sound of the thrusters started again. We were coming in for our landing.

Hiding there in the netting, I realized that I was still dressed in camouflage gear and needed a change of clothing. No use taking the bright commando or the thug, they were probably dressed like me, in U.A. Army fatigues. I needed to dress like a crewman, not a soldier. I hung in the netting, silent and still listening to the muffled roar of the thruster engines as the transport prepared to land in some new hangar. Were we touching down on land or a battleship?

The thick metal doors of the kettle split open. I could see a quiet landing pad outside. The area was brightly lit. The ground was paved with black asphalt. There were no boxes or people, and no clues about where we might have landed.

"Well, come on. Atkins and Crowley both asked to see you," the bright commando said. In saying this, he revealed a lot of information. Amos Crowley was the Army general who had defected to the Mogats. Atkins would likely be Warren Atkins, the son of the founder of the Morgan Atkins movement. That would make this a Mogat base or a command ship, I thought.

The doors ground open and white light poured into the red-lit world of our transport. Ducking my head behind a hanging fold of cargo netting, I listened as Wingate, the commando, and the thug tromped down the metal ramp, their shoes clanging against the steel. I caught a brief glimpse of their backs as they reached the end of the ramp. Wingate was short and normal in every regard compared to the tall, athletic-looking men on either side of him.

As soon as they were out of sight and out of hearing range, I wrestled my way out from behind the cargo nets. The netting itself was made of nylon. It hung like a spider's web, suspended from the roof by dozens of little metallic cables. The cables rattled as I worked my way free, causing a soft clatter that would have attracted attention if anyone else was in the kettle. One of the pilots, however, was still in the cockpit. I could see white light spilling out of the open door at the front of the kettle.

Moving slowly, stepping lightly so that my boots made

barely any noise as they touched down on the metal flooring, I stalked across the cabin hiding behind the ribbings in the wall. I got to the door of the cockpit, took a deep breath, and peered in. A lone man sat at the controls speaking into a radio. He had a data pad on his lap. If he was filling out reports, he might be in that seat for hours. He might even finish his report, fire up the engines, and fly off to some new destination.

Life would have been easier had the man sat with his back to me. Instead, he had turned his seat ass backward. Miraculously, he did not spot me.

I had a gun, the M27 that I took from the guy I killed on New Columbia, but that would be loud. I had my knife, but I needed the man's uniform. I also needed him off the damned radio, and quickly, before a maintenance crew happened by.

It didn't happen that way.

The sound of heavy shoes echoed through the kettle. A lone worker in white overalls, the uniform of a civilian mechanic, came walking across the deck. He walked right past me, no more than three feet from my face, as I lay on my side under a disturbingly narrow bench.

"I hear it was some battle," the mechanic said at the cockpit door.

"I only saw it for a second," the pilot answered. "What I saw was wild."

"Did you fly into it?"

I squirmed back as far as I could. My feet connected with the girders that wrapped up and around the kettle——the ribs. Rolling on my stomach for a quick glance, I saw the mechanic standing in the door of the cockpit. A new target, I thought. I could kill him as he left the ship and hide his body in the cargo nets.

Rising silently to my feet, never taking my eyes off the mechanic, I breezed toward the back of the kettle, the cargo nets, and the open doorway. There, I stopped.

Standing at the top of the ramp was a boy who could not yet have been in his twenties. He wore white overalls and a white hard hat. The boy looked strong. The zipper of his jumper was down to his chest. He had a stunned, slightly stupid look on his face as he stared at me. "Do you know where Fred . . . Hey? Who are you?" Never realizing the gravity of his situation, the boy spoke in a soft voice that did not carry.

I slammed the edge of my hand hard across his throat—a slow method of murder but effective in keeping a victim silent: if you crush your victim's windpipes, you render him voiceless. He will then spend a full minute thrashing about as he suffocates, but he cannot call for help.

This boy brought his hands along the bottom of his throat as he struggled for breath. His lips formed a wide, gasping O. I slung him sideways into the heavy cargo netting. The cables rattled as they brushed against the side of the kettle, but the noise was soft. Then, as he tried to wrestle free of the netting, I finished the boy by slamming the heel of my hand into the side of his neck. The whole thing was quick and silent. The sounds of the murder did not disturb the mechanic and pilot as they chatted up at the cockpit.

A moment later, a nearly naked boy lay tucked under a mess of cargo netting. No one would find him for a while, at least not until the next time somebody loaded cargo onto this transport.

CHAPTER
TWENTY-NINE

I had no plan. Here I was, on an enemy ship, probably in the center of the enemy fleet, and I was not sure what to do next. I did not make it off the transport in time to tail Wingate. I did not have a prayer of sabotaging the fleet, or even this ship. Escape seemed out of the question. My best bet would be to find a way onto the bridge of the ship and learn the fleet's galactic coordinates. If I could locate that information and broadcast it to Huang, the U.A. Navy could come after the bastards. After what I saw on New Columbia, I liked the idea of U.A. ships having a fair fight.

Looking around the landing area, I stared into the ivory horizon where the runway met the walls. Cavernous and square, this hangar was designed for transports and cargo ships, not fighters. With the exception of Harriers, which had a vertical take off, fighters took off in runway tubes, allowing them to build up speed before entering battles.

The overalls were a bad fit. Either the kid I took them from had been less than six feet tall or he liked wearing pants that showed his ankles and sleeves that did not cover his wrists. And his clothes were baggy. I did not expect a tailored fit, still they had looked snug on the boy's muscled body. With my tall and lanky frame, I vanished under the wide swath of cloth.

The worst thing was the boots. A swampy, phosphorous stench rose out of them, and they were hot and moist around my feet. Given the choice, I would have preferred to go barefoot.

I found a pair of mediaLink shades inside one of the waist-line pockets. The lenses were greasy and dusted with dandruff. I checked the three small pores at the base of each of the eyepieces to make sure that the microphones were clear. The pores were mostly clean and I blew off the hairs and dandruff.

When I reached the door of the hangar I stopped to look back. There sat the transport, alone in the center of the brightly lit landing pad. The world around the transport was ivory white. In that bright lighting, the transport was the color of eggshells. It almost blended with its surroundings; but because it did not quite blend in, it stood out even more.

What about Fred the chatty mechanic and his friend the pilot? Would they discover the little surprise I had wrapped up in the cargo bay? They might, but that could not be helped. Sooner or later, somebody would spot the body no matter where I hid it.

The hall outside the hangar seemed to stretch the entire length of the ship. The polished gray floor went on as far as the eye could see. This was a major corridor, a squared tube with twenty-foot walls. Clumps of people moved through it, but it was far from crowded. Compared to the bustling walk-ways of most U.A. ships, this corridor was deserted.

Enough time had passed since Wingate left the transport that I had not a prayer of catching up to him. In my mind, Wingate had become a low priority at this point. He had led me to the enemy fleet. But even capturing Crowley and Atkins seemed unimportant at the moment. What would I do with them this deep in enemy territory?

All I could do was go along for the ride. My first priori-ties now were to blend in and to find my way around this ship.

Navy crews had a practice called "hot bunking." It meant that three men slept in the same rack—obviously not at the same time. They had eight-hour shifts—work eight hours, recreate eight hours, sleep eight hours. That meant that at any time, one-third of the crew would work while one-third slept and another third ate and played. The thirds were not always equal. The day crew, meaning the crew on duty when the captain was on duty, was generally larger than the others.

Hot bunking caused problems for saboteurs like myself because it meant that the ship never slept. There would always be men at the helm and in the engine rooms. So what could I accomplish? I toyed with the idea of slipping a cable into the broadcast engines, but I did not feel like committing suicide.

Feeling like I needed a better disguise than these coveralls, I followed the hall toward the center of the ship. Old as this ship was, it was still of a Unified Authority design. The basics were the basics. I knew that the landing bay would be on the bottom deck and that I would have to go to another deck to find what I wanted—a gym. Fifteen minutes and two decks later, I found one.

I began unzipping my jumper even before I entered the locker room, and had it off my shoulders by the time the door closed behind me. Training did not appeal to these sailors by the look of things. The locker room was nearly empty. I heard someone in the shower and a couple of men with towels around their waists discussed the battle at New Columbia in front of the mirrors.

Both men were Japanese. I noticed that quickly. They had black hair, narrow eyes, and bronzed skin. One man stole a casual glance in my direction while his friend spoke. Had this gym been for Japanese only, I might have been caught. But a moment later, a blubbery man with white skin turned the color of rare roast beef stepped out of a steam room. The man did not have a towel. Drops of water splashed from his flabby legs as he walked.

I grabbed shorts and a shirt from a shelf and tossed my coveralls into a locker. A moment later, I walked out to exercise, the mediaLink shades hidden in my pocket. And things continued to go my way. There was only one other person working out. He did not look at me as I climbed on a stationary bike, dropped the shades over my eyes, and began pedaling.

Now that I had changed to exercise clothes, I blended in. What I needed to do next was contact Huang or Freeman;

but with another person in the room, I did not want to hold a conversation.

In this case, I went the old-fashioned route and composed letters, customizing a form letter by choosing words and phrases from a menu and optically typing words when needed.

On my own shades, I had a menu of people I contacted on a regular basis. It was a short list that included only the late Bryce Klyber and Ray Freeman. The boy's shades had a different list. Using optical commands, I typed Freeman's address on a virtual keyboard that was always present at the edge of your vision when you composed letters.

Freeman and I swapped emergency codes so that we would always be able to locate each other in situations like this. There may have been multiple Ray Freemans in the galaxy, but he was the only one who received messages sent with this code.

Optical typing was a slow process. When I switched from the keyboard to the context-sensitive letter, it was a relief. I selected an urgent document. The default letter that appeared was a request for financial assistance; but every word was interactive and as I changed words at the front of the letter, the rest of the document composed itself.

Ray,
I have stowed away on a GCF ship. I believe Warren
Atkins and Amos Crowley are on this ship. Contact
Huang and let him know that I will transmit the loca-
tion of this ship as soon as I have it. I will call when
it is safe.

Harris

I mailed the letter. When I removed the shades, I discovered that a new crop of people had entered the gym. Four men stood in the weight lifting area, joshing with each other as they pushed levers and pulled handles. Their weights clanked loudly as they lowered them. I climbed off of the bicycle.

"Buddy, you mind tossing me a towel?" one of the men called.

"Sure," I said. I picked up a gym towel and tossed it to him. He snatched it out of the air and turned back to his weights without thanking me.

I went back to the locker room and stripped for a shower. The goal now was to remain inconspicuous as I killed time and waited for the right change of clothing. I needed something I could wear on the upper decks without attracting attention. So I went in the shower room and soaped and showered, peering out whenever I heard people entering or leaving the locker room. More than an hour passed before the man I was waiting for arrived, and I counted myself lucky that he had come so soon.

I heard the door close and rinsed myself off. When I looked out of the shower, I saw a crewman walking around the floor picking up a few sopping towels that had been discarded and tossing them into the laundry cart.

Drying myself off as quickly as possible, I listened as he emptied bins filled with dirty gym clothes into his cart. As he left, I pulled on a fresh pair of gym shorts and a T-shirt.

Stepping out into the corridor, I saw the crewman moving away slowly. He stood hunched over the laundry cart, his head turning to follow everyone he passed. He turned down one hall and then another before reaching his final destination.

Capital ships had more than one laundry facility. Chances were, there was a special facility on the upper decks just for cleaning officers' uniforms; but this laundry would do.

I approached and the door slid open.

"What do you want?" the crewman asked as I stepped into the room.

"My clothes," I said, doing an impersonation of a peeved officer. "You hauled off my uniform in one of your laundry carts."

"Sorry," the man said in a flat voice. He went back to sorting dirty clothes and did not look back in my direction. Such insubordination. I was an officer. He was an enlisted man. Okay, I was a spy pretending to be an officer, but he didn't know that.

I had at least thirty carts to choose from. In the third cart, I found an officer's work uniform.

CHAPTER
THIRTY

I went to the emptiest room on any battleship—the chapel. There I could speak freely.

"Who is Derrick Hines?" Freeman's face appeared on my MediaLink shades.

"Never heard of him," I said.

"You're using his Link address," Freeman said.

"Oh, him," I said. "He was a crewman on a GCF ship."

"Confederate or Mogat—?" Freeman asked. He had no interest in Hines's fate.

Freeman was on a communications console. I could see his face. It was as impassive as ever. Judging by his non-plussed expression, you might have thought that I had called from a bar in Mars Spaceport.

"No idea," I said. "I think it's their flagship."

"How did you get on?" Freeman asked.

"I followed Colonel Wingate, the commander of Fort Clinton."

"That was the Army base that got destroyed on New Columbia," Freeman said. "What's he doing on a GCF ship?"

"He swapped sides," I said. "Turns out he was using Fort Clinton as a surplus outlet and the Mogats were his favorite customers. Think he's worth much?"

As I thought about it, I had plenty of reasons to hate Batt Wingate. He would have sold me out without a second thought when I was regular military. He'd certainly sold out enough other clones. He must have helped William Patel smuggle bombs into Safe Harbor. Did he know that I would be there or was he just after Jimmy Callahan? I would gladly kill the man myself if I got a chance.

"He's worth something," Freeman said. "The Mogats routed the Navy at New Columbia. They shot down twenty-three U.A. ships and destroyed all three military bases. The pundits are saying that Washington is desperate.

"Have you got a location on the Fleet?"

"No," I said.

Freeman waited for me to say more.

"Ray, this is too big for us. We're going to need to bring Huang in on it. Keep this channel open. I don't know how I'm going to do it yet, but I will get you a location. Once I have something, you're going to have to turn it over to Huang."

He agreed.

"Where are you now?" I asked.

"I was on my way to Little Man."

"Your family okay?" I asked.

"A carrier buzzed them last night. I think it scared them. They're colonists. Having the Navy around makes them nervous."

"Did anything happen?" I asked.

"The captain gave them one month to evacuate the planet. They'll still be there when this is over with." For some reason, I got the feeling that he was not anxious to visit Little Man. Until recently, he never even mentioned his family. Now, when he talked about them, he did not seem to exude warm feelings.

We agreed to meet in Safe Harbor once I got off this ship. Freeman would go and see what happened to Callahan and the commandant at Fort Washington. One way or another, I thought I could bring in Batt Wingate, and we would need witnesses to prove he was our Benedict Arnold.

My new uniform made me a lieutenant in the Confederate Navy. Now that I was an officer, I moved around the ship more freely. I walked the halls and looked for clues.

The first thing that struck me was the sheer emptiness of the ship. U.A. ships were crowded with personnel. Engineers, weapons officers, cooks, communications officers . . . wherever you looked, you saw sailors. Command ships seemed doubly crowded because, along with the crew, they had fleet officers and administrative flunkies.

This ship had a skeleton crew, maybe a half-crew. I walked down major arteries between engineering and weapons systems passing only an occasional sailor.

The ship itself was clean, brightly lit, and remarkably unorganized. The cables that I saw lining the walls down in the landing bay also snaked along the halls on the upper decks. They were about three inches in diameter and highly insulated, which led me to believe that they might carry a high-voltage electrical charge. The ceilings in this part of the ship were only eight feet tall, and the cables hung one foot lower than that. At one point, thinking I was alone in a long hall, I stopped to examine them. The outside covering of these cables was black with maroon strips.

"Is there a problem with the cables, Sir?" somebody asked behind my back.

I whirled around expecting to see an MP. It was a petty officer—a maintenance technician. I recognized the crossed hammers insignia on his blouse. It was the same insignia that the U.A. Navy used. This man did not suspect me of being a spy. He was worried about my spotting a flaw in the way that the cables were hung.

"Looks sound," I said.

He saluted, but he had a curious, maybe even slightly nervous look on his face. "Sir," he said, looking as if he was not sure he should continue. I thought I knew what he would say and I was ready.

"Yes?"

Now lowering his voice to a whisper, he leaned forward and said, "You forgot your bars." As he said this, he pinched the right side of his collar between his thumb and forefinger and shook it.

That was not what I expected. I pretended to be confused. Seeing that there were no bars on my collar, I acted surprised and embarrassed. "Thank you. I can't believe I missed that,"

I said with an expression that I hoped looked like a nervous grin. The petty officer saluted and left.

Of course there were no bars pinned to my collar, I had liberated this blouse from laundry. No officer worth his spit would leave his bars or clusters on the collar of a blouse that was headed for a cleaning.

My first discovery was that this ship was a battleship. I found that out when I passed a directory on the top deck. The directory showed the ship's seven decks plus a picture of the ship from the outside. A ship of this size should have had a 2,500-man crew. Now, having walked its length on every deck, I guessed the crew at no more than 800. Maybe one-tenth of the crew was Japanese. The engineering area was almost all Japanese.

The Japanese officers made no attempt to fit in with the other sailors that I saw. Most of the men on this battleship wore tan-colored uniforms. The Japanese uniforms were dark blue. Still, Japanese officers spoke English whether talking to other officers or just among themselves.

The closer I came to the command deck, the more this ship looked Japanese. Not far from the directory, on the command deck, stood an archway made of two posts topped by two beams. Under the arch was a shrine or display with three long swords stretched across a three-tiered pedestal. Since the officers I saw walk past this shrine did not stop to bow or pray to it, I decided the display had more to do with heritage than religion.

I continued toward the bridge, passing through officer country and the maze of cubicles and offices that occupies the top deck of almost any naval ship. Here I walked with a businesslike stride, acting as if I had an important meeting to attend. On a U.A. Navy ship, someone would have noticed the missing bars. I would have been stopped and questioned. On this ship, few people noticed how I dressed.

I turned a corner and saw the entry to the bridge. Taking a deep breath to steel myself, I walked to the door. The bridge was spacious and dark. Teams of sailors gathered around various consoles and workstations.

Everyone in the room was Japanese. In the dimmed light, their royal blue uniforms were black as shadows, even in the low glow from the workstations. Looking around the floor,

I estimated that there were at least fifty officers sitting at the various stations.

In the center of the bridge sat a large square table which the captain and his senior officers used to chart courses and consider battle strategies.

There was nothing else to do. I stepped onto the bridge and walked its breadth. The workstations were arranged in concentric circles. Walking quickly without a pause, I recognized each station. The computers in the weapons area, which were unmanned at that moment, had large displays showing the diagram of the battleship with its gun and cannon arrays highlighted. The engineering station had computers showing detailed maps of each deck. I would have loved to have parked myself beside one of those computers to discover its many secrets, but three men sat at that station. The white glow of the readout display flickered on their faces.

Three men sat in front of one elongated screen in the navigation section. Their screen had a map of the galaxy along the top but most of the screen was filled with the local star system. I did not recognize the system. The last area I passed as I lapped the outer circle of the bridge was communications. Voices came from a station for monitoring fleet communications. During battle, this station would be the nerve center for the fleet. Now, after the battle, transmissions between ships went unobserved.

BATTLE GROUP SIX ABLE, THIS IS BATTLESHIP SEVEN ABLE, OVER.

COME IN BATTLESHIP SEVEN ABLE. THIS IS BATTLE SIX ABLE COMMAND.

WE ARE BREAKING FORMATION. DO YOU COPY?

WHAT SEEMS TO BE THE PROBLEM SEVEN ABLE?

This particular station was more cluttered than the worst workstation in the Golan traffic tower. A stack of data pads had toppled, spreading across the desk. Pencils, pens, papers, coffee cups, and other bric-a-brac lay all around those pads. There were four cups of coffee along the edge of that particular desk along with a brick-sized box of audio chips. In the center of this mess was a large ashtray filled to capacity with cigarette ash and butts. The line of drawers along the left side of the station hung partially open. The drawers, like everything else at this station, overflowed with junk.

I passed by the station without slowing, completed my lap of the bridge and left. Not far from the bridge, I found a bathroom. A couple of men stood by the urinals; so I entered a stall and waited until they left, then I contacted Freeman.

"Okay," I spoke quickly, but in a whisper, "this is a battleship. I have no idea where we are. I am going to leave this line open. Tell Huang to have his Intel section listen in."

Freeman nodded. He did not bother telling me to "be careful" or to "watch my back." That was not his way. He stared into the console intense and humorless as ever. His eyes reminded me of a double-barreled shotgun as they stared out from that mahogany skull. He was the most dangerous man in the galaxy, and I had absolutely no doubt that I could rely on him. His very being communicated undeniable competence.

Removing the shades, I stepped out of the bathroom stall and returned to the bridge. I took another stroll on the bridge, slowing to glance at the various workstations as I passed them. I wished I could examine the strategic charts. Huang would have paid one billion dollars for the secrets that they held. But I had something even more valuable . . . the fleet itself.

As before, nobody paid any attention to me. I approached the communications area and looked over my shoulder to be sure that no was watching. I never stopped, but I slowed down as I left a little extra mess on the already cluttered workstation. A moment later, I left the command deck and never returned.

CHAPTER
THIRTY-ONE

I was alone on the command ship of the enemy fleet. I had no idea about the fleet's position. Escape was out of the question. We must have been light years from the nearest broadcast station. At this point, I had no means of communicating with Freeman or Huang or anyone else who could help me. I could, of course, steal another set of shades; but I did not know how long I would be on this scow, and I could not afford to take any more chances.

My best bet, I decided, was to return to the landing bay, a relatively empty part of the ship. There I would stow away on the next transport that came through. Sooner or later this fleet would attack another target. If I managed to dig in with the right group of commandos, I might have a way out.

I returned to the gym. The place was as dead as before. A couple of enlisted men stood in the locker room chatting as they put on their uniforms. Neither man paid much attention as I grabbed shorts and a T-shirt and started undressing. A moment later they left and I went to the lockers.

The coveralls were still in the locker where I placed them. Weeks might have passed before somebody discovered them in a forsaken gym like this one. I pulled them from the locker, stepped into the pants legs, and zipped them up. I did not bother with socks before stepping into my foul-smelling boots. If the worst I got out of this brush with the GC Fleet was foot fungus, I would consider myself lucky.

Still noticing just how bad the clothes smelled, I started down to the landing bay. The smell was strong and the clothes felt damp against my skin. I did not know how long I would be stuck in these clothes. How had I missed this smell before?

And something else . . . I realized that I was hungry. The last time I had eaten was when I grabbed a sandwich on the Marine base on New Columbia. That seemed like a long time ago until I did the math. It had only been a few hours ago.

I took a lift down one deck. As I made my way down the corridor, I passed an electrician working on a wall panel. He had removed the faceplate from the panel and now probed the circuits with a pen-shaped tool. As I walked by, he stopped to look over at me. Our eyes met for a moment, and I nodded and moved on. The man did not return my greeting, but he continued to watch me. Perhaps I was paranoid. I looked back as I meandered down the hall. The electrician remained where he was, standing on a foot-tall step ladder, probing around that open panel.

Traveling down the next two decks, I passed almost no one. Perhaps a shift had ended and a smaller crew had replaced it. Maybe it was lunchtime and most of the sailors were eating.

That last corridor that led to the launch bay was entirely empty. The thud of my boots created an indistinct echo as I walked through that brightly-lit stretch. Everything was going so smoothly, I had no doubt that I would slip off the ship soon.

The next time I saw people was as I drew near the landing bay. Two men walked silently down an intersecting corridor. They wore the khaki uniforms of regular officers rather than the blue uniforms of the Japanese, and they fell in quietly behind me as I continued toward the bay. I expected them to turn into some door or another, but they did not. They continued straight ahead, walking at the same pace as me.

I thought about turning into the next door or hall that I passed, but there were no more doors until the ones leading into the bay. I pretended to be unaware of the men. I did not look back and I did not slow down. Neither did the men behind me.

With no other choice, I entered the landing area. A lone transport sat in the middle of the hangar, its hatch hung open. A small crowd stood on the ramp leading into the kettle. I counted three medics and six MPs, and in the center of them, placed on the bare metal ramp like a cadaver on a mortuary slab, lay Derrick Hines, stripped down to his briefs.

The muzzle of a gun jabbed into my back and a voice said, "How do you like that, boys, we have our first prisoner."

If there was one kind of naval design that did not change with the times, it was brig. I once ran security for the *Doctrinaire*, the most advanced ship ever made. I knew every cell in its brig thoroughly, and they were exactly like the cells in this ancient ship . . . the one in which I was now a prisoner. Both brigs had the same kinds of bars on their walls and the same limp mats on their cots. I did not have the means to measure my floor, but if I did, it would have measured precisely eight feet by twelve feet. I knew that because that was the size of the cells on the *Doctrinaire*.

I lay on my cot staring up at the charcoal-gray ceiling. For a change of scenery, I sometimes turned to look at the charcoal-gray walls. These cells were the ultimate in ease when it came to housekeeping. You simply pulled the mattress out and sprayed everything down with a steam hose. The floor was a grating that led to a drain.

Mercifully, they had stripped me down to my briefs before throwing me in the cell. Those coveralls reeked. From what I could tell, the late Derrick Hines hadn't washed them for weeks. I might have been a bit cold in this cell, but at least I could breathe.

Had the brig been darker, I might have slept. The lights in the hall were too bright.

I think I knew why Liberators got addicted to violence, we became morose when we just laid around. I thought about the diary from Saint Germaine in which that priest and Tabor Shannon argued about whether or not Liberators had souls. I bought into both arguments and decided that perhaps we had worthless souls. I thought about Freeman. Had he arrived in

Safe Harbor yet? I wondered about his family on Little Man. What would the Navy do?

Forced to guess how long I had been in this cell, I might have said three hours. It could have been longer. It could have been shorter. With no sun coming up and no events by which to gauge time, my internal clock was all but useless.

Footsteps echoed down the hall as the men came to look in my cell. My jailors looked in on me through the bars. Both men wore khaki uniforms. One was a tall man with blond hair, the other had dark brown locks.

"Hello, Harris," the blond man said.

I glanced in their direction. I remained flat on my back on the cot. I wanted to test them. I was their first prisoner. Would they know how to treat me and how to control me, or would they make mistakes? If they were naïve enough, I could end up in charge even though I was the one behind the bars.

"Comfortable, Harris?" the blond man asked.

"Hope you didn't go to too much trouble getting my name," I said. " I would have told you if you had asked."

"Really? I always heard that Liberator clones were tougher than that," the blond man said. "You knew you were a clone, right? I mean, I would hate for you to have one of those death reflex things and keel over right here."

"Don't worry about it," I said.

"So you're a Liberator. I always thought your kind would be bigger. I mean, aren't you guys the planet exterminators?"

I looked toward the man. "You must be a Mogat," I said in as dismissive a voice as I could muster.

"The term is Morgan Atkins Believer. I suggest you remember that, Harris, or your stay here could become real unpleasant." The humor never left his face, but his voice turned serious.

Now that I stopped to look, I saw that this was not a man to take lightly. He had a broad and powerful build. His bull neck was almost as wide as his jaw, making it look like he had a pointed head. The muscles in his shoulders bulged, but this was not the beautiful physique of a bodybuilder. This man had padding around his gut.

"Learn anything else?" I asked.

The second man outside my cell, a short chubby man with

the brown hair, stepped forward with a data pad and answered. "Harris, Wayson, Colonel, Unified Authority Marines. Raised: U.A. Orphanage # five hundred fifty-three. Year of Manufacture: 2490. Clone Class: Liberator.

"How does a clone, especially a Liberator Clone, achieve the rank of colonel?" the dark-haired man asked.

"You want to know how I became a colonel?" I asked.

"I want to know why you exist at all," the man said. "How did you find your way on this ship?"

"Do you want the full story or the abbreviated version?" With this I sat up.

"Let's stick with the short one for now," the man with the data pad said.

"I caught a ride on your transport when it left New Columbia."

The blond-haired man, clearly my jailor, smiled and gave me a vigorous nod. "Know what Harris, I believe you. An honest clone, no less."

"May I ask a question?"

"Go ahead," the man with the data pad said. The jailor scowled at him.

"Is this ship part of the Hinode Fleet, or part of the Confederate Navy, or part of the Galactic Central Fleet?"

"None of your business," the man with the blond hair said.

"Confederate Navy," the man with the dark hair said. The bigger man, the jailor, scowled at him.

"It depends who you ask, I suppose," the blond man continued to glare down at him.

"So what is the Hinode Fleet?"

"Another name for the same bunch of ships," the smaller man said.

"Do you have more than one fleet?" I asked.

"No," the man admitted.

"Shut up," the jailor snapped.

"He's in jail, Sam, and he's down to his skivvies. How is he going to tell anyone?" Then the man seemed to think twice about this before adding, "We will ask the questions from here on out, Harris. We have not decided what to do with you yet. I suggest you conduct yourself properly. Execution is not out of the question."

They left me in my cell with nothing to do and no way of knowing how much time passed. I laid on the cot in my underwear staring at the ceiling and tried to piece together all of the little fragments of information I had collected. It seemed like the separatists had a genuine Power Struggle on their hands. They had an alliance, but all three sides were claiming the Navy for themselves.

Why did the Japanese officers wear different uniforms than the other men? Did the Mogats consider themselves part of the Confederate Arms? Did the Japanese? My thoughts drifted and I fell asleep.

CHAPTER THIRTY-TWO

"I knew it was you the moment I heard they had a prisoner." "Smiling" Tom Halverson, my nickname for him, stood outside my cell looking dapper in his dress whites, with the three gold stripes of a full admiral on his shoulder boards. He'd cut his graying hair into a flattop, but otherwise he looked no different than the first time I saw him, on the bridge of the *Doctrinaire*. "Hello, Harris."

"Get specked," I said.

"Watch yourself, clone." Sam, my blond-haired jailor, warned me. Whenever people visited me, Sam accompanied them.

"That's all right, Sergeant. Colonel Harris and I are old acquaintances," Halverson said. "Is that why you're here, Harris? Did you come for me?"

I did not respond.

"No comment, Harris? That doesn't sound good."

"The admiral asked you a question," Sam said in his most menacing voice.

"That's all right, Sergeant," Halverson said.

"You know, Harris, you really are amazing. The rest of them can't even locate our ships and you turn up on one of them. It's a good thing the Unified Authority doesn't have one hundred more of you. Of course if they want to win the war they can make more of you. But then, I get the feeling that all you want is a little revenge."

"Why did you kill him?" I asked, propping myself up to look at Halverson. "You and Klyber were friends."

"I should have thought that was obvious, Harris. He's with the Unified Authority. I defected to the Confederate Arms. We were on different sides."

"Get specked," I said, slumping over on my back.

"I brought you a present, Harris."

I did not respond.

"You can break these if you want, but I went to a lot of trouble to get them for you, so don't expect me to replace them if you do." He tossed a pair of mediaLink shades in through the bars.

"Bryce said you liked to keep up with current events. There should be some dandy news for you to follow over the next few weeks.

"And don't bother trying to send messages out on those. I had the sending gear disabled." With this, Halverson turned and left.

"You were stupid," I yelled as he reached the door to the brig. "Killing Admiral Klyber was a stupid mistake."

Halverson paused. "Why is that, Colonel?" he asked.

"Huang already planned to replace him with . . ."

"With Robert Thurston, no doubt," Halverson said. He watched me for a moment with that implacable smile, and then he left.

Sam, who remained just outside the bars of my cell, continued to stare at me with those narrow green eyes that looked both alert and angry. Sometimes he looked like he could barely control himself. "If you break the lenses, they'd make real sharp blades. You might be able to save us some trouble and slit your own throat with 'em," he said. "I'd like that." Then he favored me with his backside, leaving me to pick up the shades.

I picked them up and turned them over in my hands to examine them from every angle. This was an expensive pair, far more stylish than the plastic shades I took from the late

Derrick Hines. These shades had gold wire frames and honest-to-goodness glass lenses that automatically adjusted to ambient light levels.

The strip along the bottom of the lenses with the microphones had been removed. When I slipped the shades over my eyes and jacked in, I saw they had been hobbled so that the sending functions no longer worked. The browsing functions worked well however.

We were somewhere in the Norma Arm. Not only could I browse the Unified Authority-approved channels, I also found local broadcasts that were banned and filtered out of the U.A. media. Calendars were everywhere on the Link, and I knew that it was now March 26. Eleven days had passed since Bryce Klyber's death. Thirty-six hours had passed since the attack on New Columbia. It was here that I watched the video feeds of the attack on New Columbia. I got to see how both sides reported the battle.

The big story on the U.A. feeds was the unveiling of the *Doctrinaire*. Admiral Huang, now officially the highest-ranking man in the Navy after Klyber's death, could not have been any better suited for the role of tour guide. He began his tours by telling the press how the late Fleet Admiral Klyber conceived the project and spearheaded the construction of the ship.

Huang escorted a large group of reporters on a tour of the *Doctrinaire*. He charmed them with his enthusiasm as he led them into battle turret after battle turret, then showed them the observation deck from which they could view the rest of the ship.

Huang did not reveal classified secrets like the dual broadcast generators, but he highlighted many of the obvious innovations. No reporter could possibly have missed the four launch tubes that ran the length of the hull of the *Doctrinaire*, so Huang talked about the fighter squadrons at length. He pointed out that most fighter carriers had a single tube and a compliment of seventy Tomcat fighters. The *Doctrinaire*, with its four tubes, had 280 fighters. With their rounded antennas' the new shield technology was impossible to miss; so Huang told the reporters about the rounded shields and gave a cursory explanation about the technology that made them possible.

As Huang finished speaking, he was joined by the other Joint Chiefs and several senators. Hundreds of reporters sat in folding chairs, the way they might have attended the unveiling of the old Earth-bound battleships five hundred years earlier. They would have fit more comfortably in one of the ship's briefing auditoriums than on the observation deck, but Huang saw a great photo opportunity and had the media sense to take advantage of it.

This was a side of Huang that I had never known about. He stood behind a small podium looking absolutely resplendent in his white uniform with its many medals. He and Halverson had the same number of gold stripes across their shoulder boards—three, but Huang cut a more commanding figure with the gray in his hair and his athletic build. Huang and Halverson were about the same age, but Huang wore it better. Huang looked like a middle-aged man. Halverson looked like a man closing in on his sixties.

Smiling pleasantly, Huang opened the floor for questions, and every hand shot up. Reporters clambered for his attention until he finally selected a man near the front of the audience.

"This is unquestionably an amazing ship. But it is still just one ship. How can it possibly fare against an attack force like the sixty-five ships that sacked New Columbia?"

"Excellent question," Huang said. "We have arranged a demonstration to address that very point. If you are not satisfied after our demonstration, we can discuss it further."

Every reporter's hand went up again. Huang selected a woman from the front row. "Can a ship this size self-broadcast reliably?"

"I think Admiral Klyber struggled a long time with that question," Huang said. "The engines on this ship are perfectly reliable. We have tested them thoroughly . . ."

"Didn't Admiral Klyber die in a broadcast malfunction?" the reporter followed up her own question.

"An unfortunate irony, if you like," said Huang. "The broadcast equipment in this ship is completely stable."

The reporters raised their hands. Huang selected his next inquisitor.

"Admiral Klyber was going to command this ship, was he not? Who will command it in his place?"

"Admiral Klyber never intended to command this ship. He was a fleet admiral, you know. You don't assign a fleet admiral to a single ship. Rear Admiral Robert Thurston was selected to command the *Doctrinaire* while Klyber commanded the entire fleet."

"Rear Admiral Thurston?" the reporter asked quickly, before Huang could open the floor for the next question. "The commander of the Scutum-Crux Fleet?"

"Yes," said Huang. "As you may recall, he commanded our forces to victory at Hubble and Little Man."

Thurston stepped onto the dais in his whites. A few of the less experienced reporters, the ones who had never seen Thurston, laughed or gasped at his youthful appearance. Short and skinny, with spiky red hair and an adolescent's face, Robert Thurston always looked out of place in his uniform, especially standing next to a seasoned officer like Huang. The senators at the back of the dais looked like they could have been Thurston's grandparents.

The questions continued for ten more minutes. The session would have gone on for hours had Huang allowed it, but he had promised a final demonstration.

"Ladies and gentlemen, I suggest you prepare yourselves. We are about to enter a war zone," said Huang.

Smoky-colored tinting appeared in the glass ceiling and walls of the observation deck turning them opaque. The reporters spoke nervously among themselves as they saw the muted flashes of lightning all around them. It was one thing to sit in some comfortable commuter craft and pass through the Broadcast Network. This was raw. Here they sat on folding chairs on the glass-encased deck of a monolithic battleship while millions of volts of electricity danced on the glass just above their heads.

When the lightning stopped and the tinting cleared, the *Doctrinaire* was in a battle zone. Looking around the crown of the observation deck, you could see dozens of ships buzzing around it.

"Ladies and gentlemen, welcome to the Cygnus Arm. In case it has slipped your attention, this is one of the Confederate Arms. We are forty thousand light years deep in enemy territory.

"What you see flying outside our shields are twenty-five

ships from what we in the Navy call the 'mothball fleet.'
These are vintage ships. These are battleships from 2488
and newer. They are fully functional, space-worthy ships.
They were perfectly preserved for just such an occasion as
this.

"Who is flying them?" a reporter called out.

"Not to worry," Huang said, "they are not being manned
by live crews."

Knowing Huang and his disdain for synthetic life, it would
not have surprised me to learn that those ships had all-clone
crews. But even the cost of raising clones comes out of the
budget, so Huang most likely controlled these ships using remotely controlled computers.

Zipping around, weaving in and out and around each
other, the old battleships circled around the *Doctrinaire*
from two miles off.

"Before we begin our actual battle," Huang said, "you
should know that the ships around us are using live ammunition. Rear Admiral Thurston, would you direct one of those
battleships to attack?"

One of the battleships charged straight at the *Doctrinaire*
and fired. It shot a brilliant burst of bright red laser fire followed by three torpedoes. I could not believe what I saw.
This was a full-on assault. A lethal attack. The translucent
shields turned milky white where the beam hit. The laser
beam was round and red and as thick around as a tree stump,
but it stopped dead at the shields. Moments later, the three
torpedoes slammed into the shields and burst into puddles of
light that dissolved quickly in the vacuum of space.

Most of the reporters gasped and a few screamed.

"As I stated before, the attacking ships are decommis-
sioned U.A. Navy ships. We stopped using these fifteen
years ago because their technology was obsolete, surpassed
by technologies which are now also considered obsolete.
These ships were made twenty years after the ships currently
used by the Confederate Arms," said Huang.

Huang now pulled an old-fashioned analog pocket watch
from the podium. He held it up for the reporters to see. "Let
the battle begin," he said.

"Admiral Klyber spared nothing when he designed this
ship," Huang said. "He wanted to make the ship that would

end the war . . . a ship that would terrify enemies into abandoning their Revolution."

Above Huang's head, the vacuum of space looked like a thunderstorm. Hundreds of torpedoes pecked at the shields from every angle. They burst and vanished leaving no trace. Laser beams slammed into the canopy creating a crimson light show.

"I think it's time we teach these marauders a lesson," Huang said, tensing his thumb over the timer button on the pocket watch. "Admiral Thurston, return fire." The watch bobbed up and down as he clicked the timer.

Laser bursts fired from the side of the *Doctrinaire*. I had never seen these cannons tested, so I did not know what to expect. The battleships continued to fire lasers and torpedoes at the *Doctrinaire*, but nothing penetrated the shields. Seeing these fireworks reminded me of watching a light rain fall through a see-though umbrella.

The cannons on the *Doctrinaire* fired measured bursts. The cannon fire made a sizzling sound that lasted one-half of a second at most. *Dzzzz. Dzzzz.* You could see it launch if you happened to look at the right cannon just as it fired. The laser looked like a solid red rod that issued from the cannon and vanished.

The bursts traveled at the speed of light. The time that it took for the laser bursts to pass through the shields was so short that they could not be measured by any instrument. Out in the blackness that engulfed the observation deck, "enemy" ships exploded.

Lasers from the *Doctrinaire* penetrated the hulls of the attacking ships as if they had no shields. There would be a flash. A ball of fire and smoke would flush out of the injured ship precisely where the laser hit. Everything burst from the laser wound, then the injured ships went dark. They were not crushed. They simply coughed out everything inside them as if all of their innards had been sucked out by space itself.

The computer-controlled targeting system on the *Doctrinaire* wasted few shots. Lasers burst in all directions. Many of the ships in the attacking fleet were hit two and three times. *Dzzzzz*, and they burst and died. *Dzzzz. Dzzzz*, and the crumbled carcasses turned red and somersaulted in space. The lasers might melt the surface of the ships, but the absolute cold of space quenched the damage.

Soon there was so much debris floating around the *Doctrinaire* that it looked like the ship had entered an asteroid belt.

The last of the attacking ships nearly disintegrated in the laser fire from multiple cannons. The ship continued to glide toward the shields. Huang stopped the time with a flourish, making sure that the reporters knew that the battle had ended. He looked at his watch and smiled. "Two minutes and twenty-three seconds. Not quite the time I hoped for, but not far off pace."

Putting the watch back on the podium, Huang looked up at the derelict battleship that now hurtled toward the *Doctrinaire*. "This is a lucky break. Robert, let that ship fly into our shields," he said.

The battleship tumbled into the shields and stopped instantly. The collision reminded me of a small bird slamming into a windowpane. The shields held that battered hull in place, infusing it with an electrical charge. After a few moments, the charge repulsed the dead ship and it floated away from the *Doctrinaire*.

"The enemy is using the Galactic Central Fleet, a fleet of U.A. Navy ships that vanished more than forty years ago. It is an incomplete fleet. It has no fighter craft. A fleet without fighters, gentlemen, is like a boxer without a jab. In order to strike, the enemy will be forced to use battleships, and battleships, ladies and gentlemen, big and slow ships that are hard to maneuver, make great targets . . . great targets.

"The Confederate Navy is perfect for bushwhacking helpless carriers as they emerge from the Broadcast Network. It will be useless against a giant ship that hits the deck running."

As I watched this first active demonstration of the *Doctrinaire*, I began to wonder why no one had bothered questioning me about the ship. Perhaps with traitors like Crowley and Halverson, they knew more than I did. Admiral Halverson, until recently the second-in-command on the *Doctrinaire*, probably knew all about the dual broadcast generators and the rounded shields. He knew everything I knew, plus he knew about the powerful new cannons that could destroy GCF ships with a single shot—something I had not been briefed about.

Halverson assumed I had come to avenge Bryce Klyber. Since I had no means of transmitting information when I was captured, nobody worried about what I might have learned. In their minds, I was an assassin, not a spy.

I lay on my cot thinking about the demonstration I had just seen. What would Warren Atkins make of it? What would Amos Crowley, the general-turned-traitor, think?

Would Colonel Wingate regret switching sides? Wingate could not possibly have known about the *Doctrinaire*. Would he try to weasel his way back into the U.A. Army?

What could Admiral Halverson possibly say to the men around him to give them hope? I imagined him at a table surrounded by stunned officers. "Sure it looks impressive," he would say, "but we can take it. I know we can."

No one bothered to interrogate me. In fact, after the visit from Halverson, I was pretty much left alone. My jailors suddenly remembered me the following day, March 27, 2512. That was the day that the tides of war turned.

I started the day with a quick search of the mediaLink and found nothing exciting. I pinged a few channels to watch news analysts digest yesterday's demonstration. One U.A. analyst called the *Doctrinaire* the "most dominating advance in military strategy since the fighter carrier." On the Confederate Arms stations, I saw the same interview again and again—some wizened admiral I had never heard of dismissing the *Doctrinaire* as "The Unified Authority's new *Bismarck*."

"*Bismarck*," I mused. Huang had used the same historic reference during the summit.

Having grown up in U.A. Orphanage #553, a clone farm in which the term *social studies* translated to the study of great land battles and *oceanography* meant naval science, I knew all about the *Bismarck*. That was the unstoppable battleship of its day, a juggernaut with one Achilles heel—its rudder. A torpedo jammed the rudder of the unsinkable *Bismarck* and it sailed in circles as enemy warships pounded it into the sea.

"We have more than five hundred ships in our fleet, not twenty-five," said the old admiral, a man with mutton chop sideburns and a bushy white mustache. "Our ships have been reengineered. The U.A.'s new *Bismarck* is big and slow and will make an easy target for a modernized fleet. No serious military strategist believes you can win wars by making a really big boat. They gave that up centuries ago."

Irritated by that silly old man, I took one last look around the U.A. networks for news and gave up.

I laughed at that relic of an officer for pulling out an old chestnut like comparing the *Doctrinaire* to the *Bismarck*. Granted, the *Bismarck* had been sunk, but there was no overlooked rudder on the *Doctrinaire*. Apollo could not have guided an arrow into Achilles's heel had he been dipped in wraparound shields.

It did not look like much had happened during my resting period, so I took off my shades and began my morning exercises. I stretched my legs, arms, back, and neck. Placing my toes on the edge of my cot, I balled up my fists and did four sets of fifty push-ups on my knuckles. I then did sit-ups and leg lifts and jumped in place.

Just as I began to work up a decent lather, Sam the jailor came in. "You might want to put on the shades Admiral Halverson gave you," he said. "We're about to attack another planet. It's time to show those U.A. speckers what we think of their big scary boat."

My chest, shoulders, and arms had a pleasant dull ache. I felt muscle spasms as I sat on the edge of my cot and slipped on my shades. Regular programming had been preempted. In a moment, the station would show a live news flash.

"How long has the attack been going?" I called.

"Just began," Sam said.

At first I thought the Confederate Arms reporters and their Navy had become so cocky that they were talking about attacks before they happened. Then I remembered that I had been watching a Unified Authority station when I removed my shades. Somehow the U.A. knew about this attack before it commenced.

The heading at the bottom of the screen read: TUSCANY— SAGITTARIUS ARM. The scene above was a battle in progress.

The live feed was shot from the planet's surface and told me nothing. There was none of the destruction I had seen on New Columbia. People gathered along the streets and stared into the sky to watch tiny flashes of light—a distant naval battle that blended in all too well with the stars around it. Whenever there was a big flash, a momentary explosion that looked no bigger than a dime in the night sky, the crowd would "oooooo" and "ahhhh" like an audience watching a pretty fireworks display.

> *Just moments ago, a fleet of fifteen Confederate Navy ships broadcasted into Tuscany space and were intercepted by a fleet of nearly fifty U.A. ships. It is not known if the Doctrinaire, the Unified Authority's super ship, joined this battle.*

The reporter, a young woman with long brown hair wearing a pretty light blue suit, looked more like she was on her way to the bank than covering a war. Her hair was perfect. She stood calmly in front of the camera, speaking casually. Above and behind her, little lights twinkled and extinguished. They might have been fireflies, or stars on a very clear night.

> *In recent days, the Confederate Navy has attacked Gateway and New Columbia, destroying military bases on both planets. This attack marks the first time that Confederate ships have been seen in the Sagittarius Arm.*

The woman paused and touched her finger to her ear. Then the screen split into two side-by-side windows.

> *Paula, we are receiving the first still images of the battle as it appears from space. These are early images released by the Department of the Navy.*

Behind the anchor woman's desk, a large screen showed pictures of a space battle. The first picture on the screen showed ships broadcasting in. The ships were black and would have been almost invisible if not for the bright lightning halos that formed around them.

> *As you can see, at 2215 standardized time, fifteen Confederate ships appeared in New Tuscan space.*

The next picture showed swarms of fighters gathering around shadowy shapes that looked something like black holes. The attack had already begun by the time this image was taken. The only evidence that those black shapes were indeed enemy ships was the little pricks of light where missiles and lasers struck their shields.

> According to Naval sources, 350 U.A. fighters engaged the enemy ships, destroying two battleships. U.A. battleships, cruisers, and missile carriers also joined the battle.

The next picture showed four ships taking heavy damage. In the background, I saw the flare of rocket engines. While their comrades burned, several Confederate ships tried to cut and run. They had no choice.

> There are unconfirmed reports that Naval Intelligence knew about this attack in advance and that Navy spies have infiltrated enemy command. The Department of the Navy denies those reports. We do know that the Navy was ready for this attack.

There was a pause.

> I have just received a report that a total of six enemy ships have been destroyed and that nine others managed to broadcast out safely. While Pentagon sources confirm that several single-man fighter craft were destroyed in the battle, the U.A Navy lost no capital ships.

I heard the clang, but my attention was fixed on the news and it never occurred to me that somebody had stepped into my cell. "Company, Harris." It was Sam's voice and Sam's fist, which slammed into my stomach. I was stretched out on the cot, completely unaware. The pain telegraphed itself from my gut to my brain in an instant. I curled up, my arms folded over my diaphragm as I struggled for air.

My Liberator programming kicked in the moment Sam's fist struck. The problem was not that I panicked. My mind was clear and I felt that warmth as the endorphins and adrenaline spread through my veins, but I had no air in my lungs. Given a moment to breathe and climb to my feet, I might have fought back, but Sam did not give me that moment. He grabbed my hair, gave my head a hard shake, and then dragged me off the cot. I toppled onto the cold steel floor, the edges of the grating cutting into my palms and knees, and my right cheek, which landed hard. Sam's boot slammed into my jaw with enough force to partially lift me off of the ground, and the back of my head struck the metal frame of my cot. After that, everything went blank.

When I woke, I lay dressed in my briefs in what appeared to be an operating room. My neck, shoulders, wrists, waist, and ankles were all strapped to the hard, cold surface of a table. There was a strap across my forehead, but this one was loose enough for me to lift my head an inch. I could turn my head enough to see the straps around my wrists. A bright light shined on my face from above. Its glare gave the skin on my arms a bleached look. Beyond the veil of the light, I could not see much of anything.

"I am sorry I could not visit you sooner," a voice said from beyond my sight. It was a low voice, a voice filled with commiseration. A squat silhouette appeared at the edge of the light. The man stepped closer. Yoshi Yamashiro, the former governor of Ezer Kri, stood beside the table. He wore a dark gray suit and red tie, the uniform of a civilian politician.

"I guess Tuscany didn't go the way you expected," I said.

Yamashiro laughed. "I guess not."

"And you think I had something to do with it?" I asked.

"You make an excellent suspect. Obviously you could not have done it alone." Yamashiro was a short man, no taller than five-feet-six-inches. He was powerfully built with broad shoulders and a wide chest. He did not look like a man who worked out, but rather like a man who was naturally strong. He was in his fifties or sixties with gray streaks woven into his black hair. The walnut-colored skin of his face was dry but not wrinkled. His eyes were as black as olives. I saw sympathy in his expression.

"Your being a Liberator has caused quite a stir between three uneasy partners," Yamashiro said. He spoke in a hushed voice. I was pretty sure that we were alone in the room, but that did not mean there were no mikes or cameras.

"The Morgan Atkins Believers consider you a devil. They claim to respect all life forms, but when it comes to Liberator clones, they make an exception. They want you exterminated immediately.

"Sam, your jailor, is a Morgan Atkins Believer. He has offered to kill you himself."

"He damned near did," I said, feeling deep aches in my jaw and ribs.

"The Believers are not military minded. They are politically savvy. The military minds come from the Confederate Arms. They say we should torture you, find out how you learned of our plans and what else you might know. After they get what they want, they plan to execute you."

"How about you?" I asked.

"After we win this war, I think you should go free . . . provided you explain a few things" said Yamashiro.

"How I boarded this ship?" I asked.

"We know all about that," Yamashiro said, placing a chair beside the table and sitting down. He pulled a small gold lighter and pack of cigarettes from inside his jacket. "Mind if I smoke?" Before I could answer, he lit a cigarette and replaced everything in his jacket.

I lay on my back, cold in the chilled air of this operating room, watching tendrils of cigarette smoke rise in the light.

"You killed Corporal Jamie Rogers outside of Safe Harbor while he was patrolling the woods. You were alone, and you took his place on the lift that brought his platoon back to the fleet. We know you killed Rogers because he did not report after the mission. We know you were alone because we took a head count on the ship."

I listened to this and nodded. "I did not know his name."

"We've been able to trace your movements on this ship. You killed Private Derrick Hines for his clothing. Once you had it, you went to a gymnasium on the second deck. Then you went to a laundry facility and stole a uniform belonging to Lieutenant Marcus Cox. You were seen inspecting the wiring in a service hall. When asked about it, you commented that it looked secure.

"We even have a security feed of you on the command deck. You strolled around the bridge twice. A few minutes later, you were captured back in the landing bay. Presumably you were looking for a way off the ship. Does that sound correct?"

"More or less," I said. I came off sounding much more confident than I felt.

"How did you know we would attack Tuscany?"

"I didn't," I said.

"Did you hear people discussing it?"

"Maybe the Unified Authority has a spy on the ship. I came here for revenge, not information."

"There is no one else on this ship," a voice said from behind me. I could not see the man, though I thought I recognized the voice. "There are no spies on this ship . . . well, other than you."

"General Crowley," Yamashiro said. He must have meant for this to sound like a greeting, but it sounded more like an announcement.

"Governor Yamashiro," Crowley said, stepping into view. "I was not aware that you knew Colonel Harris."

"We met on Ezer Kri," Yamashiro said.

We had not actually met. I was on Bryce Klyber's guard detail and escorted the fleet admiral into the capitol building. Yamashiro and I did not speak on that occasion. It seemed unlikely that Yamashiro would remember me from that incident.

"And you took a personal interest in the colonel?" Crowley asked. A tall and lanky man with a snowy-white beard, Crowley looked down at me with an expression that was not entirely unfriendly.

"He was not a colonel at the time, only a corporal," Yamashiro said.

"Then I have known Colonel Harris even longer than you have," said Amos Crowley. "He was a mere private when we met. He was fresh out of basic and assigned to an awful planet called Gobi. Harris was promoted from private to corporal a few days after I left. Isn't that right, Harris?"

I did not say anything. If I could have broken free of the table, I would have happily murdered General Crowley on the spot.

"You must feel very special, Colonel Harris. Here you are, a prisoner of war, and an important man like Governor Yamashiro has chosen to come visit you. I would never have guessed you to have such powerful friends."

"Governor Yamashiro asked you how you knew about our plan to attack Tuscany." Crowley said. "I would be interested in hearing your answer as well."

"I did not know about it," I repeated. "How could I possibly have known about it? I was in a cell."

"But somehow, you did," Crowley said. His voice lost its native jocularity. Now it had an antagonistic edge. "And somehow you managed to communicate that information to the Navy, Colonel. I want to know how. If you do not tell me willingly, I am prepared to force it out of you."

The truth about torture was that it never failed—the victim will always give in. It was only a matter of time. I could have told Yamashiro or Crowley my secret. I believed Yamashiro when he hinted his intention to protect me and set me free once the war was won. The problem was that his position did not seem so much better than my own.

If I read this situation correctly, the Confederate Navy was suffering from an identity crisis. The boats captured by the Morgan Atkins Believers were taken so long ago that the antiquated ships would have proven worthless in battle.

The Japanese came from Ezer Kri, a planet with several prestigious schools of engineering. The Japanese must have provided the engineering talent needed to update the GC Fleet. To Yamashiro and the refugees of Ezer Kri, this was Hinode Fleet.

The Confederate Arms, with their billions of citizens, and the Mogats, with their millions of members, were willing to tolerate Yamashiro for now. I could hear it in Amos Crowley's voice. He did not like seeing Yamashiro in this room, did not trust Yamashiro to be alone with me.

Crowley's loyalties were obvious enough. He joined the Mogats movement and deserted the U.A. Army in 2507, three years before the Confederate Arms declared independence and formed their own government. Clearly he had no connection with the Japanese. As a Mogat, Crowley would want me dead.

Fortunately for me, Amos Crowley was also a military man, the kind of man who understands the importance of good intelligence. He knew everything he needed to know about the Unified Authority military complex. Hell, he helped build it. What he did not know was how much I knew about his plans and how much of that knowledge I might have communicated to my superiors.

Staring down at me, his urbane smile as bright as ever, Crowley said, "Governor, Colonel Harris and I have some matters to discuss."

"There are the articles . . ." Yamashiro began.

"Articles of agreement stipulating the humane treatment of prisoners," Crowley said, sounding bored. "Yoshi, I assure you that Colonel Harris will receive humane treatment. Now, if you would excuse us, my interrogation team should be arriving."

Yamashiro listened to this and appeared to consider his options. Lying down on the table, I felt like I was watching two dinosaurs battle above me. Yoshi Yamashiro, the short, solid man with the powerful build, was the herbivore—the Stegosaurus fighting for its life. Crowley, ever the carnivore, was the Tyrannosaurus rex.

"I will speak with you again," Yamashiro said to me. He nodded to Crowley and left.

Crowley looked away from me to watch Yamashiro leave. When he looked down again, he had an expression that reminded me of a wolf staring at a wounded lamb. "I'll give you one chance. How did you know about the attack on Tuscany?"

"I didn't," I said. There was no reason to tell Crowley the truth at this point. He would not have believed me. He would have tortured me to confirm what I said and to make certain I told him everything. I did not want to be tortured. More than anything I had ever wanted in my life, I did not want to be tortured.

"How did you warn the Navy about the attack?"

"I did not know about the attack," I repeated. I was sticking to the truth in case they were monitoring me for physical responses. I knew how I warned the Navy, but I had not known about the attack.

Crowley pursed his lips. "I see," he said. He reached a

hand along the side of the table and I heard a snap as he flipped a switch. There were several video monitors around the table, just at the edge of the light. One down toward my feet showed body readings. Multi-colored lines ran across the screen displaying my pulse, my heartbeat, my stress level, and my brain activity. A score in the top right corner of the screen showed a computer-calculated projection of the veracity of everything I said based on those body readings.

"It would be pointless to lie, Harris. You know that." He paused, waited a moment for me to study my readings on the video screen, then repeated his questions. "How did you know about the attack? How did you send your message?"

"I did not know about the attack," I said.

"I suppose it is possible that some U.A. admiral got lucky and happened to station fifty ships around Tuscany," Crowley said in a confiding voice, "but the monitor reading your vital signs does not seem to believe you."

My pulse and heartbeat remained steady, but the lines showing my stress level and brain activity had turned into saw blades.

"I think there are things that you are not telling me, Harris. I'm not good at interrogation. We have other people who specialize in it. I'm betting that you will be a lot more helpful once they have a word with you."

He stepped out of the room leaving me alone to think about what might happen to me. They would torture me. They would use every old and new technology at their disposal to make me suffer. The old forms of torture had not been forgotten. They were brutal and barbaric. The new forms were surgically precise, left little damage, and were incredibly effective. And I was going to go through this for what? To protect the nation I hated? To get paid by Huang? To get revenge on the men who killed Klyber? More likely, I would allow myself to be tortured because of neural programming. I was designed not to back down . . . and because, despite it all, I wanted to protect the Republic, earn my bounty from Huang, and kill the men who killed Klyber. But above all, I was going to be tortured because my programming would not let me help the enemy.

CHAPTER
THIRTY-FOUR

The chemical compound in the syringe was not lethal, but the medical technician let me know that having electricity-conducting toxins flowing through my veins was not good for my health. "Taken in large quantities," he said, "it might cause cancer." He did not smile as he said this, though he must have known that a long bout with cancer was the least of my worries. He also told me that the toxins would dissolve in my blood. Two or three injections, he said, should not cause permanent damage; and in his experience, no one had required more than two sessions with this particular compound.

After giving me the injection, the technician left the room and I was alone. My fingers tingled and my palms were covered with sweat. Lying alone in the darkness wearing nothing but my briefs, I noticed the air getting colder and wondered if that chill was in the room or in me. I had time to think about how I could twist information. I practiced lies and half-truths in my head and watched the way the monitor reacted as I convoluted facts.

I did not know if anyone had ever tortured or even interrogated a Liberator clone. I did not know what kind of strength the hormone—the adrenaline and endorphins—

would offer. It would certainly keep my thoughts clear, but that might make the pain more acute.

At the moment, I saw no reason to suffer for the Unified Authority, the pan-galactic republic that created me. Yes, I had been made and raised by that government, but I had also been banned by it. The Senate passed laws to outlaw my existence. Che Huang sent me out to do his bidding, but he was no friend. The patriotic stirrings that I once felt for the Republic had been nothing but a misconception.

I looked around as best I could. Everything within that cone of blinding light shining over my table was bleached white by its brightness. Everything beyond the edge of the light was nearly invisible to me, shadows at most. Time moved slowly. I thought about the orphanage in which I grew up. I had a mentor at the orphanage—Aleg Oberland. He was the man who convinced me to follow current events. He kept in touch with me after I left the orphanage. He sent me two or three letters per year over the mediaLink.

I thought about Vince Lee, my old friend from my days in the Marines. Vince and I went on leave together. We were in the same platoon and we survived the slaughter on Little Man together. He was still an officer in the Scutum-Crux Fleet.

How long would they leave me alone to think? Was this part of the process—letting the fear of torture weaken my resolve? Maybe they just wanted to wait until their chemicals spread through every cell of my body, running through my veins like a mouse in a maze. I made the mistake of staring straight up, and the light above my head shined into my eyes. When I looked away, orange and black dots filled my vision. And the room around me was filled with absolute silence.

Time continued to pass. I watched the heart, stress, and pulse lines on the monitor. Minutes done were minutes gone. I thought about the people I knew, the clones and officers in my past platoons. I did not care for the Unified Authority, nor did I feel that I owed it anything, but there were individuals who had mattered at one time or another. There was Sergeant Tabor Shannon, a Liberator. He and I got drunk together the night I learned that I was a clone. During the battle at Hubble, he and I went into a cave filled with Mogats. He never came out.

There was Captain Gaylan McKay, a natural-born who showed no prejudice against clones, not even Liberators. He died on Little Man. McKay's last act was ordering me to leave him behind. How could I ever look these men in the eye . . . even in my dreams? These men died defending the Republic. They believed in it to the last.

What about Klyber? I imagined him standing over the table and regarding me coldly with his stern face and pale gray eyes.

"How are we doing?" The man who came in was tall, thin, bald, and wore glasses. He looked absolutely ordinary. If I passed him in a crowd, I would not notice him.

My heart, stress, and pulse lines jumped. My stress reading, which had nearly flat-lined, now looked like a mountain range. I tried to roll from side to side and break free from the restraints.

Something had to happen. Someone would save me. Perhaps Yamashiro would come back. Maybe Navy intelligence had discovered the Hinode Fleet's location. Maybe . . . Maybe Ray Freeman would come. Any moment, he could pound through that door carrying his massive particle beam gun.

The man stood over me. His skin looked paper white in the bright overhead light. The thick lenses of his glasses magnified the size of his eyes. He reached into the breast pocket of his white lab coat and produced a long glass tube. This he opened, showing me its contents. The tube was a quiver for three-inch needles. The man selected one. "This will not hurt," he said.

Yamashiro or Freeman, I thought. They were my best bets. Surely Yamashiro knew that the Morgan Atkins Separatists would betray him. He would have to know that the Confederate Arms would not look upon the Japanese as equals.

Smiling kindly, as if to reassure me, the man stabbed the first needle deep into my right bicep. I flinched, but the restraints prevented me from moving my arm.

"Don't move," the man said, pressing the needle deeper into the muscle. "You would not want to break the needle. Then we might have to dig it out." His head ticked up and down as he counted to twenty. When he finished counting, he pulled the needle from my arm, wiped the blood off with a cloth, and examined it under the light. "Good. Good."

"The needle turns green if the compound has dispersed properly," the man said. He held the needle over my face so I could see it; but of course, the light engulfed it and I could not see anything.

"You're in excellent shape, Colonel Harris. Sometimes the compound bunches up, especially when a patient has bad circulation. With you, it's spread through your upper extremities perfectly."

He placed the needle on the table beside me. I twisted my neck and managed to get a look at it. The shaft of that needle had turned jade green. I imagined myself sticking that needle into the man's eye, stabbing it into the eye and pushing it all the way through until it jabbed into his brain.

The man held the tube so that I could see it. He wanted me to know what he was doing. I could tell this by the slow way he selected the next needle and held it up for me. "Now let's be sure that the compound is spreading through your lower extremities," he said cheerfully.

"Get specked," I sneered.

"Don't take this personally, Colonel Harris. I'm just doing my job. Besides, this is nothing. This is just a small pinprick. Don't get worked up. In a minute it will all be over; and I assure you, you will forget all about the pin test." With that, he stabbed the needle deep into the calf of my right leg. This was not like an injection where the medic presses the point against your skin, then neatly slides the needle into place. This man jabbed his needle in as if it were an ice pick. I winced, but the straps held my leg still. The man repeated everything, counting to twenty, pulling and cleaning the needle, and then showing me the results.

"Excellent. Now, let's just be sure the compound has dispersed properly throughout." He selected another needle, then paused. "This one may hurt. I assure you, you will forget about it soon enough." And he plunged that third needle into my stomach.

The pain was brilliant and clear, a flash of silver lightning that shot from my stomach to my brain. I grimaced as he counted to twenty. I took short, panting breaths, feeling the stitch that the needle created between my stomach muscles.

"Get specked," I hissed between gritted teeth. "Get specked you goddamned son of . . ."

He clicked his tongue at me. "There is nothing personal about this," he said.

"Oh, yes, there is," I sighed as he pulled the bloody needle out of my gut. The muscles in my neck relaxed and my head clunked back against the metal surface of the table.

"You won't believe this, but we created this compound for humane purposes. It lets us communicate pain to your brain without inflicting physical damage," the man said. "What you will feel is a very amplified version of the damage your body is taking."

"Get specked," I repeated. The hormone had not yet kicked in. I was weak and tired and scared. Would it be Freeman who came for me, or would it be Yamashiro? I would not be tortured.

"I will give you a brief demonstration of pain. Then, perhaps, we can discuss the information I am looking for before we proceed much further."

It would be Freeman. If I could smuggle myself aboard a transport, so could he. He was seven feet tall and black-skinned, which might make him easy to spot, but he would find a way in and kill this bastard.

The man held up a harness that reminded me of a bit for a horse. He showed it to me. "Colonel, I suggest that you take this voluntarily. If you don't wear this, you may bite your tongue, and that would not be good for either of us."

"Get specked," I said again. I could not think of anything else to say.

"Suit yourself," he said. Then he held up a five-inch chrome-plated wand. It looked like a fancy pen. There were no wires hanging out of it and no lights built into it. It was just a plain, silvery shaft. He held it a few inches away from my face, giving me an opportunity to take a good look at it.

"Generally we like to start out light, maybe a couple of hundred volts, but since you're a Liberator, I think that would be a waste of time." With this he ran the wand over the left side of my chest, along my ribs, and down to my naval. For an instant I felt nothing but the smooth warm surface of the wand on my skin. That pleasant sensation might have lasted one tenth of a second. Then the pain shot through me.

The pain was like a blaring noise that engulfs everything else around it. My thoughts turned into a silver-white flash, possibly a visualization of the electrical jolt splashing out of my blood and into my nervous system. Every muscle in my body contracted. I would have arched my back, but the straps across my pelvis and shoulders held me in place. Somehow I managed to arch the area of my spine that was between the restraints.

My hands balled into fists and my shoulders tensed and bunched. My jaw clenched so tightly that my teeth should have shattered. Had my tongue slipped between my teeth, I would have sheered it off.

Then, as suddenly as it started, the pain disappeared and my body dropped to the table. I lay there on that cold metal, my back no more rigid than a wet rag. And, for the first time since I had been brought into this room, I felt the hormone flowing through my body. It had probably been released during that jolt as the shock of the electricity overwhelmed my brain.

"My, you Liberators are tough," the man said. "Normally my patients start to sob about now." The man looked down at me. "Still, you did mess yourself. That's something."

It was true. During the jolt, my body had let go of all the waste it was holding. Far from sobbing, however, I would have broken this man's neck if not for the restraints. My thoughts and head were clear. My desires were violent, and this time I knew my bloodlust was not just a response to the endorphins flowing through my veins.

I chanced a glance at the biofeedback monitor and saw something interesting. My readings had flat-lined again. Calmed by the hormone, my brain activity and stress level were normal. My heart was beating a bit fast and I found that I could speed up my pulse by fighting against the restraints—isometric exercise.

"In the old days, they used to kill people with the voltage you just experienced," the man said. "Did you know that? You just experienced twenty seconds of two thousand volts. Well, actually, it was ten volts . . . the wand only has a ten-volt charge, but your neural receptors believed they were taking a two thousand-volt shock. That was the voltage they used to use in electric chairs. They would electrocute the condemned for thirty seconds at two thousand volts to make them pass out, then they would drop the voltage and finish the job.

"Now you know how those old outlaws felt just before they died. The only difference is that this won't kill you. This won't fry your brain or damage your vital organs, so we can keep you riding the lightning for a much longer time. The only thing we have to worry about is having a fear-induced heart attack. Judging by your readings, Colonel Harris, I don't think that will be a problem.

"So, think you could hang on to your sanity through a ten-minute jolt?"

I wanted to tell this asshole to go speck himself, but I did not want to show that I was in control of myself. More than that, I did not want to make him angry.

"You know, the first time I tried this procedure I killed the man. The guy died . . . my fault entirely. I had him on a table just like this one, only it had electric restraints.

"It was just a little shock, just a disabling shock. It shouldn't have hurt the guy at all, but, you know, with the compound increasing the voltage . . . Anyway, the restraints had a two hundred-volt charge, so he got the equivalent of forty thousand volts nonstop. His heart burst.

"I don't know if that would happen to you. This is such an excellent opportunity. I never imagined I could ever work with a clone of your make. You have no idea what an amazing specimen you are, and to think, they can mass-produce you."

I was not sure how to act, so I lay in place shaking my head and moaning softly. I acted as if all of the strength had left my body. In truth, a lot of it had. I did not have enough strength to make a fist or fight against the restraints.

"So let's talk about the information I need, Colonel Harris." The man sat down on a rolling chair and glided up to the side of the table so that our heads almost met. "Should I call you Wayson? Can I call you Wayson?" He laughed. "I suppose at this point I can call you anything I want. Just don't pull out my magic wand—is that what you are thinking, Wayson?"

Thanks to the hormone in my blood, I began to forget just how painful that jolt had been. I had to work to stop myself from telling the man to "get specked."

"So, Wayson, I'm going to ask you some questions. Whether you answer or not, I'm going to give you another jolt. One of the things they teach us in intelligence training is, 'Never accept the first offer.'

"So you tell me as much or as little as you want, and I'll still fry you after that. Then I will ask you the same questions again. And we'll keep that up until I think you've told me the truth. All of the truth."

He leaned still farther in so that our faces were almost touching. "Tell me, Wayson, how did you know that we were going to attack Tuscany?"

I continued rolling my head back and forth and groaning softly. My acting must have been decent enough. "Didn't know about Tuscany," I said, clenching my fists lightly to raise my bio-readings.

Out came the wand. He pulled it from his lab coat with a snap of his wrist. He did not look at me. He watched the monitor as he brought the wand toward me, and I suppose he liked what he saw. My heart rate must have been skyrocketing and now I was not acting. He placed the wand on the table beside my arm.

"Wayson, you cannot possibly expect anyone to believe that," the man said, though something in the tone of his voice made me think that he might.

"I suppose if you didn't know about the attack, the next question makes no sense. Still, you must be in contact with someone, Wayson. A bright man like you would not come out to the enemy fleet without telling somebody."

Sighing slightly, the man climbed to his feet and I saw that he had the harness in his hands. There was a plastic bar in the middle of the harness. This he slipped into my mouth, pinning my tongue in place behind my teeth. I put up some resistance; but I was weak and he won easily enough. He laced the harness around my face then synched it to the strap across my forehead.

"Is there another spy on this ship?"

I could not speak, of course; and now that my face was bound and my breathing obstructed, my pulse, heartbeat, and stress readings were no doubt off the charts.

"Nothing to say for yourself?" the man said as he picked up the wand. This time he touched the wand to my throat, just below the corner of my jaw. The pain was all encompassing. My muscles clamped and my thoughts turned into a silver explosion.

The wand traveled slowly down my neck, over my collarbone, and then paused just above my heart. The agony was exquisite. My hands clenched into fists, and my fists pounded involuntarily up and down between the table and the restraints. My jaw clamped down on that plastic bit. My eyes screwed into tiny slits, which was good because I lay staring up into that blinding light.

During the moment itself, as the stream of electricity seemed to stab into my body like an endless blade, I lost all thought and control. If the man had asked me a question and I had somehow been able to hear him and I was intelligent enough to understand and answer, I would have told him anything he wanted. I do not know if he asked questions during the torture itself. He must have known that I could not hear, could not think, could not speak. I lay on that table a straining, suffering, quivering mass, no more intelligent than the electricity that so overwhelmed my brain.

From my heart, the wand moved down across the flat of my stomach. Had I been cognizant, I would have worried about the man dragging that wand across my genitals, but he paused over my lower abdominal muscles, and then he placed the wand back on the table.

"Wayson, you just survived three minutes and twenty-two seconds of two thousand volts. If you were truly riding the lightning in an old-fashioned electric chair, your eyes would have melted and your hair would have caught on fire. Do you still say that you've never heard of Tuscany?" the man asked.

Thanks to the hormone, which likely flooded my veins in excessive quantities, my thoughts came back the moment the wand went away. I was in pain, no doubt about that. I felt worn out and weak, but I was back in control the moment the electricity stopped.

A whimper left my lips. I was not sure if it was real or I pretended it. I did not cry. I did not even whimper again. When the man removed the harness from my mouth, I whispered, "I did not know about Tuscany."

"Is there another spy on this ship?"

"I don't know," I said. "I don't know." All the strength left my body this time. I lay flat on the table without enough strength to so much as turn my head. A layer of sweat covered my body. The cold air in the office bit into my damp skin, but I was calm. The hormones left me calm and resigned.

"You know what, Harris," the man said in a voice so informal that I might not have recognized it, "I think I believe you."

CHAPTER
THIRTY-FIVE

Between the initial beating I received from Sam the jailor and the time that I woke up again inside my cell, nearly twenty-four hours had passed. The ringing in my head was the worst I had ever felt, but my body did not hurt too badly. Sam had left some nasty bruises on my ribs. That was the worst of it. My left bicep and right calf had deep charley horses where the interrogator stabbed me with his needles. As for the electrocution, some of my muscles were strained from fighting against the restraining straps. For the most part, I felt no worse than I would have felt after a really tough day at the gym.

During the time I was being interrogated, I caught a lucky break. The Confederate Arms sent ten ships to Odessa, a wealthy planet in the Sagittarius Arm that supported the Revolution. They did not intend to attack the planet, this was a blockade-running mission.

A flotilla of U.A. Navy destroyers and fighter carriers met them as they emerged. The Confederate ships tried to escape without engaging the Sagittarius Fleet. The U.A. ships followed. Two Hinode battleships were destroyed. The others fled until they could broadcast to safety.

Since I was deep in the bowels of the ship, stripped to my

briefs and strapped to an interrogation table when the battle occurred, Crowley must have decided that I had nothing to do with it. The Confederate Arms said there was a leak in the chain of command and blamed the Mogats. The Mogats said that the Japanese should have been better prepared for the battle. I personally wanted all sides to blame Tom Halverson. With any luck, they might even shoot the bastard and me with the same firing squad.

The door down the hall opened. Someone walked toward my cell, his hard-soled shoes clanked against the metal grid floor. I did not bother climbing from my cot. At any moment, I thought, Sam would step into view. If he came close enough, I would kill him. I would snap his neck. I was marked to die anyway, and dying sooner might mean avoiding another torture session. So I lay on my cot facing the far wall of my cell, curled into a ball and acting defeated.

The steps stopped at the edge of my cell. "I have a gift for you, Colonel Harris," Yamashiro said. "This is a gentleman's gift. No one else needs to know that I gave it to you."

For one wild moment I thought he had smuggled a gun into the brig. I spun over on my cot so that I faced him. Yamashiro stood right in front of my cell leaning forward into the bars. He held on to the bars with his right hand, and reached toward me with his left. That hand was cupped around something, my "gentleman's gift."

I sat up and stared through the bars at the man. Our eyes met for a moment, then he nodded down toward the gift he had offered me. I stood and approached.

"You're not supposed to stand so close to the bars," I said. "It's dangerous. A prisoner could grab your arm and pin you against the bars."

"I'm not worried about it," Yamashiro said. As I drew closer and looked at his offered hand, I noticed the calloused skin along the edge of it. A short and powerful build, sandpaper hands—these were the signs of training in judo or jujitsu.

Yamashiro turned his hand so that the palm faced up. His fingers still curled over the gift hiding it. As I approached, the fingers spread revealing their secret. I saw nuggets of glass and wadded up wires that looked like they were made of gold. Yamashiro smiled. "It was a fine magic trick."

Seconds passed as I stared at that hand filled with sparkling gems of broken glass, my heart sinking in my chest. Then I realized that the pulverized mediaLink shades he held had gold frames. The ones I left on the bridge had cheap black plastic frames. "A young ensign found them in a communications station on the bridge."

"Then you have more than one spy on your hands," I said. "I've never seen those before."

Yamashiro's smile spread. "No? The shades you left had black frames. These were the best I could do on short notice." He closed his fist again and pulled his hand back through the bars.

"Where are the real ones?" I asked.

"Right where you left them," Yamashiro said. "I thought they might be more valuable just as you left them. Having unseen ears can be a powerful tool."

I worried about Halverson setting a trap by giving faux orders in range of those shades. I imagined intelligence relaying those orders to Huang and Huang sending the *Doctrinaire* into an ambush. What kind of trap could stop a ship like that? Then I remembered that Yamashiro had called this a "gentleman's gift." Why had he come and why had he not told Crowley about my little trick?

"Who did your ensign tell about the shades?" I asked.

"He told his commanding officer, who told his commanding officer," Yamashiro said, an infectious, mischievous grin spreading across his face.

"And it went all the way to the top?" I asked.

"Yes," said Yamashiro.

"But Admiral Halverson did not hear about it?" I asked.

"He is with the Confederate Arms Fleet," Yamashiro said, as if those few words explained everything. "The ensign was an officer in the Hinode Fleet. The information came to me."

"And you don't share intelligence between fleets?" I asked.

"Sadly, no. Like you, we also suspect that our allies in the Confederate Arms may not be reliable."

"I see," I said. "In my opinion, the Mogats aren't much better. You know how they got these ships in the first place?"

Without waiting for a response, I answered my own question. "They gassed the original crew."

"So you would not trust them?" Yamashiro asked.

"If I were you, you mean? I would trust the Arms before I would trust the Mogats," I said. "You know who you should have trusted? You should have trusted Klyber. Klyber did not want to invade your planet. He tried to keep the Senate off your back as much as possible."

Yamashiro's smile did not fade, but his eyes seemed to harden and his expression became more serious. "I admired Admiral Klyber but I did not trust the Senate."

I stared straight into Yamashiro's eyes. "The Mogats would not have known how to rig Klyber's ship like that."

For a long moment, Yamashiro returned my glare, looking me in the eyes. Then he looked down at the floor and shook his head. "Klyber was an honorable man. I did not want him killed."

"But you showed them how to do it," I said.

"Yes," said Yamashiro, still looking down. He produced a package of cigarettes and lit one. "A Hinode engineer figured out how to sabotage the generators and taught some of their engineers."

"Did you know what they would do with it?"

"Yes."

I laughed. It was an angry laugh. "Is it irony or karma? Now that they know how to sabotage broadcast engines, what makes you think that they won't do it to you?"

"The Believers could barely fly these ships when they helped us escape Ezer Kri," Yamashiro said. "They had no idea how to maintain or repair them. We renovated the fleet. Our engineers did all of it."

"The Mogats learn quickly," I said, "so watch your back. Once they know enough, they won't need you or your fleet officers. As I recall, you're a student of history. Right now, your officers are playing the role of Poland to the Confederate Arms's Soviet Union and the Mogats' Nazi Germany."

Yamashiro took a drag on his cigarette, stared at me for a moment, then shook his head. Clearly his history was civil, not military.

"The Nazis and the Soviets had a shaky alliance. It ended the moment they both invaded Poland to try and get a better shot at each other. Once your war with the Unified Authority is done, you'd better have an exit plan."

Yamashiro thought to himself as he listened. He took one last long drag from his cigarette and exhaled the smoke through his nostrils in dual streams. His smile had vanished and he wore a serious and thoughtful expression. "One way or another, the war ends tomorrow. We're attacking Earth," he said.

CHAPTER
THIRTY-SIX

Time never moved so slowly for me as it did after Yoshi Yamashiro's visit. I was locked in the brig of a ship that was about to go to battle against the most powerful navy in history. This was the command ship. If the *Doctrinaire* located this ship, it would undoubtedly destroy it. With those big cannons, one shot could finish the job.

If the Secessionists won, the Confederate Arms and Mogats would agree that it was time for me to die. If the Unified Authority carried the day, Huang might execute me. For somebody who had supposedly given up on life and survived purely by instinct, I cared more than I should have.

I tried to sleep but found that I could not lie still on my cot. Sam came in to check on me every hour. He stood outside my cell and stared in at me.

"You want something?" I asked once.

He gave me a cocky smile. "Comfortable?" he asked.

"You want to come in and fluff my pillow?" I asked.

"You know, Harris, I used to want to shoot you. After seeing what they did to you in the interrogation room, I'd rather keep you alive. I might enjoy giving you the wand a time or two myself."

"Why don't you come in here and we can discuss it," I said.

"You might show me some respect after what happened last time. Maybe I went too easy on you." Sam actually seemed to believe what he was saying.

"I'd love to go another round. Maybe this time you can hit me when I'm looking." I knew I was baiting him, and I knew it would have the desired effect. Sam considered himself a pretty tough guy.

He turned red then fought back his rage. "Watch yourself," he said. "Things could go worse for you next time. I wonder how that wand would feel if you went in with a broken jaw."

"Lets find out. Why don't you come in here and break it?" I asked. Sam heard this and stormed down the hall.

The next person to call on me was Admiral Halverson. As he had before, Halverson came bearing gifts. This time, he carried a small red visor on a two-legged stand. The unit was no more than eighteen inches tall, wobbly support frame and all. Sam accompanied him. In the admiral's wake, the jailor acted more civil. "You've got a visitor, Harris," he said.

The last time he said that, of course, he caught me unaware and pummeled me. This time he stayed outside my cell, as did Halverson.

"Hello, Colonel," Halverson said.

"What is that?" I asked.

"This?" Halverson held the visor up so that I could get a better look at it. "This is how sailors used to view their battles forty years ago, back when this ship was made. This is a remote strategic display." Halverson walked to the door of my cell and placed the display on the floor.

"Be careful with it, Harris. It's an antique."

I sat on the edge of my cot, my legs dangling over the side. "So you really plan to attack Earth today?" I asked. "Doesn't that seem a bit . . . suicidal? The *Doctrinaire* will be waiting."

"I'm counting on it," Halverson said with a bright air. "I should hope that the Unified Authority's most powerful ship will come to protect its capital world. Believe it or not, Harris, we sped up our plans because of you.

"Ever since you arrived, we seem to have lost the element of surprise. So now, thanks to you, we have very little choice but to finish the war."

"May I?" I asked, looking first at the remote display, then at Sam.

Halverson nodded. I stepped off the cot and walked over to the door of the cell. Kneeling rather than bending over, so that I could keep an eye on Sam, I reached through the bars and picked up the display.

The thing weighed no more than a pound. The visor itself was made of cheap, hollow plastic. The outside of the display was convex. The inside had two eyepieces surrounded by spongy padding. A black cable hung between the back of the visor and a U-shaped control pad.

"The display is monochrome, I'm afraid. It's red against black. Old technology, but it's the best I could find."

"I can't watch from the bridge?" I asked.

"Harris, I don't know how you tipped Huang off, but resourceful as you've proven yourself to be, I wouldn't trust you anywhere near the bridge."

"So you think you can win?" I asked. "You have what . . . roughly six hundred ships? Didn't the Galactic Central Fleet have about six hundred ships? That was before Thurston blasted four of them at Little Man."

"Some of the fleet is too old or too badly maintained to fight." Halverson continued to smile. "And they've shot down seventeen more of our ships since you came aboard, Harris. We're down to five hundred and forty. Well, five hundred and thirty-nine."

"Did you hear what Huang said about a fleet with no fighters?" I asked.

"That it's like a boxer without a jab? He doesn't know what he's talking about. The man is a politician, not a sailor. He puts on a good show."

"Not as good a show as Thurston, though," I said. "You were crazy to kill Klyber. Did you really think you could stop the *Doctrinaire* by killing Klyber? Didn't it ever occur to you that Huang would replace him with Robert Thurston?"

"Harris, Bryce Klyber was a personal friend, but this is war. I hated killing Bryce, but I need Thurston in his place."

"Thurston is a better strategist than Klyber ever was," I said. "You were there when Klyber tried to match him in a simulation." Days after Thurston replaced Admiral Absalom

Barry as the commander of the Inner Scutum-Crux Fleet, Admiral Klyber challenged him to a simulated battle. Thurston read Klyber's opening move and predicted his every step, forcing him into submission.

"Klyber was more dangerous for our purposes," Halverson said. "I've served under both officers. Thurston's style is tailor-made for us."

"You're crazy," I said. "Robert Thurston is the best commander in the U.A. Navy."

"Under most circumstances," Halverson said, his smile as unfailing as ever.

"But you didn't need to kill Klyber," I said. "Huang took the ship away from him at the summit. He gave Thurston the *Doctrinaire* and moved Klyber to the support fleet."

Halverson's smile faltered. "They moved Klyber to the support fleet," Halverson echoed, and the pride and bravado vanished from his voice. "I learned about the transfer after the cable was set, but by the time I heard about it, it was already too late . . . too late." He stood silently staring at me, then turned to leave. "Enjoy the show, Harris," he called over his shoulder.

He and Sam left the brig; and once again, I was alone.

THIRTY-SEVEN

I had heard about strategic displays like the one Tom Halverson gave me. Sailors used to call them "red worlds." This was not the obsolete strategic views replaced by the 3-D holographic displays used in modern ships. This was a portable display that officers could take into engineering or battle stations.

The visor was about three inches thick. Inside its housing was a laser that could draw objects in brilliant detail. The only problem was that it could only draw them in one color—red. My eyes never did adjust to that red-and-black display.

I switched on the power and pressed my face into a soft foam ring that ran along the inside of the visor. A little sign appeared instructing me to adjust the eyepieces to the shape of my face. Using two knobs built into the top of the visor, I adjusted the display until the words in that sign seemed to float out in space.

The display showed a satellite view of Earth. I could see the side of the planet facing the sun. In the display, the lasers drew clouds and land in red. The ocean was black and hollow. The edge of the moon was barely visible in the right corner of the display. In the lower corner, a digital clock counted backward. The clock read 00:05:37.

When the clock reached 00:01:00, I heard a muffled commotion outside my cell as the ship was called to general quarters. The call to battle stations lasted the full minute. The sound must have been thunderous throughout the ship. In the brig, where thick iron walls muted most of the sound, I soon forgot about the call to general quarters and did not notice when it ended.

The visor blanked out. It went dead for just a moment then winked back to life, and I knew that we had just broadcasted into Earth space. In the red-and-black panorama, the fabric of space around the moon seemed to shatter as 540 self-broadcasting ships appeared just behind the moon. Seen in red and black, the charcoal gray Hinode ships were not visible on this display but a label along the bottom of the screen said 540 ships.

A more modern display would have offered me optical menus. I might have found a way to view the Hinode ships using heat or motion-tracking sensors. On this old relic, the most I could do was zoom in and zoom out.

Turning my attention to Earth, I saw hundreds of ships rising from all points on the globe and forming a blockade. The *Doctrinaire* was nowhere among them. There were Perseus-class fighter carriers, battleships, and destroyers. Not all of the Unified Authority ships were made for combat. The fleet included medical barges and emergency evacuation ships designed to save crews from dying vessels.

I zoomed out to see a wider perspective. From this angle, the U.A. ships looked no more significant than specks of dust in a sandstorm. As I closed my perspective, the U.A. ships took on shape and detail. My camera was still far enough out to see from Canada to the Brazilian coast. From here, the Earth ships looked like a swatch of broken glass. Panning in so close that I could make out the Rocky Mountains, I studied the Earth Fleet's formation.

I watched as an endless stream of fighter jets sprayed out of carrier flight tubes. Even this close in, the fighters were nothing more than motes as they flew into formation and moved to the front of the fleet.

Fumbling blindly with the little control pad as I watched the Earth fleet fly into formation, I accidentally pressed a button that altered my view. Earth was still formed of solid land and hollow oceans, and the open space around the moon was still black, but now objects appeared in that space.

The Hinode ships were now more marked than displayed. They were still grouped around the moon, some 240,000 miles away. The two fleets would only need a minute to cross the 200,000 miles between the Earth and moon.

Pressing another button changed my battle perspective so that I could now get a closer look at the Hinode ships. Fine vector lines traced the edges of the ships. There were only three kinds of ships in the Hinode Fleet—cruisers, destroyers, and battleships. These ships were big. They would make easy targets.

When I switched back to the Earth Fleet, I did not like what I saw. The fleet could have used Klyber at the helm. It looked untried and unready for battle . . . or, perhaps, simply unready for this battle. Whoever was in command of the Fleet had placed the frigates near the front of the formation, just behind the fighters—a textbook formation for a different battle. The U.A. did not need frigates, a class of ship designed specifically to combat fighters for this battle. The Hinode Fleet had capital ships and no fighters. I saw this and realized Che Huang had undoubtedly installed himself as Fleet Commander.

"Good going, Huang," I laughed.

Looking at how the Earth Fleet had arrayed itself, I saw that the cruisers were stationed so far out that they would be easy targets for any ships that flanked the formation.

In the bottom corner of the display, the clock now counted forward. Six minutes had passed since the enemy ships broadcasted into Earth space. The Hinode ships spread their ranks and started forward.

One of the old cruisers, however, seemed to have stalled. It inched forward, limping behind the other Hinode ships in stuttering short bursts. This had to have been the 540th ship, the one that Halverson doubted would be in on the battle. I might have thought that it was the command ship, but I was on the command ship. I would have felt that kind of engine problem.

The Earth Fleet had twenty carriers with 1,400 fighters. Those fighters dashed forward and splashed across the front of the advancing Hinode formation, parting in every direction and breaking into its ranks. The visor lit up as thousands of short-range lasers and cannons opened fire, and still the Hinode ships advanced, closing in on Earth.

I zoomed in for a more detailed view. Now I could see both the cannon fire and the toll it took on the fighters. Laser fire appeared on my visor as hair-width lines that flared out of nowhere then disappeared without a trace. Looking into the battle was like staring into a dandelion, there were so many filaments. The U.A. fighter squadrons evaporated before my eyes. The bigger Hinode ships simply picked them off as they continued their advance.

But where was the *Doctrinaire*? The battle had begun.

The front ranks of the Hinode and Earth Fleets were almost within range, and the barrage began. Missiles and long-range beams filled the air. I could not tell the difference between particle beams and lasers on this display. I knew that the U.A. ships had both particle beams and lasers, and that the particle beams were far more destructive.

Hinode ships had only lasers.

Perhaps the frigates were a sacrifice. The first Hinode ships blew them up quickly and brushed past their mangled hulls without incident. Next came the front ranks of destroyers and battleships. Running into this bedrock layer, the Hinode ships spread wide.

And then it happened. First the jagged shards of lightning appeared. I had never seen anything like the anomaly caused by the *Doctrinaire*. It was a huge shimmering bubble, as big as any two ships on the field. On my visor, it showed in translucent red.

This antique could not possibly show the bright intensity of the anomaly. On the battlefield, it would have looked silver and white. It would be the same color and intensity of the electricity that filled my head when I was being tortured, and I imagined it against the pure black background of space. Any pilot looking in that direction would have been blinded.

From that silver white bubble, the bow of the *Doctrinaire* emerged. It was huge and fierce, like a fire demon emerging from a cocoon of flames. It was the embodiment of the entire galactic military—a beast that had won every war and nearly every battle for the last five hundred years.

Huang was a better tactician than I gave him credit for. The cruisers were off on the edges to make space. As the anomaly began, the U.A. battleships cleared out of the way and the *Doctrinaire* drifted into the void that they created.

Even before it had fully emerged from its anomaly, the *Doctrinaire* began to fire. Its massive cannons lashed out quickly, appearing to pluck Hinode ships out of space. I imagined the *dzzzz* sound as the new, special cannons fired their half-second bursts. In the vacuum of space, a Hinode battleship trying to fly over the front line of the U.A. formation exploded, jettisoning anything that was not fastened down. Then the fires within the ship consumed all of the oxygen around it and the ship imploded. The crumpled ship floated sideways as it drifted away from the battle.

More cannon fire followed. Another Hinode ship exploded and imploded, then drifted away. Then two cannons fired in different directions, and two more derelicts appeared. Every time the cannons from the *Doctrinaire* hit an enemy ship, the ship exploded, taking thousands of men with it.

Across the battlefield, the reaction was immediate. Hinode ships scattered. They broke out of their offensive position and shot off in weaving evasive threads. Several ships broadcasted away. Zoomed out far enough to see the entire battle, I could not make out details. I did not know how many ships fled from the scene. I just saw the anomalies. It looked like twenty or maybe thirty ships had fled.

From the corner of my eye, I noted the time. The battle had gone on for nine minutes and twelve seconds. The entire Hinode Fleet could broadcast to safety if it wanted. Because I took my eye off the battle for just a second to look at the clock, I almost missed the decisive blow.

I saw the flash and zoomed in immediately. I was just in time to see the last of the lightning as it danced like Saint Elmo's Fire along the edges of the *Doctrinaire*. The great ship seemed to list, its bow dipping down and moving counter-clockwise as if preparing for some spiraling maneuver. Then the ship seemed to flinch. It grew brighter as light shined through its portals. Panels along its roof burst, unleashing folds of flame and vapor. Finally the *Doctrinaire*, the great ship, the leviathan, vanished in a glowing ball that hurled debris in every direction before collapsing on itself.

I pulled my face out of the visor. I needed a moment to understand what I had seen. When I looked back, I saw the wreckage of the *Doctrinaire* hanging silently in space. It looked like a giant bird lying with its wings spread. The ship was utterly dark now, with not so much as a spark flashing.

Only a handful of U.A. ships remained around the *Doctrinaire*. The destruction of the *Doctrinaire* brought even more ruin: every ship around it was smashed.

Now the Hinode Fleet regrouped. It had lost a few ships at the onset of the battle. After the Apocalypse of the *Doctrinaire*, the Hinode Fleet suddenly had a huge numerical advantage. Most of the Earth Fleet had been destroyed. Many of those U.A. ships that survived the destruction were so badly damaged that they could hardly defend themselves as the Hinode ships renewed their attack.

Part IV

REDEMPTION

CHAPTER THIRTY-EIGHT

On board the Hinode flagship, sirens blared and people shouted. I heard the muffled sounds of celebration through the walls of the brig. They had destroyed the Unified Authority's goliath ship, but they had not made the galaxy safe for themselves. U.A. ships still patrolled Perseus, Norma, Cygnus, and Scutum-Crux. They would certainly retaliate.

The door of the brig opened and in entered Yoshi Yamashiro. He looked dour as he approached. He came right to the door of my cell and spoke quietly. "The war is over, Harris." He saw the antique "red world" sitting on my cot and asked, "Where did you get that display?"

"Halverson gave it to me," I said. "How did they do it? How did they destroy the *Doctrinaire*?"

Yamashiro smiled, but I saw no joy in that smile. It was the tired smile, the man who has heard a funny joke but lacks the strength to appreciate it. "We should discuss that later."

"I'm not sure how much later I have," I said.

Yamashiro passed a package wrapped in brown paper through the bars. The package was approximately the same size as a folded flag. It was not soft, but it was bendable.

"You will need to take care of the jailor yourself," Yamashiro said. "We will be back in an hour."

"Take care of Sam?" I asked. "How do you expect me to do that?"

"Let yourself out," Yamashiro told me.

As he left the brig, I gave the door a tug. It slid open easily on its rollers. I caught it after less than an inch. There were security cameras all along the brig, three of which had views into my cell. Smiling to myself and trying to look away from the cameras, I returned to my cot.

I could have slipped out of my cell and killed Sam in his office. I knew where it was. I visited it on my way to my cell the day I was captured. The problem was that in all likelihood, he would spot me. The security cameras had motion-tracking.

"You and I have a score to settle," Sam called from the door of my cell. Instead of making me come to him, the Mogat jailor had come to me. Unfortunately, he also had a pistol in his right hand. That presented a problem.

"You going to shoot me?" I asked.

Sam pretended to give this question serious consideration, then beamed. "Yeah. I suppose I am."

"No trial?" I asked.

Sam stuck his right hand, pistol and all, in through the bars. He aimed the pistol at me. "We have a problem. See, the Japanese think they won the war. They reconfigured the boats, you know. So they think they're in charge. And the Confederate Arms, they think they won the war because Admiral Halverson came up with the idea of attacking Mars. They think they're in charge, too."

At that moment, I still did not know about the Broadcast Network. All I knew was that the *Doctrinaire* had been destroyed. I did not even stop to question why other fleets had not sent ships into the battle. "What about Mars?" I asked.

"You didn't hear? We destroyed the Mars broadcast station," Sam said. He saw the stunned look on my face. "Didn't know about that, huh? We turned out the lights on the rest of the galaxy. Now the whole U.A. military is dark and stuck in place. "

It took me a moment to understand what Sam meant. At first I thought he meant that the Network provided power to the rest of the Republic. Then I realized that he meant that there would be no communications. Without the Broadcast Network, the outer fleets would not only be stranded, they would have no idea about what had happened.

"Which brings me back to you. Halverson and the Japanese want to let you go free. Now General Crowley, he knows what's what. He figures it's easier to get forgiveness than permission, if you know what I mean. He figures, we shoot you now. Then, if Halverson and the Japanese complain, we say something along the lines of, 'Oops. We didn't know you'd care.'"

Sam stood just outside the bars at the far end of my cell, lazily pointing the gun in my general direction. His arm and hand were relaxed. I was a fish in a barrel. He probably wanted me to plead or to lunge for his pistol. What he did not expect . . .

I sprang from the cot; but instead of lunging toward Sam as he must have expected, I vaulted along the floor in the other direction. Probably thinking that I had lost my nerve and was running for cover, he did not bother firing at me.

As I reached the end of the cell, I kicked. The heavy door slid along its track and crushed Sam's arm which was resting in the bars. He did not realize what had happened until the gun fell from his hand, which remained pinned in place by the bars. He screamed in surprise or pain, or rage, or possibly fear and fell to one knee.

I did not know if anyone was watching on the security monitors, so I moved quickly.

"You son of a . . ."

". . . test tube," I finished the sentence for him.

Sam pulled his arm from the bars and charged forward. He had to know that he did not stand a chance in this fight. He could not beat me whole. With his wrist broken, he would be an easy mark, and he had to know that I meant to kill him.

As he came toward me, he rose to his feet. I chopped into the side of his neck with the heel of my right hand. Keeping my hand on his shoulder, I guided him face-first into the wall. He stumbled back, yelling as he toppled to the floor. I stomped on his neck and snapped it. Sam lay on the metal grating floor, silent and bloody, with a gash across his forehead and his neck creased at a sixty-degree angle. His left ear rested against his shoulder. His mouth had a frozen sneer that showed most of his teeth.

Alien thoughts ran through my head as I looked at Sam lying on the ground. I felt regret, though not for Sam, per se. I hated the bastard. Had the war gone the other way, I had planned to kill Sam anyway. No, I did not feel bad about killing Sam. For some reason I just felt bad about killing. It was as if life had suddenly become more important to me because I had seen so much of it wasted. I tried to ignore those alien thoughts. I had work to do.

I dragged Sam into the cell and hoisted him on to the cot facedown, then spread my blanket over him.

Yamashiro's gift was a Japanese naval uniform. I slipped it on quickly. My hour was almost over. He would return for me.

The uniform fit nearly perfectly, though it was a bit wide in the shoulders and gut. Anybody looking closely would see that I was not Japanese long before they would notice the baggy blouse.

I did not know whether I should wait in my cell or hide in the jailor's office. Yamashiro answered that question for me when he and seven officers strolled into the corridor. Yamashiro wore his customary dark wool suit and tie. He looked at Sam's lumpy body on my cot, then down at the pistol on the floor. "It appears as if we have interrupted an execution."

"That was the general plan," I said.

"Stay close to us," Yamashiro said.

"Where are we going?" I asked.

"Another ship."

All of the officers in Yamashiro's cadre were tall; three stood an inch or two taller than me. Yamashiro arranged these men in a loose formation around me, then led us out of the brig. We moved at a brisk, businesslike pace, walking like men who had someplace important to go. Confederate sailors in tan uniforms stopped to watch as we passed.

As we got farther from the brig, more Japanese officers turned out to join us. We formed a solemn parade. While the rest of the ship celebrated, the Japanese marched quietly, gaining in number. By the time we reached the landing bay, where three transports awaited, there were easily two hundred officers in our ranks.

While we officers boarded the transports, Yamashiro went to have a word with the Confederate officer running the landing bay. After a brief chat, Yamashiro returned and the transport took off.

The mood on the transport remained solemn. The men did not speak or joke. Most of the men stared at the ground as if ashamed. There was a distinct air of defeat.

"What is going on?" I asked Yamashiro, who sat beside me on the bench lining the outer wall. He stared at me for a moment then spoke. "The officers of the Hinode Fleet are meeting for a victory celebration," he said. "We will have four battleships to ourselves."

"Celebration?" I asked. "This looks more like a wake."

"After a fashion. Like you, we are making our escape. The enemy will have several hundred ships. We will have four. We view this battle as a defeat."

"You could not have planned all of this since last night," I said.

Yamashiro shook his head. "We knew where we stood long ago . . . long before you and I spoke. We have been planning our escape for months.

"One thing did come out of our conversation. I have long felt a debt to Admiral Klyber. Had it not been for him, the Navy would have attacked Ezer Kri. He persuaded the Senate to settle with an occupation. When you tried to warn me, I decided to repay my debt by bringing you along."

The entire Broadcast Network would have shut down the moment a Hinode battleship fired its lasers into the Mars broadcast station. The discs, mile-wide mirrors with little more than electrical wiring and razor-fine welds to hold them together, shattered instantly. Think of it—the Unified Authority, the largest and most powerful empire in the history of humanity, was held together by electrical wiring and a bit of welding.

Now that the Network was down, all fleets were stuck in the areas they were patrolling. When the Mars discs broke, the entire Broadcast Network shut down. The U.A. Navy ships could fly thirty million miles per hour, but that was still one-sixth the speed of light, and most inhabited planets were located thousands of light years apart from each other. The U.A. Navy had a fleet in the Scutum-Crux Arm that could have defeated the Hinode Fleet, but those ships were 10,000 light years away. Without the Broadcast Network it would take those ships 60,000 years to reach Earth.

Without the Broadcast Network, the galaxy was no longer a Republic, it was a loose collection of inhabited planets. Throughout the six arms, there were only a very few instances in which any two inhabited planets were within traveling distance of each other.

And then there was the question of communications. The discs worked as a transom, broadcasting and directing radio waves so that Earth could communicate across its empire. Now, even using laser messaging, it would take messages minutes just to reach Mars. As Tom Halverson later described it, human communications had been knocked back to the days of the Pony Express.

In Scutum-Crux, Sagittarius, and all the outer arms, Earth had suddenly gone silent. Most people would know that Hinode ships had attacked Earth. That was all they would know. Suddenly every planet was alone in the universe. No fleet could hope to go beyond the territory it was currently patrolling. Struggling planets could never hope to receive support or supplies.

Only the allies—the Confederate Arms, the Mogats, and the Japanese—could traverse the galaxy now that the Broadcast Network was destroyed. With the exception of small scientific craft designed for exploration, the U.A.'s entire self-broadcast fleet was aboard the *Doctrinaire*. Now, the alliance between the Japanese, the Mogats, and the Confederate arms was splitting. I had not lied when I told Yamashiro my dire predictions.

THIRTY-NINE

If the Confederate Arms or the Morgan Atkins Believers suspected that the Japanese planned to flee, they did not care. The Japanese said they required four battleships for their victory celebration, and the Mogats and Confederates agreed. Why not? After their losses against the *Doctrinaire*, that left them with 486 ships in their fleet.

Yamashiro's men searched their four-ship squadron for bombs and traps and found them clean. Their broadcast generators already powering up, the new four-ship Hinode Fleet flew away from the Confederate/Mogat ships. Officers on the other ships should have figured out that the Japanese planned to leave. Had they been paying attention, they would have seen that the broadcast generators were powered up.

Once we broadcasted away from the other ships, we were safe. The Milky Way was so spread out that no one would ever find us without knowing where to look. Forget the analogy about looking for a needle in a haystack. The odds of accidentally running into an enemy fleet in the Milky Way were more along the lines of accidentally finding a particular grain of sand in the Sahara desert.

The mood throughout the ship became more relaxed once all four ships materialized. Most of the crew attended a mass briefing to which I was not invited. I stayed in a ready room not far from the bridge realizing that for all intents and purposes, I was still a prisoner.

I sat at one end of a large conference table, my eyes fastened at an indistinct spot on the wall. For the last few years of my life, I had suffered from disconnect. I felt alienated. I was not a normal clone, nor was I a natural-born, and I felt I owed no allegiance to anyone synthetic or natural. Now, knowing that the Republic I had been created to defend was gone, I felt sick and hollow. The Unified Authority had been so vast and so undeniable that it never occurred to me that it could actually end. What happens when the universe comes to an end? Who knows? Who cares? We'd all be dead.

But the universe of my creation had come to an end, and I survived. I sat alone in the conference room contemplating the end of Earth-brewed beer and orphanages filled with military clones. Would the Navy's various outer fleets find food, or would they starve? The tens of thousands of men on the Golan Dry Docks would surely die unless somebody saved them, but the only ships that could reach them were Confederate State ships.

The briefing took hours, but I did not notice. I wondered what strange debt Yoshi Yamashiro thought he owed Bryce Klyber, and why he thought he could pay it off by saving me. I wondered how deep that debt extended. Was it paid off by sparing my life? Would payment include integrating me into the Hinode Navy?

The door to the conference room opened, but I did not look up. I might as well have been back on my cot in the brig. In came Yamashiro and four officers. Yamashiro sat across the table from me. His four officers positioned themselves, two on either side of him. They did not sit at the table but formed a V around him, like samurai guarding their shogun. For the next few minutes, I sat in silence.

"The second war has already begun," Yamashiro said in a whisper that nonetheless shattered the silence. "A battle has broken out between the Mogats and the Confederate Arms. The Mogats have seized control of most of the fleet."

"How can you know that?" I asked.

"We took a lesson from you and placed transmitters on every ship," Yamashiro said.

"You bugged your own ships? But that would mean we were still nearby?"

"We are five million miles from the fleet. You might say we traveled a safe distance to listen."

"Can't they detect you?" I asked.

"How would they do that?"

"Radar," I said. "Radar stations pick up the anomaly when you broadcast in."

"And transmit the information over the Broadcast Network," Yamashiro said. "Only the Broadcast Network is no more."

"And your transmitters have a direct link," I said.

"Even if the Morgan Atkins Believers detected us, we would be able to broadcast away before they could reach us. But, as you might guess . . ."

"The Mogats and Confederates have bigger fish to fry."

"I would say they are distracted at the moment," Yamashiro said.

"So where does that leave me?" I asked. "Am I now a citizen of Shin Nippon?"

"I am sorry to inform you, Colonel Harris, that my officers and I have discussed this and we do not feel it would be advisable to bring a man of your destructive capacity to our planet."

"You mean a Liberator?" I asked.

"I mean a killer," Yamashiro said. "Some of my men watched you kill your jailor. Liberator or natural-born, you are a dangerous man."

"I'm not the only killer. You and your men are wearing uniforms," I pointed out.

"We are engineers. We modernized the ships and helped fly them," Yamashiro said. "The Mogats and the Confederates did all of the fighting. We never wanted to enter a war."

"So this was just a reprieve," I said, thinking Yamashiro meant to execute me.

"I do not understand," Yamashiro said. "We will take you wherever you wish to go as long as it does not endanger our ship."

"You're joking," I said.

Yamashiro looked confused.

"Why are you helping me?" I asked.

"We owe a debt to . . ."

"Bryce Klyber. Yes, you mentioned that before. But you also showed a Mogat assassin how to kill Klyber by rigging his transport."

"We had no choice," Yoshi Yamashiro said. "Admiral Halverson said that we could not have won the war if Klyber commanded the *Doctrinaire*."

"I don't understand how that can be. I served under both Klyber and Admiral Thurston. I saw them square off in a battle simulation. Thurston ran circles around Klyber.

"Why was it so important that Thurston take command? From what I saw, you had something more powerful than the *Doctrinaire* all along."

Yamashiro looked back at the officers sitting on either side of him as if looking for permission or perhaps support. Some of them seemed not to be paying attention. The ones who acknowledged his glance nodded.

"Now that the battle has ended, I suppose there is no reason for this to remain a secret. I understand Admiral Halverson loaned you a portable display unit. Is that correct?"

I nodded.

"When the battle started, one of our cruisers remained behind."

I thought about this and remembered a ship sputtering forward and falling behind the rest. I assumed it had mechanical problems. Then, as the battle progressed, I forgot all about it.

"That was the weapon," Yamashiro said this with the self-satisfied air of a man who believes that he has satisfactorily explained a great mystery.

"That cruiser destroyed the *Doctrinaire?*" I asked, doubting.

Yamashiro looked back at his officers, then decided to give up the goods. "Admiral Klyber was a very aggressive commander. He would send his command ship into battle along side his other ships. Robert Thurston was more of an organizer. With a super-ship like the *Doctrinaire*, he preferred to shoot enemy ships as his support fleet herded them in his direction.

"Klyber would have flown the *Doctrinaire* as it was meant to be flown, like a gigantic battleship. Thurston used it like a floating fortress. Do you see now?"

I shook my head, though the pieces were starting to come together.

"Klyber would have flown his ship up and down the battlefield. Thurston remained in one place, destroying every ship that came within range. He remained in one place long enough for us to chart his position and . . ."

"You broadcasted that cruiser into the center of the *Doctrinaire*," I said. My admiration was immense. "Absolutely brilliant."

"We placed a nuclear bomb on the bridge of the cruiser."

"So the cruiser was a drone?" I asked.

"You can't self-broadcast a drone ship. You might lose control during the broadcast. We could not trust a drone ship, not with so much depending on it. We trained a crew of Morgan Atkins Believers to fly a suicide mission."

"A kamikaze mission? You trained kamikaze pilots?" The irony was remarkable, but Yamashiro seemed unimpressed. He gazed at me with a stony expression. "You taught a bunch of Mogats how to run their own broadcast computer?" I asked. "Did you give them some engineering tips?"

Yamashiro nodded.

"And they would have passed that information on to their friends," I said. "You won the war and made yourselves expendable. From here on out, the Mogats will be able to pilot their own ships."

Yamashiro pulled out his cigarettes and lit one. He drew the smoke in very deeply and held it for several seconds in his lungs. His eyes never flickered. He never blinked. He stared off into the distance as he performed the calculations that now ran through his head. He was stocky and strong, but still an old man. His allies had outmaneuvered him, and he knew it.

Dressed in his suit and red necktie, his black hair brushed back and oiled, Governor Yoshi Yamashiro considered the alliances to which he had sold his soul. Whom did he hate more, the Confederate Arms, the Morgan Atkins Believers, the Unified Authority, or himself?

"We cannot fly you back to Earth," Yamashiro finally said, after blowing a stream of cigarette smoke. "That entire system is a battle zone. Is there anyplace else you would like to go?"

"Anyplace?" I asked. "Take me to New Columbia."

CHAPTER
FORTY

I had a lot of reasons why I wanted to return to New Columbia. If I had to be stranded on a planet, being stranded on a planet with a large agricultural base and a small population was attractive. Thanks to the evacuation, New Columbia had far more food than people.

Even before the evacuation, New Columbia had the kind of economy that could survive on its own. In Safe Harbor and other cities, it had both industrial and financial infrastructures. Outside of those cities, it had large farms. The planet had started out as a farming colony. Granted, I had enemies in Safe Harbor. If Jimmy Callahan survived the attack on the Marine base, he would have a score to settle with me. There might be Marines who would consider me a deserter for not staying on base during the attack.

But I also had my reasons for wanting to go to New Columbia. The first was Ray Freeman. The last time I spoke with Freeman, he was headed to that very planet to meet with me. While he and I were not exactly friends, we were partners. I felt as connected to him as I did to any man in the galaxy. Since the Mogats destroyed the *Doctrinaire*, I had begun to place more importance on people.

My other reason for wanting to go to New Columbia was

my plane, the self-broadcasting Starliner I had borrowed
from the *Doctrinaire*. The ship was mine now, free and clear.
With the destruction of that great ship, no one even knew that
Johnston Aerodynamics had ever built a self-broadcasting
Starliner. Once I had the Starliner, I would no longer be
stranded on New Columbia . . . assuming it survived the attack.

From the bridge of the Hinode battleship, a deck officer
took a satellite scan of Safe Harbor and reported to Governor
Yamashiro. "The city was evacuated before the attack," he
said. "It still appears mostly empty. The primary targets were
all destroyed. I did locate a tank and some armored personnel
carriers moving in the city limits. I also recorded a firefight."

"Artillary?" Yamashiro asked.

"Small weapons," the officer reported.

"Are you certain this is where you want to go?" Yamashiro asked me.

"Yes," I said.

He turned to his deck officer. "Can we send a transport
safely?"

"From what I can tell, there are no people around Safe
Harbor spaceport."

"You think it's safe to land there?" Yamashiro asked.

"I doubt anyone would even see us flying in. The spaceport
is several miles out of town. Even if they pick up the transport
on the way down, we should be able to lift off again well before anyone comes within twenty miles of us."

"How does the airport look?" I asked.

"Undamaged," said the officer. "I don't think any looters
have made it out there yet. It's pretty far from town and the
roads were destroyed."

"What about the Marine base?" I asked.

"Destroyed."

"The Army base?" I asked.

The officer shook his head. "All primary targets were
destroyed."

Maybe Callahan was dead, I thought. Even as I thought
this, a voice deep in my head scoffed at the idea.

Yoshi Yamashiro suggested that I wear old Galactic Central
Fleet work fatigues rather than the uniform of a Hinode officer.

Actually, he told me to change into the fatigues, but he made it sound like a suggestion by saying, "Maybe you would present less of a target by wearing fatigues."

I knew better than to argue the point.

Yamashiro and his senior officers walked me to the landing bay and escorted me on to the transport. Yamashiro bowed and his officers saluted as I walked up the ramp. I turned and returned the salute.

The kettle was large and gloomy, big enough to hold one hundred men and entirely empty except for me. I looked around the poorly-lit cabin, taking in the metal walls and shadowy compartments.

There was a box on one of the benches. The card on the box had my name on it. As the thruster rockets lifted the ship off the deck, I sat down and opened that box. Inside it, I found an M27 complete with a detachable rifle stock. I found a particle beam pistol. I also found a combat knife with an eighteen-inch serrated blade and a blood gutter that looked remarkably similar to the knife that the Hollywood version of me carried in the movie, *The Battle for Little Man*. The knife that I had once thought no self-respecting Marine would carry, I now connected to my belt. In the quagmire of Safe Harbor, that knife might indeed come in handy. The box also held an ammo belt. Under the belt I found five spare clips for my M27 and a half-dozen golf ball–sized grenades.

The ride down to Safe Harbor spaceport only took a couple of minutes. During that time I stripped and reassembled my M27. I loved the way the snaps and clicks echoed against the walls of the empty cabin. I stuck a clip into the slot and set the safety.

"We're coming in for a landing," the pilot called from the cockpit. That was all the warning I got. I heard the thrusters, felt the padded bounce as the landing gear struck the pavement, and headed down the ramp as the heavy metal doors opened ahead of me.

The transport, with its landing light and area lanterns, created a small island of light. As soon as I stepped off the ramp, the doors closed behind me and jets of blue flame formed in the thruster rockets. Crouching out of instinct, I jogged a safe distance and watched as the bulky drop ship lifted itself off the tarmac, rotated in the air, then roared out of sight. For a few seconds, I tracked the light of the transport's engines as they shrank from view.

The air was still and humid on the tarmac. It was a warm night lacking so much as a simple breeze. Crickets or some similar insect made an electronic sounding buzz off in the distance. Other than the buzz of the insects, there were no other sounds in that liquid night.

The vast dark plateau of the spaceport runway looked as dark as coal in the moonless night. Maybe it was the torture, or maybe it was the fall of the seemingly invincible Unified Authority, but something left me feeling small and alone. Not long ago, I had avoided people. Now I felt keenly aware of some new emotion, some barren emptiness, that rose in my stomach whenever people left me alone. I considered this new emotion and decided that it had nothing to do with fear. It came from a new understanding that life was fragile.

I thought about the way I felt after I killed Sam in my cell. Regret for the murder of a man who planned to murder me was not logical. Was it loneliness? Had I somehow become untethered?

Judging by what I saw around me, there was not so much as a stray volt of electricity anywhere in the spaceport. The buildings stood mute and dark like mountains with unnaturally straight cliffs. Runway lights sprouted mute from the pavement. From what I could see through this shroud of darkness, the spaceport had not been touched during the attack. I saw the profile of the terminal building off in the distance. It appeared as a silhouette with straight lines.

The runway stretched out before me vast and smooth. I ran its length with little fear of tripping. The stark white walls of the hangars looked dark gray as I passed them. The large entry doors of the first few hangars hung open. When I peered inside, I found them emptied of everything except tools and equipment.

I had a moment of panic when I found the hangar in which I left the Starliner wide open and empty. I felt that sinking feeling in the pit of my stomach as I looked around the cavernous blackness. Just as I began to lose hope, I saw a similar hangar not too far away and realized that I might have gone to the wrong building.

Feeling my pulse quicken, I rushed to the next hangar. The door was locked on this one. I thought about pulling out my particle beam pistol and shooting the door off its tracks, but decided against it. If my Starliner was in there, I should be grateful for a door that hid it from prying eyes.

Along the side of the hangar, I found an office door and smashed the glass in with my pistol. Reaching in, I turned the lock and let myself in. The power was out. The only light in the office came from an EXIT sign that faded as it fed on the last fumes of its emergency batteries. The sign's green light formed a luminous puddle over the door. That the emergency batteries could have lasted so long amazed me until I realized that the attack on New Columbia had happened less than one week ago.

I opened the door beneath the EXIT sign. The hangar was small by spaceport standards. Despite its thirty-foot ceiling, the building was far too narrow to hold a military transport such as the one I had just come in on. It had just enough real estate to house three commuter-class ships side by side.

Wan light shown in through a window in the back wall and dissolved into the eerie blackness. My eyes could not adjust to such total darkness. The hangar was not only dark but silent. It was an auditory vacuum, devoid of so much as a cricket chirping, or a dripping faucet, or a breeze, or even a ticking clock.

Reaching a hand in front of my face to keep from smashing into something, I stumbled forward. I worried about tripping on a power cord or a toolbox, but the floor was clear. I imagined reaching out and finding something cold and dead, a victim of the invasion, but that did not happen. The only people in the spaceport during the attack were allowed to leave the planet unmolested.

I found the smooth, rounded, metal of a spaceship. It was almost too large a ship to be in this hangar. My Starliner was big by private ship standards, but it wasn't as big as this ship. This ship was tall and bulky. Brushing my hand along its nearly vertical hull, I felt my way around the floor. I could not be sure in the dark, but I felt confident that I recognized this ship.

Once again I felt my way through the darkness, walking slowly and blindly, afraid that at any moment I might bump my head on a wing or shelf. Not far from the first ship, I found the edge of a diagonal wing belonging to a second ship. I followed that wing toward the front of the Starliner. Punching my security code into the pad, I unlocked the hatch.

Now I found myself on familiar ground. I flipped a switch and lights turned on around the cabin. The cabin was long and narrow, with white leather seats and surrounded by wood-paneled walls. From this angle, the cabin looked like a miniature movie theater fitted into a tube. Instead of a screen it had a cockpit.

I switched on the landing lights and had a look at the other ship. As I suspected, it was Freeman's ship. He had come this far. I had not known whether or not he made it to Safe Harbor before the Confederate Navy destroyed the Broadcast Network. Freeman must not have realized that my Starliner was self-broadcasting or he would have taken it.

I slept in the Starliner that night. The chairs only reclined so far, but they were soft and comfortable.

Safe Harbor Spaceport was thirty miles out of town. At the first light of day, I stole a car from a parking lot outside the passenger terminal and began the trip into town. The highway was empty and still with forests lining one side of the road and open fields on the other. There were no cars along the road and no signs of people. Except for the occasional billboard or road sign, this might have been a natural path on an uninhabited planet.

Five miles down the road, however, I ran into the ruins of an armored column. Tanks, missile carriers, personnel carriers, jeeps . . . military vehicles of all makes lay burned and broken. Some were upside down, their wheels in the air.

When the enemy demolished this column, they destroyed the road as well. Ten- and twenty-foot trenches scarred the road. Rough craters pocked much of the landscape. One particularly large trough cut across a bend in the road and may well have extended beyond it. It looked like an enormous knife wound in the earth, and the exposed soil within that gouge was charred black.

Seeing no point in trying to drive any farther, I climbed out of my car and shouldered my gear. I was not the first person to park here. A civilian van was parked near the front of the convoy. Like me, somebody had stolen a vehicle and driven in as far as he could from the spaceport. I stole a luxury car. The other person had stolen a family van—a utilitarian vehicle with cargo space and headroom. It had to have been Freeman.

I went to have a closer look at a broken tank before starting the hiking portion of my trip to town. It was an Alsance-Blake, a make of tank generally used by the Army. The same powerful laser that gashed the ground hit the tank's turret and melted it. Molten metal had poured down the side of the tank like wax flowing down the side of a candle. The soldiers inside this tank would have drowned in a bath of melted steel if they were not incinerated first.

A few days earlier, I would not have equated human lives with this destruction. Now I felt something akin to pity for the men who died here. They would have been clones, like me, but not like me as well. They would have been standard GI clones. They were not my kind, but not far from it.

I hopped a small gully the lasers had cut into the road and continued to the next vehicle, a truck that had been sheered in two. This was the work of a battleship. That was the strength of attacking with battleships. You could scour the planet from above the atmosphere, using laser cannons to destroy enemy emplacements that were so far away they could not return fire. At least thirty men had died on this truck. Corpses in battle gear, their skin charred and their lips and eyelids burned away, grinned down at me.

I heard the caw of birds in the distance. Whether or not the birds had already picked over this particular carrion, they were coming now. If any of these dead had moist flesh, the birds would peck at it and strip it away. That might be good. The air around these vehicles reeked of burned meat. I doubted anyone would come out to bury these poor bastards.

A few vehicles later, I came to a spot where an explosion had blown a twenty-foot hole in the road. The blast radius was thirty or forty feet long. Judging by the debris I saw around the hole, the laser had likely struck a missile truck, detonating its deadly munitions. Had that truck carried a nuclear payload, I would have been irradiated long before reaching the convoy. I might not have made it out of the spaceport alive.

A wonderful cooling breeze blew across this scene. The tops of the trees swayed in that breeze. The wind brushed across the velvety carpet of tall grass that stretched across the fields. Beyond the fields a blue lake twinkled in the bright morning sun. And ahead of me, the scorched supply line stretched on and on and vanished behind a hill. To the best of my reckoning, the column stretched on for another seven miles.

I did not make it all the way to Safe Harbor before nightfall. Crossing the gullies and blown out sections of road slowed me down. By late afternoon, I was only two or three miles from the outskirts of the city. I was close enough to see it clearly, but I did not want to travel into that urban tangle in the darkness. As the sun set and the sky took on streaks of amber, orange, and gold, I set up camp just inside the forest and ate an MRE that I had scrounged from the Starliner.

Once night fell, I hiked out of the woods to have a look at the distant city. No lights shined in the tall buildings. Some glow rose from the street. There might have been fires in dumpsters and trashcans. Maybe a few small stores had gone up in flames. The glow suggested controlled fires, but you never knew.

When morning came, I would make my way into the city. I would travel to Fort Washington, the stricken Marine base. I wanted combat armor. The sensors and lenses in a combat visor would help as I searched for Freeman and Callahan.

Resting in the woods, sleeping in the dark because I did not want to give away my position by building a fire, I thought about Safe Harbor, and Honolulu, and the Mars Spaceport, and the city they called Hinode on Ezer Kri. These had all been busy, thriving cities. I tried to imagine what it would be like to walk through these cities today, but the only image I could conjure was a spaceport terminal packed with millions of people fleeing their homes. I remembered frightened children and crying women and general silence.

In the morning, I ate another MRE and finished the hike into town.

CHAPTER
FORTY-ONE

The last time I came into Safe Harbor, the city was empty but perfectly preserved, like a museum exhibit. Now it more truly fit the profile of a ghost town. Looters had gutted the small stores on the outskirts of town. Some buildings were burned down.

There had been few cars along the street on the night of the attack. Now I found cars parked in the middle of the streets. These cars must have been found, driven dry, and abandoned. Not that I was in any position to condemn car thievery.

Safe Harbor had become a patchwork of prime city and war zones. A few blocks into town, I walked into a neighborhood that had probably survived the Hinode attack only to be sacked and destroyed by gangs. This had been an upscale residential area with two- and three-story apartment buildings, parks with playgrounds, and hedges along the sidewalks.

Hinode lasers had not done this damage. The streets were intact but there were bullet holes everywhere.

The windows and doors of the apartment buildings were broken in. Some buildings had been gutted by fire. The windows of these buildings were blackened from smoke. Beds, toys, and clothing littered the streets. The people who sacked this neighborhood had taken everything they wanted, then, in an anarchic feeding frenzy, destroyed everything they did not want. I looked at the stuffed animals, the toy cars, the books, and the furniture and thought about the families I passed in Safe Harbor spaceport.

The thieves were like wild dogs, like a goddamned pack of dogs. Soon I would run into them, and my newfound respect for human life would not help me. I began to wonder if I would have the ability to pull the trigger when the moment came.

Without people, cities become uncomfortably quiet. Walking through Safe Harbor, I heard my own breathing and the soft clap of my footsteps. I turned one corner and heard the pop of automatic fire. This happened on the outskirts of the financial district, an area filled with monolithic skyscrapers that seemed to slide out of the sky.

One of the buildings across the street from where I stood had a circular drive lined by four flagpoles. From those poles hung flags representing the Unified Authority, the Orion Arm, New Columbia, and Safe Harbor. A strong wind pushed those flags. They snapped and waved. Holding my M27 before me, my right forefinger over the trigger and my left hand supporting the stock, I paused to look at the flags.

The financial district stretched on for blocks, three square miles of city real estate covered by fifty- and sixty-floor buildings with marble façades and glistening windows. The looters would certainly have come into the financial district; but they could not break these inch-thick windows with simple bricks and they would not waste bullets trying to decorate this part of town. Some of the buildings had protective louvers across their entries. The looters would need to find better tools before they could enter these buildings. They would need lasers or explosives. I wondered just how well armed the looters might be.

I saw snatches of sky between the buildings. It was blue and cloudless, and it glowed. The day would turn hot and humid by midafternoon; but for now, the temperature remained in the high sixties and a cooling breeze rolled through the city.

A few blocks into the financial district, I located the remains of an Army checkpoint. I smelled the destruction long before I saw it. The scents of decay, dust, and fire became stronger. Then I turned a corner and confronted it. The men who erected the barricade had prepared to face looters, not battleships. A few laser blasts had reduced their tanks and armored transports to slag. There was one spot in which a laser had dug a six-foot pit in the middle of the street.

The laser carved a perfectly round pit. The laser melted the road around the pit, heating the tar until it boiled. The tar had cooled days ago, but the acrid smell of melted tar lingered in the air.

The men guarding this checkpoint would have died at their post before deserting. They were government-issue clones, heavily programmed and damned near incapable of abandoning an assignment. A direct hit from those laser cannons could turn an entire platoon to ash, and the heat from a near hit would kill a man, but they would have stayed. If there had been bodies left after the attack, the looters carted them away.

Taking one last look around the destruction, I sighed and continued on. From here on out, I would travel through smaller streets and alleyways. As long as I continued heading north and east, I would end up somewhere near Fort Washington. When Ray Freeman arrived in Safe Harbor, the Marine base was the first place he would have visited.

After another hour, I found my way into a retail district. Going from the deserted financial district into a retail section was like stepping out of a forest and finding yourself in a pasture. As I moved through alleys, working my way around pallets and the layer of trash that carpeted this portion of town, I heard an engine growl.

Moving through the empty streets of Safe Harbor, the hum of an engine sounded as foreign to me as the roar of a dinosaur. This was not a car, I could tell that easily enough. If it was a truck, it was a large truck. If I had to guess, I would have said it was an armored transport from the Marine or Army base. No self-respecting corporation would own such a noisy truck.

I switched from my M27 to my particle beam pistol as I peeked around a corner. Ahead of me I saw a four-way intersection over which hung a blacked-out stoplight. From here on out, I would need to move more cautiously. I was entering enemy territory. This was gangland. Anybody and everybody was the enemy.

Traveling from lot to lot, hiding behind walls and fences whenever I could, I worked my way forward. I tracked down the sound of that truck engine. Soon I heard voices.

"Hey, guys, look at me! I'm a specking Marine." The man who said this had a low voice that sounded utterly without intelligence.

The buildings in this area, mostly two- and three-story commercial structures with block-length display windows and awning-covered entrances, had been looted and gutted. The glass in the display windows was shattered. In one window, dozens of naked mannequins lay piled on top of each other like logs in a fireplace.

The building directly behind me was a looted diner. The people who broke into the restaurant seemed to have had a certain reverence for it. They did not break the windows or steal the tables and chairs. Except for a missing door, the restaurant looked clean enough to open for business.

Whoever was talking was right around the corner from me when he said, "Careful with that, it's worth something."

"This thing? I wouldn't want to wear it. It's got clone meat inside it. Clone probably rotted all over it."

"I'm telling you, that helmet is worth something. That Marine combat armor, that's good shit."

"If you don't want it, I'll take it," a third voice said. "I'll give you five hundred bucks for it."

I did not recognize the voices. I knelt in a shadow to listen for clues about who these men were.

"Money doesn't buy jack," the first man complained.

"Might sometime."

"Only if the government comes back. If that happens, we're all screwed." That was the second speaker, the only one who sounded like he could read.

"I'll trade you a canned ham for it," the third man offered.

"A canned ham? No shit?" the man sounded impressed.

Staying low to the ground, I slipped over towards a broken display window. The floor inside the display was covered with sparkling shards of glass. Whatever had been on display inside this window must have been valuable since the looters had picked it clean.

I climbed into the window and found an open door that led into the store itself. This particular shop had sold gourmet foods, not that there was anything left on the shelves. Posters showing kosher this and imported that covered the walls. Banners for cheeses and special brands of coffee hung from the ceiling. Toppled refrigerator display cases, demolished shelves, and cast-away shopping carts littered the floor. The store was huge and dark except for the bright sunlight that shined in through small windows in distinct rays.

I sorted my way through the wreckage. Checkout stands were pushed over and computerized registers lay on the floor, their drawers hanging open and empty. Stepping over a register, I approached the front door of the store and peered around the edge.

The plaza did not look busy by any stretch of the imagination, but it was well-trafficked. It looked like a downtown shopping district might look on a Saturday afternoon, in a city that closed on weekends. Groups of men and women sat on walls or around a fountain. The fountain was full of sloshing blue water, but its jets were turned off.

I recognized the canned ham boys instantly. They were the ones standing around the corpse of a Marine. The biggest of the men had stripped the helmet off of the dead clone and held it in his hands. As I watched, he placed one boot on the dead man's back. I decided the man was an idiot as I watched him hold the helmet to his face and stare into the visor. "What's so good about this thing?"

I could have used that visor. In my personal opinion, Marine combat armor, with its audio sensors and lenses, was the most important innovation in soldiering since the invention of gunpowder. Also, I did not like seeing these grave robbers abusing the body of a fallen Marine.

Looking around the plaza, I noted that all of the men were armed. Most had government-issue M27s. They must have taken these from dead soldiers and Marines. I wondered if looters had found their way to Fort Washington and how thoroughly they had picked over the base.

"Why do you want this so badly?" the goliath with the helmet asked the runt sitting beside him.

"No reason, I just like the look of it."

"You wouldn't have offered a ham for it for no reason."

At the edge of the plaza, three men looked under the hood of an Army supply truck. The truck's dark green paint stood out against the cement courtyard and slate fountain. Any number of warlords had probably carved up the city and claimed sections for themselves. I had located some warlord's stronghold. There were a couple of heavy-caliber machine guns mounted on the front and back of the truck, but if that was the best this dime store daimyo could do, he and his tribe would not last long.

"Throw in some chocolate bars and you can have it," the big man said.

"I ate all my chocolate bars," the runt sounded embarrassed. "How about a half-box of Twinkies?"

I went back into the store and let myself out through a window on the other side.

The warlords with downtown territories mostly concerned themselves with survival. They held small areas, kept their gangs grouped in tight clusters, and gathered whatever small arms they could find. I passed more than one dozen similarly doomed fiefdoms on my way through Safe Harbor.

What if every city in the galaxy had degenerated this way? Had Washington, D.C. been carved up by a handful of self-appointed warlords? Maybe not. Maybe cities like Safe Harbor, cities that had been evacuated, collapsed more readily into anarchy. Cities that still had soldiers and police to keep the peace might be okay. It occurred to me that this anarchy was probably not restricted to U.A. territory, either. The Confederate Arms probably had the same problem.

As I reached the outer suburbs around Fort Washington, however, I discovered signs of a different disorder. Someone had claimed these streets, and I had a pretty good idea of who had done it. Someone painted the letters JC on signs and walls. Like a dog urinating to mark its territory, JC, possibly Jimmy Callahan, had painted graffiti around this part of town. On one larger building I saw, "JC 'Resurrection'."

"Resurrected," I thought, it had to be Callahan.

I thought about Silent Tommy and Limping Eddie, the two men who had been his bodyguards. Were they his seconds-in-command? The notion of Jimmy Callahan running this section of town should have made me laugh. Instead, it sent a chill through me.

CHAPTER
FORTY-TWO

The ruins of Fort Washington blended in with the stores, churches, and houses in this ugly suburb. I found my way into a neighborhood that could only have been officer housing. The houses were three-bedroom jobs that all looked alike from the outside, right down to the flower beds and white picket fences. These homes had no more floor space than a two-bedroom apartment. They had patios the size of postage stamps and shingled roofs. Looking up the driveways, I saw upended tricycles and plastic swimming pools. I could almost hear the children playing.

Not wanting to approach the fort in daylight, I broke into one of these homes and hid inside it until nightfall. The front door of the house had been marked with a red JC, but the contents inside had not yet been picked over. I entered a clean kitchen that was orderly except for the pile of dirty dishes in the sink. Inside the pantry I found a jar of peanut butter that I ate by the spoonful as I waited for sunset.

The officer who had lived in this home was a family man with a pretty platinum-blond wife and two little boys. I saw pictures of the family on the walls. The boys shared a single room sleeping on bunk beds with steel tube frames. Searching the house, I found a flashlight and a cheap pair of binoculars, both of which I took. I also found a book of fairy tales and a Bible, both of which I left behind. The wife had jars of fruit preserves in the garage. She and the boys had undoubtedly left the planet during the mass evacuation. Even if he was alive, her husband would never find them again. Not without the Broadcast Network.

Before leaving the house, I stowed my M27 and four grenades in the family linen closet under a stack of children's blankets. I would need to travel light and kill quietly. I kept my particle beam pistol and the ridiculously large combat knife.

As the sun dropped on the horizon and the sky turned dark blue, I slipped back on to the street and traveled the last mile to Fort Washington. A tabby cat followed me from a distance as I walked down the street. The people had left their pets behind. The cats would roam free. Dogs left in houses would likely starve to death.

Fort Washington was a large compound encompassed by a chain link fence and razor wire. No lights burned anywhere that I could see, but I saw the glow of fires around the grounds. Lasers or looters had destroyed much of the fence. Making one last inventory check, I knelt beside the chassis of an overturned bus, examined my pistol to be sure it was charged, and stole on to the base.

Since the attack on Earth, I had developed an inconvenient appreciation for human life. It was as if my neural programming had gone haywire. I had the same instincts as ever, but after seeing the Galactic Republic go up in flame, I now placed a value on humanity. I even had an idea about what was going wrong inside me. I was designed and programmed to protect the Unified Authority. My programming must have been specifically set up to do whatever was necessary for the protection of the Republic. Only now, there was no Republic. I had no trouble identifying the enemy, but the mental loop that let me justify any action had been closed.

The attack had left the base in ruins. Every building I passed was destroyed. The first building I saw was a barracks, an elongated brick dormitory for enlisted Marines. The building had caved in.

More than anything else, Fort Washington reminded me of a college campus. It had old buildings and new ones, modern structures made out of the same red brick that the minutemen would have used had they built barracks during the Revolutionary War. Tradition. A network of tree-lined lanes laced the base together. Between the buildings were long, well-mowed stretches of grass that looked like city parks in miniature.

The base landscaping also included trees. There were thirty-foot firs and groups of leafed trees. As I walked around the base, I noticed large bundles hanging from the lower boughs of almost every tree. The bundles looked like rucksacks. They hung at the end of long leads of rope, dangling perfectly still, apparently so heavy that the low summer breeze did not move them.

Strange how the mind works. Coming into the base I did not notice these cocoons. Now that I saw a few, the mental veil dissolved from my eyes and I saw that they were everywhere, hanging from the trees, from the rafters of the buildings, and two or three bundles hung from each streetlamp.

They were not rucksacks, of course. These were the Marines of Fort Washington. Pulling my flashlight from my pocket, I stole up to one of the streetlights. Three men dangled above me, two clones and an officer. The clones were clearly killed in combat. They had been stripped of their armor, but I could tell by the blistered skin of their faces and their charred bodysuits that they were killed by laser fire. Some grave robber must have found them while scavenging through the base.

The officer, however, had not died during the raid. Someone had executed him, firing a single bullet into the side of his head from close range. I could see his tied hands through the bag. Shining my light on him, I saw that the top right corner of his head was a bloody, hollow mess.

These were Callahan's scarecrows. Killed in action or put to death after the battle, it didn't matter. Jimmy Callahan strung up the bodies as a warning to other warlords that Fort Washington was his territory. If I looked around long enough, I might find Colonel Bernie Phillips hanging from a tree. As the base commander, Phillips had helped me stash Callahan. He was the one who helped me steal an Army jeep so that I could sneak into Fort Clinton. I was disgusted with myself for letting this desecration bother me.

There might have been 20,000 or even 30,000 men assigned to Fort Washington. Could Callahan and his men have strung up all of the bodies? Some of the Marines would have gone into town to fight. Seeing the hopelessness of the situation, some of the officers would have gone AWOL. The enlisted clones would have fought to the end.

I thought that many of the men killed during the attack would have been too torn up to hang, but that turned out to be wrong. Under a nearby tree, I saw a body without arms or legs or any of the familiar curves you associate with the human form. On closer inspection I discovered that it was nothing but a bunch of body parts. Somebody had stuffed this fellow into nylon netting used for laundry.

Like I said before, most of the base lay in darkness. Crossing a hill, however, I heard the mechanical drone of a power generator. I had no trouble locating where the noise came from. Off in the distance, a two-story building shown in a bath of incandescent light. Glare from that building illuminated the broken buildings around it.

You could only describe Jimmy Callahan as a complete moron. Lying on the ground at the crest of a grassy hill, partially hidden by the six Corps corpses hanging above me, I could have picked off half of Callahan's army with a single shot had I brought a rocket launcher. They had lined up in a tight group for some kind of parade.

The terrain he selected showed his lack of tactical training. He set up his headquarters in a building surrounded by hills. The hills formed a ring around him, giving me or any invading gang the high-ground advantage.

And then there was the light. Callahan felt compelled to show off to the world that he had a working power generator. The light from his headquarters illuminated his troops. I could see the men in the machine-gun nests set up on the veranda. I had a much better view of the sharpshooters on the roof than they had of me. Although they had night-for-day scopes, they would need to locate me before they could aim and shoot. I could see them clear as day.

A particle beam pistol, however, was not the right equipment for a sniper attack. It was a short-range weapon for killing people and blowing up targets within a thirty-feet radius.

So I lay silently at the base of a tree, hidden from view by dangling corpses, and I watched. Most of Callahan's men wore fatigues. Some carried M27s. Some carried pistols.

I estimated Callahan's troops at somewhere between 150 and 200 men. He had jeeps and all-terrain vehicles, and a few armored personnel carriers. How he had taken control of this territory with so few men I could not understand. Then I heard the rumble. An LG tank rumbled up the street toward the lighted building. The letters, *LG*, stood for *low gravity*. These units were made for use on planets with low gravity, obviously. Tell a Marine engineer to make a tank heavier and you can guess exactly what he'll do. He adds thicker armor, heavier guns, more durable treads, and more powerful motors. Most tanks weighed about sixty-five tons or 130,000 pounds. The extra 70,000 pounds on an LG tank was dedicated to killing.

That was how Callahan became so powerful. Who or what could possibly stand up to that tank? All of the jets on Bolivar Air Base would surely have been destroyed, not that a jet could necessarily destroy a tank like this. Whoever took over Fort Clinton Army base might have similar tanks.

I pulled out the binoculars and took a closer look at the situation. These were cheap "bird watcher" quality gear, but they gave me a better view. I could read the markings on the tank as it rolled to within a few feet of that lighted building. I was just lowering the binoculars when an officer stepped out of the building. For an odd moment I thought it might be Colonel Phillips. I brought up the binoculars again.

Jimmy Callahan, wearing one of Bernie Phillips's colonel uniforms, strutted down the stairs like a made man who owns the future. His arms swinging at his sides and his head held high, he surveyed his troops. He barked orders and strutted around the tank pretending to inspect it. I did not even need these lousy peeps to see the self-satisfied expression on Callahan's face.

"See any reason why I shouldn't cap him?" The voice was so low it sounded like a whisper. Ray Freeman knelt beside me. He held a sniper's rifle in one hand and a rocket launcher in the other.

I pretended to have known he was there all along. "I don't see the point in it," I said.

"Looks like we're going to be stuck on this planet for a long time, Harris," Freeman said. "And I don't want Callahan for president."

He raised the rifle and sighted Callahan. It was a top grade rifle with a built-in silencer. No one more than twenty feet away would hear shots from that gun. Because of our elevated location, no one would spot us.

"So you're bringing democracy to New Columbia," I commented.

Freeman, who was about as likely to appreciate ironic humor as he was to learn ballet, merely grunted.

"What about the tank?" I asked.

"You worried about it?" he asked.

"Not especially," I said. I wasn't. I was more worried about the jeeps. In this gravity, the tank would rumble along so slowly that a five-year-old could outrun it.

"I didn't think so."

"But I'm not worried about Callahan, either," I said, taking a quick glance at him through the binoculars. I was about to tell Freeman that I had a self-broadcasting ship.

"Me, either," Freeman interrupted. And with that he pulled the trigger. Two hundred yards below us, a misty red halo formed around Callahan's head, and he dropped to the ground. While the people below shouted in confusion and scattered, Freeman picked off the four sharpshooters on the top of the building. Let me rephrase that—he picked off the three snipers I had seen, plus the one that I had not noticed.

Two of Callahan's soldiers ran for a jeep. Freeman picked off the faster man before he reached the vehicle. He shot the second man as he tried to climb into the driver's seat.

Total chaos broke out below. The men in the machine-gun nests fired into the hills. Only one of the guns fired even near our direction. Freeman shot that gunner first, and then he took out the gunners in the other nests.

"You here to watch or help?" Freeman asked.

"You have things under control," I said as I picked up the rocket launcher and aimed at the tank. Thinking this rocket would destroy that tank was the only miscalculation Freeman made. A shoulder-mounted rocket like this might damage that LG, but it sure as hell would not stop it.

"Do you know what to shoot?" Freeman asked.

"The tank?"

"Not the tank, the fuel depot."

Located at the edge of the darkness was the fuel depot that the late Jimmy Callahan used to fill his vehicles. Somehow it had survived the Hinode Fleet's attack. I aimed the rocket at a fuel tank and fired, triggering a grand explosion that lit up the night. The explosion was deafening.

Hidden up on that hill, I heard it and felt the percussion. The force of the blast shook the ground and the sound thundered in my ears so that the vibrations became intermingled as one in my head. A fireball shot sixty feet into the air. It towered over smaller eruptions as underground tanks, pumps, and piping blew into shrapnel. Flames shot in all directions lighting the area with a golden glow.

The rocket set off a chain reaction, igniting a network of underground fuel tanks that extended below the road. Fuel tank after fuel tank exploded leaving huge craters in the road. Made for use in a low gravity theater, that LG tank could not possibly come out after us.

Callahan's troops were thugs, not soldiers. They would not regroup as quickly as Marines, but they would regroup. They would send scouts and assassins out to find us soon enough. We did not wait. Once he was sure that the tank and the jeeps could not follow, Freeman turned to leave.

I watched men running around near the flames. The muffled bang of underground explosions, so different from the crackle of gunfire, echoed through the night air. The late Colonel Callahan's men would not get their LG tank out of that cul de sac anytime soon. They might fill the craters if they became desperate or ambitious enough to mix tons and tons of concrete. That might work. They certainly did not have enough technical know-how to build a bridge over those pits.

Looking back behind me as I left the rise, I saw the tree under which I had hid. I saw the bodies dangling from its lowest boughs like strange black fruit against the orange hue of the fire.

"You didn't have to kill Callahan," I said as we crossed the fence and left the base.

"I wanted to," Freeman said. He led me to a house on the same street as the house I had used.

"My Starliner is self-broadcasting," I said, sounding even more annoyed than I felt. "We can leave anytime that we want."

Freeman stiffened and looked back at me. "Self-broadcasting? We're getting off this rock."

"It wouldn't have mattered if Callahan was president of the friggin' Orion Arm," I said. "He wouldn't have been able to touch us."

Freeman thought about this for a moment then grinned. "So killing him was a bonus."

Ray Freeman did not talk much. When he did speak, he seldom talked about himself. I gleaned some of what had happened from things he said over the next few days and constructed the rest of it in my mind. This is what I think happened when Freeman landed in Safe Harbor.

Freeman came in a few days before me. He arrived before the Hinode Fleet defeated the Earth Fleet and destroyed the *Doctrinaire*.

Freeman stole a van at the spaceport and drove until he reached that stretch of road that was too destroyed to pass. He left his van and hiked into town and found his way to the Marine base. Like me, Freeman did not believe that the Hinode Fleet could survive a battle with the *Doctrinaire*. I think he hoped to find Callahan and bring him to Earth for safekeeping.

When he got to Fort Washington, he found men wearing fatigues and armed with M27s gathering bodies. Here Freeman made a rare mistake. He assumed the men with the M27s were Marines. When he asked about their commanding officer, they took him to go see "the colonel." Freeman did tell me that Callahan referred to himself as "the colonel."

Alert as he was, Freeman would have noticed that Callahan's thugs did not carry themselves like real Marines. He would have noticed the casual way they handled their firearms, the way they spoke to each other, and the slow pace at which they worked. Real enlisted men were clones. Unless all of Callahan's men wore officers' insignia, Freeman would have noticed that the men around him were not government-issue.

They took Freeman to the building Callahan used as his headquarters. That was a mistake. Freeman quietly surveyed the field, looking for strategic locations and tactical advantages. He had an eye for this. He would have spotted the tree at the top of the rise and known it was the perfect spot for an attack.

By the time Callahan came out to speak, Ray Freeman knew how many snipers Callahan had on the roof and where they were positioned. He knew how many machine-gun nests were along the veranda. He would have seen the LG tank rumbling around the parade grounds, and he would have taken note of the fuel depot as well.

Callahan decided to have Freeman killed. He must have decided that since he and his thugs had the guns, they would have no trouble executing the gigantic black man. They probably took him to the same field where they did their officer executions. The moment Freeman decided the odds were right, he killed his would-be executioners.

Freeman never left an attack unavenged. He hiked to Fort Clinton the following day. Knowing that the Army base would be under gang control as well, he presented himself with a winning offer. In exchange for a sniper rifle, a rocket launcher, and a ride back to Callahan territory, Freeman offered to cripple the gang holding Fort Washington. How could the gangsters at Fort Clinton refuse? They gave him a stealth jeep and the best sniper rifle they could find.

That night, as he returned to even the score with Callahan, he found me.

CHAPTER
FORTY-THREE

Freeman had a stealth jeep, but he did not want to use it. The gangs whose territories bordered the Marine base would have heard the shooting. Anybody within thirty miles would have heard the fuel depot explode. Our attack would have touched off a feeding frenzy in Safe Harbor.

"How long did it take you to get in from the spaceport?" Freeman asked.

"Two days," I said. "One day to reach town and one day to cross town."

"Two days," Freeman repeated.

"We could cross town in less than an hour in that jeep," I said. "We'd be at the spaceport by sunup."

Freeman shook his head. The house was dark inside. We were in a basement with only subterranean windows. We could see up and down the street from our ankle-high perspective. The street was dark and still, but we expected marauders to follow soon. Callahan's troops would come looking for us. So would his enemies.

"How did you come through town?" Freeman asked.

"On foot," I said.

"Did you cross main roads?"

"Alleys, mostly," I said. "I hiked through a couple of department stores to avoid being seen."

"The main roads are broken up," Freeman said. "We'd end up driving through the neighborhoods."

"We would be sitting ducks," I said. "There are gangs everywhere. All it would take is some hotshot with a road-block and a bazooka."

Freeman watched me figure this out. Too silent by nature to help me catch up, he was often one step ahead of me. There was a flicker of movement on the street. He rose to his feet and moved toward the window, his massive body forming a black silhouette in the thin light.

Up the street, five men moved slowly toward us. Four of them formed an uneven picket line, with the fifth covering their back. These were, as I said before, thugs, not soldiers.

They walked right up the middle of the street apparently giving no thought to cover. They had torches attached to the barrels of their rifles, and they swept the ground before them with the beams of those torches. They made splendid targets.

"Think those are the scouts or the hunting party?" I asked.

"What difference does it make?" Freeman asked as he raised that sniper rifle and pointed it out the window.

"They'll be looking for us," I said. "However many men Callahan had in his gang with whatever weapons they have left, they will be looking for us."

Freeman nodded. In the waning light, I could just make out the features of his face. "Smashing a crippled gang is easier than smashing a whole one."

"So do we stay here tonight?" I asked. I could not help wondering when the killing would end.

We could simply hide in the basement and pick off gang members as they approached. Freeman could hold down the fort, but one of us, meaning me, would need to check the street. I pointed this out, then ran up the stairs and slipped out of the house.

It was a silent, balmy night with the first hints of a cooling breeze. The snap and crackle of the fire on the base carried in the air, but it was far away and the big explosions had stopped. It now sounded like a large bonfire. I moved along the edge of the house then crossed twenty feet of grass to crouch behind a hedge. Maybe eighty feet away, the men with their glaring flashlights marched up the street. Their whispering carried so well on the soft breeze that they might just as well have been shouting.

Sprinting to a tree, then crawling behind a hedge, then kneeling beside a garage, I advanced along the street. From where I hid, I could see the dark barrel of Freeman's rifle poking out from the basement window.

As I watched the white eyes of the torch beams travel up and down the street crossing and tangling and illuminating bushes and lawns, I realized that I was about to do what I was created to do. I was designed for combat and for killing. This would be murder. These men had no chance of saving themselves.

I recounted their flashlight beams. There were five of them.

Freeman and I needed to kill these men so quickly that they would not make a sound. There might be another party of five searching the next street and another five on the street after that. There might be an army of thirty or forty men waiting to hear what happened with these five scouts. I remembered the soldier with the rocket launcher slung over his shoulder. Now, with Freeman hiding in the basement of a house, that rocket launcher was worth a dozen machine guns. Fire a rocket at a bungalow like the one in which Freeman now hid, and no one could possibly survive the attack.

"I'm not sure what we're going to do about that damn tank," I heard one of the men say. "Maybe we can take it apart and rebuild it on the other side."

"What? And carry the parts? That specking thing must weigh one million pounds. Just them treads weigh a ton!"

"What about fuel?" a third man asked. "They got the depot."

"Shit, there's more gas," the first man said. "It's a big base. There's got to be more fuel."

They were so wrapped up in their conversation that they did not even notice when the man in the rear got hit. He had been walking a good twenty paces back from the rest of the group. Freeman picked him off with a shot to the head, and he fell in the deep grass. No one even looked back for him.

Freeman's next shot was not so skillful. He hit the man in the head, but the man managed to yelp as he died. He staggered forward and dropped his machine gun on the road. It did not fire, but the racket was jarring on this otherwise silent street.

I fired my pistol and hit the two men closest to me. The green beam caused their torsos to burst. The kills were neither silent nor pretty. Both men dropped their guns, causing more racket.

The last man turned and tried to run. Freeman's silent shot struck him from behind, tearing away two-thirds of his neck. He flopped to the ground as if there was not so much as a rigid bone in his body.

Others would come. If they did not locate us, they might burn the entire neighborhood down.

We needed to put a couple of miles between us and Callahan's remaining soldiers before daybreak. We started down one street, saw men with lights, and then went down the next street. We zigged and zagged our way through the sleepy officer's suburb hiding beside houses and sometimes dashing into backyards.

Like the base itself, this housing area was a maze. Roads formed cul de sacs and concentric circles. Tall brick walls separated communities that should not have been divided. Coming to an intersection of two small roads, I heard voices and stopped Freeman. I pointed to a hedge, and we both hid behind it. Seconds later, a parade of forty or fifty men walked by. These men carried rifles and pistols. They were not dressed in fatigues but in a variety of civilian clothes.

These men did not speak. They meandered ahead. They did not use flashlights or bright lights that would give themselves away. Hiding a mere five feet from these ghostly soldiers, I watched them pass then turned to Freeman. "Those aren't Callahan's," I said.

"Scavengers," Freeman said, "coming to see what caused the explosions." He did not need to say more.

The first signs of daylight showed on the horizon. The sky brightened behind distant buildings. We traveled through an exurb, then a suburb and finally the metro, winding our way through alleys and small streets. Once in the city, I had an idea about climbing down a manhole. I lifted the lid from the manhole, and Freeman watched skeptically. The problem was that we did not know where the tunnels might be collapsed. In the end we continued above ground.

We never did run into gangs as we passed through Safe Harbor. I saw a man once. He watched us from the top of a three-story building. He sat on the ledge of the building with his feet dangling over the edge, and calmly watched us walk. Whether he was resting or maybe a guard on watch, I could not tell. But he seemed to be more interested than concerned about us.

It took a day to reach the outer edge of Safe Harbor and another day to make our way down the highway. When we reached the vehicles we'd stolen, we hopped into Freeman's van and drove to the spaceport.

I had not slept much since landing on New Columbia, neither had Freeman. We decided to rest for the night. He slept in his ship and I slept in the Starliner. As I made my bed, I found an old book with dried-up leather binding. With all that had happened, I did not immediately recognize it. Then I saw the words, *Personal Journal of Father David Sanjines*, and remembered reading the book the night that Bryce Klyber gave it to me. This was the diary of that Catholic priest who hated Liberators but made an exception for Sergeant Shannon. I reread the passage and wondered what this man would have thought about me.

Considering his prejudices, what would Father Sanjines have thought if he had lived to see the entire Republic fall? What would he think of the chaos in Safe Harbor? Liberators had not caused this entropy, though some had died trying to prevent it. As a priest, Sanjines would have agreed that evil can come from natural men. Would he also have agreed that good can come from synthetic soldiers?

CHAPTER
FORTY-FOUR

While I slept, Ray Freeman went scavenging around the spaceport. Most of what he found was packaged food, cookies, candies, and pastries that tasted like plastic. He got it by breaking into vending machines. He loaded this food into a galley at the back of the Starliner. He also brought a few changes of clothes, some combat gear, and a couple favorite guns including the sniper rifle they gave him at Fort Clinton.

We had not yet opened the hangar doors. The lights under the wings of the Starliner cast a faint red glow around us. Other than that, the area around the ship was as black as space.

For a man who prided himself in not caring whether he lived or died, I spent a lot of time fussing over safety checks. I examined the housings around the broadcast generator and the broadcast engine. I checked the instrumentation. I also refueled the Starliner, siphoning thousands of gallons of fuel from an underground tank outside the hangar. Space flight required very little fuel and the energy I needed for self-broadcasting was created by a broadcast generator, but atmospheric flight ate into my fuel supplies and I had no idea when or where I would be able to refuel.

Freeman sat silently in the copilot's seat through much of

this. The seat was a squeeze for him. It was too close to the controls. The wheel brushed against Freeman's massive chest. He had to curl his tree-stump legs under his seat because the niche under the dash was both too small and too short to accommodate them.

Freeman sat in that seat, staring out the window and looking like an adult in a child's playhouse. It took a moment before I realized what had so captured his attention. He was looking at his plane, which he had owned for years. With the Broadcast Network out, his ride could no longer attempt anything more ambitious than continent-hopping.

I knew better than to inquire about it. Ask him how he felt, and Ray Freeman would simply stare at you.

"Any suggestions about where to go?" I asked as I powered up.

"Delphi," Freeman said.

"Never heard of it," I said.

"You've heard of it," Freeman said. "The neo-Baptists renamed the place. Before my father arrived there, the planet was called Little Man."

"Little Man?" I asked.

"I was headed there before you called me."

So much had happened over the last few days that I forgot all about Freeman's family. They had set up a colony on Little Man. The U.A. Navy had sent a fighter carrier to the planet to tell them to leave. And then . . . and then the Republic went dark.

"A fighter carrier dropped in on them," I said. "How long ago was that?"

"Four, maybe five days," Freeman said. "Why?"

"I might be wrong about this, but if I remember correctly, it takes over a hundred hours to travel from the nearest broadcast disc to Little Man . . . and that is at top speed. If that carrier only left Little Man four days ago, it would not have made it to the discs in time to broadcast out."

"Yeah," Freeman said, rising to his feet. "I figured that. I'll open the hangar." He climbed out of the cockpit. The low ceiling of the Starliner was an uncomfortable fit for me, and I was only six-three. Freeman, who stood at least nine inches taller than me, had to bow his head, curl his back, and waddle sideways to wedge himself through the cabin. To climb in and out of the hatch, he had to drop into a low squat.

I turned on the landing lights as he walked across the hangar, bathing the floor in bright white glow. The door was still locked. Freeman pulled out his particle beam pistol and shot the locking mechanism, blasting a hole in the center of the door through which a beam of bright daylight stabbed.

When Freeman tried to slide the tall metal door along its track, it still did not budge. There was a mechanical roller with heavy metal cogs along the top of the doorway, just above the track. Freeman shot the roller and it dropped to the floor. He tried to roll the door open again, and it still fought against him. This time he pulled his particle beam pistol and shot the track from which the top of the door hung. There was a loud yawning noise as the tonnage of the door, which was at least thirty feet high and a hundred feet across, pulled itself free from its supports. The metal door quivered in place for a few seconds, then twisted and fell flat against the tarmac outside the hangar. The resounding crash reverberated through the hangar.

A torrent of bright daylight flooded in through the gap that the door had once blocked. His expression still as inscrutable as ever, Freeman turned and walked back to the Starliner, pocketing his pistol along the way. He did not rejoin me in the cockpit but took a seat in the cabin.

I drove out of the hangar, rolling over the fallen door, and took off. Streaming up into the horizon, I chanced a glance down at Safe Harbor. From here, the city looked no different than it had the first time I came. Five miles up and rising quickly, I could not see the burned buildings and broken highways.

The atmosphere thinned and darkened as we entered outer space. I did not have to worry about radar or traffic controllers tracking me. As soon as we left the New Columbian atmosphere, I engaged the broadcast computer and worked out coordinates for Little Man. Lightning danced outside the cockpit, and we emerged in the Scutum-Crux Arm a short thousand miles from the target.

CHAPTER
FORTY-FIVE

Something in my programming had gone haywire and rendered me sensitive to the loss of human life. I still had the ability to kill, but it bothered me. Now, seeing Little Man, my head filled with memories of the Marines who died in that awful battle. I remembered Captain Gaylan McKay . . . the personable young officer over my platoon on the *Kamehameha*. I remembered the ranks of idealistic Marines and the march that led to their deaths. Strange as it sounds, I felt an involuntary shiver. What I should have felt was anger.

"When was the last time you saw your family?" I asked.

"It's been five years," Freeman said.

"This should be some homecoming," I said.

"They don't want me here," he said. He did not elaborate. Freeman never elaborated.

We kept flying into the green and blue horizon. Using sensors to search for metal and heat, we located the colony in a plains area. They were building their settlement on the edge of a forest and not far from a clear-water lake. In the distance, a mountain range filled the horizon. It was not on the same continent on which we fought that final battle.

The first thing we saw was acres and acres of plowed land. Beyond the fields was a small and primitive town that

consisted of warehouses and unfinished apartment buildings. Even when the apartment buildings were complete,
they would only be temporary shelters meant to hold people
for days or weeks. Work had already begun on larger, more
permanent buildings as well.

Women and children in simple clothing emerged from
the temporary shelters as we landed. Men in overalls came
from the construction projects and from the fields. If there
was one thing that stood out about the people on Little Man,
it was their industrious nature.

The people did not approach my ship, but huddled together inside the borders of their town. They did not seem
scared. They simply stood in place, curious to see who we
were.

"I guess the welcoming committee has arrived," I said,
and turned to see that Freeman had already opened the
hatch. I followed him out.

"I should have known it was you," a man called in a voice
drenched with loathing. Freeman did not answer.

When I stepped out of the ship, there was a collective
gasp. I guess they were used to a seven-foot-tall black man,
but the sight of a clone was strange and new. I turned to look
at these people and got a jolt of my own.

I had always taken it for granted that Ray Freeman was
unique in the universe. He was, I thought, a one-of-a kind,
like me. It never occurred to me that he could have come
from a colony of men and women similar to himself. The
men and women of Delphi were very much like Freeman.
They were tall and dark-skinned. One of the woman later
told me that they were pure-blooded African Americans. As
far as I knew, they were the last people anywhere who referred to themselves as American at all.

"What are you doing here, son?" an old man asked. The
man was tall and solidly built, but he looked underfed. He
did not have Ray Freeman's broad, wrestler's physique. His
shoulders were square, his back was erect and the parts of
his arms that extended beyond the short sleeves of his shirt
looked strong and well formed. He removed his hat. An even
layer of gray berber hair covered his head. His dusty skin
was far darker than Ray's, almost a true black. It looked dry

and leathery from decades of toil under a burning hot sun. "What are you doing here, Raymond?" he repeated.

Silence hung between Freeman and his father like a curtain. I could almost feel the hostility. The people around the old man stood silent and staring. They stood unflinching and unmoved. Like Freeman's father, these people were tall, dark, with skin that had dried to leather in the sun.

Freeman took nearly one minute before he began to speak; and when he did speak, he spoke so quietly I could barely hear what he said. "The Broadcast Network was destroyed."

"Destroyed?" the elder Freeman repeated. For the first time since we landed, the people behind him showed concern. They began to speak quietly among themselves.

"I wanted to make sure you were okay," Freeman said.

By this time, however, the elder Freeman's attention was no longer on his son. He had turned to me. "You are a friend of Raymond's?"

I nodded, wondering if Ray Freeman had ever really had a friend.

The old man turned back to Freeman. "How could anybody destroy the Broadcast Network?" It was a fair question. In U.A. society, the Broadcast Network was a given as constant as sunlight and water. No one, with the exception of Rear Admiral Thomas Halverson, had ever stopped to consider its fragile nature.

"There was a war. Some of the arms declared independence," Freeman said. His father should have known this. Of course his father would have known this. It was the biggest news in history. And yet, looking at the old man's surprised expression, it became clear that he had not known about the war.

"A civil war?" the old man asked.

"It's a civil war if you lose," Freeman said. "It's a revolution when you win."

"They won?" A younger man stepped forward. This man was far shorter than Freeman and not as broad along the chest and shoulders. He had a wiry build, but he looked athletic.

"They destroyed the Mars broadcast station," I said. "Without the Mars discs, the entire system shut down."

"For how long?" the old man asked, turning back to Ray. "How long before they fix the broadcast station?"

"They won't fix it," Freeman said.

"Of course they'll fix it," the younger man said. "They'll send over the fleet . . ."

"Earth doesn't have a fleet," Ray said. "The Earth Fleet was defeated, and they can't send ships from other fleets without the discs."

The older Freeman stood still as a statue, his gaze boring into his son's eyes and then mine. "Man has finally turned his back on us," he mumbled. Then louder, he added, "God has cleared the way for us to stay in this promised land."

There were 113 people living on Delphi. I know the exact number because the entire population, or perhaps I should say *congregation*, assembled in their meetinghouse—a building meant to be used as a sleeping and eating facility during large evacuations. The people sat on plastic benches. Archie Freeman, Ray Freeman's father, looked down on the congregation from behind a very plain pulpit, over which hung a fiberglass cross.

There were two women with infants in the congregation. One woman threw a blanket over her shoulder and nursed her child. You could hear it sucking when the conversations lulled. The other woman cradled a sleeping baby in her arms, rocking it softly as she stood in the back of the meetinghouse. I noted the tenderness with which she treated the child and envied it. Having grown up in U.A. Orphanage #553 with other clones, I had never seen tenderness of this kind.

The people of Delphi attended this meeting as families. Husbands and wives sat together with their children. Near as I could figure, there were eighteen extended families. The whole of them only filled the first four rows of the meetinghouse. For the most part, the next twenty rows sat empty—an ambition unfulfilled.

"My son says that we are in danger," Archie Freeman began the meeting with those words. He stood at his pulpit as austere and grave as any man I had ever seen. He had washed and changed his clothes. He wore a black suit, white shirt and black necktie. He dressed like a businessman.

Now that he had washed up, the color of Archie Freeman's face was almost onyx. His skin had the texture of parched leather, his reward for fifty years of trying to start colonies on uninhabitable planets. Having finally landed on a productive planet with plenty of water and healthy soil, he did not want to leave.

Archie was bald at the top, with a very short layer of gray-white hair that looked like a macramé cowl. His eyes were bloodshot from his day out in the sun.

"Raymond, come up and speak your piece," the elder Freeman said.

Ray, who had been sitting with a woman near the back, stood and walked to the front of the chapel. No one reached out to shake his hand or pat his back. Seeing the reception these people gave him, you might have thought he had never lived among these people. But he must have lived with the people before they moved to Little Man. He was their 114th citizen. He probably knew every one of them by name.

Archie Freeman did not step away from the pulpit as his son joined him on the stand. The two men stood a few feet from each other. Ray, as I have mentioned before, stood at least seven feet tall. His father appeared to be three or four inches shorter than him, and a lot thinner.

"Tell them what you told me, son," Archie Freeman said in his handsome baritone.

"There was a war," Freeman said. "Four of the arms wanted to leave the Unified Authority. They had a fleet of self-broadcasting battleships. They attacked Earth and defeated the Earth Fleet." Here he paused for just a moment. "And they destroyed the Mars broadcast station. Without the Broadcast Network, Navy ships cannot travel between systems. The ship that came here a few days ago is stuck out here, too. It will be back."

Until that last sentence, the room remained silent. When Freeman told them that the fighter carrier would be back, the people started talking among themselves.

"How can you know that?" an old man on the first row yelled. It sounded like a challenge.

"It takes four to five days for a carrier to fly here from the discs," Freeman said. "The one that came here didn't have enough time to reach them before they went dark."

I heard shouting and crying. I saw men yelling at each

other, then turning and yelling at the women beside them, and I realized that these people had just been told that their world was doomed.

Archie Freeman put up his hand to calm the crowd, but the commotion continued. "Raymond and his friend have offered to move us to another planet."

That last sentence quieted the crowd.

I had this strange feeling, like I was intruding on a family matter. I was an outsider. Hell, Ray was an outsider, and he was born and raised among these people. They had something special, something I could never have. Looking around the congregation, I knew that even if I moved in among these people, I would never be one of them. They were family . . . and I was a clone. I took one last look at Ray standing tall, mute and confused, and maybe even intimidated, on that stand. Then I quietly got up and left the meeting.

It was early evening. The sun had set but the sky was bright. All the blue had faded from the sky. The horizon showed orange and red, and the sky above me was white. The temperature had dropped to a comfortable seventy degrees. Little Man was always a hospitable planet. It was the inhabitants that worried me.

A soft breeze blew in from the fields, carrying the scent of freshly-turned soil and fertilizer. I stood and stared at the ground with its rows and furrows. Beyond the fields, a red and green forest stretched out as far as a man could see.

"It looks so pretty at night," a woman said. "I almost forget all the sweat and hard work that goes into it."

"It's beautiful," I said, turning back. The woman walked in my direction. She had brown skin. It was the same color as Ray Freeman's skin, but more tanned. Her skin was parched, but not as badly as Archie's.

"You're not going to stay for the meeting?" I asked.

"They don't care what I have to say any more than they care what Ray has to say. We're pariahs, and decision-making is a job for God's elect." She wore a long-sleeved white blouse and her plain gray skirt went all the way to her feet. These must have been her church clothes. They looked clean and pressed. "I'm Ray's sister, Marianne." With this, she put out her had for me to shake.

"Wayson Harris," I said, shaking her hand.

Her palm and fingers were hard and rough, far rougher than mine. I had climbed ropes and dug trenches in school, but the life of a Marine is mostly spent in combat armor. This woman had spent her days plowing and digging with tools, not equipment. Her palms were calluses.

She had broad, manly shoulders, and her wrists were as thick as mine. She stood only an inch shorter than me. Her lips and skin were almost the exact same color. Her hair was black and long. It hung down to her waist. She was elegant and strong, and I thought that in the proper setting, dressed in soft clothes with her hair done up, she might be beautiful. In another world, where she was perfumed and pampered, she might be exquisite.

"Why are you and Ray outcasts?" I asked.

"Raymond couldn't stand living in a religious colony. He never believed in Jesus, and he and Archie hated each other. When Raymond was old enough, he caught a ride on a supply ship and got as far away as he could. I think Archie was glad when he left." I noted that she called her father Archie, as if he were a friend or an acquaintance. "He wanted someone to follow in his footsteps and lead the armies of God. That wasn't Raymond."

I tried to imagine Ray Freeman as a minister and found that I could not picture him without his armor and his guns. "Does Archie know what Ray does for a living?" I asked.

"We don't talk about that," she said.

"But you stayed," I said. "What makes you a pariah?"

"I stayed, but my husband didn't. I have a little boy named Caleb. He's in the meeting, sitting with his grandmother. I don't know how Jesus feels about divorced women, but I can tell you how the women on this planet feel about them. If I so much as talk to any of their men, tongues start wagging."

"So you'd be glad to get off this planet?" I asked.

"Mr. Harris . . ."

"Call me Wayson."

"Wayson, I don't think we'll leave this planet. Our little colony might not look like much, but we've worked night and day to build it. Delphi is a lot nicer than the other planets I've seen. Frankly, Wayson, starting all over again scares me more than that carrier out there."

Easy to say when you haven't seen what one of those ships can do, I thought. But I did not say this.

Darkness spread across one side of the horizon. The air continued to cool. I felt a pleasant chill in the breeze. "You haven't been here that long. Your crops haven't even sprouted. How hard could it be to start over again?"

Marianne laughed and smiled. Her teeth were white and even. "That field . . . We worked on that field night and day. We still haven't cleared it properly. We got out most of the rocks, but there's a lot more we can do. We've planted almost every seed we have in that field, Mr. Harris."

"Wayson," I said.

"If we leave that field . . . I can't speak for everyone, Wayson, but the people I have spoken with would rather die than leave.

"And it's not just that we are neo-Baptists. We used to do this for the church, but that ended a long time ago. Now we're colonists first and neo-Baptists second. The church wanted to create colonies just like the Catholics. That was their deal. Us, we wanted to make a home. Now that we finally have a planet that will sustain us, you can't really expect us to turn it over."

"Why did your husband leave?" I asked.

"He thought there must be a better life on other worlds, so he flew off on a supply ship, just like Raymond. He asked me to come with him, but I didn't want to go. I believed God wanted us to build a colony. I had my boy, my Caleb, and I wanted him to grow up in a righteous colony. I believed that God would bring us to our promised land, our Goshen. I believe he has.

"Do you believe in God, Mr. Harris?"

There was a loaded question. She had to have known that I was a clone. I thought about the conversation about clones and souls that Tabor Shannon had with that priest on Saint Germaine. "I don't know if I believe in God," I said. "And I don't know if he believes in me."

It was not love at first sight. It probably wasn't even love, but I felt attracted to Marianne. I liked her. I only had one other woman with which to compare her, a girl named Kasara whom I met on leave. Kasara had been beautiful, irresponsible, self-centered, and fun. She was a girl. Marianne was something else. She was raising a boy on her own; she worked hard on a farm; and she kept her head straight in a lethal situation. If Kasara lived to be a thousand years old, I doubted she would ever grow into the woman Marianne had already become.

"It doesn't seem like anybody here knows about the war," I said.

"We hear things. Well, truth be told, we all heard things. The missionaries that flew us here told us about it, but it didn't sound serious. It didn't sound like more than a little uprising."

"You never followed the war on the mediaLink?"

"And what would that be?" she asked.

"What would what be?" I asked feeling thoroughly confused.

"You said something about following the war on something or other."

"The mediaLink," I said. "That's the news source."

"I can't say I have ever heard of it," she said.

"It's too late now," I said. "It receives communications signals sent through the Broadcast Network. You do know about the Broadcast Network."

"Yes," she said, feigning that she was offended. "I know about the Broadcast Network."

"When they destroyed the Network, they shut down communications as well as travel. Close as I can figure, it would take a laser signal 70,000 years to get from Earth to Delphi. Without the Broadcast Network, they might as well be sending smoke signals."

"So it's all true. The entire Republic is shut down," Marianne said.

"Everyone is on their own," I said. "It's just that some planets are better off than others."

"So why did you come here?" Marianne asked. "You have that self-broadcasting ship. You can go anywhere."

"I asked Ray where he wanted to go, and he said he wanted to come here."

"And you went where he asked. 'Where you go, I will go . . . Where you lodge, I will lodge also . . . Your people shall be my people.' You're a modern version of Ruth, Mr. Harris."

I didn't know what that meant and I had never heard of Ruth, but Marianne's smile charmed me. "Maybe we should look in on the meeting," I said. "I don't want to start tongues wagging."

"Are you worried about my reputation?" Marianne asked. "Don't worry about me. Those tongues are already wagging. That's how life goes on a small planet."

"How did it go?" I asked Freeman as we settled down to sleep in the Starliner. Archie could not find beds for us. He could not find sheets for us, but he did have pillows.

"They don't want to leave," Freeman said. He stripped off his chest armor and stepped out of his coveralls. Stripped down to his boxers, he stretched out as best he could. "They think they can talk their way out of this."

"They want to reason it out with a fighter carrier?" I asked.

I had never seen Freeman stripped down. The massive muscles in his chest and arms looked powerful, but not defined. He did not look like a bodybuilder. He had the build of a blacksmith or a construction worker. "They think God delivered them here."

Marianne had said as much when we were talking. Images of Marianne ran through my head. Was I infatuated, I asked myself, or just lonely? So many new emotions clouded my thinking since the fall of the government that I no longer trusted myself. I wanted to ask Freeman about his sister, but I was afraid of tipping him off to my thoughts.

We slept on reclining seats that only reclined to a forty-five-degree angle. The weight of our heads never left our necks.

"You landed on an engineered planet once, didn't you?" Freeman asked.

"Ezer Kri," I said. "That's where we caught Kline. You were there, remember?"

"No, an unpopulated one," Freeman said.

"Ronan Minor," I said, remembering the mission.

"It wasn't called something Kri?" The term *kri* denoted a planet with an engineered atmosphere.

"It was a shitty place." I rolled over in my seat and hit the panel to turn out the lights. "What do you think is happening on Earth?"

Freeman thought about this. "Depends who comes out on top. If the Confederate Arms win, they'll fly in armies. The outer arms always had good ground forces, they just couldn't protect them.

"If the Mogats made out, it will be worse. The Mogats, they don't care about colonizing. They don't want to occupy Earth. All they want is to erase every vestige of the Unified Authority.

"It's only been a few days . . . The Mogats and the Confederates may not be through killing each other yet," I said.

"Harris, you think we could relocate these folks on Ronan Minor?"

"They wouldn't like it," I said. "It was a jungle and the only life on it is cockroaches and rats."

Freeman understood what I meant immediately. Ships are not allowed to land on engineered planets until they are declared stable. When squatters trespass on these planets, vermin escape from their ships. On a planet like Ronan Minor, where the vegetation is profuse and there are no natural predators, rat and cockroach populations proliferate.

CHAPTER
FORTY-SIX

Talk about your flat-world society . . . Archie Freeman did not believe that there could still be a fighter carrier floating out somewhere around his planet. It took some arm-twisting, but Ray talked him and three of the elders into a trip to the broadcast discs. We would show them that the discs were dead, do a radar sweep to see if we could find any trace of the fighter carrier, and maybe look around. Ray Freeman did not come for the ride.

Archie and his brethren were novices at space travel. They had never been in a self-broadcsting ship, and the idea of it scared the hell out of them. The old man had to brace himself just to climb into the copilot's seat of the Starliner. He did not complain or ask me to be careful. He looked around the cabin nervously and tried to sound comfortable.

"You know," he said in a confidential tone that suggested this was a big confession, "I always wondered what it would be like to go up in one of these." He laughed. Now that he was in true confession mode, he went on. "Self-broadcasters remind me of the early days of airplanes and daredevils flying through barns. Ho, ho, ho." He laughed a beautiful baritone laugh.

The elders, men in their thirties if I had to guess, sat in the first row of the cabin. They strapped themselves in and did not speak. They seemed to share Archie's outer fear of self-broadcasting ships not his inner enthusiasm.

"Do you understand how self-broadcasting works?" I asked Archie as we strapped ourselves into our seats. I, of course, only had the shallowest grasp, but a farmer/colonist like Archie would not care about the specifics. All he cared about would be the base fundamentals.

"It will be just like flying into a broadcast disc," I said.

"The broadcast discs were destroyed," Archie said.

"Not destroyed . . . just unplugged," I said, for lack of finding a better way to explain myself.

"They don't have power?" Archie clarified.

"Right. This ship can broadcast itself. There will be an electrical field around the ship right before we broadcast. It's supposed to be there. There will be a bright flash, and when we come out, we'll be near the broadcast discs."

"What if we run into that carrier?" Archie asked as I powered up my console.

"We could," I said, "but I'm betting that they went to the discs, found them dead, and have already turned back toward Little Man."

"Delphi," Archie said.

"Excuse me?" I asked.

"We call the planet *Delphi*."

"Right. Sorry."

"What happens if we run into that carrier? I don't see any guns on your ship."

"I don't have any."

"Can you outrun a carrier?"

I hit the button to start charging the broadcast engine. "Not a chance. Those ships hit thirty million per hour. I might be able to do six million miles at best."

"So what will we do?" Archie asked.

"Look, Archie, it's a big galaxy. You don't run into ships out here by accident. You can go out looking for other ships and never see them. If you and I were the only people on Delphi, what do you think the chances would be of our accidentally running into each other? The galaxy is a billion times bigger than Delphi."

We took off at a steep angle and left the atmosphere quickly. Now that we had left the ground, Archie gripped the sides of his chair, his bony knuckles curved in like cats' claws. He seemed unable to look away from the window. The sight of the planet below us seemed to hypnotize him.

I looked back in the cabin and saw that the three elders had the same reaction. They leaned into the nearest windows and stared.

"Okay, I am going to broadcast us now," I said as I brought up the tint shield.

"What's that?" Archie asked. "The window went black."

"It's a tint shield. It protects your eyes," I said. "Things get bright out there when we broadcast. Unless you tint the windows, the brightness will blind you."

"Oh, okay," he said, sounding somewhat reassured.

Strings of electricity showed through the blackened windscreen, then the flash showed through. Archie was startled. He looked around the cockpit nervously. His legs, which did not fit behind that seat much better than his son's, went stiff, and he lifted himself part way out of his chair. In that moment of fear, he lost partial control of his body. He did not wet himself or drop a load, but he farted something loud and smelly.

I had started to say, "We're here," but seeing the shocked look on Archie's face, I could not stop from laughing.

"Oh, you think that's funny?" Archie asked. "You goddamned clone."

Some things you regret saying even before you finish saying them. I saw embarrassment and anger on Archie's face. He settled back in his seat and stared straight ahead.

Out of habit, I started up the generator to charge the broadcast engine the moment we arrived. That habit saved our lives.

We arrived just a few miles from the broadcast discs and drifted over to see them. Coming to an almost dead stop, I took the Starliner around the defunct discs.

"Those are the discs?" Archie asked.

He probably did not see the discs when he came to Delphi. He and his fellow settlers had most likely traveled in a cargo ship. Even if they flew in a commercial craft, the tint shields would have been up long before they came this close to the discs.

"That is the broadcast station," I said.

"You fly into it?" Archie asked.

I remembered that he lived on a planet without modern conveniences. "You fly toward it. It sends out an energy field to transport your ship."

"I see."

"If the discs were live, they would have a white glow. There would be traffic lights and warning lights along the top. There's not so much as a volt of electricity in this station." My broadcast gear included an enhanced radar display. As I reached to turn on the display, the Harrier buzzed us. It was a gray-white blur that streaked past the cockpit and totally vanished.

"Good God! What was that?" Archie yelled.

Red lights flashed in the canopy and on my heads-up display. A warning sign flashed on my instruments. Alarms buzzed. I switched on the radar with one hand and pulled the wheel sharp to the right with the other. "Hold on," I yelled.

"What's going on?" Archie yelled. It was not a scream. He had control of himself. "What was that?"

"You asked me what would happen if we ran into that carrier," I said. "We just did."

He pressed his face against the cockpit and stared out the window. "I don't see anything."

"Archie," I said, as I stared into the radar, "that ship travels thirty million miles per hour. They could come right up our nose and ram us before you see them if they wanted."

"Do they want to kill us?" Archie asked.

"We'd already be dead if they did. That was a fighter. The pilot could flame us with a single shot if he wanted." I glanced at the broadcast gear. It would need another two minutes of charging before I could use it.

The Harrier did not came upon us from behind. It slowed so that we would see it, flashed over the top of the Starliner, and vanished into space. The radar tracked its path.

"They're not going to shoot us yet," I said.

"How do you know that?" Archie asked.

"They're stuck out here and the broadcast station is down, right?" I asked. "They'll want to know how we got here before they start shooting. If they figure out that we're self-broadcasting, they'll want to capture our ship."

"Unidentified space craft, this is the U.A.N. *Grant.* Identify yourself."

"The *Grant*," I whispered to myself. I knew the ship.

"What are we going to do?" Archie asked.

"They want to know how we got here," I said. "I'm going to show them." An amber light winked on above the broadcast engine to show that it was ready. I had already programmed in the coordinates for Little Man, and now I initiated the broadcast.

They had no way of knowing where I broadcasted to, but they could certainly make an educated guess. If I had come from within this galactic sector, I could only have come from Little Man—Delphi as Archie called it. That was the only habitable planet in the area.

With that short visit, I set events in motion. I started the countdown. Archie could no longer evacuate his colony. We had time to fly his people to safety, but he would need to leave his buildings and equipment behind. But Archie did not want to leave. He believed that God had deeded him Little Man and that God would protect him. All he needed was faith.

FORTY-SEVEN

"Raymond was right," Archie said in a soft voice to his people. He looked dejected. His arms hung at his side as he spoke, his head hung at a slight tilt. "That carrier did not make it through the broadcast disc. It will not arrive at Delphi today, and it may not come back for a week; but sooner or later, it will return."

The congregation let out a collective gasp. "Deliver us, Lord," one woman yelled. She stretched her arms above her head, her fingers extended, imploring.

I sat alone in a corner in the back of the town hall ready to leave. Freeman sat with Marianne and her son. They sat one row behind the rest of the congregation. They were with the people but not part of them.

"Raymond believes that we should leave this planet. He believes that the Philistines are at the gate, and we must abandon our promised land.

"God has promised us deliverance. We will not abandon our planet. I have seen the enemy with my own eyes. His fighters are as fast as light. But we must not fear the puny arm of man, for God will protect us."

As the congregation let out a collective hiss, Freeman

looked back at me, and our eyes met. In the silence that passed between us, we communicated disbelief.

If they wanted to call Little Man their "promised land," well, they had the right to interpret it any way that they wanted. Saying that God would deliver them from the *Grant*, however, that was bullshit. No one could deliver them from the *Grant*, and the only ones who might try were the "goddamned clone" and the colony pariah.

The thing was, I couldn't leave them. Klyber once told me that military clones were programmed with an altruistic streak. We were made to serve and protect, especially when it meant killing enemies of the Republic. But now my programming was twisting in on itself, I was programmed to fight for the Unified Authority. In the back of my mind, I constantly reminded myself that the Unified Authority no longer existed and that whoever was flying the *Grant*, they were not receiving orders from Washington D.C. I did not know if I could convince myself of this. I would not know until I either performed in battle, or froze because my programming would not let me continue.

I watched these people and I hated them. I regretted coming to Delphi. All of the anger I felt for the Unified Authority now focused itself on this congregation. And yet, none of them had done anything to harm me. Not even Archie.

Archie launched into a prayer. In that prayer he gave thanks for the planet of Delphi. Still praying, Archie said that Ray and I were led to the planet by God so that we could be instruments of deliverance. We were "tools in God's hand."

When the meeting ended, I asked Ray how he could ever have lived with these people. He shrugged his shoulders and walked away.

"Wayson," Marianne said as she watched Ray leave, "this is Caleb. This is my boy." She rested her hands on the shoulder of a young man who stood just a tad under six feet tall. His head came up to my nose.

"Good to meet you," I said, trying to sound like I was comfortable around kids. I did not know what to say to the boy.

"Nice to meet you, Mr. Harris," said Caleb.

And then we had an awkward moment when none of us knew what to say next. Archie came and tapped me on the shoulder. "May I speak with you?" he asked.

I nodded, grateful for the escape.

Archie led me to a quiet corner of the building. We could see people filing out the door. No one came to speak with us. I think they could read in Archie's posture that he had serious business to discuss.

"Mr. Harris, I owe you an apology," he said. Speaking in that baritone voice, he sounded truly humbled. He looked down at the ground as he spoke and rocked back and forth on the soles of his feet. "I don't know what came over me."

As I heard this, I could not help but remember the journal entry that the Catholic priest wrote about Sergeant Shannon. "I should not have laughed," I said.

Archie looked up at me and smiled. "It must have looked awfully funny . . . me farting with that stunned look on my face."

I returned the smile. "It did."

"Mr. Harris, you and Raymond did not need to come here. No one asked you to help us, but you came. And now, once again, we are asking you to extend your generosity."

I put up my hand. "It's okay. Coming here was Ray's idea. You should thank him."

"He says it's your ship."

I nodded.

"Well, I wanted to thank you." Archie turned and started to walk away.

"Can I ask you a question?" I said.

"Anything," Archie said.

"You don't believe I have a soul," I said. I did not really care about whether or not I actually had a soul. I had made it this far without one. But the prejudice bothered me. I had come to help these people. If they considered me less than human, that bothered me a lot.

Archie Freeman stood silent and still as a tree and stared into my eyes. He had dark brown eyes that had yellowed. His eyes were bloodshot and appeared tired and full of intelligence. Staring into those eyes, I decided that Archie Freeman might give in to prejudice, but he would never knowingly lie.

"No, son, I don't believe you have a soul."

"Science can create life, but it cannot create a soul?" I asked. "Is that what you believe?"

"Science cannot create life," Archie said.

"I'm alive," I said, "and I'm a work of science."

"I am not trying to judge you, Mr. Harris. I'm sorry for what I said. It was an awful thing to say. I don't suppose I can ever take it back. No man can tame the tongue. It is a little member that boasts great things." I did not know if this last bit was poetry or philosophy or scripture, but Archie sounded sad as he quoted it.

"Don't judge me, judge science. I crawled out of a tube, not a womb. What does your gospel say about that?" Yes, I was spoiling for a fight with a man who had come to apologize to me. I was mad. I was offended. I knew I was wrong, and I did not care.

"Mr. Harris, I don't pretend to understand cloning. I am a minister, and I have spent the last fifty years of my life on barren planets cut off from men and the galaxy."

"But you don't think science can create life through cloning?" I asked.

"Cloning doesn't create life, it duplicates it," Archie said. "If I have a fire, and you hold a stick over the flames until it catches on fire as well, you haven't created a new fire, you've simply borrowed a flame from me.

"They didn't create life when they made you, Mr. Harris. They borrowed genes from one of God's creations . . . somebody who had a soul. You got his hair and his skin, and his eyes, but I do not believe you got his soul. I don't believe his soul was embedded in that DNA.

"Now I think it's real nice that you and Raymond came to rescue us. And I am grateful that you have been so generous. You appear to be a man of great virtue, though if you are associated with my son, you are probably a professional killer. But unless science has identified the gene that holds the soul, I see no reason to believe that you are anything more or less than a temporal man . . . a body with an Earthly spark of life and no chance for eternity."

I thought about Shannon quoting Nietzsche to that archbishop, telling him that no man has a soul. I thought about pointing out that there was a time when white men thought that black men had no souls. None of this mattered. I asked Archie what he believed, and he gave me an honest answer.

"I came to apologize for what I said, Mr. Harris. I am extremely sorry about what I said on your ship. I hope you will accept my apology." Having said this, Archie turned and walked away.

"That's not exactly what he told everybody else about you," Marianne said as she came around the corner.

"You were listening?" I asked, feeling ashamed.

She smiled at me; and her dark eyes, so much like her father's, seemed to stretch wider with her smile. "He is my father."

"And that makes eavesdropping alright?"

"Yes," she hesitated and spoke slowly as if trying to make up her mind. Then, with more certainty, "Yes, it does."

"What did he say to everybody else?"

"The night you landed, we held a town meeting."

"I know. I was there for some of it. I left and you followed me and we talked."

"No," Marianne said, "that was an open meeting. After you and Raymond left, Archie held a closed meeting, just for the men."

"And you listened in?"

"Do you want to hear what he said or not?"

"What did he say?" I asked.

"People were scared of you. They said that cloning is an abomination. Archie said that incest is an abomination."

"That makes me feel better," I said.

"You don't understand. Do you read the Bible?"

"Do you follow current events on the mediaLink?"

"Wayson, you're such an ass."

"Sorry."

"Have you heard of Lot?" Marianne asked.

"Sodom and Gomorrah," I said. "His wife looked back and turned into a pillar of salt. You don't need to read the Bible to know that story."

"Do you know that after his wife died, Lot's daughters got him drunk and seduced him? They had two sons and both sons created nations."

"Unless they were cloned, I don't see what that has to do with me," I said.

"One of those nations was Moab," said Marianne. "A

woman from Moab married a Jew. Her great-grandson was King David."

"So?" I asked. I had heard of David and Goliath. I knew he wrote the Psalms. "What does any of that have to do with cloning?"

Jesus was a descendent of David. Had it not been for Lot's daughters, Jesus would not have been born.

"Don't you see, Archie justified you? He said that righteous ends can come from evil means."

CHAPTER
FORTY-EIGHT

The errand was not dangerous. All I was doing was broadcasting out to the middle of nowhere to take some radar readings and locate the *Grant*. I would not broadcast anywhere near its course, and unless they were looking for a broadcast signature, they would not detect me. If they did detect me, I would broadcast out before they reached me. If they reached me, they still wanted my ship intact. They could not risk shooting at me.

Ray came into the cockpit. Marianne loaded some food in the Starliner's galley as I prepared to take off. The last people on the Starliner were Archie and Caleb, Marianne's son. Over the last few days, Caleb had become my shadow, my helper, and my unofficial second-in-command. The boy was twelve years old, far too tall for his age, and headed toward another growth spurt. He liked to ask questions and watch his surroundings with great curiosity.

"Where do you think you're going?" Marianne asked.

"I'm going along for the ride," he said.

"You're not going anywhere," Marianne said.

"That's what I told him," Archie said.

"He's with me," I said.

She stared at me as if making sure I was serious. Caleb

grinned like a child and squeezed around her as he made his way toward the cockpit. Marianne gave me a nasty look and climbed out of the Starliner.

"Go sit back there," Ray said, pointing back to the cabin. Caleb and Archie sat on the same row. Caleb sat by the wall and stared out the window. Archie sat by the aisle and watched Ray and me.

"He's adopting you," Ray said. "You know that, don't you?"

Taking a break from my instruments, I looked back at Caleb. I could only see the back of his head. I imagined that he was smiling, excited to fly into space.

"I don't know much about families," I said. "Is that what they call it?" I flipped a switch and brought the controls on line. I would take off in another minute.

"When a fatherless boy starts following you around, he's looking for more than a friend," Ray said. He glanced at Marianne, who was standing in the door of the meeting-house. "She and Caleb are alone. Unless you want to live here on Little Man, you'd better let Marianne know you're not here to stay."

"You lost me," I said. "Let's square things with the *Grant,* then we can talk family."

So Ray sat cramped in his seat and watched me. I stole a peek at Caleb. Had he pressed his face into the window any harder, he might have broken the glass. Seeing the boy made me laugh.

"Harris," Freeman said, "this colony is a different world from your old clone farm. Nothing goes to waste here."

"Meaning?" I asked.

"Marianne is looking for a husband," Freeman said. "Her boy needs a father and you're available."

"I'm a clone," I said.

"You see any other options?" Ray asked.

Stewing over Freeman's warning, I looked back at Caleb. Archie was glaring at him, but he looked out the window and pretended not to notice. So now Ray wanted to play the role of the protective brother.

I did not want to settle down on a cozy little planet with a family. It might have been my military upbringing or the neural program that made Liberators what they were, but I could not imagine life on a farm.

"She could come with us," I said, thinking I had found a workable alternative. "We could take them to Earth or to . . . some other planet."

Freeman shook his head. "She doesn't want to get out. She wants to bring you in."

"Ray, the boy is just coming along for the ride," I said.

"Just know what you're getting into," Freeman said. "Marianne isn't just scrub you met on the beach." Having delivered his warning, he left the cockpit and climbed out of the ship. His job was to scout the area around the farm. We needed to know where the *Grant* would send its landing party and how we could defend ourselves.

"You want to sit up here?" I asked Caleb.

His smile brightened and he trotted into the cockpit. He sat in the copilot's seat.

Archie stood hunched in the door of the cockpit. Caleb and he watched every move I made as I pressed buttons and flipped switches. "What is that for?" "How about that one?" Caleb asked questions like a six-year-old, but he stored up the details like an adult. Archie watched in silence.

When I powered up the broadcast computer, Caleb's face lit up. "What is that?" he asked.

"This," I said, "is the reason we can still travel when the rest of the galaxy is stuck in one place. This is a broadcast computer. It lets us go places without having to fly there."

"Without having to fly?" he asked.

"I tell this computer where I want to go and it puts us right there."

"That's the part that scares me," Archie said.

I was afraid Caleb would ask for details, but he didn't. Instead, he hovered over the computer and pieced together how it worked. "How do you tell it where to go?"

I showed him how to translate interactive maps into coordinates. "Going to a planet is easy. The computer has coordinates for every star and planet in the galaxy." I thought I would impress the boy. I mostly ignored Archie. "The hard part is if you want to fly to a pinpoint location, like a certain spot right above a planet. You don't always aim at something big like a planet. Sometimes you have to fine tune it."

"Like into deep space?" Caleb asked. "Like where we are now?"

"There used to be a space station called the Golan Dry Docks," I said. "It was top secret. If you wanted to broadcast yourself there, you needed to put in the coordinates yourself."

And then I remembered a story that I thought he would find interesting. "You heard there was a war, right? That was the reason your uncle and I came to Delphi."

"A war against Earth?" Caleb asked.

"Yes, and Earth had this giant ship called the *Doctrinaire*. It was bigger and stronger than any other ship in the galaxy," I said. "It was so strong that it could destroy whole fleets of enemy ships. And it had special shields so no other ship could hurt it."

"So Earth used it to win the war," Caleb said, his eyes wide with excitement.

"No, Earth lost. The people attacking Earth destroyed that ship with a single shot," I said. "And they did it with a computer like this."

We spent two hours on this trip. Caleb and I spent the entire time talking. We could have returned the moment we finished taking the radar readings. Instead, I showed Caleb how the Starliner worked. This fine young man, this kid whose company I so enjoyed, I told him stories from the war. Freeman might have said that I adopted the boy back.

"How can you destroy a ship with a computer?" Archie asked.

"The shields of the *Doctrinaire* were so strong that nothing could get through them, right? And its cannons were so powerful that it could pick off any ship that came within range. But the captain of the *Doctrinaire* kept the ship in one place while the smaller ships in his fleet chased the enemy."

"Why did he do that?" Caleb asked.

"He was smart. Big ships are not maneuverable. They get into trouble when they move out of position. So Thurston, he used the *Doctrinaire* like a floating fortress. He wanted to trap the enemy with the *Doctrinaire* on one side and his cruisers and battleships on the other.

"You never saw anything like it. It looked like the *Doctrinaire* was falling . . . falling asleep. The ship slid out of formation." I held my right hand flat to imitate the ship, then let it list the way that the *Doctrinaire* had done.

"And all of a sudden it just blows up. See, the Mogats, they knew Thurston liked to leave his ship in one place."

"You're not saying that they broadcasted another ship into it?" Archie asked. "They killed themselves?"

"And they took the whole damned Unified Authority with them," I said. "They had a nuclear bomb onboard, but that was just overkill. The anomaly from the broadcast engine probably killed everyone aboard all on its own."

"Wow," said Caleb. "And ships can pass through shields when you broadcast them?"

"I don't understand how it works," I admitted. "I guess they kind of just appear. I don't think that cruiser passed through the shields. I think it just appeared inside the other ship."

Caleb, his eyes still wide, could not think of anything more to ask. He thought about this for several seconds. "So it's like you're dead when you're broadcasting. It's like you don't exist for a moment and then you come back to life." He sounded a little scared.

"It's safe enough," I said. "Billions and billions of people have done it. I must have done it a hundred times."

"But you couldn't just point to a spot and aim using the computer. How did they know they would hit that ship?" Caleb asked.

I told him about triangulation and how you can calculate an exact target using X, Y, and Z coordinates. Caleb was twelve years old, and he understood the math far better than me. Archie didn't seem interested. He went back to the passenger cabin.

Caleb asked me if we could manually select a spot near Delphi for our broadcast home. I let him pound out the calculations, enter the coordinates and initiate the broadcast home. If Archie knew who flew us home, he might have prayed for salvation.

CHAPTER
FORTY-NINE

Clones are sterile. The military class was never meant to have children. This idea was old when Christ was born. Plato, upon whose writings the Unified Authority's social structure was based, believed that warriors should live in communes and that their children should be shared. In modern days, military clones were raised in orphanages and they were incapable of having children of their own.

Marianne provided me an escape clause from Plato's society. She came with a ready-made family, and best of all, I liked the boy.

Five days had passed since the day Archie and I had flown out and seen the *Grant*. Marianne and I began taking late night walks every evening. We would sit and I would stare into the sky and tell her stories about planets and battles. I told her about Ezer Kri and the Japanese. I told her about Bryce Klyber and how he died so needlessly.

Sometimes I searched space for signs of battles between the Mogats and Confederate Arms. They were out there somewhere, killing each other. More than once, she asked me if I cared who won that war, and I told her that I did not. I lied. I wanted both sides to destroy each other; but if one side had to survive, I preferred a universe with the

Confederate Arms rather than Morgan Atkins and his fanatics.

But on this particular night, she said something that sent a warm thrill through me. She said, "Caleb talks about you all the time. He loves you, Wayson." And she took my hand in her calloused and leathery hand and said, "And I love you."

I turned toward her, and we kissed. It was an innocent kiss, the kind of kiss that I would imagine grade-school boys give grade-school girls when they decide to be a boyfriend and girlfriend. My lips were closed and my eyes were open, but I felt her warmth and tasted her breath. I had not had tender contact with another human being in years. It made me weak inside.

Had this been Kasara, the girl I met in Hawaii, we would have made love. She would have led me back to her apartment and I would have removed her clothes. Kasara was young and beautiful and had no cares. I felt no longing for Kasara, though I sometimes fantasized about her.

With Marianne, things happened more slowly. We remained outside, sitting on a bench overlooking the farm, exchanging childish kisses and holding hands. She may or may not have known that I wanted more, but she did not offer it to me.

"I love you, Wayson," she said again.

The sky was dark and the stars showed clear, like pinprick diamonds laid out on a black velvet sheet. A cooling breeze traveled across the field. I wanted to tell Marianne that I loved her, but I was not sure I knew how to love.

"How do you feel about me and Caleb?" she asked. There was a note of desperation in her voice. It was as if she had given me her best offer and would give up if it wasn't enough.

"I've never had a family," I said. "I don't know about love or father-son relations. I like spending time with Caleb. It's funny. I like to teach him things. I like it when he asks me questions."

"You're the closest thing he has ever had to a father," Marianne said.

"How about me, Wayson? How do you feel about me?" She punctuated that question with a longer, more passionate kiss than the childish kisses she had been giving me. I put my hand upon her waist, but fought the urge to let it travel. Our eyes met and we kissed again.

"Will you stay?" she whispered, and we kissed again.

I wanted to tell her yes. I believed that if I said I would stay, she would have let me make love to her. But at that moment I did not know whether or not I would be able to stay. There was a war going on in the galaxy. There were many wars. The Mogats and Confederate Arms were fighting. Unified Authority fleets still patrolled every arm. The Unified Authority still had the most ships and the most troops, even if the government itself no longer existed. What would have happened if Rome had sunk into the sea and left its legions in Gaul and Carthage?

"Will you stay, Wayson?" she repeated, and her hand brushed against my thigh. Her breasts rolled across my arms as she leaned over and kissed me again.

A life of farming . . . She might as well have asked me to spend the rest of my life in prison. Her lips were dry but soft. Her breath was sweet. Her touch was warm. Marianne was thirty-two years old. I was only twenty-two, but I considered myself much older. All I had to do was promise to stay and she would give herself to me. I suddenly understood that life held more experiences than killing. In her way, Marianne knew far more about life than me.

But the velvety night and the sparkling stars still called to me. "Stay with us," she whispered. "Stay with me." And she kissed me. Her hands stroked my chest and stomach. The night was warm and her hands were hot. It should have been uncomfortable, but her touch felt good.

My mind raced. I flashed through memories of making love to Kasara, but willed myself to imagine Marianne in her place. And I realized that, yes, maybe I did love Marianne. And as I thought this, I realized that I could not lie to her. "I don't know," I said.

"Oh, Wayson," she said, and her voice was not angry but sad.

"I was made for war. I don't know if there is anything else in me. I can't become a neo-Baptist farmer. I simply don't know how."

She pulled her face away from mine, but she did not pull away. I saw tears running down her cheeks. In the faint light that came from the compound, her skin looked dark gray and smooth. Her eyes remained on mine and I could not look away from her. Yes, I thought to myself, I do love her.

"I'll take you and Caleb with me wherever I go," I said. "It can be just like Ruth. 'Where thou goest, I goest.' Something like that."

She sighed and placed her face on my shoulder. "Oh, Wayson," she sighed again. "You don't understand."

I did understand. I just could not do anything about it.

CHAPTER
FIFTY

They might have attacked earlier except they could not risk hurting my Starliner. For the last week, Caleb and I had broadcasted out and located the *Grant* every day. It was coming closer. Sometimes it traveled at a mere ten million miles per hour, one-third of its best speed. A few times it stopped all together. The crew was taking its time.

The congregation slept as families in dome-shaped temporary dwellings that looked like blisters on the ground. I would have liked to have slept with Marianne, but no one offered. Ray and I continued to sleep on the reclining passenger seats inside the Starliner. Caleb slept with us.

Caleb was fast asleep. Ray and I did not sleep so soundly. We had our seats back and our feet up. Perhaps I unconsciously noticed the movements through the window beside my seat. Something woke me from my sleep, and I turned to look.

Outside, the moon lit the clearing with pale gray light. We were on the edge of a forest, and I saw the silhouettes of trees swaying in the background. I saw rows of dome-shaped temporary housing shelters—sophisticated tents—rising out of the ground like snowy moguls. Lights burned in a few of those tents.

It was not the tents or the trees that I focused on when I woke up. It was the phantoms that caught my attention. They looked like phantoms. Men dressed in U.A. Marine combat armor sifted their way through the tents. To me, they looked like the ghosts of the battle of Little Man, risen from the valley and come to collect us.

When I woke, there might have been fifteen of these spectral Marines moving forward slowly, carrying M27s with the rifle stocks attached. As I watched, more of these men emerged from the woods behind the camp. Apparently they had hiked in from a landing site on the other side of the trees.

"Ray." I did not whisper. They would not hear me through the Starliner's thick walls. Knowing that Freeman slept light, I did not bother repeating myself. He woke up alert. I asked, "You seeing this?"

"How many?" he asked, already in combat mode.

"I'm guessing forty-two." There were forty-two men in a platoon.

Watching them move, I felt strangely annoyed. These men seemed to have forgotten everything they learned in basic. Platoons divide into fire teams with a rifleman, an automatic rifleman, a grenadier, and a team leader. They flank their target. They don't just walk in a haphazard picket line.

Freeman fitted his armored chest pad over his head and shoulders, then pulled out his arsenal. He chose an automatic rifle, a pistol and three grenades. I took my M27. We both knew that we could not outshoot an entire platoon of Marines, even a platoon that had forgotten the basics.

Some of the Marines waited at the other end of the campsite, M27s at the ready, in case the people in the tents came out. The rest of the men walked in past the tents and started across the open ground toward my ship.

I knew the Marines outside the ship would not be able to see into the Starliner, not even with all of the nifty lenses in their helmets; but I ran to the cockpit in a crouch. "I'm going to level the playing field," I said.

"Turn on the lights?" Freeman asked.

Neither of us bothered to tell the other what we both knew—they had come for the Starliner. They had come to take my free ticket to any place in the galaxy. I powered up the control console and looked at the readout. Sure enough, it showed a U.A. battleship flying above the atmosphere.

"Anything on the radar?" Ray asked.

By now the men were close, less than ten feet from the ship. I could see them squatting, hustling into position.

"They have a battleship about a thousand miles up." I lit the landing lights, flooding the entire settlement area with bright, blinding light. Tint shields in the Marines' visors would protect their eyes from the glare. They could stare right into the light and it would not bother them.

Most of the Marines dropped to the ground or looked for cover. Three ran to the ship, and Ray accommodated them by opening the hatch.

Standard Marine training—you don't walk into a situation blind. You flank the enemy. You always pin the enemy down and flank him. These boys had forgotten that. Guns drawn, they rushed up the ramp yelling something. I have no idea what they said, however, because Freeman picked them off immediately. His automatic rifle had a silenced muzzle. The noise that the armor made as the dead Marines rolled down the ramp was louder than Freeman's gunfire. The dead men formed a small pile at the base of the ship.

Outside the Starliner, people climbed out of their tents looking absolutely terrified. Seeing the dead Marines topple down the ramp, women screamed. One young wife collapsed to her knees and wailed. Her husband stood beside her, obviously confused whether he should help her or stand still.

I never knew that negotiation was among Freeman's skills, but his technique was impeccable. First, he dropped a grenade down the ramp. It rolled smoothly, plunked on the three dead men, then continued to roll to the ground.

The Marines scrambled back and waited.

Seeing the grenade, a man jumped out of his tent only to be hit across the top of the head with the butt of a Marines' rifles. The men and women of Delphi were settlers, not soldiers. This was more than they could handle. They were desperately scared.

Caleb, who had slept through most of this, woke and placed a hand in front of his face to block the glare.

"That one still has its pin," Freeman yelled.

"What's happening?" Caleb, now more awake, shouted.

One of the Marines ventured forward to verify this. He picked up the grenade, examined it, then tossed it in one hand like a kid with a baseball. Freeman shot him in the head.

"Oh, God!" Caleb screamed when he saw the Marine fall.

"This one doesn't have a pin!" Freeman shouted. He did not scream. Freeman sounded like a man in control. But he did not toss the grenade down the ramp this time, he tossed the pin. "Do I have your attention?"

Freeman and his grenade remained in the Starliner. Caleb came out with me. Most of the Marines acted nonchalant as I stepped down the ramp. A few trained their guns on me, but most stood their ground, carefully watching my every twitch. The Marines may have been chatting over the comLinks in their helmets, but I could not hear them.

Caleb stood right behind me, a boy working so hard to be a man. If he wanted me to hold him or protect him, he kept it to himself. He walked at my side, a couple feet away from me. He did not whimper or cry. He did not cringe, but he took tentative steps like a man walking on thin ice.

"We have a standoff," I called.

"It's not such a standoff," one of the Marines shouted for me to hear. He bent down and grabbed a man out of a tent. The Marine held his M27 to the man's head. He started to say something more, and I shot him.

The ring of Marines in the front raised their guns, then lowered them immediately. Whoever was giving the orders, he did not want to test me.

"What do you want?" one of the Marines asked.

"I want you to leave," I said. This, of course, was impossible. They had no place to go. Little Man was the only livable planet around. They could fly one hundred light years in any direction and not find a suitable planet. "But you can't do that, can you?"

A Marine stepped forward and removed his helmet. I did not like what I saw. He held his M27 in his right hand. In his left, he gripped his helmet by the lip as if it were a bucket.

He was a clone, of course. The man may have been in his late thirties, a veteran so to speak. His eyes had that calculated confidence you generally saw in the eyes of veteran Marines.

But there was something odd about him. His eyelids rode high on his eyes, showing whites both above and below his pupils. He had a nervous tick which caused him to glance to the sides.

Like me, the man had brown hair and brown eyes. He stood just under six feet tall. Something else caught my attention. The man looked emaciated, as if he hadn't eaten for weeks. This was not the thin face of a man who eats sparingly, this was the bony face of a man who had lost a lot of weight in a very short time.

It had only been two weeks since the Network was destroyed. Even on a ship trapped in a remote part of the galaxy, the pantries should have had enough inventory to last for months.

"You think you're in control, don't you, asswipe?" the Marine asked. He acted as if the entire situation struck him funny.

"That depends how badly you want my ship," I said.

"Who says I want your ship?" He made a strange, high-pitched whinnie. "Maybe I just want to poke a few women and go home."

This, of course, was not the way Marines talked to outsiders. Had the man not been a clone, I would have thought he was a pirate or a guerilla wearing stolen combat armor.

Marianne stood outside her tent, watching all of this anxiously. She took little stuttering steps as if she wanted to start running to Caleb then she pulled herself back. She looked at me with a pleading expression.

"This your boy?" the Marine asked, pointing his rifle at Caleb. I loved that boy, and I had no idea what this crazed Marine might do. Bringing my right hand up, I batted the rifle away from Caleb, then grasped the muzzle and thrust it backward as hard as I could. The rifle butt struck the Marine in the shoulder.

"Watch yourself," he snarled at me.

"Yeah, you're here for the ship," I said with a sneer as I let go of the rifle.

Tension showed in his face. He wanted to shoot me, but he couldn't. If he shot me, he would lose the Starliner. Thanks to Ray Freeman's opening gambit—shooting three Marines then tossing out the pin of a grenade, no one dared accuse us of bluffing. "I could kill you," the man's gaunt face with its hollow cheeks and bulging eyes contorted into a snarl.

"Mad Dog," I said, "you wouldn't even be a warm-up."

He raised his M27. The other Marines all raised their M27s. For a moment I had no idea what would happen. Then I heard *clink, clink, clink,* and a second pin dropped out of the Starliner.

"Why don't you put me in touch with the officer in command?" I asked.

The guns did not go down. The Marine continued to stare into my face. "I'm going to pull your brains out through your ass," he said.

"You know, you do a lot more talking than thinking," I said. "There is at least one man on that ship holding live grenades. Unless you want to set up permanent residence on Delphi . . . Little Man, I suggest you lower that specking M27 and get me your commanding officer."

Eyes still fixed on mine, the Marine lowered his rifle again. "You want to speak to the man in command? I'll get him for you. But you won't like him. You won't like the general, but he might have some fun with you."

The Marine replaced his helmet so he could use the com-Link. I was glad not to see his face, it took the edge off the situation. I looked over at Caleb and told him to go to Marianne. Without saying a word, the boy ran over to his mother and they hugged. She kissed him several times on the head and looked at me.

Combat helmets drowned out sounds. They had an external speaker that let you communicate with people around you. "You want to come up to the ship?" the Marine asked using the speaker.

"Sure. I'll just hop in the kettle of that transport you have hidden somewhere in the woods, and we'll all fly off to the mothership like we're best friends. Get real, Marine."

There was a pause while the Marine relayed my message. "Okay, General Lee says that he will come down."

I did not know the name of every general in the Marine Corps and I did not know every officer in the Scutum-Crux Fleet, but I took a gamble on this one. "General Lee?" I asked. "Would that be General Vince Lee?"

There was a pause, and then the Marine said, "The general thought you might recognize the name, Harris. He also says you'd better have a damned good reason for being here."

CHAPTER FIFTY-ONE

The three of us, Ray, Archie, and I, met alone in the Starliner. Either Ray or I had to remain in the ship at all times. With their satellites and observation equipment, the crew of that battleship could watch us closely, and they might yet have commandoes or snipers around our camp. As long as one of us remained on the ship, grenade in hand, they could not gas, rush, or shoot us.

"We were better off before you came," Archie yelled in his booming baritone. He stood a couple of inches taller than me, and despite his age, there was a menacing quality to his angry stare. His eyes were as dark as shotgun barrels, and when he frowned, the wrinkles formed concentric Vs on his forehead.

It was still night outside, but now no one slept. The congregation sat around a bonfire. I could see them through the window. The fire glowed bright and warm. Its sparks rose into the sky.

Archie paced back and forth in the aisle as he thought and spoke. "I should have known better than to trust professional killers. I should have known you would start a war."

Maybe he was right. With the exceptions of Ray and myself, no one had fired a shot, but that would undoubtedly change.

"All they want is your ship," Archie said. "I say you give it to them."

I wanted to remind Archie that I was not a member of his congregation, but I fought back the urge. I also wanted to tell him that this wasn't just a question of me giving up my ride to help build his clone-hating kingdom of Christ. Before I could do that, Ray told him what I should have been thinking.

"You think they'll take the ship and leave?" Ray asked.

Archie did not answer for a moment. "There's no reason for them to stay," he said, watching the members of his congregation through one of the windows. "There's no reason for them not to leave once we give them what they want."

"How many people do you think they have up there on their carrier?" Ray asked.

Archie shook his head. "Couple hundred?"

"Have you ever seen a carrier?" Ray snorted. He turned to me. "Harris, how big is the crew on a U.A. carrier?"

"Full crew? Twenty-five hundred," I said.

"A couple thousand," Ray repeated. "And how many people do you think could fit on this little ship?"

"A dozen, maybe two," Archie said.

"How long do you think it would take those Marines to fly a couple thousand men to whereever they want to go? Five months? Six months? That's assuming the broadcast engine holds up under the strain of extended use. What if it breaks? You saw that Marine. Do you think he would be able to repair it?" Ray spoke in actual paragraphs. I was used to him speaking in single syllables and an occasional sentence.

"Some of those Marines are going to have to stay here for a long time. When half of them are gone, they won't even have enough of a crew to man their ship. Sooner or later they are going to need to leave it. Do you think they're going to make good neighbors? Do you think they're planning on sharing this planet or taking it?"

"I bet they are planning to share," I said. "Who's going to plant the crops and grow the food? Those clones are programmed for combat, not farming." I remembered that clone quipping, "Maybe he wanted to poke a few women," and hoped Archie remembered it, too.

"So after six months of servitude, we would be free. Our

lives for six months as slaves; that sounds like a fair trade," Archie kept on arguing, but he sounded desperate.

"You think they'll behave themselves for the six months?" I asked. "They're clones. They're the ones with the guns. You can bet that the commanding officers will be the first to go, so the enlisted men will be in control. They're sterile, not impotent."

"Harris means that there are going to be rapes," Freeman said.

"Copulate, not populate," I said in a glib tone. "It's a Marine Corps motto."

That got through to Archie. He heard this and froze, wringing his hands as he thought. "And you think you can get them to leave without giving up your ship?" Archie asked. "They may just decide that if they can't have your ship, neither should anybody else. They may decide to simply kill us all."

"They won't," Ray said. "They need the ship whole or they would have mowed us down last night."

By this time, Freeman had replaced the pins in both of his grenades. We only needed to maintain the illusion of live grenades.

"They need the Starliner," I said. "You and your congregation may want to stay here for the rest of your life, but they don't. The only reason they haven't attacked so far is this ship. Do you really want to hand over our only bargaining chip?"

Archie sighed. "So what do we do?" His spirit had finally broken. His shoulders slumped and his head hung. When he looked up, he had the face of a tired old man. "We can't fight them."

"I don't know," I said. "Ray and I got four of them already. That only leaves two thousand four hundred and ninety-six to go."

Archie did not notice the humor. Neither did Ray. No surprise there.

Ray gave me a cold glare, then said, "Let's see what their commanding officer has to say. Then we can talk about next steps."

Outside the ship, the first morning light began to break. The congregation did not waste daylight. We were close to a river. Three young men, Caleb among them, went to fetch water. A team of men resumed clearing a field they had begun the day before. Others worked on the temporary housing.

"You know the commanding officer . . . this General Lee?" Archie asked. "Is he a reasonable man?"

"Lee was my best friend when I was in the Corps," I said.

"Are you still on good terms with him?"

"The last time I saw Vince, we were on fine terms," I said. "He thought I died in action a few days later, so he probably considers me absent without leave and a traitor to the Marine Corps."

"That's bad news," Archie said.

"Vince doesn't think much of your son, either," I said looking over at Ray. He must have known what was coming, but he did not so much as blink. "The last time they met, Ray paid Vince twenty dollars to put on my combat armor."

"I don't understand," Archie said.

"Ray told him he wanted to play a joke on a mutual friend by having me wear somebody else's combat armor. Only it wasn't a friend, it was an assassin. There was a man hoping to shoot me. Ray used Vince as a decoy while we snuck into a building and caught the bastard."

Archie took in these words, then brightened. "But you didn't step out of the ship when those Marines were here, Raymond. He won't know you are part of this."

Freeman pointed to the cola-colored skin on the back of his hand. "He'll figure it out."

Most of the day passed and we still had not seen Vince Lee. He may have thought that making us wait would give him a psychological advantage. That was what I thought he had in mind until I saw Lee in person.

His invasion force had come in the dead of night. It was early evening when Lee's transport first appeared in the sky. By that time, many of the congregation had given up on him. The women toiled in an already-cleared field with hoes. Men cut down trees with saws and axes. Ray's mother, a woman in her late fifties with long pearly hair, taught the children math, reading, and religion by the dregs of the bonfire.

I was in the cockpit mulling over my options and feeling guilty about relaxing while everyone else toiled. When I glanced over at the navigational computer, I spotted the transport.

"He's coming," I called to Ray. "One ship, headed straight for us."

"Think he'll be reasonable?" Freeman asked, preparing the grenade and stashing a few pistols around the back of the cabin.

"Archie would love Vince Lee," I said. "Lee was the most anti-synthetic clone I ever met. I think he suspected he was a clone. He protected himself from the death reflex by hating other clones."

"Any chance we could just say, 'Lee, you're a clone,' and kill him off?" Freeman asked.

"Maybe we could start a chain reaction?" I said, only half joking. This idea might have had a shot at working. If we could convince enough of Vince's Marines that they were clones, maybe we could start a mass death reflex. If one clone believed, maybe they all would. The glands in their brains would secrete their deadly hormone, and the whole crew might die. Maybe we did have a weapon, if enough of them were watching.

One minute later, a silver-gray speck appeared in the blue, cloudless sky. For a moment it looked like an apparition, perhaps the sun reflecting off of a cloud. The transport continued to drop. When we first saw it, the ship may have been twenty miles up and far off in the icy blue horizon. It dropped out of the sky and flew over the forest, and then seemed to float over the camp. All work stopped. The men and women dropped what they were doing and gathered in a group.

I ran down the hatch and gathered Marianne and Caleb. "Wait on the ship," I said. "You'll be safer there."

Marianne nodded. She looked more unhappy than scared. Her forehead was creased with lines, her lips were tight, and her eyes had pleading intensity. Without saying a word, she nodded and turned to the Starliner. Her hands remained on Caleb's shoulders. She kept her hands on him as they ran to the ship.

I rushed through the crowd and found Archie and his wife standing near the fire pit. "You'd better come with me," I said. He followed without a word.

Transports were large, clumsy birds, with bloated bellies designed for carrying soldiers. They had powerful shields, thick armor, and nearly indestructible engines, but no guns.

The transport landed in a field in which some women had been planting seeds. First the thruster engines fired to soften the landing. They emitted fiery-hot plumes that baked the soil as the transport rotated in midair so that its ass end pointed toward the camp.

The plumes from the engines dusted over two hoes that were left in the field, lighting their handles on fire. Then the ship settled on its heavy iron skids, packing dirt beneath it. The ship must have weighed thirty tons. Seeing her work ruined, one woman buried her face in her husband's shoulder and cried.

By the time the ship landed, I had returned to the Starliner. I sent Archie and his wife, Marianne, and Caleb into the very back of the passenger cabin. Turning the other way, I joined Ray in the cockpit to watch.

The rear hatch of the transport opened with a mechanical yawn that reminded me of my past. Out came eight Marines in blood-red combat armor. Government-issue combat armor came in one color: camouflage green. The red armor made no sense. They must have painted it red, but why? Then I remembered the Mogats during the battle for Little Man. They had worn red armor. Lee was emulating the superior forces.

Someone had stenciled THE KING OF CLONES in gold letters above the ramp that led out of the kettle.

I watched this from inside the cockpit with Ray Freeman. "Guess he figured out he's a clone," I said.

"You ever get tired of being wrong?" Freeman asked.

The eight men in the red combat gear formed lines on either side of the ramp, their M27s held tight across their chests. Next came the entourage, twenty men in officer uniforms who formed a line at the base of the ramp. As far as I knew, only seven clones had ever been bootstrapped to officer status, and only one of them served in the Scutum-Crux Fleet. But here they were, twenty men with the exact same face, skin, and hair, standing in a perfect row, all dressed as officers.

This ceremonial offloading had a familiar ring. I thought about it for a moment and remembered the way Klyber and his entourage disembarked the time that Lee and I accompanied them as their honor guard.

Last came Vince Lee, dressed in a general's uniform. He could not have been a general, of course. He stood at the top of the ramp, his bottom lip pursed, his eyes squinting, and surveyed the lines of men before him. Then, walking in a slow, magisterial gait, Lee proceeded down the ramp. It had to be a joke, but I was too afraid to laugh.

The men and women around the camp looked too stunned to speak. One man fell to his knees as if praying, but his eyes were wide open. His wife stood beside him, trying to pull him to his feet. The man ignored her.

One of the men in Lee's honor guard climbed into the Starliner and shouted, "General on deck!"

Freeman shot him. His body slid down the ramp and landed just about where the other three bodies had landed. Lee looked down at the dead man with a bemused expression.

"I don't remember inviting anyone to come aboard," I yelled.

Lee smiled, nodded to his guard, and started up the ramp. "Permission to come aboard?" he yelled. He had a sardonic tone.

"You know what, Lee," I answered, "I think I'll meet you down there. I could use a little fresh air."

Ray, pulling the pin from a grenade, sat down in the copilot's seat. I walked across the cabin and said, "Archie, do you want to come with me?"

He nodded and we headed down the ramp.

The Vince Lee I knew would never have let his hair grow beyond regulation. He was the ideal image of a Marine with his powerful physique. The man was fanatical about bodybuilding, and not just bodybuilding, but old-style weightlifting.

As Archie and I came down the ramp, I saw the new Vince Lee. This man had hair over the tops of his ears. He had the same glassy-eyed look as the Marine who led the raid. He also had the same recently-starved look about his face. His skin was sallow. He had large dark pockets under the eyes. He also had a few days' stubble on his cheeks.

"Hello, Wayson," he said with no enthusiasm as I approached. Then his sneer broke and he smiled. "You're looking good for a dead guy." He did not reach to shake hands or salute.

"General Lee?" I asked.

"Let's see. Two years back I heard you died. A couple of weeks ago somebody told me that you made colonel. I also heard you went AWOL. And here you are alive and well, and trespassing on Unified Authority territory out of uniform. Good men died defending this planet." His eyes narrowed into slits, then he smiled and his face relaxed. "Give me your ship and we'll forget you were here."

"You'll just fly off and pretend you never saw me?" I asked.

"Something like that," Lee said.

Behind him, Lee's entourage stood in a single row. They did not stand at attention, and they whispered among themselves. They all had Vince Lee's face, though none of them had his muscular physique.

A moment passed, both silent and heavy. "What does 'king of clones' mean?" Archie asked.

Vince laughed. "You noticed that, did you? I'm glad." He turned to me. "I wanted to make sure that you saw it, too. Let's go for a walk, Wayson. How does that sound?"

"You mind if Archie comes along?" I asked. Vince should have known Archie from the first time the *Grant* visited the planet.

"Just you and me," Lee said.

"Isn't that how they used to kill political prisoners? They'd take them out in the woods and shoot them. You still have a transport filled with Marines out there, don't you?"

"I guess I do," said Lee.

I turned to look at Archie. "It might be safer if you wait in the ship."

He nodded.

"Lock it up until I come back," I said.

"Glad to see that we trust each other, old friend," Lee said.

"Semper Fi Marine." I answered.

Lee laughed. At least his guards did not follow us as we went into the woods.

We crossed into the woods. These were not the same woods we had marched through before the great battle, but they had the same tall trees. Scattered rays of light penetrated the canopy of leaves and needles forty feet above us. The woods were dark and shadowy, and the light formed distinct shafts that slanted here and there.

During our march to the valley that Archie Freeman called "Armageddon," snipers picked off our scouts and officers. I did not forget this as we walked through a dim glade.

"What happened?" Lee asked. "One moment I heard there was a big naval battle near Earth. I heard they sent their entire fleet, but I figured the *Doctrinaire* would take care of all that. Then the Network went dark."

"That just about describes the whole fight," I said. "The *Doctrinaire* broadcasted in, and the Mogats zapped it. They sent some ships to shoot the Mars broadcast discs, and the Network went dark, just like you said.

"Vince, I was there. Huang sent me to infiltrate their fleet, and they caught me. I was in the brig on Halverson's command ship."

"Halverson? Rear Admiral Halverson?"

"He was the one who killed Klyber," I said. "He defected."

"Shit," Lee hissed. "What happens if somebody starts up the Mars broadcast station again? Will the Unified Authority come back to life?"

"You make it sound so easy," I said. "The Confederates have their whole fleet there, last I heard. That was over five hundred ships.

"I haven't seen the station, but I'm guessing that they destroyed the discs. That would be a hell of a build job. You'd have to start from scratch."

"Sounds grim," Lee said. "Halverson defected? I served under him. I can't believe he would do that. No wonder they beat us, he and Klyber wrote out the whole playbook together."

Vince's sanity seemed to come in and out in waves. He had lucid moments when he acted and sounded like the Corporal Vince Lee with whom I had served. There were also moments when he could not stand still, when his eyes darted in every direction as if we were in a frenzy, and when he cackled loudly at nothing in particular.

This was a lucid moment. We walked together silently as he digested what I had just told him.

"So what does 'king of clones' mean?" I asked

"You, of all people, should not have to ask," Lee said.

"You mean it's me?" I asked.

"Well, it was you. Now it's me. Now I am the king of clones."

The trunks of the trees around us were about fifteen feet in diameter. The leaves overhead were a mixture of green and red. I saw birds and scampering animals in the branches above us.

"You might have been the greatest hero the Corps ever knew," Lee said. "I mean, the battle on Little Man, and Hubble . . . and when you killed that SEAL clone in Hawaii. I think that was the best one. The only problem is that except for us, no one ever heard about it.

"You know what was even better than that, Wayson? You remember how you found out you were a clone and it didn't even phase you? God I envied you! You were the specking perfect Marine. Nothing could kill you, nothing could stop you. Not even the goddamned death reflex.

"Me, I was just another general-issue clone. You were a specking Liberator."

I stopped.

"Yeah, I know I'm a clone. Everyone on my ship is a clone. It's the only all-clone crew in the history of Unified Authority."

"What about the . . ."

"The death reflex?" Lee interrupted. He did an expert job of steering the conversation. "Interesting thing. Once the Network went dark, the natural-borns began to panic. I don't know if you knew this, but I always sort of suspected I was a clone."

"I knew," I said.

Lee cackled, and I regretted admitting it.

"The officers were in a panic. You remember Captain Pollard? You met him on the way to Ravenwood. Remember, that was the place where you supposedly died?" No sign of sanity remained in Lee's voice by this time.

"Pollard really lost it. He parked our ship next to that broadcast station and he wanted to just sit there until it switched on again. I told him he was dreaming . . . that thing wasn't ever coming back online. We waited, and waited, and waited. Everyone could tell that it wasn't coming back . . . at least the clones could.

"Pollard said I became worse every day . . ."

"Worse?" I asked.

"He used the word *unhinged*," Lee said.

"Because of the waiting?" I asked.

"Because I could tell that the frigging Unified Authority was gone. I could feel it. And we were going to wait there until the goddamned *Grant* was nothing but a box of bones.

"So Pollard makes me take some medicine for the stress. He gives me this serotonin inhibitor, and you know what happens?"

You lost your mind? I thought. "No."

"I look in the mirror and see a guy with brown hair and brown eyes. And I figured, damn, I'm just like you now, and if I'm going to be like you, I need to be able to take over in a bad situation. I was going to have to lock the officers up, but if I locked up the officers, sooner or later the enlisted men would figure out that the only people not locked up were clones."

"Not unless you told them," I said. "They never figured out that they were clones when they were in the orphanage. If that wasn't enough to show them, I would think they'd never figure it out."

"That's true," Lee agreed, and he laughed hysterically.

"So I took a bunch of clone sailors to the sick bay, and I had them try the same medicine I was on. Know what happened? Give a swabbie enough serotonin inhibitor, and nothing happens when you tell him he's a clone. You get it? You lude them up, get them stoned out of their specking minds so that they don't get stressed about anything, and there's no death reflex."

Lee laughed and laughed. "Pretty specking obvious. My entire crew is on some drug called Fallzoud. The joke around the ship is that they're so friggin' stoned, they wouldn't care if their dick falls off.

"The only problem is that they're not supposed to take it

for more than three days straight. I've been on it for nine days."

I did not know what to say. An entire crew of cloned Marines, stoned out their minds, and fully aware that they were clones . . . they would be a danger to themselves and every one around them.

"What happened to Pollard?"

"I had him arrested, of course. Once we started taking Fallzoud, we sort of restructured the chain of command. We were in charge, and we didn't need natural-born officers screwing with us, so we put them in the brig."

"Is he still in the brig?" I started to form a plan. If Freeman and I could slip on board that ship, we might be able to free the officers. Maybe we could put together a counter-mutiny.

"No, you saw to that," Lee said without any sign of emotion. "Once we spotted you in space, the officers decided to break loose so we had to kill them."

"You killed them?" I asked. "In their cells? Unarmed officers could not possibly break out of those cells."

Lee stopped to consider this. "I never really thought about it," he said, sounding mildly surprised but not at all bothered by this comment. "I sent a platoon to take care of them, and that was the last I heard of it."

Sunlight poured through the trees in the distance. We had walked near a large clearing in the woods. Here the buzz of cicadas or something similar filled the air. In the distance, the bare metal hull of a military transport sparked in the sunlight. For a moment I thought Vince might have lured me here to shoot me. But that was the last thing on his mind. He was on a drug that shut down his emotions. All of his men were on that drug.

They probably did not eat or sleep much. They just overmedicated in the mornings and lived with the side effects. Paranoia, mood swings, lack of appetite . . . I knew what was wrong with Lee and that other Marine—they were insane and I had no way of knowing how long their drug supply would hold out.

Lee turned and started back in the direction we had come from. "So what do you say, Wayson? Are you going to give me your self-broadcasting ship?"

I had misunderstood the situation, and it was by sheer

luck that we had not all been killed. No sane man would destroy a space ship he needed just because he could not have it. An insane man, however, might. "Can I have a couple of days to consider my options?" I asked.

"Sure," Lee said, sounding magnanimous. "But if you so much as power your engines, I'll blow that specking ship of yours into the next galaxy. Do we have a deal?"

CHAPTER FIFTY-TWO

I had that ridiculous combat knife, two M27s, and a particle beam pistol. Ray had one pistol that fired bullets and another that fired a particle beam, assorted knives, an oversized particle beam cannon, a sniper rifle, and a satchel filled with grenades. Of course, if the battle went right, we could pick up more weapons as we went along.

"If they're still living by the book, they're luding up in the morning. I think that was why it took Lee so long to come down. He had to take his Fallzoud then wait for his brains to unscramble."

We were holding an emergency conference in the Starliner—the closest thing we had to a war room. Archie and the three elders sat in the front row of the Starliner. Of the 113 people in the congregation, only twenty-three were men of combat age. I held an informal census and found sixty-nine women (girls included), thirteen boys below the age of sixteen, and eight men ages fifty or older. The twenty-three combat-aged men were wedged into the cabin of the Starliner. Three of them sat on the floor.

"Luding?" one of the elders asked. "What is that?"

I had just explained everything I knew. I told them about Fallzoud, and how it had enabled Lee and the other clones to cope with the knowledge of their origins. I told them about how Lee had murdered the natural-born officers and that I thought he was insane.

"Medicating . . ." Archie said. "They take their medicine in the morning . . ."

"Fallzoud? You ever heard of that drug?" Archie looked at Ray whenever he asked questions. So did most of the other men in the cabin. Ray and I were in the cockpit leading this huddle.

Ray shook his head.

"Vince said it was a serotonin inhibitor," I said. "I'm no doctor, but if he's taking it to stop the death reflex, then Fallzoud is some kind of relaxation drug."

"And you think the drug leaves him weak?" Archie asked.

"I'm guessing that the drug leaves him limp," I said. "We wait until they're strung out, and then we attack."

"You've got to be joking," one of the elders said. "How many men are on that ship?"

"That ship is the *Grant*," I said. "It is a U.A. fighter carrier. Fully staffed, it has two thousand and five hundred men, one fifth of whom were officers. All but one of those officers are dead. Ray and I took care of five of the enlisted men. That leaves us with one thousand and nine hundred and ninety-five, give or take a few.

"To have narrowed the odds down that far before even getting started . . . well, I'm feeling pretty confident," I said.

No one responded.

"Do you have a plan?" Archie asked, rising to his feet.

"I saw the transport that the Marines came in on last night. It's a couple of miles away through that forest. I suggest we slip in and spy on the transport tomorrow morning. We wait until we are sure they've luded up . . ."

"And kill them?" one of the youngest elders asked. He might have been twenty years old. Just a kid, I thought. He was tall and wiry with broad shoulders and long arms.

"We kill them or they kill us," Ray said in his familiar flat tone. All expression had left his demeanor. "Sometimes those are your only choices."

Ray always seemed slightly embarrassed around his people, and the haughty way they acted around him did not help matters.

"Levi and Simeon killed thousands of Hivites in a single day," Archie said. "They did it just like Raymond and Mr. Harris have suggested." I did not know the story, but everyone in the congregation apparently did. Whether it was Archie's story or just his support, the tenor of the meeting changed. The elders nodded, and I'll be damned if I didn't hear a couple of quiet hallelujahs.

After the meeting, Marianne told me what happened between Levi, Simeon, and a Hivite prince named Shechem. It was from the Bible, so she knew I wouldn't know it.

This man named Jacob had 12 sons by different wives. Two of the boys, Levi and Simeon, and a girl named Dinah, came from the same mother. Sechem raped Dinah then asked Jacob, her father, for her hand in marriage. Levi and Simeon told Jacob they would allow the marriage as long as Shechem and all the men of his city got circumcised. Shechem agreed and managed to convince all his men to follow.

So Levi and Simeon waited until the men of the town were foreskin-less and helpless, then they grabbed their swords and rode into town. None of the men in town could stand up to them, so to speak, so Levi and Simeon killed every man in the town.

Archie equated Ray and me with two conniving murders. Hallelujah.

It was late at night by the time we adjourned. Stars twinkled in the sky. A distant moon showed in the darkness.

"Do you think one of those stars is their battleship?" Marianne asked me. She, Caleb, and I all sat on the large boulder overlooking the river. She had her hands wrapped around my bicep.

The night was cool, her hands were warm. She rested her body against mine. This night might be the night, I thought to myself. She had that kind of sparkle in her eye.

"It's a thousand miles away," I said. "You might not even spot it with a telescope. It's too small and too far away."

"Are you scared?" Caleb asked me. He did not know the details, but he knew we planned to attack.

"No," I said. Then I thought about it. "Yes. Yes I'm scared. But this is not the first time I've been scared. And I don't think this is the most dangerous thing that I've ever done."

The water rushing down the river made a cool, crisp churning noise. The sound conjured old images in my head. I thought of Tabor Shannon and Bryce Klyber, friends who had died. I thought of Klein, the clumsy one-handed assassin who tried to shoot Vince Lee because Freeman talked him into wearing my helmet.

The air was cool and the fresh scent of pine carried in the breeze. At that moment, I wanted to live on this planet with Marianne as my wife and Caleb as my son. It was the best offer anyone had given me.

"You have seven guns and a knife," Caleb said. "And you're going to attack forty Marines in combat armor. I'd be scared."

"*Shhhh*," Marianne said. "Someone could be listening out there."

"You ever heard of David and Goliath?" Caleb asked.

"Yes, I've heard of David and Goliath," I said. "Goliath was the giant and David was the shepherd king."

"It's from the Bible," Caleb said.

"So I hear."

"Just making sure," the boy said.

"Christ is from the Bible, too," I said. "I've heard of him as well."

"Anyway," Caleb said, ignoring my comment, "You guys going against those Marines, that's kind of like David fighting Goliath."

"I wish it was that easy," I said.

"Easy?" Caleb picked up a stone and tossed it into the water. "Goliath could have killed any man."

"You've got it all wrong," I said. "King David was never in danger. Every Goliath has a weakness. David just knew what it was."

"He knew Goliath's weakness," Caleb repeated. "Man, that's smart."

Sure it was smart, I thought, *I was a synthetic Bible scholar.*

A few minutes later, Marianne took Caleb to sleep in the Starliner. Archie was in the ship. He was the man with the grenade, just in case Lee's men came before we got to them.

I sat alone on the river bank thinking about Marianne. I imagined taking off her clothes and feeling her warm bo imagined her lying down with her long hair forming a sheet beneath her back. My body responded to the fantasy.

When Marianne returned, she walked slowly. I could see her clearly in the moonlight. Her skin was smooth. Her eyes remained on mine. She seemed to catch the moonlight in her hair. Without saying a word, she sat beside me and pressed her mouth against mine. She was breathing hard now. The kiss was warm and wet. I reached through her hair, wrapped my hand around her head, and held her close.

It happens like this, I thought to myself. *Just like this*.

The kiss ended and she pulled her face a few inches from mine. "Wayson," she whispered.

I could have had her on that night. Instead, I stood to leave. "I love you," I said, "but I cannot do this. I cannot stay on this planet, and you're looking for someone who will stay."

"It's all right, Wayson," she said, taking my hand. "I know and I understand."

By this time, I had already made up my mind, and the mood was gone.

I could have made love to her that night. I should have made love to her that night. As things turned out, we would never make love.

CHAPTER FIFTY-THREE

Ray Freeman crawled forward on his stomach, brought up his sniper scope, and checked on the guards. The scope had night-for-day vision and powerful magnification. The guards were 300 yards away, but that hardly mattered. Using Freeman's scope, I could have counted the hairs on their heads.

Of the twenty-three combat-aged men, we only brought twenty with us. One was too scared. We left two to guard the camp in case we never returned.

We hid along the edge of that primal forest. We heard the scratch of tiny animals running among the branches overhead and the occasional howl of something larger marching upon the forest floor, but we never saw anything creeping or climbing. These woods were dark in the sunlight and black in the night.

"Have a look at this," Freeman said.

Two Marines guarded the clearing sitting on a log. They did not have a fire. They did not need one. The night-for-day lenses in their helmets gave them better vision than a fire could ever offer. The ventilation in their bodysuits kept their environment a comfortable 75 degrees.

I lay down on the ground beside Freeman and s̶h̶⋯

weight so that I could peer through the scope. In the distance, the sun had just begun to rise, and that part of the sky was a rich blue. Behind the sentinels, the kettle door was open, and I could peer up the ramp and see the Marines milling about inside.

White light blazed within the kettle. Most of the men inside it wore their body armor, with their helmets off. Then I saw him. A man in a medic's uniform walked around the kettle distributing plastic cups. The men drank the content out of these cups then crumbled them up.

"This looks promising," I said.

The medic walked out to the guards and handed them cups. They emptied the little cups like shot glasses, snapping their heads backwards and spilling the liquid into their mouths.

I handed the rifle back to Freeman and knelt beside him. "Give the medicine a few minutes to take," I said.

We could not use the particle beam pistols because we could not risk damaging the transport. That left us with my two M27s, Freeman's pistol, and my oversized combat knife. I thought about the knife that Hollywood Harris used in *The Battle for Little Man* and smirked.

"Get in position," Ray said. "I'll wait for your signal." I nodded and took five men with me. I brought these elders along as scavengers. They would take weapons off the bodies that Ray and I left behind.

We moved just inside the tree line, crouching, stealing behind thick trunks. When we stopped at one tree, the guards were no more than fifty feet away. They sat slumped on their fallen log. Their helmets were off, so I could see that they were not speaking to each other.

I handed an M27 to one of the elders, a young man who would have looked athletic had he not been so skinny. Then I told all five of them to stay behind the tree.

Things move slowly when you begin stealth missions. ⸢No⸣thing ruins stealth like impatience. I might have taken ⸢only⸣ five men with me, but when the adrenaline starts to ⸢flow, be⸣ginners become impatient.

⸢I moved s⸣lowly, taking long, shallow breaths that made no ⸢sound within⸣ twenty feet of the guards. They sat on ⸢the bench⸣, their eyes staring straight out without blinking. Their hands hung down by their sides. They were not comatose exactly, but they were strung out. One of them turned and looked in my direction. I was pretty well hidden between some ferns and a tree trunk. He would have seen me if he had his helmet on and might have seen me anyway, but he showed no reaction. His brown eyes seemed unfocused and his jaw hung open.

I pointed my forefinger straight up in the air, then brought it down as if aiming a pistol and pointed at the guards. The report of Freeman's rifle was no louder than a man spitting, but it scared two large black birds that had settled a few feet away. The first bullet tore through a guard's head, blowing off his ear and most of his forehead. The man fell off the log. The other guard fell a moment later. Neither man made a sound as they died, but their armor rattled as it struck the ground. The log blocked my view of the bodies, but a puddle of blood spread into view.

The hormone already started to flow through my veins. I looked around the clearing, took a deep breath, and ran to the transport. Hiding behind one of the doors at the base of the ramp, I knelt to think out my next move. The morning sun beat down. I felt heat reflecting off the ship.

The men inside the kettle were not as dazed as the guards we had just killed. I heard them talking softly among themselves. They sounded mellow, not strung out. Had I not needed this transport, I would have tossed a grenade up the ramp. A grenade in the hole would have killed every one of them. Had any tried to escape, Freeman and I would have shot them as they left the ship. But I needed the transport in working condition.

I signaled for Freeman to come. The elders came, too. I did not want them to see this bloodbath. They looked so young. Most of them were in their thirties; but with their wide eyes and scared expressions, they looked young and vulnerable to me just the same.

"Stay here," I whispered to the man beside me.

"I can help," he said.

I pointed to the two dead guards. We could see them very clearly from beside the ship. The tops of their heads were blown off. One of the men had fallen in such a way that his face had turned in our direction. Below his eyebrows and to the right of his nose, everything was intact. Everything else was a wad of soft, bloody meat.

The man beside me looked at the bodies and swallowed. He started breathing hard. I knew the expression on his face. He was imagining himself falling just that way. Fortunately, Freeman arrived before the man could panic.

"I'll take the left. You take the right," I told Freeman. "We'll both start in the middle."

He nodded. He took his pistol. We edged our way to the bottom of the ramp and ran up shooting. There were thirty-six men on this transport, two pilots and a platoon—less the four men we had killed earlier and the two downed guards.

Most of the men did not even have their guns with them. They turned and looked at Freeman and me with stunned expressions as we opened fire. A man in the back jumped for the bench where his M27 lay. I hit him three times as he flew through the air. His head cracked the bench and he fell to the ground. Another man whirled around and leveled his gun on me. I shot him in the chest and the face, then shot the unarmed man who stood beside him.

Some of the Marines hid in the shadows. As I walked past one of the steel girder ribs, someone reached out and grabbed me by the shoulder and neck. I spun and slammed the butt of my M27 into his chest with so much force that the detachable stock broke.

The force of my blow did not hurt the Marine inside his armor, but it knocked him off balance. He fell to the deck, and I shot him in the back as he tried to climb to his feet. By now the hormone ran thick in my blood.

The noise of our guns was deafening inside the kettle and flashes from our muzzles looked like lightning. A Marine leaped at me from behind. I saw him at the last moment and pistol-whipped him. Shards from the broken rifle stock stabbed into the man's cheek and lips. He screamed in pain. Blood streamed from the wounds. I shot him.

Another man ran toward the ladder that led to the cockpit. He may have wanted to hide. He may have wanted to call for help. I shot him between the shoulder blades, and he dropped to the floor.

And then it was over and I never did use that damned knife. It was a one-minute storm that rained intensely and went away. I looked around the kettle with its bitter stew of dead Marines. The walls were covered with blood. The floor was littered with men in dark green armor. With all of the blood and flesh around them, they looked more like squashed insects than like men.

They had once been my comrades. A few years earlier, I would gladly have stood shoulder-to-shoulder with these men. Time draws great gulfs.

We only had a small window of time. The first men we shot had barely moved. They sat lethargically by and let us butcher them. As we moved into the transport, the Marines we encountered became more aware. Some of them seemed to awaken out of their drunken stupor entirely. That meant we had to get to the *Grant* as quickly as possible. If that fighter carrier was already filled with alert clones, it was time to surrender.

I invited the elders to come have a look. Most of them vomited as they came up the ramp, but that was expected. They did not know the workings of death; they were farmers.

The elders—carried the bodies out of the ship. They worked in groups of two, holding the corpses by their feet and hands. They tossed the bodies into an untidy pile just outside the ship. These elders became acclimated with death quickly. When they first began clearing the bodies, the elders handled them gently. By the time they finished clearing out the kettle, these good Christian men lugged the corpses no more reverently than they would handle a sack of grain.

My job was different. I was the grave robber. I mixed and matched armor from the dead guards, wiped away the blood, and put together a full combat suit. This was the exact same thing I had done to Derrick Hines, the technician on that Confederate Arms ship, but it bothered me more. In fact, this entire bloody mission left me unnerved.

Ray climbed into the pilot's chair. He had never flown a transport before, but he had flown some pretty big ships. As for me, I had never flown anything but a couple of private spacecraft. Everything I had ever flown was made by Johnston Aerospace.

The rest of the mission lasted only four minutes. I followed Ray up the ladder and into the cockpit. He had no trouble figuring out the controls. I heard the whine of the ramp doors closing. I heard the hiss of the thruster engines as we performed a very smooth vertical takeoff.

"That went well," Freeman said, taking his eye from the wind screen for just a moment.

"Did it look like the medicine was already wearing off?" I asked.

Freeman nodded. "There are almost two thousand men up there. It's not going to be this easy."

"We need to go wholesale . . . sabotage the ship and kill them all with one big bang," I said.

We stared at each other in silence, both of us knowing that we did not stand a chance of pulling this off, both of us knowing it was far too late to back out.

"Transport Pilot, this is *Grant*. Fred, what the speck are you doing?" The voice came over the radio and it sounded lucid and irritated. There was no trace of the drug slurring his voice.

We were only half way between the planet and the ship, but they had already spotted us. The sky around us had thinned. In a matter of seconds, we would leave the atmosphere.

"Fred, respond. Transport pilot . . ."

In the distance, I could see the *Grant* hovering in space like a great white moth. Radiant light from the atmosphere glowed on its underbelly. The top of the ship was lit by external lights. Beyond the ship, the textured blackness of space stretched in every direction.

"Fred, your orders were to remain on Little Man. Come in."

Freeman and I exchanged glances. I went to the communications console. By this time I had checked the virtual dog tag on the combat armor I took from the guard. I was now Private First Class Thomas Cain. "Grant traffic control, this is Cain. Our pilot is down," I said. "He got sick last night. We're bringing him in."

Clap. Clap. Clap. The sound of somebody clapping his hands three times in sardonic applause rang from the communications console. "If Fred's sick, who is flying the transport? Fred's the only enlisted man on the *Grant* who knows how to fly a transport.

"Wayson Harris. You never change." I recognized the voice. It belonged to Vince Lee.

"Harris, their shields are up," Freeman whispered. By now

we were close to the *Grant*. Shields were invisible in space, but their energy reading showed on our computers. More importantly, their cannons and missiles must have been locked in on us.

"Lee?" I asked, "that you?"

"You're making this too easy, Wayson. I pretty much decided I would have to take you out, but you're coming to me. Whoever heard of anybody raiding a carrier? And in an unarmed transport, Wayson, that's great."

And that was when it happened. Flames burst out of several areas along the length of the *Grant*. The entire hull seemed to breathe in and out like a bellow. Then the ship exploded. It looked nothing like the grand explosion of the *Doctrinaire*. This explosion was not nearly as big nor as bright. Twenty-foot fireballs ignited from the hull and extinguished in the vacuum of space. Pieces of the ship crumbled and flew off into space.

The superstructure of the Grant never fell apart. The ship just seemed to turn off. The windows in the bridge went dark, and the ship listed slightly, then floated out of position.

We landed the kettle and hiked back through the woods. As expected, the Starliner was gone when we returned.

The congregation assumed I had flown off in it. Upon seeing me, Marianne started a frantic search for Caleb. She found him out in the field. Only then did I understand.

Archie must have listened when I taught Caleb how to broadcast a ship. Caleb said that Archie ordered him off the Starliner early that morning. It must have taken the old man a long time to program the location of the *Grant* into the computer. Once he did, he started up the ship.

Around the camp, people compared Archie Freeman to Samson and said that he died a martyr. I don't think he saw it that way. He would have described himself as a shepherd protecting his fold, the bastard. But he had left me stranded on goddamned Little Man. Marianne and Caleb would adopt me, and I thought I could love them, but I was made for space, not farming. Ray, I thought, would have even more trouble adapting than me. He'd abandoned this life once before.

EPILOGUE

"This is a short-range transport. It isn't made for long trips," I told Ray as he sealed the rear of the kettle. "It's going to take us a month just to reach the broadcast station if we reach it at all.

"Even if we get there, this will probably be a one-way trip. You don't really think we can make it work."

"Death in space or the rest of my life stuck here on Delphi," Freeman said. "I'll take my chances." Less than one month had passed since our battle with the *Grant*, and he was already going stir-crazy. Dying out in space might have been easier for him.

His plan was a shade shy of suicide. He wanted to fly this navy transport out to the broadcast station. I had never seen a kettle fly for more than a day, and we would be out for a full month. If we made it to the broadcast discs, Freeman hoped to strip the sending gear out of them and adapt it for this ship.

The shuttle's engine produced the energy for it. It generated joules and joules of energy for its shields. But this shuttle wasn't designed for the stresses of self-broadcasting. It did not even have tint shields. Even if we made it to the discs and somehow Ray adapted the broadcast equipment to work, it could all go wrong. I had first-hand knowledge about what happens when broadcasts go wrong.

"Even if this works, we'll be lucky to get one flight with this," I said.

"I'm willing to risk it," Freeman answered. So was I, if it meant I could get back in the war.

THE ULTIMATE IN
SCIENCE FICTION AND FANTASY!

From magical tales of distant worlds to stories of
technological advances beyond the grasp of man, Penguin has
everything you need to stretch your imagination to its limits.

penguin.com

ACE
Get the latest information on favorites like
William Gibson, T.A. Barron, Brian Jacques,
Ursula Le Guin, Sharon Shinn, and Charlaine Harris,
as well as updates on the best new authors.

ROC
Escape with Harry Turtledove, Anne Bishop,
S.M. Stirling, Simon Green, Chris Bunch, Jim Butcher,
E.E. Knight, and many others—plus news on the
latest and hottest in science fiction and fantasy.

DAW
Mercedes Lackey, Kristen Britain, Tanya Huff,
Tad Williams, C.J. Cherryh, and many more—
DAW has something to satisfy the cravings of any
science fiction and fantasy lover.
Also visit dawbooks.com.

*Get the best of science fiction and fantasy
at your fingertips!*

Penguin Group (USA) Online

What will you be reading tomorrow?

Tom Clancy, Patricia Cornwell, W.E.B. Griffin,
Nora Roberts, William Gibson, Robin Cook,
Brian Jacques, Catherine Coulter, Stephen King,
Dean Koontz, Ken Follett, Clive Cussler,
Eric Jerome Dickey, John Sandford,
Terry McMillan, Sue Monk Kidd, Amy Tan,
John Berendt…

You'll find them all at
penguin.com

*Read excerpts and newsletters,
find tour schedules and reading group guides,
and enter contests.*

Subscribe to Penguin Group (USA) newsletters
and get an exclusive inside look
at exciting new titles and the authors you love
long before everyone else does.

PENGUIN GROUP (USA)
us.penguingroup.com